CH00823201

Sea Cliff

Sea Cliff

A Love Story

Mary Deal

Books by Mary Deal at Amazon

FICTION
The Ka, a paranormal Egyptian suspense
River Bones, the original Sara Mason mystery
The Howling Cliffs, 1st sequel to River Bones
Down to the Needle, a thriller
Legacy of the Tropics, adventure/suspense
Sea Cliff

COLLECTIONS
Off Center In the Attic – Over the Top Stories

NONFICTION
Write It Right—Tips for Authors—The Big Book
Hypno-Scripts: Life-Changing Techniques
Using Self-Hypnosis and Meditation

CONTRIBUTED TO:
Killer Recipes (Susan Whitfield)
A Book and A Dish (Martha A. Cheves)
25 Years in the Rearview Mirror (Stacy Juba)

*For **Doug and May Robinson***
…whose love endures

Chapter 1

Rachael stomped on the brake. The car jolted to a sudden stop with a sharp desperate squeal of the tires as the amber light changed to red. She nearly missed seeing it. "Whew!" She could have bought it just then as cars whizzed across the intersection of Lake Street at 26th Avenue in San Francisco's Richmond District.

That Matthew what's-his-name, if he comes onto me again, I'll…

She needed to concentrate on driving and not get preoccupied by that insistent guy in the park. She never sought his attention but saw something in him she could write about. Inadvertently, she had let down her reserve and allowed a conversation, somewhat. Her new novel and the hot lead character occupied her thoughts. She had secretly watched that guy in the park. Emulating some of his characteristics and mannerisms would help flesh out the love of her lady story character's life. Writing was something she could accomplish without the hassle of dealing with annoying people, like that Matthew what's-his-name.

Why are guys always hitting on me? I don't put out that kind of vibe. Dressing down in sweats and my old hoodie should discourage anyone's interest.

Rachael Connor was comfortable with her life, didn't need to be out showing the world what she was about. So what if men thought her aloof or reserved? The few men she had known were turn-offs. Men always made her feel the same. Hit on. Their comes-ons made her skin crawl, and that insistent Matthew with his easy flowing conversation distracted her.

What was it about him? Said his name was Matthew Knight. I didn't need to know his name to put him into my story.

A brown-haired knight with an inquisitive gaze, and wearing gray designer sweat pants and red tank tee came to her rescue. A man and woman arguing near the pond caused her to have an abreaction to her own tragic memories. Rachael loved visiting the pond and sitting inside the tree circle to work on her laptop. Then that ugly fight began, that couple almost coming to blows as they verbally sparred while walking in fits and starts along the footpath. Belligerent, like her mom and dad. Panic welled up and glutted in a lump in her throat. Her senses tingled in a warning of fight or flight. Then Matthew appeared by her side as she crouched behind a tree trying to hide.

In a few moments, he had shown more interest than merely wishing to calm her. He helped her nerves to settle down, but stayed longer on the pretense of wanting to make sure she was okay. That, she was sure of. She avoided looking at him but caught a glimpse of his sparkling eyes. Without hesitation, he reached over and picked fine pieces of tree bark out of her brassy red hair. Other guys were quick to comment on her hair and eyes. If he had mentioned it, and added that her eyes were green as emeralds, if she heard it one more time, she'd have walked away and left him with his mouth hanging agape. Red hair and green eyes were not that rare anymore since others dyed their hair and used non-prescription contacts. Her hair and eyes were natural. She wished people would stop calling attention to them. She also wished the guy who knelt beside her would have left, but his coaxing and conversation seemed inviting, trying to show he really cared. Yet, she wanted to be left alone to work.

Mountain Lake Park off Park Presidio Blvd, barely inside the Presidio grounds, was a place she spent many hours keying away, writing her stories. Days were becoming sunnier and warmer, perfect for being outdoors. Since seeing Matthew and his half naked body in a tank tee the previous summer, the main male character in her latest story was now graced with that fantastic physique. Rachael also wrote in her journal. That always helped her get clear of some of the lagging residual effects of old abuses at the hands of her mother and father. Actually, she considered herself well-healed, until something like that couple arguing set her off before she could stop herself from teetering into the abyss of fear.

Matthew had kept the conversation going. Rachael hadn't disclosed much about her herself though Matthew pried. She tried to nicely discourage his interest, yet he persisted, being friendly. He said he worked as a part-time counselor with troubled teens and understood more than just kids. He seemed genuine and caring, but her gut intuition kicked hard, advising caution. This guy could be using her abreaction as a pretext to get to know her. She wasn't dumb, had learned her lessons well, thanks to her tyrant father and domineering mother. After leaving their overly-protective shell, she had two relationships since moving to San Francisco; two that consisted of meaningless, juvenile conversations and hand-holding that made her feel like a high school girl. Had she not ended those fledgling relationships early, she'd have let herself in for more disappointment, like during her teen years. Those years were part of the past she wished to keep buried, yet tapes of old memories often times replayed spontaneously in her mind, uninvited.

After that first encounter with Matthew, Rachael changed the description of the secondary character's eyes in her novel. Hunter Lockwood would be graced with Matthew's amazing eyes. Rachael gave the auburn-haired protagonist, Melissa

Turner, a couple of lines expressing the way she felt about Matthew.

Hunter's hazel eyes carried a look of knowing, like he was seeing into her soul. His eyes contained gold specs around dark pupils. The outer irises seemed sometimes blue, other times green. Depending on which way sunlight shined in, they turned a light teal color. His eyes were exquisite, but Melissa wasn't about to comment on them and encourage him to chat.

To her, he seemed gregarious, maybe too sure of himself, an in-your-face kind of guy, not a person to hold back when he wanted something. He exhibited one good quality, at least. He did not comment on her hair and eyes. Surely, he saw her as a person, not as a unique set of colors.

More alert to traffic, Rachael finally found a parking spot on 22nd Avenue near the corner of Lake Street's scenic neighborhood. Then she walked up to Tina's Italian Deli and Cafe on the corner of 22nd and California Street.

Chapter 2

"Going back again today?" Tina asked, teasing Rachael from behind the counter. "Sometimes I wish I had your schedule."

"I work full days. I can take my office anywhere." Rachael lifted her laptop above counter height and drummed it lightly with her fingertips. She carried the expensive computer in a flat brown leather envelope rather than leave it in the car.

"Ha! Every day, to the park? What keeps calling you back?"

"Do I need a reason?" Rachael asked, smiling and rolling her eyes.

Tina glanced quickly out the window. "The weather's warming up, but I'll bet spring's not the reason."

"Thanks for the hot tea." Rachael never ordered what she wanted. She was a regular and the counter crew knew her preferences. Tina was also a personal friend.

"Hm-m, Greta?" Tina asked. "Someone's drawing you out of seclusion." She looked Rachael up and down. "You usually wear your grubbies to the park, with that thick head of hair pulled back in loose braids. Today you're all designer. What's his name?"

Rachael was always amused at the pseudonym Tina tacked onto her, claiming she was reclusive, like *Garbo*. Tina playfully nicknamed everyone and the names usually fit. "C'mon," Rachael said, "I love working in the park when the weather's mild." She rolled her eyes sideways at Tina and familiar neighborhood patrons within ear-shot.

"What's on your agenda today?" Tina asked. She was usually busy at the deli. She understood Rachael worshipped her seclusion. "I'm taking a breather. No catering orders today, just the usual cafe business, so I'm giving myself a day off. Wanna go somewhere? Shopping, stretch your legs?"

"Can't on Mondays. I go to my brother's to do his bookkeeping."

"Oh, too bad. Guess I'll walk the neighborhood for some exercise." Her disappointment echoed Rachael's feelings about not having a friend around during the few times she chose to do something other than work.

"Come with me," Rachael said. "You can explore the fields around my brother's property while I do my work."

"Go to your brother's house? No, I'd feel out of place."

"You kidding? We'll be alone. He's never home."

"I'll pass."

"C'mon, you're always telling me to break out."

Tina seemed pleased. "Well, it might be nice to do something different. I seldom get out of *The City*."

"Can you go now, ready to leave?"

"Anytime, I guess. I'll change into my shorts."

"Bring a sweater."

Traffic on Geary Boulevard was start and stop till they connected to Hwy. 101, and then to Hwy. 80, which was a straight shot toward the San Francisco/Oakland Bay Bridge. She managed to get through the access section of freeway quite quickly. Some Mondays, the mid-morning traffic both in and out of San Francisco was as congested as any of the worst rush hours.

On the elevated freeway and skirting the downtown skyscrapers of the Financial District, Rachael glanced intermittently over the skyline. She smiled and let out a long sigh.

This was her city. San Francisco represented transition, personal freedom, peace, and opportunity.

Progressive jazz oozed from the radio. Fresh salt air circulated through the sunroof of her two year old Porsche Carrera. The weather warmed passing through the East Bay. On the open road, and not having to think much about the mechanics of driving, Rachael's mind was free to wander.

"You get paid for doing this work for your brother?"

"That's the deal."

"I know one reason no one sees you much. You're always working. That's how you can afford that house, your gorgeous clothes, and this dream car."

"You have a lucrative business."

"And huge overhead."

"You live well, too."

"I always wondered how you did it," Tina said with a wry smile.

"I don't make that much."

"But you buy expensive things."

Tina became a friend from the first time Rachael visited the deli soliciting donations for Lisbeth House, a safe center for abused women and children. Rachael withheld telling anyone about her financial picture and Tina never pried. Yet, they had the kind of rapport that allowed them to confide in each other. "It was an inheritance, Tina, quite a while ago."

"I didn't know."

"When people know what I have, they think my father was some sort of swell guy."

"Oh, the abuse thing, yeah, but to leave you an inheritance? Some little part of him must have been good."

"I tried to get my brother to believe that. He thinks if Dad could have warmed up to anyone else, he'd have left everything to them."

"No-o!"

Life changed when Rachael moved away from home. Before high school graduation, she went through a bout of depression. "Dad sent me here to stay with Amanda, a family friend, till I got my senses back."

Tina leaned forward and lowered the volume of the music. "Your senses? Was your dad living in the dark ages?"

"He was so behind the times, had no idea what was going on with me."

"I'll bet there was a high school sweetheart in the picture," Tina said.

"I hid a two year relationship with a guy named Rodney that ended two months before graduation."

"Oh, bad timing."

"I went through graduation like a zombie."

"What about friends, someone to talk to?"

"Never trusted anyone. If you knew the way I grew up..." Rachael shook her head while keeping her attention fixed on driving. "I wasn't allowed to date, lost out on friendships, school activities, everything." She learned bookkeeping from her dad's business of hauling and drayage in the farmlands of the Sacramento River Delta. "I worked every evening after homework and most weekends."

"Yuk. No social life. I can't imagine."

Rachael laughed softly. "What are you saying? With your fourteen hour days at the deli, you're no gadabout."

"While growing up, that's different. How did you manage a relationship that lasted two years?"

"Once in a while I got to stay at my best friend's house overnight. Her parents understood. Dad never figured it out. Celine and I went to dances and parties."

It was then that Rachael would sneak away to be with Rodney. Painful memories of him flooded her mind as her sleek little sports car sailed in and out of traffic as if safely guided by an invisible hand.

"Hey, Rach, you're not gonna' go soggy on me, are you?"

"Sorry," she said, though she kept alert to the highway signs that passed overhead. She dabbed at her eyes and wiped her fingertips on her chic navy blue sweatshirt.

"Who was this Amanda lady?"

"Someone my dad knew for years."

"His girlfriend?"

"I don't think so, maybe business related in some way." Until Rachael told her about the abuse, Amanda never suspected anything like that. It hit her like a bomb blast. "She had the same perfect image of dad that others had." What anyone knew was that her dad was a hard worker and a good provider for his family. "Wise soul that Amanda was, she took it in stride." Rachael smiled again. "She'd do anything to help me. Even took me for a psychic reading."

"No kidding. What did you learn?"

"Among other things, I'm supposed to have two, maybe three kids." She chuckled in disbelief.

"You laugh?' She laughed. "That many kids, it'll take time for that prediction to come true."

"Tina, I don't want kids, don't know if I have enough knowledge to raise them right. Don't even know if I want to be married. Relationships and me don't work."

"You don't put much stock in the reading?"

"I'm sure Amanda wanted to lift my hopes." She shrugged. "I'm not sure about marriage. None of the reading's come true."

"Too bad. Amanda sounds like my kind of person."

"Amanda was pretty much out there, you know? She wore this ring with a huge *Marquis* cut stone, must have been 10 carats. Said people thought it was a *CZ* because it was too big to be a real diamond."

"And it was?"

"Yep, about the only thing in life I ever coveted." Rachael snickered. "It was gorgeous." She smiled secretly to herself. If she were ever to marry, she wondered if her guy would be able to give her a Marquis diamond, even half that size. "Long before I lived with Amanda, she and her guy got engaged. He owned a brokerage firm. He gave her the ring. Two weeks after that, he had a heart attack and died on the street."

"Oh, poor Amanda. Poor guy!"

"Remember I showed you the little dangly diamond earrings I have?"

"Yeah?"

"They're from the 1940s. Amanda left them for me in her will when she died."

"She must have loved diamonds. They're classy without being garish."

"Such beautiful sparklers, but no chance to wear them."

Chapter 3

Amanda was in real estate. She had taken a listing on a Sea Cliff house even though it desperately needed renovation. She knew that one day it would become a gold mine. Once renovated, the old building could easily sell for an exorbitant price because of its location on the cliffs behind the Richmond District. "Amanda told me to get my dad to buy the house. She convinced him in subsequent conversations that he needed the tax advantage that house afforded since his dependents would soon leave home. I live in that house now."

"And the rest is history."

"Not quite, but he bought it. Then, for the first time in my life, Dad thanked me for something." Rachael was shocked when he let her stay in San Francisco with Amanda to oversee the renovation. "Me, he left the whole renovation to me," she said, tapping her chest. "Made me promise to consult with Amanda on everything though."

"Rachael, your dad did have a good heart."

"No, actually without me there to thump on, he used my brother."

"He abused your brother, too?"

"I didn't realize it then. I was ecstatic about being away from home."

All her life, her father reminded that she didn't know how to do anything competently. He'd painfully flick her ears, or slap or kick her when he was frustrated. He's use a board if he had one in his hands. He destroyed what little self-confidence she had and denied her any opportunities to prove her abilities. In one way or another he'd convince himself he was right. Other than Amanda's coaxing, Rachael couldn't guess what motivated him to allow her to manage the renovations, let alone leave home.

"I'll bet you went to great lengths to win his approval."

"I did. I worked hard on his books. Paper work was a burden he struggled with. The Sea Cliff house gave me the opportunity to do something almost completely on my own that would please him."

"That was right after high school. How old were you?"

"Seventeen. I desperately wanted to prove I was more than just his dumb daughter." Renovations were progressing well. Amanda organized a gigantic birthday party for her that October. Rachael felt vindicated.

"Did your dad follow your progress?"

"No, he didn't call on my birthday or Thanksgiving." Rachael finally called Brandon. He wouldn't say much. His pretentiousness told her something was wrong. The week before Christmas, she took a bus home and experienced the saddest two weeks of her life. Her dad continued to gripe about raising two kids alone. He cursed her mother for having died, then mumbled something about it being better anyway because she was another burden to him. "He was vicious and self-serving. Brandon's grades were poor. He had a broken arm and made excuses about how it happened."

"I can understand how everything would look normal to outsiders," Tina said. "I'm guessing the abuse happened when no one was around."

In the week that followed, Brandon admitted he was glad the Sea Cliff house was progressing well. All he wanted was for

Rachael to come home. He admitted he wasn't good at doing her bookkeeping.

"Your dad made him do the books?"

Brandon wasn't yet sixteen but trying desperately to be the man their father demanded he be. Brandon cried when they spoke. He was planning to run away.

"Never did I think about moving back there."

"Don't tell me you did."

"A neighbor told me I could report my father to child abuse authorities. There were agencies in Sacramento that would investigate. She warned it could be a long losing battle."

"After being away a while, were you emotionally strong enough to handle your father's wrath?"

"I left the Sea Cliff house sitting idle with Amanda to look after it. I hadn't done all the renovations I wanted to do. Dad wouldn't rent it out for fear someone would damage the upgrading I did. I mean, the kind of people who can afford to rent a house in Sea Cliff are not the type to trash it. I went home till Brandon completed high school, then planned to bring him back with me after he graduated."

After she returned home, two miserable years passed. Her dad never laid a hand on her again. He yelled and complained and cursed. Brandon would have occasional bruises and make flimsy excuses. He was afraid to complain and quietly worked hard. His grades were failing.

"You know, Rach? This sound like reality TV. Where does it end?"

"Oh, that wasn't the end of it. Brandon refused to come back with me after graduation. He was bitter about my having left him behind in the first place." She couldn't convince him of the impossibility at the time and he blamed her for the abuse he'd received.

"There's got to be a positive end to this. You're a different person now."

"Maybe positive after a while."

Just days after Rachael and Brandon had their talk, in an explosive argument with one of his drivers out on the loading dock, her dad turned to leave. In his rage, he walked right off the end of the platform. He hit the concrete hard, chest first, and sprawled out, disoriented, anger and blood pressure raging. They say he struggled to stand, and then suddenly thrust his shoulders back sharply several times before collapsing again as blood spurted out his nose and mouth.

Rachel and Brandon stayed at his hospital bedside. Past midnight, he went into cardiac arrest and expired. Later, the doctor said his flaccid respiratory organs were unable to supply his heart with life-sustaining oxygen. The diagnosis was that the shock of the fall made both his lungs collapse, possibly weakened from a life time of breathing crop pesticides and other toxic residues that permeate the croplands.

"I know that whole scene, Rach," Tina said while squirming in her seat, as if the emotion of it made her feel as trapped as Rachael had felt. She gestured with her hands. "You and your brother standing at his bedside, trying to show your dad you loved him, and with his dying breath, he made no effort to repent."

Tears welled up in Rachael's eyes as she reminded herself to drive safely. "When the heart attack came, he went into deep spasms and twitched till his wretched soul shook loose."

"How did I know that?"

A will was found in a safe deposit box. They learned she and Brandon would each inherit half of a large double indemnity life insurance policy, and equally half of the business or half of the proceeds if the business would be sold. Money from their mother's life insurance policy, when she died, was invested in a broad stock portfolio. "We were to divide shares equally or liquidate and split the earnings. Brandon received the Walnut Grove house and I got Sea Cliff."

Tina had tears in her eyes. "All bittersweet recompense for the years of battering and abuse."

Brandon offered his share of their mother's stocks in exchange for sole ownership of the company. However, he agreed to pay Rachael a nice fee for doing the accounting in order to avoid more costly expenses from a CPA firm.

"So he'd picked up some business savvy."

"More like selfish motivation. He'd allow me to do the bookkeeping, even though I can do more. A CPA firm would pull the monthly Profit and Loss statements. He was afraid I'd have too much control."

Brandon wanted to keep the business alive in Walnut Grove. He hadn't been trained for anything else. His grades were barely enough to allow him to graduate. He had his special kind of emotional difficulties from growing up with a tyrant. With the help of the business, he saw the chance to make a reputation for himself by carrying on where his father left off. With his share of the inheritance, he should have been able to do it quite comfortably.

At the turnoff in Walnut Creek, Rachael headed south on Hwy. 280. The flow of traffic changed from expensive SUVs and sports cars to pickups, larger trucks, and other commercial vehicles glutting the road.

"You taking the long way to the Delta?" Tina asked as she noticed the sign.

"No, we're going to Lathrop, south of Stockton. Brandon only stayed in Walnut Grove through two crop seasons." There was ample work servicing farmers who needed heavy equipment, truck motors, or spare parts and over sized tires transported. About every farmer in the Delta communities hired George Connor's Hauling and Drayage at one time or another. Moving cumbersome equipment, transferring of animals, even transporting of crop overloads to the processing plants in Clarksburg and Sacramento had to be done by someone. "But Brandon wasn't prospering. He had taken on Dad's temperament and abused the drivers so much, finding willing help was nearly impossible. When people spoke of his temper…"

"Like father, like son, right?" Tina glanced out the side window studying the open fields that flowed into the distance. "What made him choose that area?"

"The best work Brandon could get to keep his trucks running was by referral from Manchester Trucking out of Modesto." Manchester couldn't come that far north in the Central Valley and make it a profitable trip at the same time. They pushed their overruns to Brandon because George Connor gave them referral business when they were a startup company years earlier.

"Sounds like your dad was a good businessman, at least."

"Someone told Brandon about an old mansion for sale outside of Stockton sitting on six commercial acres that could house his equipment." The isolated mansion was run down, being sold for virtually pennies. People in the area hoped a private party would buy and restore it, rather than see a developer demolish it. Selling the Walnut Grove house allowed him to purchase the old mansion and acreage. He'd have enough capital left over to pump fresh blood into his floundering affairs. The flood of images paraded through Rachael's thoughts as clearly as if they happened yesterday. She was thankful for Tina's friendship and understanding.

"And?" Tina asked, as if impatiently waiting for an update on a missed episode of a favorite reality show. "Did his business improve after the move?"

"He thought his trucks would stay busy being deeper into the crop lands. Moving was just another excuse." George Connor built a hard reputation, managing to prosper right there among the farms on the Sacramento River Delta islands. Brandon chose to move away from bad memories.

"Rachael, your history, I thought I knew you."

Rachael remained silent. The reverie took her to the days when she and Brandon were much younger. They would romp through the tall weeds and wild flowers that grew between the rows of pear trees near where they lived. After the orchards were flooded, when the water receded and the ground dried out, they'd walk in the powdery soil and feel the fading coolness of moisture in the dirt under their bare feet. Soft powdery dust would fly up between their toes as their feet slapped soft drifted mounds of top soil. They would laugh discreetly, without making noise, afraid of being accused of doing something wrong.

Rachael's memory slipped farther back, to one of the many times when her parents thought she or Brandon had done something wrong. Her dad taught her mom how to punish. She would rip a thin new branch off a pear tree, run her hand backwards over it to strip off the leaves, then use it to whip them as punishment.

Another memory flashed through her mind; her father holding her three month old brother's naked bottom over the kitchen stove to dry him out because he wet his diaper too much.

A car honked startling her. Rachael gasped, drew her attention back to driving. She looked up through tear-filled eyes, in time to catch a glimpse of the overhead sign for the junction to Highway 680.

Tina remained quiet for many miles, surely absorbing what she had just learned. Judging by the way she studied the countryside, she was thankful to be out of The City for a while. Rachael wondered if what she disclosed would affect their friendship.

Chapter 4

Occasional homes along Manila Road resembled the weathered way she remembered farm houses always looked. Farm equipment sat here and there on the properties. The shaded lawns beneath tall pin oak trees invited.

Rachael tapped the button to close the sunroof, dust being prevalent in the farmlands. Pulling into Brandon's dirt and gravel driveway, she eased to the right edge, as her brother insisted. Parking closest to the side door was his spot. He didn't appreciate having the space blocked. Brandon's pickup was gone.

Tina leaned down to see out Rachael's side window. "What a gorgeous old place."

Rachael glanced around the property. The tractor and trailer rigs remained in the same spot where they stood idle for more than a month. Weeds grew tall under the beds and around the tires. Trucks not rolling out on a regular basis was a bad omen. Certainly, there was enough business in the Central Valley to keep each truck on the road.

A feeling of unrest came over her. Brandon would have to do something soon, if only listen to her or his financial advisor. Idle trucks meant bills would not get paid. Creditors might cut off the privileges they extended to Brandon on his father's reputation.

She wondered how much Brandon remembered of his father's work habits. If trucks are sitting for any length of time, they should at least be moved to rotate the tires. Over winter, they'd be driven onto planks of wood or onto concrete to prevent the tread from rotting in damp soil.

Rachael sighed heavily. "Brandon's suppose to renovate this house. From the look of things, it's not happening yet."

They climbed out of the car.

Tina seemed awed by the size of the house. "What a decorator's dream."

Rachael laughed. "Well, don't be too surprised when we go in. He hasn't done anything inside either. It's always a mess."

"I'm not going in. I'm gonna walk about as far as I can see down this great country road." She leaned forward against the car, stretching her calves.

"I'll be about an hour."

Tina removed her sweater and tied the arms around her hips. "Don't hurry. I haven't seen this much open space in ages."

Rachael let herself in at the kitchen entrance and her mouth dropped open as the smell of stale food assaulted her nostrils. Dirty dishes were left stacked in stale water where soap had gone flat. Pans used for food preparation, not even rinsed out, sat on the greasy stove. Fingerprints were everywhere. The black and white checkered floor desperately needed to be mopped and waxed.

She looked in the refrigerator for a bottle of cool water wondering if anything in the house would be safe to put to her lips. A few bottles were pushed to the back behind a large covered container that looked to have something growing inside. She twisted the cap off and wiped off the mouth of the bottle on a paper towel. She sipped as she made her way around the front of the staircase to the den on the opposite side of the house. Everything looked more unkempt than ever. In four years time,

Brandon remained living in only two rooms of the sprawling old Victorian that once stood as a grand lady of the croplands.

Sighing, she sat down and booted up the old desktop PC. Brandon insisted on paper invoices and receipts because he hadn't learned anything about electronics. Putting a batch of invoices in order by date, she came across one from a florist for eighty dollars and another from a jeweler for one hundred twenty five. Who could be worth that much? Did he find a girlfriend? Brandon's frantic conversations about women led her to believe he'd settle for nothing short of a royal princess. What it looked like was that he was trying to bribe one.

Entering his checks and expense account items, she found more restaurant receipts than usual, tell-tailing expensive dinners. Various business meetings were scribbled on the backs, mostly with women. Having learned long ago not to ask questions, she shrugged and entered them. As more and more evidence turned up, and with vehicles standing idle in the field, it was plain to see Brandon was doing more playing than working. She wasn't going to question him. She had long ago grown tired of his excuses. She was there to update the books. Later, the CPAs could approach Brandon about anything that might be questionable. Hopefully, they could put some sense into his head.

Rachael paused. She really understood her brother. He was too far gone to listen to reasoning. He had grown paranoid and expressed no fear or remorse about lying to cover his actions and shortcomings. His attitude was that he owed no one an explanation. The business was his and his alone.

She sat quietly, lost in thoughts that drifted back to other men she knew, namely the two disappointing young men she once dated. Her mind flashed onto Matthew in the park. He arrived one day driving a white pickup loaded with construction equipment. He evidently had a job and worked out, judging by his physique. He seemed to have more purpose than any other guy she remembered. Brandon seemed having lost his.

She was about to shut down when she remembered she meant to run a check on the system. His old computer had little capacity and responded sluggishly. As far as she knew, the accounting program she'd installed was the only one on the system. Brandon was intimidated by computers and wanted nothing to do with them. If it was malfunctioning, he wouldn't know.

Keying up the directory, she found a word processing program added. The CPA or someone must have installed it for him. She brought up the directory found and numerous women's names appeared in a column. There must have been at least three dozen. Internet services were added and he had many bookmarks. Rachael's curiosity wasn't above letting her take a peek.

Dishes and pots and pans rattled from the kitchen. Brandon must have come in. Certainly he wouldn't come into the office for fear of having to explain his expenses.

Rachael clicked a link. A file came up revealing her brother's response to a girl who ran a personal ad to meet men. Rachael scanned it briefly finding it boastful, long and boring, typical of those ads. The rest of the files must have been the same. Rachael didn't bother to check further. Brandon's grammar was atrocious. In order to meet women, he was probably forced into learning the PC and keyboard because he hadn't learned to write well by hand. At least, he seemed to be learning word processing. She visualized him struggling pathetically through dyslexia to finish the emails. She sighed heavily. She loved him so much. She keyed out and shut the system down. If only Brandon could find a nice girl he could care for. In love, someone might get through to him.

After straightening the office, she went immediately into the kitchen to find Tina wiping down the cleaned counter. A lot of dish soap had freshened the air somewhat.

"You didn't."

"I started as a waitress, remember? I own a restaurant."

"Brandon's mess? I hoped I'd finish before—"

"Never mind. I'm not one for sitting around doing nothing."

Regardless how her brother became more and more indifferent, Rachael would do whatever she could to help him. She'd have done the cleaning before leaving and was glad he wasn't home to know a stranger did it. Or maybe, it might have shocked him into remembering a little more self-respect.

During therapy, Rachael worked through the pain of losing the closeness she remembered sharing with her brother in times long past. Having to admit they were far from being as close now was a traumatic experience that brought a lump to her throat. "In that case, let me wet Swiffer before we go," she said.

Tina went to sit in the car with the door open. On the way out, Rachael left a note hanging outside the back door.

Pausing on the back steps, Rachael glanced again toward the aging pickups, tractor-trailers, and flatbed trucks. She imagined her father puttering around his equipment, servicing or hosing them down. She remembered Brandon doing those same tasks beside him. How much his actions resembled those of their dad. While Brandon's hair and facial features looked like those of their red-haired mother, especially her green eyes, the rest of him was nearly a carbon copy of their father. While Rachael had sparkling brassy hair and clear skin, Brandon's thick hair was rust red and he had freckles. Kids in school use to bully him, saying freckles were for girls.

She wished she could get through to her brother. In therapy, she had worked her way clear of the effects of abuse, or at least understood their residual effects and how to deal with them. She could see that Brandon, not having help or understanding of any kind, was sinking more and more into assuming their father's belligerent personality. That alone would not allow him to submit to therapy.

"Well, I'll be damned."

Rachael turned quickly. "Brandon, you startled me."

"I never thought I'd see the day you got close to these old trucks again."

"I didn't realize I'd walked over here."

"Don't tell me you're missing Dad."

"No, actually I was thinking how much you remind me of him."

"Oh, thanks a lot." Brandon said, voice heavy with sarcasm.

"What I meant was that you remind me of him. You're thin like he was and you've got his height, and the trucks—"

"I'm six feet, and I've been taller than him for a long time."

This seemed definitely not a day when Brandon was relaxed and civil. Nor was it a day for conversation. Sibling respect from him had dwindled to cautious apprehension. Each meeting proved another example of how far apart they had grown.

"Did you just get here? You aren't taking your friend inside, are you?"

"I'm ready to leave. I've finished."

He glanced back toward the house, seeing the note taped to the handle of the screen door. "Something important?"

"I wanted to let you know the floor might be wet."

"Again? Why do you do that? Why don't you let me live the way I live. I'm not part of your snobby upper crust city life."

She didn't dare tell him Tina cleaned, didn't want to hurt him in any way, though maybe he needed a little shame. "Brandon, you don't need to live like that. We, at least, grew up clean. As long as you don't have help, I'm probably going to straighten up each time I come. There's no way I can walk away and leave you to—"

"Hey," he said, interrupting and smiling suddenly. "I might have a new girlfriend."

"Don't expect your girlfriends to clean up after you."

He raised his eyebrows. "Maybe you're right."

"And maybe they won't go out with you again when they see how you live."

"I never thought of that. Who's your friend?"

"She's too old for you. Brandon." Rachael said, trying to smile. "What am I going to do with you?"

"I don't think you're supposed to do anything."

"You want to go to lunch with us? Let me treat you."

He let out a sharp breath. "Why are you always trying to be one up on me? I don't need to be treated."

"Oh, forget I asked," Rachael said, blurting it out and then regretting it. "We don't get to see each other very often. I thought it would be nice to sit somewhere and talk for a while, like we used to when we were kids."

"Kids? I don't care to remember much of that. I'm better off the way I am now. You live too much in the past."

Rachael did not live in the past. She had gotten on with her life. He hadn't taken the brotherly courtesy to learn how she fared. There was no getting through to him. She turned to leave. "I guess I'd better be going." She reached for his hand and gave it a squeeze.

"Well, thanks, Rach. I hope the paperwork wasn't too messy."

Hearing him express some appreciation was a surprise. She stretched up on her toes to give him a quick hug. He didn't respond and pulled away as soon as he could.

"You'll always be my brother, Brandon," she said quietly.

Chapter 5

The next day, Rachael walked to Mountain Lake Park and stayed several hours. Thankfully, Matthew didn't show up. She was well-aware of his interest. What would it take to discourage him? Hopefully, he had other lady interests. At times, he sat with various girls in the park. He'd demonstrate a little yoga for them, seeming to like the attention of ditzy little loud-talking females hungry for attention.

Occasionally, a tall blonde would walk into the park and call his name. Matthew would hesitate, then walk over. She'd talk. He'd listen. At other times, that same blond would drive up to the end of 11th Avenue and honk. Sometimes she'd be in a Mercedes, sometimes a BMW. What it looked like was that they might have been a couple that broke up but she had more to say. It didn't look like he was too enthused, but he always went to have a conversation with her. Maybe she was his ex-wife. At other times, as Rachael discreetly watched, Matthew would walk back to his truck to leave and find a note on the windshield. She couldn't read his expression from the distance. His body language and tearing up the paper said it wasn't a parking ticket. Outwardly, Matthew seemed having himself together. That may not be the case. Rachael was settled in her life style with no thoughts of allowing intrusions.

While the thought of Matthew sometimes cause sudden sparks of excitement, she awarded the emotions to her story characters. She had written a new scene for Hunter, the character now more fully patterned after Matthew. The rest of the week passed without him gracing the park. She made great progress on her story by emulating his gregarious personality and speech. Her two previous novels were simple stories. Maybe what her characters lacked was meaningful descriptions and a little mystery to further flesh out their personalities. Her thoughts dwelled on Brandon and his crudeness. She thought of Matthew with his caring attention and sensibility. She would use whatever traits she could in her story.

Returning home from the park that Friday, she found a message on her office answering machine from ConverTech in Santa Clara in the South Bay. They warehoused and wholesaled electronics. The company offered a temporary position in response to her query for consulting work. Rachael wished to complete the refurbishing of her home that was left unfinished after her dad died. She could easily afford the cost but preferred to work temporary assignments and paying cash for any repairs or redecorating. In that way, she wouldn't have to delve into her savings or investments.

The message requested she fill in for a secretary taking a pregnancy leave of absence. "Duration would be two months and we are willing to pay your standard fee," the woman's voice said. Rachael charged higher rates than the agencies for computer time. This firm was aware of the precision and accuracy of her work performance. "We prefer you instead of hiring an unknown we'd have to teach from scratch," the speaker said. "If you want the position, we need you to show up this Monday." Rachael left a message on her brother's cell phone message center saying she would be coming to Stockton on weekends for a while instead of Mondays.

That weekend, Rachael wrote feverishly. Her characters began to learn they must know themselves before they could know anyone else. They needed to know who they were, apart from their parents, siblings and peers.

Rachael was developing unique personalities in Melissa and Hunter as she maneuvered them through heart rending sequences toward resolving their deepest issues. She gave Melissa the same type of tyrant father and submissive mother she grew up with, and wove in about as much of that situation as would fit into her fiction. She endowed Melissa with the same confusion she possessed about relationships and how they didn't fit into the picture her father painted about life. Melissa was reclusive and needed to be drawn out.

Work on the book progressed rapidly despite recently rewriting many portions and nearly starting over from scratch. In a zealous fit of over-eagerness, she put together a query letter accompanied by the story outline and the first three chapters and sent them to Dennis DeBaer, her literary agent. She also mentioned two additional manuscripts which were in outline form in her computer.

"To keep me alive in their memory," she said aloud in the solitude of her office. If they remembered her previous attempts to make a name in the book business, she wanted them to know they shouldn't count her out. So what if they were the people who have the last word? If they didn't like this book, publishers were plentiful. Yet, there was something special about this story. It was different from her first two with their simple plots. She could feel it and hoped they would recognize it too. Having accomplished a great measure of progress on her story, she felt ready to start the temp position at ConverTech.

The commute to and from Santa Clara each day was arduous. Thankfully, her car was dependable. Each day, she'd leave home at six o'clock in the morning and return home again around seven or even eight o'clock in the evening, and that would be dependent upon whether there were accidents slowing traffic along the way. Time to visit the park didn't exist. The two hour commutes each morning and evening left her dwelling on thoughts of Matthew and Hunter. Matthew consumed much of her thoughts and his book character much of her story line.

By the time she completed the two month contract, she had talked herself out of needing to see Matthew again for any last details she might glean for her story. Her muse would conjure anything else needed.

Two months of long commute hours had been productive. It gave her time to think seriously about the content of her novel. She had purchased a mini-recorder to make story notes so no brilliant bits of information would be lost. With the temporary work assignment behind her, she looked forward to catching up on transcribing those recorded ideas into story material.

Frustration had set in about not being able to write continually. Yet, though now she could, she found herself staring at the small bulletin board beside her desk. She had long ago drawn the features of the man in her story. He looked similar to a dashing young Sean Connery. Somehow that image no longer fit. More and more, she thought of how much the features of the man in the park should be thumb tacked in front of her. She needed to rethink her character. How had Matthew slipped into her thoughts to consume them and take over her plot? How had he become such an intrusion?

The next morning, the sun shone brightly. Rachael thought about taking her work to the park. If Matthew was there, he'd try to talk. Judging by the way he held on and tried to keep that first conversation going, he'd wanted more. She just knew it. If he approached her again, it would change her mood. She wouldn't get any writing done. Finally, she struck a key, opened the file, and started to work.

She stayed home the rest of the week, working straight through the weekend. With ample time available again, progress on her book happened rapidly. Her short simple novel had grown. When finished, it would become a longer, more intense story than ever imagined. This filled her with glee. The following Monday, she made the regular trip to Brandon's home. As she drove in silence, remnants of a vivid dream of ballroom dancing with the character in her story filtered in. They floated around the floor and as she looked into the man's eyes, the dancer became Matthew.

Chapter 6

The scent of the evergreens filled the air on the small hill at the park entrance.

"Where have you been?" The voice coming up behind her was Matthew's. He skipped around in front of her and walked backwards as she proceeded on.

"I beg your pardon?" she asked, startled out of concentration.

His face took on a look of astonishment when he realized the accusatory tone in his voice. "I'm sorry," he said. "I came looking for you and you haven't been here for months."

"Oh?" she asked, smiling curiously and wondering how many times he'd looked for her.

He shook his head and smiled back. "You're late, too."

He wore white painter's pants with a bib front and shoulder straps over a ratty white tee shirt. They were spattered with paint and other stains. He bent forward, slapping at his usually silky hair, shaking out powdery construction dust as they walked to the tree circle.

"Dad and I've been trying to complete these two jobs in the Sunset. We've gotten busy since the weather warmed." He spoke casually, as if they had been friends for ages.

The least she could do is be nice till she could get him to leave her alone or herself leave. "I thought people were holding back on major expenses. You know, the sluggish economy and all."

"Tell me about it. The market for new houses is depressed. People are remodeling existing homes instead of building new ones.

"What do you do when construction slows?"

"Hustle, I mean, really get out there and create some work. I've put my earnings away. I'm not hurting. Dad had some hard times a few years back, though. He was ready to sell his old boat. We might be looking at slow times again if we don't get some contracts."

"Would you help your dad if he got strapped?"

"Goes without saying. Dad followed me here from the jobsite. He's on his way to Marin."

"Here?" She cringed and looked around.

"He's getting us something to drink. I was hoping you could meet him."

Meet his father? What for? She barely knew Matthew, had only a meager conversation with him. Now she worried about how much she may have disclosed about herself. Then his father arrived.

Matthew stood straight and proud beside his dad when he introduced him. Then he said, "Dad. This is Rachael Connor, the girl I told you about."

Rachael nearly swallowed her tongue. Told his father…? She smiled nervously and offered her hand as she learned his name.

"We finally get to meet," Cameron said with eyes searching hers.

Why did he look at her so seriously? His gaze was piercing.

"Let's rest here a while, Dad."

Cameron motioned for Rachael to sit before he did.

How strikingly alike they seemed. They could pass for brothers with a few years in between. Matthew was slightly taller than his dad, and more muscular. In his younger years, Cameron must have been as fit as Matthew. The years had gently softened his angular build, but there was no doubt he remained strong and agile. Matthew's facial features were as his father's might have been as a young man, except his nose. Cameron's nose was a Roman type, more sharply pronounced. Rachael wondered what Matthew's mother must look like. Her genes must have contributed the gentleness to Matthew's features. She wondered how much of this new information she might use in her book.

"Did I tell you about our names?" Matthew asked. She simply waited, knowing he would explain. "Dad's name is Cameron Matthew. Mine is Matthew Cameron. Mom and Dad didn't like the way Cameron Matthew sounded so they switched names around for me."

"Yeah," Cameron said. "I kind of liked the idea of naming my son after me. I think my parents didn't say the two names together enough times before they settled on it. It didn't sound right, Cameron Matthew."

These two men, near-strangers, talked and treated her as if they had known her for eons.

"That's a pretty fancy piece of equipment you've got there," Cameron said as he studied the laptop.

"I had to buy this, or stay indoors night and day working on the desktop.

"You write that much?"

"Sometimes fifteen to twenty hours a day. Until I bought this, I could go days without stepping into sunlight."

"My, my." Cameron fumbled for his glasses and cocked his head back and leaned closer, studying her computer through bifocals. "You any good?"

"You mean writing or computers?"

"I'm interested in this gismo. You good at running these?"

"I guess."

"Oh, come on." Matthew said. "You ought to see her, Dad. She's so good—"

"You don't know that," she said.

"Sure I do. I've been watching you since last summer."

Her eyes widened in surprise. She struggled to keep her composure. "A lot of people do what I'm doing."

"Don't underestimate yourself."

"Once you learn the basics, the rest is easy," she said. She felt uncomfortable and a little embarrassed. Compliments for her were few and far between, not often enough for her to learn how to graciously accept them. "How's the home building industry?" she asked awkwardly of Cameron. Then she felt ridiculous again. People didn't build homes in San Francisco. Bare land in The City was nonexistent. People added floors atop existing buildings or they remodeled.

"We hit a slump a few years back. It was Matt who scared up some renovations. Kept the shirts on our backs."

"Aw, Dad." Matthew seemed both embarrassed and proud.

Cameron finished his soft drink and announced it was time to go. Rachael stood with them, offering her hand to Cameron to say goodbye. He looked deep into her eyes again with a stare that made her shrink inside.

"I'll be seeing you again, I guess," he said. He sounded like he wasn't sure he liked the idea, had to make an effort to be accepting. She smiled weakly as he turned to say goodbye to Matthew, shaking his hand and walking away.

Matthew stood looking after his father with a proud expression. "He's so great, Rachael."

"He seemed a little aloof."

"He doesn't understand your situation."

"My situation?"

"You know, the abuse part."

"You didn't tell him, you didn't."

"It's no big thing. Dad and I have no secrets."

"Matthew, that's private."

"He wanted to know about you."

"You could have told him anything, not that." She took a breath and felt her face heat up.

"And hide from the rest?"

She was seething. "You had no right! I'm just a girl in the park."

"Aw, Rachael, don't you see? It's no big thing to me. If you have flashbacks and stuff, well, deal with it. You're not going to get clear of it if you're in denial."

"Now I know why he looked at me like he knew something he didn't want to know." She didn't know what else to say and certainly couldn't change anything now. She didn't want to keep the abuse a secret. She simply wanted to get beyond the stigma. Yet, the idea of anyone discussing her problems, especially in her absence, made her feel weak. Why did Matthew feel privileged? Was his family open about intimate details and no one had privacy? The thought was appalling.

"I understand abuse from the volunteer work I do." He looked into her eyes without blinking. "I have a feeling you're not one of those sad statistics."

That, from a person she had not enticed and even avoided? "What makes you think I—"

"Come walk with me," he said, offering his hand. She didn't take it. "C'mon. I want to walk over there through those shrubs to the golf course. My stockbroker is usually at that tee about now. I need to pass a message to him."

Rachael was surprised. Her stock broker played on the same course. "You go. I need to get some work done." No sooner had she keyed up and opened a file when Matthew returned.

"You're not going to get much writing done anyway, now that I'm here." He smiled a big wide teasing smile. His mannerisms were natural. He exuded caring, his extroverted nature even cute, though he seemed overbearing.

She felt a pang of anxiety at putting her writing aside again. She gave in to the conversation, vowing not to get caught in the same predicament in the future.

Matthew kept up a barrage of leading questions about her life and family, and talked about his parents as well. He seemed to hang onto every word she spoke, as if anticipating the pieces of a puzzle coming together. She saw empathy in his expression, and acceptance, but she remained careful not to discuss intimate matters. He was trying to develop a relationship with her and he was headed for disappointment.

He asked about her mom, who died when Rachael was ten years old. Female problems was all Rachael could utter in embarrassment. They spoke briefly about Brandon and Amanda. Matthew took it in stride. "Your friend, Amanda, has sort of taken your mother's place?"

"Oh, no. Amanda passed away, too, but she was the person who helped me turn my life around."

Rachael didn't mention being involved in buying and remodeling the house she lived in. "Amanda helped put me in touch with something inside myself. She pushed me into therapy, then college. She had a stroke right after I graduated from City College. She lingered a few weeks, then died in her sleep."

They were silent. Matthew slipped side glances, studying Rachael's face. Suddenly, he said, "You know? You look fragile, but I'll bet you can be tough as nails."

She shrugged it off. She learned to protect herself by knowing herself. Was he referring to the hesitation he claimed to notice in her? Developing a strong sense of self-preservation made her cautious.

His facial expressions were at times intense. She sensed the power of the man. She began to like his easy nature and quick smile. She forgot about her computer and writing and found herself enjoying their conversation. She had not disclosed as much to anyone she barely knew. Now she was beginning to feel comfortable because she was talking with someone who sincerely expressed an interest in her, who didn't look down on her. He welcomed anything she shared and hadn't caused her to feel like a child, cowering, anticipating reprimand or punishment. Feeling inconsequential was something she had difficulty working through with most people. Like his father.

Suddenly, a feeling of guilt and caution overwhelmed her. He can't be real. This was too easy. Maybe that's the way he saw her. She'd been too forward. She needed to end the conversation and flee.

Chapter 7

"You know, if we keep talking every time we're here, neither one of us is going to get much done, my writing and you getting back to your jobsite." She intended to leave.

He seized the opportunity. "That's why you have to let me see you at other times. I remember you saying something about some of your evenings being free."

"I do allow myself time to *rest* after a full day's work." She hoped he caught the hint.

"So, honor me, Rachael." He was serious again.

Honor him? He was placing her on a pedestal and she knew it. Her dad had warned about the approaches men might use. Some tried to touch while acting nonchalant. Some moved quickly toward sexual conversation. Others sensed her rigidity and would back off. Her Dad was right about one thing, and that was about men's overtures. Yet, Matthew chose his words wisely and his attitude seemed genuine. He made no attempts to touch her. She still felt uncomfortable and wanted to be alone to think. "Darned." she said.

"What is it?"

"I need to pick up something on the way home." She hoped the excuse would help her escape. "I'll stop at Tina's."

"Good. I'll walk with you." He shrugged and looked smug. "It's not the kind of date I had in mind, but it's a beginning." He looked back toward his truck parked on the street as if looking for someone. Then he turned his attention back to her.

Her plan had back fired. Now he'd linger at Tina's. She just knew it. The position of the sun said it was well past noon. She would probably have to delay any further writing till evening. He picked up her back pack, hoisting it over his shoulder, then offered a hand to pull her to her feet.

Tina's Italian was a neighborhood kind of place frequented by a variety of people living in the area. Some were retired building owners. Others were career types living in rental flats and who relaxed reading books or newspapers over a cappuccino or herbal tea. Gourmet Italian deli foods were on the menu. Once in a while, some of the younger generation dressed in black, with multicolored spiked hair, would hang around. That corner was a great place to people watch. Maybe in the future, Rachael would forego the park and sit at Tina's for a change.

The sun's rays beat down and took the bite off breezes from the ocean and was comfortable enough to stay a while. They bought hot herbal teas and almond biscotti and sat outside at a white resin table on the sidewalk. They talked for the better part of an hour. Rachael sat with her back to the sun, keeping the harsh light off her face and in shadow. She wondered what Matthew saw when he looked straight at her. Despite feeling self-conscious, Rachael found a lot of enjoyment in their conversation and wasn't aware of time slipping by.

"We're going out this Friday," he said, placing a hand on top of hers. He made a statement, not a question left open for an answer.

"Not that I know of."

"Rachael," he said quietly, leaning forward over the table. "Don't you know the difference between someone who cares about you and someone who doesn't?" She simply stared back, feeling like a frightened child. "I'd like to see you at other times. A few snatched hours in the park seeing you at a distance is not enough. You know I'm interested. Have I done something, said something? Or are you completely turned off?"

The meaning hit her hard. She sighed and launched into a lengthy dissertation about how she preferred to live like a hermit. Anxiety welled up. She wanted to discourage Matthew's interest.

"I dated a couple of guys. It didn't work. I mean, they both wanted something. That is, one of them even tried to move in with me. He was broke. Not that I would have allowed him to…" She sighed. "Those guys didn't know themselves, or me. They assumed…" She shrugged. "We weren't that close. I guess I'm not ready for a relationship. Too busy. Like my privacy. Have a full life."

Those two hopeful guys wanted something from her. One couldn't look her straight in the eyes. The other couldn't afford anything more than a hamburger date. Yet, they were the strongest two men she had attracted. Now here was Matthew, making a huge statement. He looked her straight in the eyes when he spoke and he seemed honest.

Matthew waited patiently. His eyes focused on hers as she spoke. "I'm trying to understand what motivated those excuses," he said when she finished. Then he took both of her hands and held them firmly. "Well, you've met a decent guy… me. I think it's time you learn to trust someone." He leaned farther toward her and brought his face within inches of hers. "Write down your last name, your address and your phone number and give it to me." His smile softened the demand.

The thought of being close enough to kiss made her face heat up in a rush. Surprised, she pulled away, then obediently fumbled in her pack for a pen and paper. No luck. He couldn't come up with them either. His things were in his truck back at the park. He playfully slapped a paper napkin down on the table in front of her. Unable to hold back a smile, she said playfully, "I'll get a pen."

"Go… go," he said, completed surprised.

He relaxed backwards in his chair and stretched his legs out in front of him, clasping his hands behind his head and lifting his face toward the afternoon sun.

Inside the deli, Tina stood with mouth agape sending a clear message of envy. A waitress asked loudly from behind the refrigerated deli case, "Hey, Rach, who's that muscle mass?"

Heads turned and people grinned. This was a community gathering place where mostly everyone knew everyone else and the atmosphere and attitudes were laid back.

"Do you think I should go out with him?" Rachael pretended indecision to her friends behind the counter. She'd already made up her mind to do so. She teased, playing the part, gloating.

"Go out, Rachael, anytime, anyplace." Tina sighed long and slow. "On second thought, he might not be right for you. Leave him here. I'll check him out. I haven't seen anything like that in years."

"Why go out?" a younger waitress asked breathlessly. "I'll bet he's great at indoor activities."

"It's no wonder you live such a private life," Tina said. "If I had someone like that, I wouldn't want to share him either."

Back outside, Matthew had attracted two girls, which was probably common for someone like him. One was a small unremarkable looking blond, the other, a black-haired girl with boobs too high up under her collar bones and too much eye makeup. They chose the table next to Matthew and the black-hair girl kept rocking back in her chair toward Matthew, maybe to get his attention. She straightened up when Rachael sat down again. Rachael wrote and handed Matthew the napkin. He studied it while she watched. Then he held it at arm's length, glanced at her and back to the napkin, then to her once more. "You live right here in Sea Cliff?" His voice carried a tone of disbelief.

"Uh-huh."

"Now, I have a few more questions," he said with a curious grin. "But because you're so secretive, I'll be patient and learn things first hand."

"I'm not that secretive, Matthew. I'm just not a public person."

"Okay. Friday evening, Rachael Angeline Connor." He spoke her name warmly, eyes sparkling mischievously again. "I'll pick you up at six."

"Six o'clock?" she asked, enunciating.

"I want to stop in at a basketball game before we go to dinner. Do you remember when we first talked, I told you I was involved with some kids at the Haight Rehab?" She nodded. "Well, I don't have to coach this Friday, but some of my kids are playing in a game in the Mission. I want to show up, to see if they do. After that, we can eat. Okay, Angel?"

It seemed important that she approve what he was planning. "Sure," she said, shrugging and raising an eyebrow.

"Where would you like to have dinner? Do you like that little seafood place at 26th and Clement? It's called…"

"The Inland Harbor?"

"That's the one. We'd be right back here in the area, in case you felt uncomfortable and decided to bail out on me." He couldn't stop himself from smiling.

"Inland Harbor's fine," she said, rolling her eyes. "The food's superb."

"You mean we're finally doing this?"

As she and Matthew said their goodbyes, out of the corner of her eye, Rachael saw Tina and the others watching wistfully from inside the deli. The two girls at the next table mumbled together but continued to watch him walk away.

Matthew would probably make it back to his truck at Mountain Lake Park without having felt his feet touch the pavement.

Hoping for a short cut home, Rachael walked down the wrong block and ended up temporarily disoriented on a dead end street.

Later that evening, Rachael entered a note, intending to find a place in her story to attribute more of Mathew's characteristics to Hunter.

In everything Hunter said, he seemed assertive, totally sure of himself, like he had no hang-ups. His motivations seemed pure. He seemed like a guy who went after what he wanted, and would work to the nth degree to get it, no matter how long it took. How could he express himself any other way except to say what was on his mind? If only Melissa could grasp what gave him such assuredness.

Chapter 8

"Hi, it's me," he said through the phone, his voice upbeat. "I want to confirm tomorrow evening."

"I thought it was confirmed."

"No unanticipated changes that I'm going to have to talk you out of?" His smile came through on his voice.

"That's not funny."

"I'm not trying to be. I'm counting on you."

"I realize that," she said. "You can find my place if you watch for the mailbox with the shingled roof."

"Your mailbox?"

"It's between some shrubs at the corner of the brick wall. It'll help you find the driveway."

On Friday, Rachael felt restless most of the day. She wasn't able to sit or concentrate long enough to write anything of substance. She thought she should back out of the date. Instead, she telephoned her brother and learned he was going to liquidate their father's business. She spoke with him at length which transferred her anxieties, temporarily.

Somehow, she had to calm down. On the lower level of her cliffside home, she had built in a small gym, and lap pool with a hot tub at one end. She managed to concentrate enough to exercise through her usual strenuous routine. She swam several lengths in the pool as much as her hyperactive energy would allow, then sat in the hot tub till her nervous energy calmed. She showered and styled her hair, and finally dressed for the evening.

Access to the house was a narrow driveway that gently slanted down the cliff side between two large street level homes. A portion of her roof, top floor and tree tops, were visible from up on Sea Cliff Avenue. The narrow driveway leveled off at the bottom in front of the house.

Standing hidden behind the kitchen curtains with the room lights off, she saw a yellow T-Top Corvette appear across the top of the driveway. Matthew in a Corvette? She wondered what kind of car he might drive. He seemed together, sure of himself. He seemed pampered. Yet, his conversations never disclosed any real greed. She found herself envying Matthew's self-assuredness. She was having trouble identifying and maintaining that characteristic in herself. Anyway, she was sure Matthew would not be driving a clunker.

After parking, he sat a moment and studied the house, probably with curiosity about how she might be living. Smiling as if pleased, he climbed out and leaned against the car, studying the house. "Get a good feel for the place, Mr. Builder," she said, whispering to herself as if teasing. He walked around studying flower beds nestled in rock gardens. He bent down and touched the weathered piece of driftwood that lay near the front door on which was carved the name Sea Cliff.

She watched every move he made. Looking taller than ever, he wore brown slacks with matching soft leather dress loafers. His long sleeved beige designer dress shirt was open at the throat exposing his rugged upper chest.

He looked toward to doorway at the far end past the garage. Then he turned his attention toward the opposite end.

"Wow." Rachael said softly, retreating quickly when her breath began to fog the window pane as he looked in her direction. What a difference from the gym clothes and dirty painter's pants. "Wow," she said again, a hand over her mouth to muffle her voice and breath. This hunk of a man was coming to take her out.

Double tones chimed throughout the house. With legs turning to rubber, she went to answer.

He was straining to see inside through the sparkling multicolored floral and bird designs of the custom stained glass windows bordering the front door. Rachael paused momentarily and took a deep breath, then opened it slowly. She hoped he wouldn't notice her shakiness. Instead, the gold specks in Matthew's hazel eyes danced. He looked as if preparing to pounce on her. He studied her from head to toes and back again.

Her thick hair was no longer gathered back in unbraids. Instead, soft curls fell gently across her forehead and continued loosely over the top. The sides were brushed outwards, away from her sculpted cheekbones, falling shoulder length at the sides and longer down her back.

Her slender figure did justice to a simple shirtwaist dress in rich burgundy silk with long sleeves and the skirt cut just above the knee. Her earrings were 14K, as was the exquisite baroque ring that sparkled on her right pinkie. The chic image camouflaged her questionable self-confidence.

Matthew stepped into the foyer. He put both hands on Rachael's waist, lifted her into the air and swung her high in a circle. "Geez," he said. "Is this the same girl I met in the park?"

"Matthe-e-ew!" Rachael said, squealing.

Though she occasionally burned *Nag Champa* incense, her home always contained a hint of it in the air. Just then, her being swung around fanned her *Balahe*, the French cologne she always wore.

He let her down gently. "You're beautiful, Rachael."

Beautiful was not the way she pictured herself. In one of his better moods, her dad told her she was. His mixed messages didn't make sense. If she was beautiful, why had her father always told her to keep her body covered, as if she had something to be ashamed of. Whatever she might wear, repercussion was anticipated and her father doled it out. Certainly there must be something wrong with her.

He stepped back and looked down. "You've got gorgeous legs." His mouth hung open in disbelief. His response took her by surprise. She blushed. He hugged her and kissed her cheek, then stood there shaking his head and breathing her scent. Finally, curiosity getting the best of him, he began to look around. "Ah, tropical decor. I love it."

Rachael felt conspicuous. She needed to distract Matthew or risk more embarrassment. "C'mon, I'll show you the house." Matthew being a home builder, the offer was merely a gesture of friendship.

Crossing the family room on the east side of the entry foyer, he glanced at the walls. "Love the minimalist floral art."

"These rooms are small. Trying to fit in really busy artwork would make the place feel stuffy." Yet, she didn't have to remind him. In his business, he'd probably seen many decorated homes.

He walked to the windows overlooking the Pacific Ocean, the mouth of *The Bay,* and across to the Marin Headlands State Park. He impulsively unlatched the sliding door and stepped out onto the balcony, which ran the length of the house. She followed.

"What a view."

"The whole back of the house is glass. Each room has a spectacular view. Even the fog is a study."

"Every room has windows like these?" He glanced up and down the length of the house. Any good builder knew the more glass you have in a wall, the less strength the wall contains. Rachael knew it, too.

He leaned over the balcony and spotted the lap pool and hot tub. Gesturing toward the long, shallow pool, he said, "It's enough. Who would have thought a place on the cliff would have any kind of a pool at all?" He breathed in deeply, savoring the salt air, while looking around the grounds. They re-entered the room with him curiously examining everything.

"The rooms are pretty small, and they're side by side, like boxes in a row." She meant to tease, having once purposely told him she lived in a box when he pried wanting to know too much about her. "The contractor said that was the only way this much glass could be used, because the rooms are small, they support each other, and because the glass is only on one wall. The previous owner built in some heavy duty support columns along the back. He was terrified of earthquakes."

Matthew's curious smile asked how she knew that much about the house. Looking around the room, he mentally measured footage. He was a person whose life's work involved making the best use of space. He crossed to the east wall and opened a door behind tall bookcases. "Oh, the powder room," he said, rolling his eyes. Then, having seen a group of photos on some book shelves, he picked up one showing three young women singing and playing instruments.

"Anybody you know?" he asked facetiously, teasing. "Wait, don't tell me. The redhead at the piano. Your mom?" Rachael smiled. "Must have been talented. Was your dad jealous?"

"He might have been."

"Was your mom abusive, too?"

"Sometimes. She was mostly helpless."

"That's usually how it goes."

"No, helpless. Didn't understand much. She was a savant."

"I think I know what that means."

"Means she couldn't comprehend much. Her mind was different. The one thing she knew was music."

"Was she good? Were they good?" He gestured to the picture with the opposite hand.

"Sing and play any instrument around. Mom could hear a song one time on the radio, then play and sing it without ever forgetting the words or the music."

"How did the two of them ever..."

"I'm sure they married before Dad had a chance to know her. She was thirty-five when they met. My grandparents must have dumped her on him so they wouldn't be stuck with her the rest of their lives."

"Did she ever go professional?"

"Oh, no. That picture was at a private party. Those are her sisters. They were called *The Country Girls*. That's as far as her career went. Her parents thought night clubs were sinful and Dad put an end to her career when they married."

"Too bad."

"Yeah, she was good and it's all she knew." Rachael said, momentarily sad.

"How did the abuse affect your mother?"

"She got an equal share. She used to say she'd have to whip us when we were bad, or Dad would beat her for not doing it."

"Repressed talent and self-preservation. What a life," he said, staring at the picture. "Must have been some mean years." He replaced the picture on the shelf.

"Well, without sounding like a bleeding heart, you're right. There was always a bribe or a punishment for everything."

"Your mom's condition, can that be inherited?"

"I don't know."

"What would you do if your baby was born a savant?"

She raised her eyebrows. "I would help my child become everything he or she could be, given the circumstances. Mom could have had an exciting career. She was truly gifted. What would you do if—"

"I've haven't thought about anything like that." He seemed to absorb every word of the conversation. Then he smiled suddenly, gesturing to the picture again. "Neat photo. My dad's great with a camera, you know."

She smiled, waiting another moment as he looked at more photos. Given that her mother was a savant and she carried her mother's genes, that and the history of abuse might be more than any man could accept. Sighing, she asked, "Wanna see more of the house?"

"What's on this side?" He opened another door. "Oh, it's the garage," he said, answering himself after turning on the light switch. "Who's green Carrera?" Standing in the open doorway and looking straight at her, he seemed more and more curious about everything.

She smiled, hesitating, then answered. "The owner's. It belongs to the owner. Can't you tell?" She gestured toward the pale green carpet.

Rachael led him past the stairwell and through the living room on the west side. A brick fireplace on a raised hearth stood at the junction where the living room and dining area met. He sampled the views through each window, then looked around the kitchen and breakfast nook. As they proceeded, she described the changes that were made to the original house, careful not to disclose who designed and managed the renovations.

They back tracked to the polished oak staircase at the front foyer and descended carefully down the steep U-shaped stairwell, typical in San Francisco hillside homes. A large wall mirror greeted them at the bottom.

"Normally, I'd ask you to remove your shoes. Since they don't look like they've been to a construction site, you can leave them on… this time." She stepped onto the thick, plush white carpet of the lower level and motioned to the right. "This was a bedroom, now my office." A desktop and peripheral equipment sat on a white laminated Scandinavian desk bordered by bookcases. A cell phone, a Kindle, and a printer sat on an adjacent table. She went to retrieve the phone and her evening bag.

"You're too neat," he said, smiling and noticing the rocking chair in the tiny sewing nook by the window. He went to examine one of the hand embroidered chair pillows. She turned, heading for the staircase again. "Wait," he said. "What's through that doorway?" A white enameled pocket door on the west wall was closed.

"That's my room," she said quietly.

"You mean I don't get to see it?"

"Only the cleaning lady and I get to see that room."

Matthew glanced at her sideways as if he didn't appreciate the implication of her statement.

She led him through the guest bedroom on the east side of the stairwell, then out onto the ground level terrace through the sliding glass doors. They paused, staring at the water in the lap pool, faintly disturbed by the bottom scanning filtering system and an occasional breeze fluttering across the glassy top. "This way next," she said.

They entered the recreation room situated below the garage. Indoor-outdoor carpeting covered the floor. The furnishings consisted of two redwood chaise lounges and a small table. A limbering barre ran along a mirrored wall. A complete home gym stood behind.

She began sliding a louvered partition. "The laundry and re-stroom are back here." Rachael tried to draw his fascination away with the home gym. He reclined, trying a bench press not caring one iota about the wash room. For a moment, Rachael slipped back into a negative thought and wondered why she was showing her home to a complete stranger. Well, almost a stranger. He was a home builder after all and she was proud of her house.

Chapter 9

They walked outside again, crossing the narrow stretch of lawn beyond the lap pool to the edge of the yard where the rocky cliff side dropped off steeply. He stood looking out over The Bay and down the hillside. Bush poppies and rock roses were blooming among the budding Spanish broom. Wire vine bushes grew helter-skelter down the rocky slope and even weeds found their places.

"How far does the property line extend?"

"Almost all the way down," she said, walking over to join him. "There's an access lane down there for the Parks Department. That's where the property ends. It's the edge of China Beach.

Suddenly, he spotted the entrance to a small arbor in the corner of the lot near the cliff. He went to stand beneath the trellis, thickly intertwined with Himalayan honeysuckle. Tall white oleanders at the back marked the property line.

"Who'd ever believe a place like this existed along these cliffs," he said, beaming his approval.

"You should be here when everything's in bloom," she said proudly. "The scent is intoxicating."

"I hope I can be," he said, looking up and down the length of the house.

A pale shade of green blended the house with trees and shrubs on each end. Muted darker shades of the same color accented the exterior doors and woodwork trim. The room Rachael said was hers on the south end contained the most glass and seemed to be the largest room extending farther out into the yard than the rest of the house. A small table and two chairs sat on the walkway near the outer entrance to that room near the hot tub. He squinted and pinched his lips, about to ask something.

"The whole upper balcony is actually part of the roof of the lower level," she said, hoping to distract him.

Then he turned toward the other end. "What's that section beyond the garage?"

"That's guest quarters."

"Let's see," the builder said.

She caught his arm before entering to point out that the entire house was once two separate cottages that were used by care-takers of the larger homes at street level. Those larger houses sat level with Sea Cliff Avenue with the service quarters hidden from sight behind and down the cliff a bit. After children of the families in the larger homes grew and moved away, yards were no longer needed. New property lines were established and the two cottages were then sold off. The buyer joined both of the cottages by adding a garage at the driveway level above, and a laundry room below the garage, creating a single long structure.

"This is not up to the same quality as the rest of the house," she said, stepping inside. "The renovations were never finished." A queen sized bed with two night stands and a dresser occupied the lower level in front of the window. Doors to a bathroom and large closet were at the back. "There were tenants in here for a while. They trashed the place. I was always afraid they were going to break a window, or worse."

"You worry that much about your landlord's property?" She said nothing. Matthew kept looking around, cocking his head, like he was on to something. "After you," he said, motioning for her to climb the black metal spiral staircase by the wall. She declined, motioning for him to go first. Recognizing she didn't want to be above him in her short skirt, he respected her wish and obliged.

Upstairs, they entered the open living, dining, and kitchen area. There was a love seat and chair, an occasional table between, and a dinette set. A wrought iron railing held them safely as they looked out over the bedroom below.

"Pretty spacious floor plan for such a small space," he said with much enthusiasm. "This can be renovated into a cozy hideaway for someone."

"I'll bet the pictures automatically pop into your head."

"If the owners decide to remodel, could you influence them to let Dad and me bid the job?"

Rachael looked at the floor. "I think the owners might have received a quote from the company who did the original renovations." She glanced out the window.

They exited through the upper front door of the guest unit. Low brick retaining walls lined both sides of the driveway extending down toward the house from up on Sea Cliff Avenue. They spread outward in either direction creating a narrow parking space in front. Slate slabs paced off a walkway beside the retaining walls and led downward through the shrubs on either end of the building.

"The pathways give access to the lower level without crossing through the house," she said as he opened the car door for her. She climbed in, sniffed the air and smiled. *Umm! Definite not a dollar store cologne.*

He climbed behind the wheel. "Before I forget," he said, taking a business card from his shirt pocket. "This is for you."

"Oh?" she asked, unsuspecting.

"I've written my phone numbers for you. The boat, Mom and Dad's, and Mom's store are on the back. The office and our cell numbers are on the front."

How incredible that he'd be doing this for her. "Thank you," she said as she slipped it into her tiny purse.

He grabbed her wrist and held it gently. "I mean it, Rachael. Call me anytime, anywhere." Then he turned to study the house again. "The guest house makes the whole building seem larger than it actually is."

"Sparse furnishings give the illusion of bigger rooms. What do you think? Is this a builder's nightmare, or what?"

"How many people live here?" he asked, switching on the ignition.

How naive if he thought she had found a single room for rent in a house like this in the Sea Cliff neighborhood. "Did you like the house, Matthew?"

"Of course. You live in tropical splendor. You should have shown me your room. I'm interested to see how you live too." She smiled, pleased with herself. His expression grew more intense. "How is it you were fortunate enough to find a room to rent here?" Why don't you live in the guest house instead? She shrugged. "The place is neat, almost like no one lives here. Except for your office," he said, teasing again. "Who are the other people you share with? How did you find this place?"

At first, Rachael felt denigrated at being thought of as a struggling female who paid rent in someone else's home. She took a deep breath and let it pass. Her response would set him straight. She smiled as his look became more inquisitive. Quietly, she said, "I live here, Matthew, by myself. This is my house."

A look of surprise and then recognition slowly appeared. Suddenly, he thumped the steering wheel with the heel of his hand. "I should have known. After the things you said about the house and how well you know its history, and… and your bedroom is, or course, the master bedroom."

"I thought you'd get it sooner." She couldn't help but smile.

"And the Carrera?" he asked, blurting it out. "It's yours, too!"

"Yep."

"You will let me drive it once, okay? Just once, Rachael. Okay?" She smiled. "On second thought, maybe twice?" Rachael shook her head, relieved he was not upset with her deceit. Then, another look of realization seemed to come over him. He smiled uncontrollably again. "Aha!" he said.

"What is it now?" she asked, smiling at the success of her little charade.

"What was it you said? No one gets to see your bedroom except you and the cleaning lady?" Maybe he understood that to mean she wasn't seeing anyone else. He made a sharp gesture doubling up his fist and thrusting it forward in mid-air, exclaiming, "Yes, yes!"

"What is it, Matthew?"

"Nothing, Rachael, just feeling proud of you." His eyes twinkled.

"This was part of my inheritance when my dad died." She spoke softly as they started on their way. I got this house and Brandon got the one where we grew up." Matthew was silent. She felt awkward. "Do you remember what I said about the two guys I used to see?"

"Yes?"

"They both seemed to covet what I have. Carl, a guy I dated two years ago, always put me down, saying I was young and dumb and, sooner or later, I'd lose everything."

"Some guys are like that. But you're what, twenty-six, and you employ a cleaning lady? He should see how you've held your life together."

"The other guy, Les, tried to move himself in with me. I came home one day and there he was, his truck loaded with stuff, backed up to the front door, waiting for me to arrive and let him in."

"You mean, he was just there? You didn't talk about it first?"

"No, we weren't having a relationship or anything. We'd only met a few months before." Her voice elevated, expressing how ridiculous the entire situation had been. "I saw him a couple of times after that. He acted sheepish, embarrassed, sorta slunk away."

"You see him anymore?"

"Not since then."

Matthew snickered. "He might have found someone to take him in."

"Those guys, everything was a big game to them."

She told him about Carl and Les hoping he'd see she wasn't easily fooled. She purposely withheld much about her life, hoping Matthew was attracted to her as a person, and not to her possessions. Something inside hinted that Matthew was different, yet, she needed confirmation of it. One thing she knew instinctively was that from this moment forth, knowing what he now knew about her, she would begin to see his true motivation.

Chapter 10

They talked as they drove toward the Mission District. Matthew smiled all the way. He kept bringing the conversation back to Rachael, her house and her life. "Everything you've done, everything you've told me, seems complex, mysterious," he said. "I want to know everything about you."

Now, feeling more relaxed, Rachael told him about the inheritance she'd received and how Amanda helped her invest.

"You mentioned a cleaning lady?"

"Oh, yes. Rosa," Rachael said. "Rosa Gutierrez. She's from Mexico. She lives in the Mission District in an apartment building filled with middle-aged widows."

"Widows? I'll bet that place rocks."

Rachael laughed. "They each do something to supplement their pensions. Rosa does cleaning. Margarita is a part-time nanny. Consuela is a seamstress. Felicita does bookkeeping. I don't know them all. There's at least six of them."

"No lonely old widows there. I'll bet they eat their meals together too."

"They do, they do. They take turns cooking so each of them doesn't have to cook every day."

"By the looks of your place, Rosa's immaculate."

"Yeah, kind of feisty, dedicated. She comes on Thursdays and Fridays. You just missed her." As Rachael spoke, she noticed

Matthew check himself several times from placing a hand on her thigh as he drove.

"So your abusive father always said you wouldn't amount to much?"

"Yeah."

"He should have lived so long."

"What do you mean?"

"Well, I didn't know you back then. Seeing the way you now live and your dedication to writing, what I see in you is a wealth of creativity and perseverance."

"It's always been there." Matthew understanding her seemed suddenly overwhelming. Rachael's emotions fluctuated up and down nearly out of control. "Oh, Matthew, you give me too much credit."

"I'd embarrass you if I told you what I see," he said, waiting for an answer. She sighed. "Gentle, fragile, vulnerable…"

"Matthe-e-w."

"You haven't met anyone who showed you how important you are, have you?"

"Not in those terms." Now she was totally uncomfortable. She needed to change his train of thought. He drove as if he and his Corvette were part of each other. "This work you mentioned doing at the Haight Rehab, emotional issues, you said?"

"And a whole lot more. I work with adolescents and teens going through drug rehab programs."

"That's pretty heavy."

"Actually, I teach and coach sporting events which are part of the guys' rehabilitation process. Along with that comes dealing with their emotional issues too. I didn't think I was qualified. The kids are always interested in my physique," he said, leaning over the steering wheel and playfully flexing his powerful shoulders and arm muscles. They looked like they could cause his shirt sleeves to burst.

"I imagine that's a big attention getter."

"Yeah, I've been able to get a lot of kids into body building, aerobics, gymnastics. We did a fund raiser and got a lot of equipment donated to the Rehab." Pride and excitement filled his voice when he spoke of his involvement. "I can't wait till I have a son. I hope it doesn't happen too late. I sorta want to grow up with him." The comment seemed to come from deep inside his heart.

"We have something in common, sort of," she said, then paused. Why had she chosen those words. They made her look too eager, too naive.

"We do?"

"I volunteer at Lisbeth House, the abuse center. You've heard of it?"

"That's part of your therapy, right?"

"In the beginning it was. I know a lot about what's going on in those women's lives."

They slowed down in front of an old run down red brick building on the corner of Fair Oaks and 15th Streets. In earlier times, it must have been a thriving elementary school. The windows were now boarded up. They and the outer walls were covered with graffiti. A sign placed high up the wall at the side entrance displayed the name, *Woodland Sports Center for Teens.*

"This building's been condemned for years," he said. "The Rehab petitioned and got the gymnasium reapproved for use."

"Is that a neighborhood gathering place?"

"Actually, no. Use was granted strictly to accommodate sports events for teens and young people working their way out of drug and alcohol addictions."

"Boys only?"

He shook his head. "Girls too. Basketball, badminton, tumbling, aerobics and so forth, all take place at different times."

"This is where you spend your spare time?"

"Many hours, mostly coaching weightlifting and boys basketball. Dad and I submitted a proposal to The City to renovate this place for the kids," he said with a dubious expression. "The City couldn't afford it and said the school wasn't needed."

"That's too bad, considering the kids are more important."

"We're keeping their eyes open for another location. This place doesn't even have heat." As they came around the block again, a car pulled away from the curb. Matthew edged into the parking space. "Synchronicity," he said, snapping his fingers. "When things are going the way they're supposed to, everything falls into place."

Chapter 11

As they climbed out of the Vette, he threw a red bulky knit sweater over his shoulders and tied the sleeves loosely across his chest. They made their way through the side gate on a path leading to the rear entrance. The gym was in back at ground level. Sounds of a basketball game in progress spilled out. Crossing a small lobby and entering the gym, they found seats on the sideline as a few of the teens waiting to play yelled greetings to Matthew and whistled and hooted at Rachael. Several of the guys joined them. Matthew seemed proud to introduce her to everyone.

Another young man wearing sunglasses strolled over and squeezed into the crowd that gathered around. Matthew stood. They shook hands. When the guy sat down on the bleacher, the crotch of his droopy knee pants crossed near his knees. How did those guys keep from wearing their pants around their ankles? Matthew introduced the man as Fernando. He wore a hoodie sweatshirt with the hood thrown back. His dark hair was slicked back and he wore a red band around the top of his head and tied behind. Despite the sunglasses, he looked mean. He and Matthew sometimes talked in hushed tones. Rachael watched the game and allowed them their privacy. Then Matthew excused himself to talk to one teen farther down the sideline leaving her in the company of Fernando.

Suddenly, Fernando turned to her and drawled, "Ooo-whee. You're so fi-i-ine, Rachael." He flagged a hand loosely in the air. "Now we know why 'da smile on 'da man's face a'gin."

Rachael felt her face flush. "Why aren't you suited up with the rest of the guys?"

"No, baby. Nobody gonna' make me wear them shiny shorts? It ain't cool." His speech was exaggerated, hand gestures sharp. "Gotta' stay loose, chickee. Gotta' be cool."

A break was called. A tall, lanky young black kid dribbled the ball past Rachael, rolling his eyes and bouncing his head and shoulders up and down in a manner that exaggerated his body movements. He smiled with sparkling white teeth. His arms and legs were all over the place. His even brown skin glowed from perspiration. His face shined with it. He eyed her, checking her out, dribbling in place in front of her. In between dribbles, he clapped his hands. The bouncing ball and clapping beat out a rhythm as he began to rap.

"I like basketball, and exercise, too. I score lots of points, and this one's for you." As he finished, he leaped into the air and heaved the ball backwards over his head with one arm. His entire body turned in follow through. All heads turned in unison to follow the ball. The whole place went silent as the ball sank into the basket to the whoosh sound of the net.

"Yay," Rachael said, yelling and clapping loudly like the others.

"That's Dooley. He's some kind of ball player." Fernando said.

Someone called out to get Matthew's attention, directing him toward the lobby. He passed in front of Rachael, bending to tap her knee. "I'll be right back," he said, hurrying toward the doorway.

Soon he returned, saying it was time they leave. The game was almost over and he only wanted to check to verify that a couple of his kids actually showed up to participate in the game. They said their goodbyes. Dooley and Fernando, in their own comical ways, made a point to let Rachael know they liked what they saw and that Matthew was a lucky guy.

"Ooh-whee," Fernando said as he bounced around on bended knees, like he couldn't stand still. "Ain't no cold weather gonna bother you two. You two together gonna make some real San Francisco heat!"

She shook her head in disbelief of his antics.

Back out on the street, as Matthew opened the car door for her, he said, "Oh, not again." He let out a sigh of frustration. At the same time, Rachael saw the note stuck under the wiper blade. She remembered watching Matthew find notes on his truck at the park. He walked around and snatched the pink slip of paper off the windshield and read, then climbed into the car flicking his wrist and waving the note.

"I'm sorry," he said. "She does this all the time." Rachael remained silent. She knew what the note meant. "It's from Linda, the girl I used to date." He flipped it open with his thumb, holding it up for Rachael to see. She didn't look. "She wants me to call her. She wanted to know why the guys wouldn't let her in."

"Oh?" Rachael forced a half nod. It would seem that Matthew and Linda were still involved. Rachael felt small. What had she gotten into? She wasn't the type to go after another woman's man. It was overwhelming just going out on a date, and now this.

"One of the guys told me she was here and making a big issue about needing to see me. They sent her away, then came and got me. They didn't want to say anything in front of you."

"I see."

"Linda's playing her childish games and it's irritating me." He seemed to feel great discomfort with the situation. "I hope this doesn't put a damper on our evening." He looked at her hopefully.

"It doesn't bother me," she said dryly.

"She's never been in there, Rachael."

"Oh, c'mon. You and she sound pretty tight if she knows where she can find you. You want me to believe you didn't share this important part of your life with her?"

Matthew seemed to deflate, knew he was walking on thin ice, knew he'd better clarify. "We went together about three years. You might have seen me leave the park with her a couple of times."

"Well, no, I never noticed." What would it matter if she had seen? It wasn't a lie. Rachael never saw him leave with her. "You used to date her. You still see her?"

His expression was grim. Then Rachael realized what was going on inside his mind. They were getting progressively closer since meeting in the park. She was someone he didn't want to lose. Like she described Hunter in her novel, Matthew might go to the nth degree to get what he thought was worth it. It didn't matter that they were new to each other. With him, conversation came easy, as if he had no hang-ups, yet now he struggled. "Linda could make a scene if she was in the mood." He looked her straight in the eyes again. "I could get embarrassed, too, you know."

"Did you try telling her to get a new life?" Everyone had someone in their past. Meeting Matthew, then talking about Linda wasn't something she conjured for her story plot. If she was patient and listened, maybe she could learn more about love trysts to put her story characters through. Her book was in first draft format. She could change or add anything to spice it up. "Are you still seeing her?"

"She'd like to think so. Actually it's over for me."

"So you say."

"No, really. She tries to act like we're a couple. Her real interest is in anyone who can further her career or keep her in nose candy."

Rachael winced and lowered her gaze. Not drugs, too. That was a characteristic she wouldn't include in her story. "That life style, that's not for me."

Like the coolness of their conversation, air inside the car was chilly. He started the engine and adjusted the heat level. Still they sat. "Yeah, I guess it's the crowd she runs with. She's a top model at Stage Center. You heard of them? She's trying to get into acting, done lots of commercials, would do anything to get into the movies."

"She any good?"

"She's great looking, a natural blonde, gorgeous. Her lifestyle didn't always include me though, and her aspirations leave me empty."

"Have you done drugs?"

"Of course not."

"You're telling me you've been dating someone for three years who does, and you haven't?"

"She had stopped before we got together."

Nose candy. He did say he worked with people with emotional issues. What was he doing alone in the park? Maybe their relationship isn't as bad as he claims and he fills the hours till they can be together.

"Are your lifestyles that different?"

"They are now. We met at the Haight Rehab, when Linda began a series of lectures as part of therapy in overcoming her addiction. I do some volunteer work there. By the time I met her she seemed to have control of her life. She was getting lots of breaks re-establishing her career." He shook his head slowly, sadly.

"You were willing to overlook her past?" That was commendable. What kind of guy was he? He was in the mood to talk and that was good. She could learn what she needed to round out her character's demeanor. Matthew could provide some first-hand information she could use, if not in this story, a future book. That's as far as she could allow this friendship to go and she didn't care about her ulterior motives. If need be, she'd find another place outdoors to sit and write. She could climb down the cliff to China Beach. Shouldn't be too difficult.

"There was always something," he said. "We got engaged but that didn't make her happy. Soon after that, everything fell apart again. I'm sure she got back on drugs."

"Couldn't you tell?" Rachael couldn't help her lack of sympathy.

"I guess I kept making excuses for her. First she wanted to see me. Then she didn't. She got sick for a while. Someone told me she had an abortion." His voice cracked. He looked away, pain clearly evident in his expression.

A pang of sorrow shot through Rachael's nervous system. "Oh, I'm sorry." She flinched at the thought of Matthew and Linda sharing a bed.

"She started seeing other guys, to promote her career, she would say. By that time, I wanted out."

"But you still see her. You jump every time she comes around."

"She doesn't return my texts. I never know when she's going to show up. She lives in Marin. He thumbed the direction across the *Golden Gate Bridge*. "San Anselmo."

"She wants to see you but doesn't return your messages?"

"Not always. She stays somewhere in The City with friends because of long working hours. Her house is a junky place anyway. She keeps it so she can claim to live in Marin."

"I wouldn't have patience for pretense like that."

"Maybe I'm a pushover, I don't know."

Rachael felt a bit of empathy and didn't know why. "You aren't that easy, are you?"

"I hope not." He shook his head. "I brought it on myself, though, the deceit."

All this talk about Linda, a beautiful model. That part of Matthew's life wasn't anything she could give to her character.

Surely, it wasn't over if Linda knew where to find him. Rachael wanted to wind down the conversation until she could end it amicably and send him on his way. Other than physical description, Mathew and her story character would have little in common.

Chapter 12

Rachael thought about her own weaknesses and not being able to end the conversation. "If you're willing to keep in contact, doesn't sound like you're ready to end it."

He sighed and seemed to cave in. "She has my ring. That sounds petty. I went way over my head to please her. Way over my head." He paused, as if waiting for repercussions. "The ring's expensive. I'd like it back, if she hasn't hocked it and sniffed the proceeds up her nose. I'd like to know…"

"What?"

"If she aborted my baby."

"Sounds like you two have a lot of history together. If you could talk, get her back into therapy, arrange your schedules, you'll probably be back together before…"

"I'm telling you, it's over." Even he seemed shocked by the tone of his voice.

"I see," was all she dared say.

Evidently he held a lot of anger that should have been worked out long ago. Surely he hadn't meant to express it toward her. Rachael remembered herself expressing anger toward innocent others till she got into therapy and understood. She wasn't about to let that happen again. Living alone assured it.

"The last time we got together, over a year ago," he said, continuing in softer tones. "She was damned moody. Then, just as quick, she got real cuddly. Later, she fell asleep right in the middle of, you know, in bed."

"That's embarrassing, Matthew. I don't need to know that." Rachael wasn't sure how to receive that kind of conversation. She looked away. The people and era when she grew up were not of the same mentality. Today people seemed willing to air their dirty laundry wherever they found an ear.

"You know what something like that does to a guy? When I tried to wake her, she mumbled something about going to the cabin next weekend. Then she went out of it again." His words came out in a rush. "That blew me away. I don't have a cabin. She was out of it, didn't have a clue who she was with. That confirmed she was on drugs again, and seeing someone else." His words tumbled out like he needed to expel them.

Rachael wouldn't know how to detect someone doing drugs. "How could you tolerate knowing?"

"More of those excuses I made for her," he said regretfully. "That last time, that was it for me."

"But you're still making excuses. That's why you run over every time she honks at the park." Fat chance her story character would be a pushover. She envisioned her story character to be like the man of her dreams and being a pushover wouldn't be written into his demeanor.

"Rachael, it's been a year since I made my decision. I wasn't about to rush into another... I need to get my ring back to end this ridiculous charade. I leveraged a lot of my holdings to get the ring she wanted. Besides, when I get involved again, it's going to be with someone who isn't afraid to let me into her head."

That sounded like both a challenge and a threat. "You do need to heal."

The look on his face said he knew he had allowed the conversation to go too far astray. "Look, I didn't mean to burden you. You have your own difficulties to contend with." He sounded truly sorry. He was too eager, too open. He straightened up in the car seat and grew pensive staring off in the distance.

Rachael thought of Matthew continuing to see Linda even though he said he was not interested in that relationship any longer. Her thoughts and fears were confusing. A man like Matthew must surely know how to take care of his needs. That might be why he was interested in getting involved. The relationship with Linda was ending and he didn't want to sleep alone. He had to be assertive. She stared straight ahead through the windshield beginning to seethe inside.

"Rachael," Matthew said, taking her chin. "Listen to me. Linda's a druggie. She's not allowed in there. Those kids are rehabilitating. Some of them knew she was going through rehabilitation when she lectured at the Rehab. Now they know she's probably using again. I told them a long time ago not to let her in. It's too tempting for the others. The guys here, they know I'm not seeing her anymore."

Explained that way, the whole thing did sound plausible. "Do you think she flashes your ring around so your friends will think you're still together?"

"She may have hocked it and can't afford to retrieve it. That's why I buried the cost in my business expenses."

"Business expenses... how?"

"Linda filmed part of a series of TV commercials for my dad's business."

"Is her picture now a permanent fixture around your office?"

"Would you be jealous?" he asked, smiling, pressing his luck.

"Not in the least," she said. Why should she be jealous? If Matthew wanted to cling to a past relationship, then so be it. She didn't have to see him again.

"We weren't able to use the commercials. Linda felt she was given too small a part for someone of her reputation."

"What?"

"She wanted to speak and act. She tried to dictate the entire filming and, finally, refused to continue. Nothing was finished. Her agent even threatened to sue if we used any portion we might salvage. We took a loss on the whole thing. Dad and I buried the cost of the ring."

He seemed sad about the predicament with Linda, angry and frustrated as well. He spoke in past tenses, like a man who knew he had been had and was determined not to let it happen again.

"I'm sorry, Matthew. I have no right to pass judgment on anything you do."

"Yes, you do," he said. He turned the motor off again. "When we're together, you have every right to express what you feel in any manner you wish."

"This doesn't concern me."

Icy silence filled the car though the air had warmed. It seemed he sensed her interest slipping and he needed to do something to save the moment. Slowly, he continued. "Look, do you remember Fernando?" He thumbed toward the gym. "In there?"

"The hoodie guy?"

"And Dooley?" She nodded again, wondering what he was getting at. "They're cops, Rachael." Her mouth flew open. "They're cops who look much younger than they are, working with kids like they're some of the gang. The kids know them as counselors from the Haight Rehab, which they are. The kids don't know they're cops too. Do you remember seeing another guy who wore a hair net? He was playing."

She squinted trying to remember, then nodded. "The one who seemed stand-offish?"

"He's a narc." Rachael listened and looked at Matthew with her mouth hanging open. "His name is Juan Carlos, and those guys are as normal as you and me. They work undercover, especially Juan Carlos. He gets right into the thick of drug deals and everything else. And Dooley, the tall African-American? You know that big act he put on for you, dancing around and rapping and shooting the hoop? That's exactly what it was, an act, but mostly for the kids. He's a great ball player. He acts cool, but he's an ordinary person and just as refined as you and me."

Rachael sat in silent astonishment, thankful she had not mistakenly commented on the guys' antics. Anything she might have said would have proven to be quite embarrassing had she mentioned how phony they seemed.

"You see, Angel, Linda's not welcome here. She pops up on a whim wherever I am and makes everything go wrong."

"She's stalking you then, knows your car and where you hang out."

He didn't comment but started the car again, shifted, and pulled out into the street.

Rachael's thoughts worked overtime. Matthew didn't have to disclose anything about the undercover cops. Why had he? The idea of Matthew telling her was stunning. Matthew trusted her. How could he trust so easily? Not that she wasn't trustworthy. It was simply not part of her sensibilities to divulge secrets. Matthew must have looked inside her mind. He had to somehow know that he could trust her, and here she was, holding him at an emotional distance because she hadn't allowed herself to trust him. Suddenly, she began to see Matthew as being wiser and more intelligent than she imagined. The thought sent a flood of warmth through her nervous system. Just as quickly, she wondered if he was open-minded about everything, maybe that's how Linda was able to snag him. Could he be so naive that he didn't know his openness could hurt him and others as well? She began to wonder if anything she and Matthew shared would become public knowledge due to his in-your-face attitude.

Chapter 13

"Look, there's the usual Friday night lineup," he said, cruising slowly along Clement Street. "Being pacified with free wine."

"It's crowded," she said, straining to catch a glimpse. "It'll take forever for that line to get inside."

"Want some wine? It's worth the wait."

"I don't like to eat late. It's past eight thirty."

He looked at his watch. "You going somewhere? It's Friday night."

"How about across the intersection?"

"The Pier? Some friends once recommend that place."

"The seafood's fresh catch."

Their conversation was light through the soup and salad courses, mainly talking about the many great eating places in San Francisco. In the immediate area alone, Rachael named seven or eight other restaurants she favored with ethnic menus and each superb.

"Um-m," he said, savoring another bite of Mahi-Mahi. "This delicate white fish stirs up memories of being in The Islands."

"You've been to Hawaii?"

"Been there." He shrugged. "It's a good escape."

"I keep saying I'm going totally vegetarian," she said, ravenously devouring the tender grilled salmon. "Then I have a meal like this."

"Can you be that disciplined?"

"Can you tell by my plate?" She had almost finished with her meal.

"What motivates you?"

"To improve my meditation."

"I've thought about it some," he said. "I don't know if that's something I'm ready to tackle. Food's too tempting. Good food, that is."

"If you desire deeper meditation, maybe you should fast occasionally."

"You're a great deal more relaxed," he said, smiling. "Are you finally getting used to our being together?"

"Will you stop scrutinizing my every move?" It was half a demand and half light-hearted.

They stayed and talked for another half hour over hot teas. Then Matthew said, "Oh-oh. Look at that waiter by the kitchen door."

"Patiently waiting with towel draped over his arm," she said playfully. "An impatient look on his face. What's that tell you?"

"Hey," Matthew said, looking around. "This whole place is empty."

"I think they want to close."

"So much for quiet conversation."

Crossing Clement Street to the car, Rachael said, "I've eaten at a little French place, down a ways. They have a fireplace with sofas. I'm pretty sure they have a bar, so they must stay open after dinner hours."

"Point the way," he said, eagerly.

"Go slow, Matthew. We might miss it," she said as they crossed 10th Avenue. "We'd better take the first parking space we come to. It'll be impossible to find something right in front."

They dodged cars weaving back and forth across the double lines to bypass others double parked.

"There it is," she said, pointing. "*La Fleur*, on the right."

They circled around the block looking for an open space, a precious commodity in the Clement area on a Friday night. They drove up one more block and came around again as another car squeezed into a small vacated slot. They looked at each other under raised eyebrows. Then passing again right in front of La Fleur, tail lights flashed at the corner of the block ahead. Matthew threw Rachael a look and smiled out of the corner of his mouth.

"Synchronicity," Rachael said.

He eased alongside the car at the curb as it started to pull forward into the intersection. The driver behind Matthew honked. Rachael looked back as the driver behind pointed to the parking spot indicating he wanted it. He tried to ease his car toward the open space to take it the second Matthew moved up to jockey backward into position. His bumper seemed breathlessly close to Matthew's polished yellow.

"I'm not moving," Matthew said stubbornly. "And I dare him to nudge my Vette."

"I can solve this," Rachael said. In true San Francisco manner, she grabbed up her purse and jumped out of the car. She stood in the middle of the empty parking space until Matthew pulled forward and then backed into it. The other driver waited and watched in dismay. As Matthew climbed out of the car, the man flagged him the finger and sped away.

"Gee," Matthew said and shrugged. "Must be his favorite toy."

The fireplace sent out its warmth. Rachael had only been in the place once before when Tina wanted to scout it out before accepting a date. Rachael remembered they were both disappointed that the fireplace was gas and not wood burning, but this was the only place to come to mind for this evening's purpose.

Velvet sofas of forest green were thick and soft. No others were in the lounge area. Others were at the bar toward the back, and some noise could be heard from the few remaining patrons in the dining room. Soft sultry French ballads wafted into the room. Occasionally, mellow tones of a jazz saxophone lulled in the background. For the moment, they were alone.

Hot decaf tea with lemon wedges arrived. Settling in, Matthew pulled up a small ottoman and propped his feet. As Rachael removed her jacket, he reached for her, pulling her backward against him. Her hair fell against his face. His arm lay across her upper chest. She relaxed against him. He breathed in deeply and nuzzled her.

"I'm enjoying this time with you, Rachael Angeline," he said in a special voice. "I hope you're well aware I intend to see a lot more of you."

"You mean you haven't found anything to put you off?" she asked, with a hint of teasing. He might later find lots to change his mind. For the moment, she felt greatly at ease.

"Sounds like there's a scared little girl inside of you."

Rachael bolted upright turning to face him. "What?" She was about to say something sarcastic, then realized he was right, and held her tongue. She dropped her gaze and fumbled with the fabric of the sofa letting out a sigh of frustration. What was it that made her feel small when a truth was revealed?

"It's okay, Rachael. When someone's interested, you share. If the interest is genuine and sincere, you work things out together."

Again, he sounded like he was talking from experience. Of course he was. He freely donated his time helping troubled teens. He seemed to have more than an average understanding of human nature. He certainly must have something to offer, but he was moving too fast.

"Don't you hear enough about people's problems?" she asked, nervously forcing a smile. "You don't need to take on mine. Can't we keep it light."

"Not on your life." He was adamant. "I intend to know a person I care about. The outward appearance attracts, grooming, speech, table manners and such." He paused, thinking. "If nothing in the outer expression turns me off, what's left is to get into the person's head. And heart."

"Sounds methodical."

"You gotta admit. Something pulls two people together. If you can get past the outer trappings, you find the real person inside." He studied her reaction. "It's my belief that couples need to understand more of what makes each other tick, what motivates them to be one way or another. That includes any faults or shortcomings." He spoke cautiously as if trying to get a point across.

Then she understood. He was laying out what he expected of any relationship they might have together. She listened, staring directly into his eyes. One thing they always shared was great eye contact. At a time like this it unnerved her. "This is not the time nor the place. I don't know you, Matthew."

Chapter 14

"You'll like me," he said with a most conceited grin. Then as quickly, he was serious again. "I need to understand what that person inside of you is trying to tell me."

The tension was too much. Rachael began to feel the same apprehension she experienced in therapy. She needed to do something to relieve it. "Do you want to learn everything tonight?" she asked with another feigned smile. She felt cornered, wanted the conversation to end. She wished she were home alone.

"Can't happen all at once," he said. "I don't intend to let it drop though." He studied her. "This is something we have to get past, if we're to have a spontaneous relationship."

He was talking long term. What could he be seeing in her? And so soon. It wasn't the house, or her inheritance, or anything like that. He expressed an intense interest in her from the day they first spoke, even admitted he wished to meet her months before, in the fall of the prior year. Back then, he'd only seen her dressed down for sitting in the grass by a tree as she worked on her laptop. She shrugged, confused, felt a calm excitement knowing someone seemed truly interested. And he just happened to be the person she dreamed wouldn't show her the time of day.

Great at practicing avoidance of revealing anything about herself, she surprised him with a very direct question. "What about you, Matthew, what makes you so intense?"

"I refuse to believe problems are unsolvable. Get to the heart of the matter, then go on from there." He was thoroughly relaxed. He put his hand gently on her shoulder as they sat close. "I have many questions about you. About everything and everything. I hope you feel the same about me. And don't worry," he said. "I'm not going to learn something I can't deal with, then...," he said, snapping his fingers sharply, "I'm out of here. That's not me, so relax. I intend to know you better than your therapist." He smiled quickly as light from the fireplace lit up the devious twinkle in his gorgeous eyes.

"Okay, you'll get to know me as much as I feel confident letting you know. If you're leading me on," she said, teasing and slanting her eyes at him. "If you're leading me on, when I'm through with you, you will flee." They laughed. They needed to do more of it.

"You'd love my parents," he said suddenly. "Mom's name is Mona, Ramona Lee."

He told her about how his mother went through an unhappy spell a few years back and how his mom and dad separated. "Dad was like a zombie," he said. Then his father realized that Mona needed to have her own life. She wanted her own business. He agreed that if she would return and give their marriage another try, he would finance the business she always wanted.

Rachael turned sideways drawing her legs up under her, leaning on her arm on the back of the sofa, absorbed in what Matthew had to say. It was good to hear him talk. She could, at times, be too full of her own thoughts.

"I remember a time after they got back together. Even I knew there was some tension between them. Their anniversary was coming up. One night, Mom told me to stay in my room because they were going to have a late dinner and a private talk. Well..."

he said, smiling. "Do you know what happens when you tell a twelve year old to stay in his room?"

"You peeked."

"Mom fixed a candlelight dinner for their anniversary and got dressed up in this long sparkling blue dress. She was trying to show Dad everything was okay. Dad was always worried about losing her for good. While they were eating dinner, I saw them hugging and kissing." Matthew seemed to delight in telling, the devious child in him showing through. "I stayed in the shadows in the hallway. I wanted everything to be okay between them. I loved my mom, but I didn't want to move away from my dad again. I wanted them to stay together. I watched."

"I hope you're not going to say what I think you're going to say."

Matthew watched Rachael's expression for some sort of approval as he continued talking. "Right in the middle of dinner, Mom took Dad's hand and led him to the sofa. They started fooling around and before long, Mom's dress fell to the floor. Mind you," he said. "I was twelve. I couldn't have stopped watching if my life depended on it. They got stark naked and made love, right there on the sofa and on the floor. I watched. They were hugging and clinging together. They were holding and kissing each other and I was glad." He sighed. "I guess, soon after that, I started asking Dad to tell me everything about sex. That blew his mind."

"He told you everything?"

"Over a period of time. I don't know if he suspected I might have watched. To this day, I don't think they know."

"How did that episode effect you, Matthew? You were pretty young."

"Dad and I got real close. I thought he might get angry at me for wanting to know too much. Guess he figured if I was old enough to ask…"

Light from the fireplace flickered around the dimly lit room. He seemed intent on keeping the conversation on close personal matters. She felt hot and swallowed hard and looked downward.

Suddenly he said, "I suppose we should leave. It's almost one o'clock, and I've got to be at work at six."

"At six… this morning?"

"Actually, Dad and I are trying to finish these two jobs. We have a huge project coming up in three or four weeks and want to get these two houses out of the way. We're working seven days a week now."

After the short drive to her home, he waited while she unlocked her door. Not expecting him to follow, she stepped inside and turned to face him. He stepped right in after her, smiling.

"You can't say goodbye and expect me to walk away."

Her heart began pounding. What could he have in his mind? Certainly he wasn't going to turn out to be one of those guys who thought their dates owed them a little sex for having bought dinner. She felt a surge of panic and disappointment and backed away.

"I want to hug you, Rachael." He didn't wait for her reaction. "It's to show you I enjoyed this evening. I want to make sure you know it, then I'm out of here." His hands were on her shoulders holding her at arm's length. He smiled warmly.

With eyes wide open, she stared up at him, not knowing what she should be prepared for. He pulled her closer as she resisted. Feeling the strength in his arms, she wanted to melt against him. She felt confused again. Slowly, he bent down and left a gentle kiss on her mouth. She took in a sharp breath and couldn't move. He looked at her lovingly, then wrapped his arms snugly around her pulling her against him. He kissed her fully, covering her lips gently, and lingered.

Rachael wondered what kissing his sensuous mouth would be like. Suddenly it was happening. Her hands were flat against the front of his shirt. She felt them slipping around and onto his back and was powerless to stop them. She felt her breasts flatten against his strong chest as he pulled her tighter against him, his kiss insistent, while hers hesitated. Suddenly, she felt the tip of his tongue running over her lips, exploring. His breathing quickened. Hers did too, and she trembled. He was going too far. She had to stop him. She had to stop herself!

With great effort, she pushed away, covering her lips with her fingers.

He didn't resist her stepping back. He seemed as surprised and shaken. "Rachael..." he said, whispering huskily.

"You should go, Matthew." In a flash, thoughts raced through her mind. She wanted his kiss and nothing more. She didn't want him to stay. She wanted them to be in love. It was too soon for that. Maybe he just wanted sex. Maybe he was a little more polished than the others. Suddenly, her father's words thundered through her mind. *"Don't do those things! You'll turn into a whore!"* Sensing she could lose control, she had to end it. Now.

He simply let go and stepped back. "I understand." He spoke quietly in his straight forward manner, sincerely and without shame, letting his breath calm. They looked at each other for a short while. She said nothing. "I'm disappointed, but this doesn't change anything." He forced a crooked smile and squeezed her hand as he turned to leave. Then he let go and walked out the door toward his car without looking back.

Chapter 15

Rachael worked the hotline at Lisbeth House that Saturday and Sunday evenings. Being in service to others brought home the fact that her life had changed drastically. While volunteering, she selflessly devoted time to the caller's emotional care. Hearing a troubled woman's voice was all she knew at that moment. Being needed and able to help in return was helping her to like herself. She became someone who made a difference. The more time she spent with the abused, the more she realized abuse was a role she would no longer experience personally.

When she first began volunteering, she was constantly reminded of her own history. She struggled to turn the knowledge around to shed some light into another person's noxious existence. Except in rare instances, she wouldn't share information about her past with incoming patients. In their fragile mental states, they would see her as more fortunate. When some learned her story, they first felt resentment for her having gotten her life together. If someone asked why she was there, she would carefully divulge some of her experience.

On a couple of special occasions, Dr. Melton asked her to address a small group of women who were ready to hear another person's success story. Other than those instances, she concentrated on the patients. After a while, she didn't have to consciously think about how her experiences could be utilized to enlighten others. She simply got better, gaining experience and knowing exactly what needed to be said or done.

After a busy evening at Lisbeth House, Rachael returned home, spent and quiet. She read some meditational material to change her focus, then went right into deep meditation. Experience was slowly helping her realize she had no momentous problems of her own. She determined to keep herself safe from harm forever, from anyone. She would strive to find ways within herself to promote healing from any negative effects left over from childhood.

Through the years, however, memories would plague her. She'd find herself entangled in moods and fears, the source of which she had difficulty identifying. She struggled to understand the intense rage that sometimes welled up inside, seemingly from nowhere, and at the most inopportune times. Though the rages happened infrequently now, she dug deeper within trying to understand herself, knowing everything had a cause. Fortunately, her frustrations were fewer and quite diminished in severity. She was no longer being abused. That, and her commitment never to allow abuse to happen again, fed the knowledge that her healing would be completed. She learned to trust her judgment and determined to help those at Lisbeth House discover that same truth for themselves. Yet, each successful moment was diminished somewhat by the fact that she couldn't help Brandon overcome his emotional scars.

For the next three days Rachael remained sequestered, exercising, doing yoga and writing, pouring out her feelings in a make believe romance too perfect to exist, except to tantalize a reader's senses. Writing stories helped create the perfection she hadn't been able to attract into her own life.

Matthew hadn't called. Every time she thought of him, she felt a little more confused. His attention and affection excited her. Sometimes she would pace the floor of her office, or stand staring out the window over The Bay remembering his every word.

He told her to call anytime. That was earlier the first evening, before he turned and walked away without looking back. That one act probably meant he wouldn't call her again, that she would have to call him if she wanted to see him. He made it clear. He wanted more than a kiss. Did that mean she would have to take him to her bed if she wanted to see him again? Sex was out of the question. Getting that close that soon wasn't going to happen, if she had anything to say about how a relationship might develop. She waited for him to call.

Rosa, her cleaning lady, came on Thursday. As usual, she arrived as Rachael was showering. A habit by now, she had hot water ready by the time Rachael walked into the kitchen.

Rachael opened a paper bag sitting on the counter and peeked in. "Rosa, you didn't bring those Mexican pastries hoping I'd eat one, did you?"

"No, *senorita*. Not me." Rosa was a little heavy and had a full head of short salt and pepper hair. Her weight might have kept her face filled in. She wore no makeup and had only a few wrinkles around teasing dark eyes. It was amazing how she could navigate the stairs multiple times and never be out of breath.

"Rosa...?"

"No, no. I pick it on the way here. I put aside till time to go *mi casa*. Sure you no like?" At times she could have an incredibly playful personality.

"Don't tempt me."

Rosa removed one of the pastries for herself, then tucked the bag at the corner of the counter.

"Your Darjeeling, senorita," she said, sitting a cup and saucer on the counter. She gently pinched the skin on Rachael's arm. "Why you no eat more? *Muy flaca*. Need more meat."

"Eating sweets isn't going to put on muscle. If you think I'm weak," she said, teasing, "you're welcome to come and watch me in the exercise room."

"You like breakfast now?"

"I can get it."

"I fix. *Que queres*?" When she spoke her language, she could pronounce the r letters that seemed to vibrate off the end of her tongue.

"Grapefruit slices and one of those big fresh tomatoes will do."

"*Dios, mio.*" Her diet was something that caused Rosa to frown.

"I'll go dry my hair first."

Preparing food or meals for Rachael was not part of Rosa's duties. She was simply there to clean the bathrooms and kitchen and dust and vacuum the house and guest unit. She would polish the stairwell banister once in a while. Sometimes she took it on her own to wash all those windows on the balcony side. She insisted and it unnerved Rachael to see her on a ladder up there.

Those chores were enough for two days work. Rosa managed to change the sheets and get the laundry done and sometimes putter in the flower beds. Often she'd take a dip in the pool or hot tub. She fussed over Rachael like a mother hen. She learned to fix Rachael's vegetarian meals when she was there and did everything without batting an eyelid.

"How's your daughter?" Rachael asked, returning to the kitchen.

"Ah, *si*. She love *Nueva York*. Husband good. Good life."

"Have you thought about moving there?"

"No *gracias*, senorita. From here, closer to *mi Jalisco*. Besides, no find job like this anywhere." She smiled her ridiculous smile that said she wasn't afraid to admit the truth.

Rachael was probably taking the place of Rosa's daughter. If Rosa wanted to do the little extra things for her, she would allow it. Rachael always made sure to compensate Rosa for her efforts with birthday gifts and Christmas bonuses, and even financial help when more was needed. Once Rosa caught bronchitis and Rachael paid the doctor's bills which Rosa's meager insurance didn't cover. Little favors made life a whole lot easier and Rachael was always intuitively aware when help was necessary.

Rosa, likewise sometimes verbalized happiness for Rachael in the form of a man. *I could introduce you to some of my young acquaintances*, she once said. She didn't ask a second time. Rosa was well aware her younger party-loving friends wouldn't understand why Rachael chose to refrain from eating meat or drinking alcohol or caffeine. Certainly, they may not slow down long enough to understand her yoga and meditation.

Rachael once tried to explain to Rosa that she had a rough childhood and wasn't in a hurry to place her life at the mercy of yet another man. Every once in a while, she would catch Rosa looking at her sideways as if trying to figure out what was wrong with her.

"Senorita, why you no smile today?"

"Rosa, I… uh… went out with the guy in the park."

"*Por fin*," Rosa said. Rachael had told her a little about Matthew, what he looked like and what his personality seemed to be. Rosa was anxious to meet him. "Finally," she said again, then frowned. "Was it so bad to give you this kind of face?"

"I don't know. Everything went okay, till the end."

"*Que mas, que?*"

"He might be like every other guy looking for a good romp."

"So soon?"

"What do you mean 'so soon'? It's not going to happen, Rosa."

"Ah, *pues…* not right away."

"Rosa!"

"Give him time to show his colors," she said. "Then?" She rolled her eyes and swooned.

Rosa worked extra hard for the next two days, lingering past quitting time, assuring the house was immaculate for this special man. Yet, by the time Rosa left on Friday evening, Matthew hadn't called.

Sunday arrived. He hadn't called. Rachael toyed with the idea of calling him to chat, then asked herself, about what? She didn't have a clue as to what she might say to him on the phone to make him want to talk for any length of time. She didn't want to invite him over, thinking he would interpret that as her invitation to resume where they left off. She decided waiting for him to call would be best. That's what her father would have advised.

The four day July Fourth weekend arrived. Only Brandon called. He asked Rachael not to drive up that Monday. He was having friends stay over.

Each morning on that holiday weekend, Rachael walked to Tina's alone to quietly enjoy a light repast. She always carried her laptop. She chatted briefly with a lot of the regular customers she hadn't seen for a while. People watching was a favorite past time.

The younger people from the area who congregated at Tina's talked about important topics like environmental or political issues, computers, and the arts. Of course, there was always talk about who was dating whom. A few even knew something about meditation. Meditational techniques weren't something a true meditator learned from anyone else, even though Rachael would like to have known one person with whom to share spiritual experiences.

Though Rachael knew many of the people who frequented the corner, she preferred to remain distant. She avoided lengthy, mind-bending conversations and usually sat alone. That way, she wouldn't have to explain herself or prove anything. Sometimes, at an outside table, she would prop her feet on a chair and tip her face backward to soak up sunlight.

After a while, she would walk home and get right into exercising or yoga. In mid-afternoon, she'd resume writing till way past midnight, sometimes neglecting to eat anything more. Finally, in the middle of the night, she'd flop into bed exhausted.

The phone rang a few minutes after noon on Wednesday.

Chapter 16

"Hi," he said, sounding upbeat. "You haven't called me, Rachael. I was hoping to hear from you."

"Well, I wasn't sure what would be a good time to reach you," she said, lying.

"C'mon, we have cell phones." He paused. She didn't respond. "Are you not interested, Rachael? Did I come on too strong?"

Not interested? Her heart began to fearfully pound. "No, no, you didn't." She hesitated. He waited. She struggled to keep her voice even. "I'm not sure I'm ready to get involved with anyone, Matthew. I think you're way ahead of me, I mean, I would like to develop a relationship before…" She couldn't finish.

"Rachael, come on. You can talk to me." He spoke softly, prompting her.

Rachael took a deep breath and mustered her courage. "I'm not ready for a physical relationship. I don't believe in starting a relationship based on sex." She felt proud, a little astonished, at having said it out without her voice quivering.

"Is that what you think? All I want is sex? Angel, getting into your secret bedroom isn't the way I want to start to know you."

"Really?" she asked, her tone expressing doubt. The fact that he referred to her secret bedroom, which she hadn't shown him, evidently played on his mind. She wasn't dumb. His remark was a dead giveaway. She sighed into the phone. In the least, he was thinking about her. She was learning to read him. Yet, she wondered why he hadn't called, but dared not ask. He said he started dating again after his breakup with Linda. He was probably seeing other girls, too, and that was deflating to think about.

"Well? I'm waiting, Rachael. Are we going to do a thing together or do you want to let it drop?" There was a hint of teasing in his voice again.

Rachael's heartbeat started fibrillating. What did he mean, *do a thing together*? "I, ah… yes, I would like to see you again." She wanted to ask when, but was sure it would be too forward of her. After therapy and achieving a great measure of self-confidence, something inside still wouldn't allow her to take command of the situation and ask when they might get together. Her telling a man she'd like to see him on such-and-such date and time would be akin to placing herself on the proverbial sacrificial altar.

A man's voice came through the phone from the background calling Matthew's name. Then someone started the motor of a noisy piece of equipment.

"Rachael," Matthew said, speaking louder. "I'm calling from the jobsite. If you want to get together, call me tonight and we'll talk about it, okay?" He seemed distracted. "Call about nine," he said, yelling into the phone.

"Okay, I guess. Nine o'clock," she said, raising her voice.

The rest of the afternoon was spent at her computer. Her thoughts kept returning to their noontime conversation. Matthew sounded genuinely curious as to why she hadn't called. Over and over, she thought about every word he spoke, the inflections of his voice, and how he seemed to be able to cut their conversation short at the end. She'd better call this evening if she counted on seeing him again. "Somehow, you'll find the courage," she said out loud. She tried to perceive how calling him would not be a wrong thing to do. At best, the concept was difficult to comprehend. Unable to grasp the fact that it would simply be okay for any reason at any time, she put subject out of her mind.

Sunlight faded quickly. As nine o'clock drew nearer, Rachael became more and more hyperactive. Earlier in the evening, she had eaten more than usual in an effort to keep her nervous stomach quiet. Now she was paying the price with anxiety and acidity. She wondered why she hadn't been able to master the art of yoga and meditation during times of exceptional stress. The techniques always worked when she felt peaceful. She made a mental note to try to discover stronger techniques to help her calm down when she needed most to rely on them. Finally, at nine fifteen, she picked up the phone and tapped in the number.

"Hello…" a sleepy voice mumbled on the other end.

"Hi. Matthew."

"Oh… hi. I guess I dozed. I'm beat, totally zonked." He must have been. Even his words sounded exhausted. She wondered if he pretended to be tired so he could end the conversation quickly again, or if he was that spent. "I wanted you to call this evening to give me a chance to check with my parents before we spoke." He sounded like he was beginning to wake. "We're going out on the boat on the seventeenth. Would you like to come?"

"You're taking the boat out? The one you live on? Where are you going?" Rachael was beginning to ask questions the same way Matthew did when he was excited or curious about something.

"We're going up through the Delta, your old stomping grounds, along the Sacramento River."

"Re-e-ally?"

He yawned into the phone. "I'm sorry. Dad and I are pushing these two houses. Actually the crews can do the rest from here on. We're due to start this job remodeling a big apartment complex in Daly City. Did I tell you about that?"

"You mentioned it."

"Dad wants to make one good trip on the boat before we start that job. He takes the old boat out about once a month. With this job coming up, we've got to stay with it. The housing market hasn't picked up and this is a gold mine for us when other people can't find work."

Rachael loved to hear him talk. He was thorough about explaining everything, like he always learned the details of anything in which he became involved.

"The Delta?"

"Well, Rachael? You going to keep me up all night wondering?" Even though he sounded bone weary, he joked. He purposely snored loudly through the phone, teasing again.

"Yes, I'd love to go."

The thought of being on the water again in the Delta sent Rachael's emotions skyrocketing. Was it possible some dreams do come true? Brandon wouldn't share the family boat and a long time passed since she'd last been on the water.

"You sure you can free up some time?"

"Mattheeew!" She could sense his wide teasing grin through the phone.

"It's a week from this coming Sunday. We're going up for one day. Usually we like to go for the weekend, but not this time. Anyway, if you're going, you have enough time to get a couple of things together that you might need."

"Like what?"

"A light wind breaker and some deck shoes. If you have sneakers with good tread, they'll do."

"Got 'em."

"And, of course, I get to see you in your bathing suit, don't I?" he asked, teasing again. She didn't respond. He yawned again. "Don't think we'll be doing any water skiing though." His voice began drifting off again.

"Are you falling asleep?"

"Angel, I'm tired," he said, stifling yet another yawn. "Can you call me sometime in a few days, a little earlier. I'd like to talk a little longer. I've been missing you." His words trailed to nothing more than mumbling.

His breathing was labored. Surely, he was nodding off. She whispered good night just loud enough for him to hear. The sound from the other end was a slow sigh of a sleepy person before the connection went dead. With emotions beyond recapture, she went right to her computer expressing her joy through writing.

When Rosa arrived the next day and noticed the difference in Rachael, she became caught up in her mood and baked a carrot cake. Rosa helped Rachael pick out what they judged to be a proper bathing suit to wear for the first time with Matthew as well as please his mother and father. Definitely, a skimpy bikini was out.

"The boat Matthew lives on must be larger than a ski boat in order to sail that far north from the Bay Area," Rachael said thoughtfully. "It'll be close quarters and I don't want to be near naked in front of his parents."

"You're too shy," Rosa said.

"I can't remember a guy ever being in my pool." Rachael dreaded any man should see her in a swimsuit.

Rosa flicked here eyebrows. "Maybe when you're eighty."

The next Wednesday arrived and Rachael realized she hadn't yet called Matthew after saying she would. She had to settle down, collect her thoughts, make the call. Simple. Matthew would see her in a bathing suit. Maybe she'd wear shorts and a shirt or some kind of cover up. Maybe not wear the swimsuit, but pack it in a tote bag. At least she'd made up her mind to go. The thought of having an opportunity to be on a boat again, in the Delta, kept her emotions soaring.

Then she remembered if she and Matthew were getting into the water, she'd have to remove her make-up. Without it, her auburn lashes left her eyes looking quite pale, like an adolescent girl. She dreaded the thought of having to remove her makeup and at the last moment thought about trying to find something indelible that wouldn't wash off in water.

She had yet to meet Matthew's mother. Panic lodged in her throat. If they didn't hit it off, they'd be stuck together in close quarters for the whole trip. A feeling of uneasiness ran through her.

By the time she picked up the phone to call Matthew again, she had almost talked herself out of going. With reasons conjured from nowhere, she nearly convinced herself she'd be out of place on board. Then Matthew answered the phone with a positive voice that told her he was elated at hearing from her. Rachael's resistance vanished.

They talked briefly about what was going on in their lives. Later, he said, "I'll be over early on Sunday, by six. Can you be ready?"

She hesitated. If he picked her up, that meant he'd have to bring her home again. She dreaded the thought of going through a repeat of saying goodbye after their first date.

"If there's a lot to do to get under way, I can drive there. Yes, that's probably better. Why don't you tell me how to find your boat."

"Actually, Dad and I will trim the boat on Saturday. You might have trouble finding the right slip. I'll pick you up. It's just a hop over the bridge."

She could find her way around most any place and not get lost. Matthew seemed adamant. Finally, she decided she could handle him if their parting at the doorway went that far again. Who would drive was a silly thing to debate.

In the next couple of days she mulled over what he might have been doing. He hadn't called. First, she convinced herself he was seeing someone else, then told herself she shouldn't wonder. Even so, it upset her. Yet, why was she feeling possessive?

"Maybe does much physical labor," Rosa said reassuringly the next day. "Not only being the boss."

"I hadn't thought of it that way."

He wasn't quitting at noon or three o'clock. He worked from five in the morning till sometimes after six in the evening, dragging himself home bone weary every night.

"Also has volunteer service at Rehab… every week, like you say."

"That's right," Rachael said. "Maybe he was too busy to call or too tired when getting home late."

Maybe he waited to see how assertive she could be by calling him for a change. Rachael's programming didn't allowed her to dwell on such things. If he were interested, she expected him to call, and that was that.

"You want relationship, no?" Rosa asked.

"A meaningful relationship, on my terms." Having some control of the situation was one way she could feel at ease and not let anything happen that she couldn't get out of.

He asked her to accompany him and his parents. Certainly, that meant he considered her special. He wouldn't try anything with them along. Somehow she'd get through the day and enjoy the trip too.

Chapter 17

Matthew was right on time again. He wore white Jamaica shorts and deck shoes, minus any socks, and an open hooded sweat shirt jacket over a blue tee with some sort of Hawaiian logo across the front.

"What kind of watch is that?" Rachael asked.

"It's a tidal chronometer. It's my dad's. I lost mine somewhere." He slipped it off his wrist and handed it to her. "I'll show you how it works once we're under way."

Excitement about sailing again was exemplified by his hurried attitude. He looked rugged and ready and too good to be true. With someone like that, he might lose interest in someone not thrilled about setting a public image.

Rachael wasn't like most people her age. Keeping up with the crowd wasn't for her. She didn't do any socializing. In time, Matthew would probably find her boring. She knew things would happen that way. Yet, for the time being, she'd enjoy the boat ride and pray he wouldn't notice how out of place she felt.

She carried a canvas tote containing her bathing suit, makeup and other essentials. She wore white denim knee shorts and a print cotton shirt left open over a blue halter. Matthew's glances followed her every move. Being appreciated was nice, though made her jittery to the point of wanting to scream at him to keep his attention on driving.

The ride to the boat would be a short one, over the Golden Gate Bridge and down into Sausalito to the harbor. Now it was Rachael's turn. She couldn't keep from peeking at Matthew's bare legs as he drove. When he began to speak she was thankful for the distraction.

"You haven't met my mom yet. I know you'll like her. She's a pretty fine lady," he said proudly. Till then, he hadn't spoken much of her.

"Are you close to your mom?" Rachael felt slightly intimidated. She didn't know what to expect and her stomach was queasy. On top of everything, his family might be too sophisticated. They owned a boat big enough to live on, they hired models for advertisements for their flourishing businesses, and had built a presence in the Bay Area. Rachael thought of her few accomplishments and felt like an outsider.

In fact, she didn't know what to expect of the entire day. Originally, Matthew said he lived on his dad's boat. Rachael guessed that he tolerated a small cramped space because he didn't want the responsibility of a house or rent.

They entered the harbor parking area and Matthew waved at two guys walking by. One leaned down to see who Matthew had in the Vette with him. Rachael felt conspicuous and yet, excitement filled her knowing she was being seen with someone like Matthew. They continued on, past the smaller sailboats, to the far end of the harbor where some empty slips looked much wider.

"This is *Basin Two* of *Clipper Harbor*," he said.

Boat sizes were getting much larger in the direction they were headed. He pulled into a numbered parking space, got out, walked around, and opened her door. He grabbed her bag while watching her, as if expecting to see something in her eyes. His sparkled mysteriously. He walked fast pulling her by the hand through the maze of boats as they headed out toward the end of the dock.

The size of the boats was mind boggling. They were beautiful and well maintained and each one was larger than the last. Rachael couldn't believe her eyes as she looked from one to another and another. Finally they arrived at the slip farthest out.

"Here we are," he said, like an announcement.

Rachael's eyes opened enormously and her jaw dropped as she studied the boat from end to end. "This is your dad's old boat?" she asked, in total disbelief. "You live on a yacht?"

"Welcome to the Mona Lee II," he said, gesturing with a wide sweep of an arm. Her name was painted in large flowing blue script across the stern. He smiled broadly at Rachael's look of bewilderment. "You don't have the corner on surprises, Angel." He put his arm around her shoulder, gave her a squeeze, then helped her climb astern.

What Matthew casually referred to as his dad's old boat was a fifty foot motor yacht, white with medium blue trim and didn't look very old either. "What is this little boat?" she asked, shaking her head.

"A *Chris Craft Constellation*. Dad traded his old '73 *Hatteras* for this one." He turned quickly as someone approached.

"Hi," Ramona said, greeting them.

Matthew introduced the two women.

"Call me Mona, please," she said, clasping Rachael's hand. "At last. We get to meet you." She smiled and wrapped an arm around her son's waist. "I'm happy you could join us on Matt's birthday."

"Mom!"

"You didn't tell me this was your birthday."

"It's no big deal, Rachael. I don't make an issue of my birthdays."

"I'd have loved to surprise you."

"You're here, you're my surprise," he said softly, looking into her eyes.

Mona teased, clearing her throat conspicuously. She wore a lavender sweat suit that fit utterly perfect. It could have been tailor made. Standing side by side, Rachael discovered similarities between herself and Mona. Both were thin and the same height.

"I've always wanted to straighten my hair," Rachael said, noticing Mona's dark, silky shoulder length cut.

"Then you should try it. It's easy to care for," she said, as smile lines appeared around sparkling almond shaped blue eyes.

Her nose was straight with a soft tip which may have been the softening factor that kept Matthew's nose from being fully like his father's Roman type. Mona was quite a striking person, with high cheek bones and a classic face not easily forgotten.

"Please be comfortable here, Rachael. We're going to have a lot of fun today," Mona said with an almost childlike excitement in her voice. "Cam's not back yet. He went to his office up on Caledonia Street." She smiled warmly at her son. "Matt will want to show you around before we get under way." Mona seemed a woman with absolutely no pretenses. Her glance at Matthew was the look of mother's pride. Rachael hoped the look meant she approved of his choice of sailing partner.

"Come with me. I'll give you the grand tour," he said, motioning for her to follow. She dropped her tote bag in a corner. They climbed to the next level.

"What we have here is the aft salon," he said, mimicking a tour guide.

The aft saloon was decorated in varying shades of peach. Everything possible was convertible to a bed. The boat had air conditioning. They climbed a short stairway to the Pilothouse. The floor, made of reddish hued teak planking, shined free of dust. Two pedestal seats looked out of tinted wrap around windows at the helm station.

Next they climbed to the fly bridge, where he explained a lot about the yacht's specifications. They climbed back down to the lower salon and passed through to the galley, which was fully equipped and completed in light beige wood tones. Not an inch of space was wasted. Counter tops covered major appliances.

"I didn't know anyone cooked enough on a boat to require a complete kitchen."

"This boat was equipped to service fishing trips at sea. Dad doesn't fish much. This is the way it was when he got it. The fly bridge was still decked out."

"Why would he buy such a large boat if…"

"It's dad's toy. He said rowboats were for kids."

They descended a few steps down into a hallway in the bow with doorways opening into other rooms.

"There's more space here than I imagined."

"These are staterooms. This is the master suite," he said with an unexpected twinkle in his eye.

"Oh, wow. This is the best."

A queen sized platform bed covered the water supply tank. There were night stands, even a long dresser against one wall, ample closets and what looked like a rather spacious bathroom tucked into the bow beyond another opened doorway. Wall treatments, bed covers, carpeting and other furnishings were in various shades of peach and green.

"Mom coordinated the interior. She took her time and worked with a decorator. You'd be amazed what can and can't go onto a boat."

"Why not?"

"Mostly because of the moisture that's always present."

Rachael poked at the bed with her fingertips.

"Go ahead, lay on it," he said.

She did, being careful not to place her sneakers on the spread. "Your mom and dad have a pretty cozy nest here," she said, pleased, forgetting herself momentarily. "I thought a bed on a boat would be like sleeping on a slab. Is your bed as comfortable as this one?"

Matthew's smile widened. "Angel," he said cautiously, barely able to contain himself. "I'm the person who lives on this boat. You're laying on my bed."

"You-r-r bed?"

There could well have been a hydraulic lift under her pushing her upward. She sprang straight upright to a standing position seemingly without bending.

Matthew broke into hysterics. He hugged her and laughed uncontrollably. Finally, lost for words, all she could do was laugh along.

Chapter 18

"Sorry for the delay, folks," Cameron said, hurrying on board. "Let's get under way."

Although the air was a bit brisk and thick fog hovered over the Bay, the sun's rays began to leak through the haze.

"This should turn out to be a perfect day for a cruise," Matthew said. "The weather's always better inland."

"Yeah," Cameron said. "We need to get beyond San Pablo Bay before the glut of sailboats start proliferating on the waterways."

Matthew turned to Rachael. "I wanted to explain what goes into getting under way. This fog's too risky for much talking right now. Dad and I'll be preoccupied for a while."

"I remember a lot about being on the water."

"Then you know there's too much involved manipulating a vessel this size through fog to become distracted in conversation."

Matthew untied ropes from the cleats on the dock, threw the ropes on board, and hopped on. "This is starboard," he said, gesturing along the right side of the vessel. He pulled down a long awkward white pole from its mount on the outer wall of the lower salon. "Push against the dock, like you see me do," he yelled over his shoulder as he took down another pole and made his way toward the bow. She positioned herself, imitating to his stance. Leaning into the pole, he pushed against the dock and watched to see she did the same. The craft floated free from its moorings. Another long push for ample clearance and Cameron started the engine.

After remounting the poles, Matthew leaned over the side. "These inflatable bumpers are called fenders," he said, pulling them onto the deck. "Always haul up the fenders when you put out." That done, he wiped his hands on a towel Mona brought, gave Rachael a quick peck on the cheek, and headed to the helm leaving her alone with Mona in the lower salon.

"I watched you fend off," Mona said. "You learn fast."

"That's easier than it looks," Rachael said. "I didn't know such a large boat would float so easily."

They stayed below moving from one side of the vessel to the other watching the harbor pass by. Then they went upstairs to the pilothouse and looked out from behind Matthew and Cameron at the helm.

Rachael was surprised. "You can barely hear the motor up here."

Mona began to explain what she knew the men would be doing. There was quite a bit involved in getting under way and Rachael was excited about learning. Mona smiled warmly, studying Rachael.

Rachael smiled, silent momentarily, pondering Mona's scrutiny and thinking about the two men at the helm who acted more like best friends or brothers than father and son.

After a while, they passed majestically under the Richmond-San Rafael Bridge.

"There are a couple of places along the way where we'll have something to do," Mona said.

"I'm ready." Rachael was excited.

Mother and son were thorough and well versed in their chosen activities. Mona talked more about the river, then coaxed the conversation toward the subject of relationship matters.

"Have you and Matt been doing some exciting things?"

"Actually, no, I mean, we met… went to dinner once."

"I thought you met several months ago. I'm sorry, didn't mean to pry. The way he talks about you, I thought you see each other often."

That was good news, hearing that she had been in Matthew's thoughts.

Now Mona seemed awkward and changed the subject. "You've got to come visit my store. Matt said you write and read a lot." The store was evidently something she was quite pleased with. Her face took on a whole new light when she spoke of her business. "Matt's my best customer." She smiled. "You both do yoga, don't you? I mean, Matt said you do too." She seemed embarrassed admitting things Matthew related.

Slowly, Rachael nodded agreement and smiled cautiously, not knowing whether she was about to hear something for or against her chosen beliefs.

"Matt has read every book on every kind of yoga I can find for him. He's the main reason I started carrying books on Eastern philosophy."

"Every book?" Rachael hadn't known how deeply Matthew was involved in yoga. She watched him practice in the park and he mentioned having read a few books. That explained why he seemed adept at his exercise regime. He wasn't doing only the physical postures. More than likely, he was consecutively performing the mental ones as well.

"Once I started carrying those books," Mona said, interrupting Rachael's thoughts. "I was amazed to learn how many people are interested in the eastern cultures."

They sailed through San Pablo Bay, then passed under the Carquinez Bridge. "I didn't know San Pablo Bay was this big."

"C'mon. Let's go topside."

Grabbing her jacket, Rachael followed Mona to the main deck. They sat and looked out over the water as the yacht sailed under the Benicia Bridge in its state of never-ending reconstruction.

They skirted Suisun Bay, the graveyard for antiquated rusting military vessels sitting dead in the water.

Matthew could see her and Mona from the helm. If he was honest in his intentions, deep down inside, he must wish she and his mother would become friends, good friends.

Making good time, they sailed past the southern-most tips of Honker Bay and Chipps Island, and then past Point San Joaquin and the mouth of the San Joaquin River. A strong bay breeze was pushing into the Delta and clearing away the inland tule fog.

"We've entered the Sacramento River Deep Water Channel," Mona said, waving an arm and pointing from bank to bank. After another half-hour, they veered to the right. "Now we're in the Sacramento River. It'll be pretty much of a smooth run up to Rio Vista from here."

The mention of the familiar childhood place in the Delta caused Rachael's anxiety level to rise.

As the tip of Grand Island passed port side, Mona led Rachael out to the bow.

"I didn't know about this part of the river when I grew up here," Rachael said. "The water was usually too choppy to take our small ski boat to make it this far south."

"Cabin cruisers towing skiers zip through this area," Mona said. "To expect to maneuver this big tub as easily would be ludicrous."

They inched alongside the river bank. The trip was going smoothly. Mona continued explaining as they sailed. Ahead, northeast of Freeport the channel was filled with shoals and wing dams. Wing dams were installed to scour out the channel bottom. They would be under water at high tide. They could hit one if they sailed too close to the banks. "I'd hate to think what would happen if we bashed into one of those." Mona grimaced, paused, thinking. "Oh yes, there are many bridges along the way. The guys will radio ahead for clearance."

"So much to do."

Matthew called through the PA system for Rachael to come up and join him in the pilothouse. On the way, Mona insisted she change into her bathing suit. The sun was beginning to beat down and glare off the pristine white of the boat. She said they might sun on the deck or swim later, so they both washed off their makeup. Rachael felt comfortable enough to do so because Mona had no qualms about washing hers off first.

Mona looked at Rachael's clean face. "Geez," she said. "Not even a wrinkle."

Rachael began to feel uncomfortable knowing Matthew was about to see her as plain as she could be. She hid behind sunglasses and wore a loose beach shirt over the bathing suit.

Despite feeling self-conscious, Rachael felt proud, even a little smug. Being with Matthew was like being with someone who knew everything. He was sure of himself in the right kind of ways. He could even make mistakes look like part of a plan. To think he cared enough to want her company.

He was perched in a pedestal chair. She stood leaning against him. If was amazingly quiet in the pilothouse, unlike the outside where she heard the motor, wind and water, and other noises. Mona and Cameron sat behind in the aft salon and were probably watching. She could feel their curiosity without having to look back. She felt nervous. From bits of information, she gleaned that Mona and Cameron were greatly interested to know what was going on in their son's life. They seemed a positive, loving couple, and of course they'd peek, probably every chance they got. They were concerned for their son's happiness, and from a couple of vague comments Mona made earlier, they didn't want him hurt again like he was with Linda.

Of course, Rachael had no intention of hurting him, yet she wasn't about to try to appease him to win him. She felt great anxiety when thinking about how much time a relationship would take from her work days. She became absorbed in her thoughts watching the river flow by. Matthew threw her a teasing sideways glance. Rachael wondered if Mona and Cameron knew or even cared that their voices were carrying forward.

"Cam, do you think he's serious about her?" Mona asked. "They've just met."

"I think he's more serious than she is," Cameron said. "Matt told me he's been eyeing her in the park since way back last year. Just when I think he's a copy of his horny old man, I hear him say a thing like that. I mean, what's taken him so long?"

Matthew glanced at Rachael again and squeezed his eyes closed, flinching at the truth. Rachael threw him an *Aha!* look.

"I think he's serious, Mona. Look at the way he's always looking at her. If he doesn't watch where he's going, we'll run aground."

Both Matthew and Rachael fixed their attention straight ahead and tried not to laugh. Matthew put a finger to his lips instructing Rachael to listen. He evidently didn't care that she learned some truths. He seemed to get a kick out of his parents speculations.

"You spoke with her first. What was your opinion?"

"I spent thirty, maybe forty minutes with them in the park that day. She seems like she's got a good head on her shoulders," Cameron said, sounding thoughtful. "I saw the way she looked at him. We got dirty that day, covered with construction grit. Still, she couldn't keep her eyes off him."

This time, Rachael glanced up at Matthew knowing she'd been found out.

"I don't know though, I don't think they're doing anything, you know, sleeping together. If they were, Matt wouldn't have that hungry look every time he gets close to her."

Matthew pulled Rachael closer. "Talk to me," he said. "I don't want you to hear all my secrets."

"Watching the water pass is hypnotic," she said, teasing. "Stay focused on the water."

"I don't know though," Cameron said, speaking low. "This abuse thing, sort of scares me."

Rachael stiffened. Evidently Matthew told them everything he knew about her. Her heart fluttered. She tried to contain her anger. She looked up at Matthew. "How could you?" she asked, whispering. She was almost in tears and wanted to pull away from Matthew's side. She felt paralyzed.

"We haven't had anything like that in our family," Cameron said. "How could he—"

"Maybe it's not as bad as you think," Mona said. "Give her the benefit of the doubt."

"You know, Matt's—"

"Cam, I don't think Matt's the kind to elope or anything like that. Good heavens. He's thirty-one years old. If he does, that's his business. We brought him up right."

"He's dying to have his own son, Mona. I hope it doesn't make him do something he'll regret."

Matthew squeezed her shoulders again as if he wanted to distract her. Rachael sneaked a look in the overhead rear view mirror. Mona sat stroking Cameron's cheek with the back of her fingers as she talked, relaxed with each other, with them being present, too. Rachael stared out at the water and let her mind drift.

"I hope so," Cameron said. "You know, I look at her, and I see a real deep streak of something running through her. I can't put my finger on it."

Again, Rachael wanted to scream. *What does he think he sees? What would he know?*

"I sensed it, too," Mona said. "I interpret that as will and quiet determination. She's a little resigned. She might simply be passive aggressive."

Rachael raised an eyebrow. Was that another label for her… passive aggressive? Her therapist said she was. Was she that easy to read? She needed to do something to stop Mona and Cameron from talking.

"Wouldn't that be a change?" Cameron asked with a smile in his voice. "Matt falls in love with the first quiet girl he's ever met and she leads him on the chase of a lifetime?"

Rachael couldn't help smiling as her emotions bounced up and down.

Matthew cleared his throat real loud. "Hey, Dad," he said loudly. "When's the last time you went fishing up here?"

Mona and Cameron looked forward suddenly as if they had forgotten they weren't alone.

"Last time we came up with the Claytons," Cameron said.

"And where were you just now, Rachael?" Matthew asked quietly near her ear.

"What do you mean?"

"Staring out at the water watching the river pass by? Did you hear all of their conversation?"

"I-I guess I didn't," she said, lying. "Did I miss something?"

"It's better that you did," Matthew said with a sigh of relief. He smiled to himself, taking peeks at his mother and father through the rear view mirror as they moved around in the cabin.

"These are your old stompin' grounds, aren't they?" Matthew asked. "Are you remembering?"

"Lots of things," Rachael said wistfully.

He tugged at her shirt tail, playfully billowing it upward. Suddenly she jerked away, frightened.

"What are you doing?"

"Rachael, I'm teasing."

She read the questions in his eyes and pulled her shirt tightly around herself and stared straight ahead.

"What is it, Rachael? What was that mark on your back?" Before she could move away he grabbed her arm and held her wrist securely. Rachael thought she had chosen a bathing suit that would have hidden the mark. Evidently she didn't. He began to lift the edge of her shirt.

"Matthew, don't!"

He did. Now he was seeing the long, jagged scar on her back at the lower side of her rib cage that the bathing suit should have hidden.

"Where did you get that?" he asked, exasperated. She couldn't speak. "Rachael?"

"From my dad," she said quietly.

"What? How?"

"He hit me with a board, when I was seven or eight." She turned her face away. Anxiety made her throat close.

"That son-of-a-bitch!" Matthew's gentle, mild-mannered nature hadn't till then included foul language. "That sickens me! That son-of-a-bitch!" He enunciated the words through clenched teeth.

Not meaning to seem pathetic, and not wanting to go through other surprising discoveries, she said, "I have others and I don't want you to make a big issue of it."

"Where?"

She wasn't about to go through a total expose of her marks. "On my hip and the back of my head.

Matthew gently placed his arm around her shoulders and looked down at her. "I hurt for you, Angel. I am so angry." After a while, he glanced at her. Suddenly, he said, "Take off the glasses. You're beautiful."

She wished she felt that way. Bravely, she removed the sunglasses and looked up at him, pathetically fearing rejection. Instead, he pulled her to him and held her snugly and kissed the top of her head. For quite a while, he remained silent looking straight ahead, clenching and unclenching his jaw.

She clung to him with an arm around his waist. finally pulling away and looking up at him again. His hand was on her shoulder as he looked down at her. Neither spoke. They simply looked into each other's eyes. She was afraid the visible reminders would repulse him, cause him to see her as ugly. Evidently they hadn't. She was more than thankful and wanted to tell him. She shook her head. The words wouldn't come. He pulled her close again and Rachael felt sheltered.

Chapter 19

"Tell me some things you remember about this area," he said.

Rachael looked out trying to identify their location. It was difficult to determine from water level after not having been on the river for years. Until she saw a familiar pump house on a pier out over the water, she pacified him with talking about farming and trucking and how people lived in the rural communities along the river.

"What amazes me is how you can remember every minute detail."

"Well, I grew up here. I was a part of this culture."

"Must be the writer in you."

Mona appeared on the bow making her way from side to side watching the water.

Rachael was finally able to point out various familiar larger homes and buildings that showed over the top of the levee, She hadn't wanted to start talking about the Delta. Surely, he'd been there many times and made his own history along the river. Talking about her memories was difficult at best, if not depressing and mood altering.

He began playing with the ends of her French braids, absentmindedly rubbing the back of her neck. This was turning out to be a very good day for them. With his parents present, there was no threat of her and Matthew getting caught in a clinch again.

Matthew always seemed to need to touch her. At times it was difficult pushing him away. She loved his gentle touches and knew he'd expect the same once they were alone again. She sneaked a glance at him and found he was absorbed in piloting the craft.

Suddenly, he looked down at her and said, "Why don't you give me a big sloppy kiss, right now, and give my dad a thrill." Rachael pulled away laughing. He playfully motioned for her to come close again. "How much do you want to bet he's watching us?" Matthew asked, whispering.

"I'm not going to look back there." Rachael stiffened and held her breath.

Quickly, he pulled her tightly to him and made a move like he was about to kiss her. She squealed and pushed him away. He let go and they both laughed.

Mona motioned from the bow that Matthew should guide to craft toward the left bank. Soon a drift appeared near the middle of the river as they sailed smoothly past. Then Mona motioned toward the middle again.

"Now, what do you think that looks like to your dad?" Rachael asked, trying not to be overheard.

"Angel, Mom and Dad would like nothing more than to see me happy with someone and finally…" He stopped mid-sentence, then turned to look straight ahead again. After a while, seriously, he asked, "Tell me about this big mistake you once made."

"What big mistake?"

"When you were telling me about the guys in your life, you said…"

"Oh, that." She became pensive and hesitated. He encouraged her to talk. Slowly, she told him about the older guy she saw while she was in high school and about how she and Celine sneaked out to parties and dances. Rodney was twenty-one, she, fifteen. Rachael choked up, remembering. She remembered part of the therapy she taught others, that talking about things that bothered them was a good way of getting clear of the effects. This memory bothered her.

"Was there something more between you two?"

"I thought so," she said quietly. "I guess he was too old for me, too experienced. I looked forward to graduation, thinking after that we'd get married."

"Did you love him that much?" Matthew's voice expressed empathy.

Memories flooded her mind again. Being in the Delta brought back feelings she'd suppressed. "You need to understand, Matthew. No one in school was interested in me. I didn't mix like the other kids. I was something of a mystery, I guess. I thought I looked funny or different from everyone because no one cared. Rodney and his friends dated younger girls because in the small Delta towns, there just weren't that many girls to choose from."

"He took advantage of your innocence and you fell in love with him because he was older and seemed more mature."

"During the school year, he used to meet me in the park at lunch time. About anytime I could stay at Celine's, I got to see him. Once, my friends and I participated in the Holy Ghost parade. So did almost all the girls in school," she said, shrugging. "Dad encouraged that. Rodney chauffeured me in the parade so I could sit on the back of his convertible. Dad didn't put it together." She smiled at the memory. "During the dances, we used to sneak away, lots of us. We'd drive to some deserted field out among the gas wells. We'd synchronize our radios and dance in the headlights. The guys usually drank beer. Some of the girls did, too. I tried it once and got horribly sick. Some of the kids smoked weed."

"Ah, to escape, to escape."

"They tried to get me to do it, but I couldn't. Sneaking out was bad enough. If my dad caught me..."

"Bad, huh?"

"I'm sure he would have beat hell out of me. Then he'd have taken me to a doctor to see if I was still a…" Rachael bit her lip. She wished she hadn't mentioned that bit of information. She didn't want Matthew to ask about the intricacies of the relationship. A few months before the end of her senior year, with graduation activities beginning to happen, and the time consuming studying for finals, and then tests, she saw less and less of Rodney. She never once entertained the idea that she might be losing him. They had discussed what it meant to move forward to graduation. He had already been through that period in his school years.

One day, Myna, a girl, sort of in Rachael's circle of friends, announced she was getting married two weeks after graduation. She confided to a couple of friends that she started dating this guy about mid-year and had gotten pregnant. She flashed his picture around in the hallway between classes.

"Oh-oh." Matthew grimaced in anticipation.

"I didn't know Myna had a steady boyfriend. She was known for making the rounds, dating anybody who'd take her out."

Sometimes Myna was seen with a whole carload of guys cruising Main. She used to tell stories about taking uppers and downers and whatever else happened to be the in thing. She looked a lot older than her age and was known to frequent some of the bars out in the hills.

"No one ever told you about him and her?"

Rachael shook her head. "I walked over to look at this picture she was flashing and got the shock of my life. It was her and Rodney looking lovingly at each other."

"I'm sorry, Angel," he said, again pulling her close. He stayed silent. Rachael imagined that he could be understanding. She couldn't tell him everything, and wouldn't.

"I barely made it through finals. I was still managing my father's archaic bookkeeping system."

"Have you seen this Rodney guy since?"

"They're divorced now. That marriage couldn't last. I heard they were both drinking a lot. They used to have these big drug parties. What a waste. It would have been different if he and I married."

"Then, Myna did you a big favor."

"A favor… for me?"

"If you continued in that relationship, you might have ended up like him.

"No way."

Matthew paused, glanced at her quickly. "Is there a chance you'd try to see him again?" he asked. "I mean, if his condition were different? What if that changed? What if he got his life together, Rachael? What if one day you saw him and he told you he realized the big mistake he'd made?"

"That's a lot of *what ifs*. What are you asking?"

"I think you haven't gotten over him. Even though a lot of years have passed, you're emotional when you talk about him. What I'm asking is, if the whole situation could be made right, would you see him again?"

"No," she said. "I'm reliving the hurt and need to get clear of it."

"Wouldn't you try to recapture what you lost back then?"

Rachael waited a moment getting her thoughts together. She should toy with Matthew, let him think he might have some competition. Let him know Rodney might have a chance if he cleaned up his act. That wasn't her way. If having no competition was boring to Matthew, she would at least not lose him to game playing. She wanted to make a point, one he needed to hear.

"No, I wouldn't go back, not ever," she said. She had put her heart into that relationship. She lived to be with him as much as possible. Her voiced quivered. "I took chances sneaking out to see him. If my dad would've caught me, he'd have killed me. I had to sneak out because that tyrant of a father wouldn't let me

117

date." She took a deep breath. "Then while I wasn't around, Rodney was out screwing someone else. She had his baby." Rachael nearly lost her composure. She put her hand to her mouth and swallowed hard, fighting off a choked feeling. "No, no way would I go back."

It took a lot for Matthew to listen to her talk about the love she once had for someone else. "Angel," he said finally. "How can we put this thing behind us?"

"Understanding, for sure." They both knew someone they needed to get over. She looked straight at him, wanting to make a point, knowing her every word would sink in though he was preoccupied piloting the boat. "I learned in therapy, that the anxiety I feel at times, is not about losing Rodney. He's a small part of it now. My anxiety is about being taken for granted and then cast aside."

"Okay, that's why you have trouble expressing your feelings," he said.

"Maybe," she said, not wishing to be diagnosed. Suddenly she felt as if a lightning bolt struck her. Her dilemma had not reached completion in her thought processes and understanding. That was most likely one of the main factors blocking her from having a successful relationship since then. That, and her father's censorious upbringing.

"I need to know something," he said.

"What's that?"

"I need to know if there is any curiosity left in you that could pull you back to Rodney, even briefly."

"What on earth for?"

"To challenge and put to rest those unfinished feelings."

"How absurd."

"Don't be so sure, Rachael. You said things weren't worked out. What makes you feel sure you wouldn't at least see him if you had a chance?"

She paused, disturbed at his persistence. Then she went on. "Rodney left me, or rather, he cheated on me and got someone pregnant, then had to forget about me. That scarred me emotionally. I felt helpless, desperately hopeless. I became less than second best. I became… nothing to him. Maybe always was." She swallowed hard, finding it difficult to speak. Her lips quivered. Tears rolled down her cheeks. "I won't let that happen again. I felt like I was losing my sanity. I don't want to risk that much hurt ever again. And what he did," she said more quietly, "deserves nothing more out of me, nothing."

"That's how I thought it was," he said.

"W-what?"

"You're afraid of the risk."

Chapter 20

Cameron came up behind them. "Need a break?" he asked. "We're going to put in at Rio Vista for a while."

Rachael discreetly wiped her eyes and slipped away.

"Is everything okay with that one?" Cameron asked, almost whispering.

"Her name's Rachael, Dad."

The secretive way Cameron posed his rude question begged Rachael to listen. She paused in the aft salon. Earlier, she heard Mona and Cameron's conversation from behind. Now Matthew and Cameron's voices floated back from the helm. She scooted to the side of the small space hoping not to be noticed.

"Sorry," Cameron said as he placed a hand on his son's shoulder.

"I've got a lot to think about," Matthew said.

"Wanna talk?" Cameron asked, taking the wheel and perching himself on the pedestal chair.

"I... uh... I care a lot about Rachael. You know that, Dad."

"Well, it's a small boat, son. I can see the way you are with her. Is she good to you? I mean, your last relationship left you dangling at the end of a rope."

"I know. That was my fault." He leaned against the other pedestal chair and crossed his ankles. He watched Mona on the deck signaling them occasional directions.

"This Rachael, does she treat you right?"

"Dad, it isn't like you think." Matthew's mood shifted into straight forward again. "We haven't had sex. It hasn't gone that far and I'm not sure it's going in that direction real soon either."

Rachael was stunned at hearing their conversation. She was about to learn some truths about Matthew and his family and couldn't pull herself away.

"Oh?" Cameron threw his son a sideways glance.

"Dad, Linda and I haven't been close for more than a year. It's been over between us longer than that. I've seen her a few times to try to get my ring back. That's not the point. I don't think I ever loved her. I was infatuated with her public image. I was wrong about who she was." He threw a hand in the air. "To this day, I don't know who she is."

Cameron was silent, most assuredly listening to his son maturing. Then he asked, "What else?"

Matthew shrugged. "I need time to think this through, about Rachael, I mean." He leaned forward to peer out the windshield.

Cameron nodded. "Well, you never rush into anything. I'm glad for that."

"Dad," Matthew cautiously began again. "Rachael seems unspoiled, even after the abuse. I don't know how many guys she's known. She's innocent about everything. There was a time when that would have been a challenge I'd have conquered and then moved on."

"You're learning you have needs other than your shorts."

"There must be something I'm supposed to learn from this," Matthew said cautiously. "Rachael won't let me touch her."

Cameron threw another sideways glance. "Oh?" he asked, then continued watching the river.

"I learned why. You saw her in tears just now?"

"Yeah, what was that about?"

"Most of her memories are painful ones. She hasn't worked through some of them. I'm sure she believes if everything's painful, why bother."

"You'll have to take it slow with that one."

"The real person she is, is buried beneath the pain. She needs someone to believe in her."

"That's pretty complex, son."

Rachael strained to hear. She picked up a magazine and opened it quietly, pretending to read should either of them notice her behind them. For the first time, she was hearing other peoples' opinions about her. Yet, neither Matthew nor Cameron were addressing the fact that she had come a long way on her own. She had grown strong on her own and they needed to recognize that without being told.

"Could be," Matthew said. "The first thing she has to do is face the fact that she got dumped. I don't know why she clings to that particular memory."

"Maybe parts of it are the few good ones she's had."

"Maybe," Matthew said, shrugging.

"You're right, though. You gotta' take this slow. If she's known abuse, any more added on top of that, well, it could send her over the edge."

"She's not going over the edge."

"There's nothing wrong with what you're feeling, son. You'd better analyze your intentions first though."

"Me? I'm not trying to do her in."

"Look, it's like this," Cameron said. "This Rachael, if she's been abused, then every other bad thing that happens to her is like one more trauma heaped on the rest. It grows and grows until she gets lost in sorrows. You follow me?"

"I hear you."

Rachael's emotions see-sawed. First, she felt exasperation about being discussed. Then she felt disgust at Cameron being fatherly. Then delight filled her as Matthew stuck up for her and the person he saw her to be, albeit not knowing much about her yet. She wanted to jump up and join the conversation and give Cameron a piece of her mind. That could incite an all-out argument, which she wanted to avoid, though her anxiety seemed ready to explode.

"Okay, listen to me. If you're stringing her along so you can claim another victory, when you drop her, it could be the thing that makes her snap."

"Don't hang that on me, Dad. It's not like I'm intentionally planning to hurt her."

"What I'm saying is, if you're looking to get laid, find someone else. This Rachael, with her abuse, you can't play with something like that."

"She's not going off the deep end."

"You don't know that. Your mom and me, we want to understand, too. We've been reading some."

"I'm attracted to her. I like her. She's been through rigorous therapy. It's not like she isn't trying to turn her life around. She works at it all the time."

"Well, you're old enough to know what you're getting into. Remember what you've been through with that other one." Cameron was visibly upset. He threw a hand in the air, ending the conversation.

Rachael had heard enough. She eased out of the cabin. She shook nervously. She had some plans for her life before Matthew came along. She wasn't throwing her life away. Then something clicked. Rachael knew she was different, at least from Linda, not that she needed to compare herself to anyone. In fact, she was most successful on her own. Whether or not Matthew remain in the picture, she possessed an exceptional mind, and never had, and never would, use drugs.

Chapter 21

As they approached Rio Vista, Mona and Rachael took turns looking through binoculars. Diehard wind surfers with multi-colored sails and boards glided effortlessly on the season's last remaining wind currents across the river below the east levee. Soon, there would be no Delta breeze at all, with more waves from boats than wind. Inescapable sweltering stillness of summer heat would permeate the region.

After docking, Cameron said, "Mona and I are going to visit some friends at *The Submerged* over there on Main. Wanna come?"

"No thanks," Matthew said. "We're headed to *Boaters Only* on Montezuma Street to do some shopping."

Once there, to Rachael's amazement, she found that her former high school friend, Celine, with whom she failed to keep in touch, owned the dry goods store.

Rachael and Celine talked fast about bits and pieces of their lives as Matthew dragged Rachael by the arm around the store.

Celine and her husband leased a cubbyhole and opened their business on a shoe string and prospered. They catered to the needs of the many boaters in the area as well as the wealthy who arrived on the water from elsewhere.

At the shoe rack, Matthew examined a pair of deck shoes for her and spotted a pair for himself. He slipped the shoes on her feet himself, to make sure they fit, while she and her friend chattered on. Leaving the store, Rachael and Celine promised to write and keep in touch. Matthew told Celine it was nice seeing her again and nice that she and Rachael knew each other. "We'll be back," he said.

Each time Matthew said something implying he and Rachael would be together again, she wondered if that was truly possible. She knew the moment must look to Celine that she and Matthew were going together or might even be married. Rachael felt uncertain. Celine knew what she went through with Rodney. Now, to have Celine see her with a man who was definitely one big eye full was a thrill. To top it off, Celine knew the Knights owned that big yacht.

As they sailed up the river, passing Isleton, Rachael was visually reminded the area northward was where many boaters and skiers would be on the water this time of year. She remembered a time she and her father and brother were in their ski boat when a large yacht sailed by. She always wondered what it might feel like being aboard one of those behemoths that seemed to monopolize the river.

Just then, a smiling bronzed young man on a single ski, pulled by a fast ski boat, aimed himself at their yacht. As he veered away, he intentionally sent a glassy spray of water high onto their decks. Rachael laughed, called out and waved, remembering some of her own antics that she caught hell from her father for doing.

Quite often, as was the case throughout the Delta, when people saw one of those big boats sailing by, they'd honk their horns and wave from the levee. Now, Rachael waved back every chance she got. That was the way of the Delta. Suddenly, she felt happy again.

In a short while, they were docking in Walnut Grove. Cameron and Mona made many friends on their frequent visits up river. Another couple was coming on board. The air was dry hot, almost stifling to breathe.

"We're going to stretch our legs," Matthew said to the others. They walked up and over the levee and past the draw bridge. "Tell me more about this area."

The sun beat down, bringing with it reminders of school finishing for summer vacation. "I went to elementary school back there," she said, gesturing toward the back of the small old town.

"Across the tracks? Let's go." He tugged at her hand.

"Now?"

"Yes, let's go. I want to see."

"We don't have time."

"They'll wait for us, Rachael. C'mon."

That was it. A little Delta area school that hadn't changed, not even the color of the paint. Rachael stood stoic trying not to remember her memories, finally shaking her head.

"Painful?"

"These were not some of my best years. This reminds me of my dad. I don't know why I mentioned this place."

"I'm trying to picture you here," he said, studying the long single story building.

"What kind of pictures?"

"In grade school," he said. "You were a skinny little backwards girl with fluffy red hair, who passed her days in a frightened confused blur."

She gasped. "How did you know?" The image was too much to think about and she didn't want anything more to spoil the rest of the weekend. "This is such a dry heat compared to the Bay Area," she said.

"Yeah, I'm parched."

She breathed a sigh of relief. "Barney's Place is back at the levee."

He was already moving in that direction. They enjoyed a quick drink in the air conditioned bar, then left. At a nearby grocery on the levee, they bought fresh Bartlett pears grown right there in the Delta to take to the boat.

"Guess we'd better get back," he said.

"How much farther?"

"To Old Sacramento, have lunch at The Paddle Wheel, then head home.

At the far end of the dock, they paused. Rachael studied the river from a water level vantage point she hadn't enjoyed for a long time. Once again, she smelled the pungent odor of murky green river water.

"Being back here with you, this time, it's special."

"I'm glad."

"It's because of you." She forgot herself and hugged him, fully, bodily.

He welcomed it. Dropping the bag of fruit onto the wood planking at his feet, he drew her tightly to him.

A ray of light and hope broke through. They were free together and the moment was exhilarating. As they pulled apart, wearing that ridiculous grin and unable to control the impulse, he suddenly picked her up and tossed her far out into the water!

Her scream of surprise was sharply cut off as she sank beneath the surface. By the time her head appeared above water, the four on the boat were laughing heartily and Matthew was swimming out to her. The below surface current was not to be taken for granted.

"Matthew!" She threw a fist in his direction as he swam toward her. "We're going… to lunch," she said, while spitting out mouthfuls of silty water. "My hair!"

Grinning from ear to ear, he dragged her back to the dock like one would haul a drowning victim.

"You see?" he said between powerful strokes. "You've tried my bed. Now you can check out my shower."

Chapter 22

Days later, Matthew called leaving a message on Rachael's answering machine asking her out. He and his father were well into the renovation of the apartment complex in Daly City.

She and Matthew had agreed not to bother each other at work by using cell phones. Rachael returned his call, telling his answering machine she would be working full weeks at a small bank in the Financial District. A couple more contracts like the present one and she would be able to remodel her guest unit. She would drive to Brandon's on the weekends. Him deciding to liquidate meant that she needed to spend a little extra time on the books in Stockton.

Two days later, Matthew left another message on her answering machine. A guest speaker from India would be at the yoga center that Friday on Arguello Boulevard near Clement Street. The center was where he sometimes attended yoga classes. There would be a meditation after the lecture and was she interested?

Rachael always wanted to attend classes there but could not bring herself to go alone. She wished she knew others with like interests. She knew of a small elite group of people in San Francisco who were serious about meditation, and who made it a way of life, as she did. She longed to meet some of them but didn't know how. She'd have someone to talk to for reassurance in her own development. Excited that Matthew asked her to go, she would attend even if to do so meant becoming adamant with her boss about leaving early. As she picked up her cell phone to call Matthew, it rang and she almost dropped it.

"Well, are you going?" he asked hopefully.

"Yes, yes. Maybe I'll learn something that will help me measure my progress." She drew a quick breath. "I didn't know you knew of that place."

"I told you before, I have a few surprises too."

She imagined his broad smile as he spoke. She felt nervy, didn't want any more surprises for a while. He was moving too fast. It was, however, helping her see that she had a life of her own, something she failed to notice much as she bumbled through her days alone.

They talked for a while arranging details for the evening. Matthew asked about Brandon and the work she needed to finish for him.

"I'm glad that's winding down," he said. "I want to be able to spend more time with you. Occasional dating isn't enough for me. At the rate we're going, how are we ever going to get to know each other?"

"Well, without the income from Brandon, I was thinking about taking on more contractual work to get my house done."

"Excuses," he said softly.

"And after that, I must return to writing."

"If you're that upset about not having enough time to write, why don't you pay for the renovations from your savings and be done with it?"

"I promised myself—"

"I want some of your time. How can you hope to develop any kind of a relationship if you don't make time for us to be together?"

Rachael evaded the question, again, in no certain terms. "Can we just do Friday and take it from there?"

He sighed into the phone. "I'd like to know when you're going to make more time for me in your life. I think we have something special."

"How can you say that after such a short time?"

"You can't say you don't have feelings for me. I'm not going to let myself get to the point where I start begging to see you. I've been there."

Rachael gasped at the implication. "What? Say that again."

As soon as he said it, surely he was regretful. He sighed again. "I'm sorry, I apologize. I didn't mean to compare you to anyone."

Rachael realized Matthew was giving it his all, not afraid of showing his feelings. "Since we'll be seeing each other Friday evening, I can delay going to Stockton till noon Saturday," she said. "If you want to stay and talk for a while, we can find a place for tea after the Yoga Center."

"Yes, yes," he said. "I'm bearing my soul for you, woman. Can't you see that?" His voice had a smile in it.

He'd better not have any ideas of getting cozy over tea in her kitchen. Nothing will be that simple. He'd surely feel encouraged to take over from there. She knew what he wanted. She'd have to be careful.

Matthew arrived at Rachael's about a half hour earlier than planned. Regardless, she was dressed and ready and spending time wrapping up her writing for the day. She, too, read many books on Eastern philosophy and was aware of changes happening to her in deep meditation. Solely, the outcome of meditation was more support than any she found through therapy or from anyone else.

At the Yoga Center, as the group moved into mediation, her hands and arms began to tingle. A flowing sensation filled her torso and rose up her spine. Her head began pulsating gently at the top. She slumped slightly, into a more relaxed position, sinking deeper into trance, enthralled and completely without regard for how she might look.

After what seemed too brief a time, she moaned softly, moving stiffly and looking around the empty room in surprise. Matthew and the Swami and two others sat cross-legged in the circle, waiting for her.

"Wow, how long have I been...?"

"You zoned out," Matthew said.

"Meditation's over?" The last thought she remembered was one of thankfulness for such a splendid opportunity. "Was it short?"

The others laughed. She rubbed the back of her neck and Matthew moved over to massage her shoulders.

He drove her directly home. "Did you know it's past one in the morning?" He smiled sadly. "I almost envy you..."

"Envy's not allowed. You'll get there someday." She was amazed to hear how much time had passed while she sat entranced.

"Maybe I'm too, too out there. Now I know why you spend time alone."

"Practice, Matthew. If you want to progress, you have to give more time and effort to it."

He smiled wryly. "Been listening to my worldly needs, I suppose. I had no idea how intense and capable your mind is."

At the front door, she led him inside. Strangely, he hesitated. The door stood open. He began to close it, then left it ajar.

He drew her closer. Rachael put her arms around his neck and hugged him. He seemed almost afraid to reciprocate.

He sighed heavily, then said, "What on earth does one do with a perfect woman?" He kissed her cheek, looked deep into her eyes, and then turned and walked out the door.

Rachael knew he'd drive home deep in thought, wondering if he'd have to compete with her devotion to meditation. She wondered if he could make such an adjustment or would he think his masculinity was undermined. If that be the case, he wouldn't have gotten the message.

Matthew called several times leaving messages inquiring as to her welfare. Then, one evening later than usual, she called him. That evening, he wasn't home. She finally made an effort to call later in the evening so she might speak with him instead of his message center. Still, she got the too familiar recording.

She listened to his voice. The futility of the situation stopped her from saying much. She was in the mood to talk and Matthew wasn't available. She asked how he was doing and reminded him to stay in touch, then tapped the phone to end the call.

Chapter 23

Rachael hadn't decided to put Matthew out of her mind. She was curious how he could be attentive one week and then disappear for another two. Trying to keep up with him seemed futile. Then one night, deep in thought about how to solve Hunter and Melissa's new plot dilemma, she decided to give her novel a rest and turned on her cell phone. No one had called. No one ever called except Tina, when she had a day off. She punched the number for Matthew.

"Hello…" he said, sleepily, then yawned noisily into the phone.

"Hi, it's me."

"Rachael?" The sound of covers rustling came through the phone.

"I'm sorry for calling this late. I didn't want to talk to your machine again."

"What a surprise." The sound of a door closing came through from his end.

She thought about Matthew's insistence on seeing more of her. She teased. "You can't say I never phone you."

"That's not the reason you called." His voice seemed to echo and he talked in hushed tones.

"No, actually we're supposed to be talking about us. We should get together."

"Don't worry about us. We're doing fine."

"I owe you," she said. "A promise is a promise."

"Now? Over the phone?" Again, the sound of a door opening and closing came through the phone.

"Well, not if you don't want to talk." Of course her timing was off.

For some reason Matthew was now avoiding the issue. The sound of a door opening and closing seemed curious considering the rustling bed covers sounded like he was laying bed. Did he have someone with him? Was she just paranoid, expecting the worst? She didn't press the matter further and her self-assurance plummeted. Moments like this were what made her feel inadequate and made her want to walk away. "Well, it is late."

"Hey, I have an idea. How would you like to join me for a day on The Bay this weekend?"

"Are you sailing again?"

"No, it's *Fleet Week*."

As quickly as Rachael's emotions plummeted to the depths, they now soared to the heights in a heated rush.

Again, Matthew insisted on picking her up and they would begin by watching the air show from the Marina Greens at the foot of Webster Street.

When they arrived, the aerobatics performed by the Blue Angels in their F/A-18 Hornets was in progress. Noise levels increased many decibels with each fly-over.

A constant stream of various colored aerobatic biplanes flew just above the water and tall masts.

After the first air show, they drove to Fisherman's Wharf. Since early morning, areas bordering any part of The Bay was glutted with cars and pedestrians. People were trying to get snapshots of everything that moved. Camera mounts with gooseneck arms were plentiful and poked above the crowds.

People were everywhere, some sitting on blankets on the tops of their vehicles.

A huge air craft carrier, anchored in the middle of The Bay, created the illusion the water was much higher than normal. Closer to the San Francisco side and seeming to dwarf Alcatraz Island, the aircraft carrier was immense and bigger than anything else out there, and it was floating.

"Nothing's that big," Rachael said as Matthew dragged her, awe struck, onto a ferry headed for Sausalito.

The ferry made its way much slower than on other days. Vessels ranging in various sizes and shapes imaginable glutted the Bay. People in sailboats and yachts maneuvered to avoid hitting one another. Coast Guard vessels sounded occasional warnings and instructions.

Amidst the prolific array of vessels, a string of rag-tag dinghies, tied end to end, jostled through the choppy waves. Protesters aboard the dinghies held up signs to remonstrate the activities of Fleet Week and the military effort. The water was rough and unpredictable. The ragged little boats were fortunate not to capsize in the choppy water.

The fog was thick. At times, vision was restricted to a couple hundred yards ahead. As the ferry passed close to the air craft carrier, the Navy's F-35B test aircraft could be seen demonstrating its short takeoff and vertical landing variant from the flight deck.

"Wow!" Rachael had never seen anything as awe-inspiring.

"Some of your expressions are childlike," he said.

"Thanks a lot."

"I meant at times you express childlike delight."

A Coast Guard cutter crossed behind where they were standing on the rear deck of the ferry. Rachael's hair billowed in the gusty air and mist. The pilot of the cutter sounded his horn. The guys waved at her. Beaming, she waved and yelled a greeting, completely surprising Matthew. He quickly moved behind her and rested both hands on her shoulders as the cutter pulled away.

The grand impressive sight of the Golden Gate Bridge could be seen every now and then beyond occasional clearings as fog drifted. Matthew stood behind Rachael with his arms wrapped around her. The ferry reduced speed for the last quarter mile due to thickening fog, then finally docked in Sausalito.

Walking hand in hand, they peered into storefronts along Bridgeway and browsed through a couple of art galleries.

"Here we are," he said as they reached the foot of Princess Street.

"What's this place?" she asked, looking for the sign.

"The Book Corner. Mom's store."

"No kidding."

They stepped inside and found many people milling about and finally spotted both Mona and Cameron chatting with various customers.

"Business is brisk, as usual," Mona said, greeting them.

Both Mona and Cameron looked surprised to see them together. She wondered why they looked at her like they weren't expecting to see her. Rachael sensed something different. Between customers, Mona managed to talk about Fleet Week and how the festivities drew more people to the store.

"Cam, why don't you drive the kids up the hill and show Rachael the house you built?"

"Oh, you'll lose your parking place, Dad," Matthew said quickly. "We're going to have lunch on the boat anyway. We should get going."

It was a quick jaunt to the harbor. Aboard, Matthew admitted he was starving and went right into the galley to prepare lunch.

"Do you always eat in?"

"No, long hours, you know. I eat on the road or at Mom and Dad's because they always have food in the house. Do you cook?"

"Not much."

He continued chopping vegetables. Rachael wondered why he brought her there when it might have been as much fun, and not as time consuming, to eat in a restaurant on one of the piers.

The flashing red light on the answering machine caught her attention, but evidently not his, even though it sat near his work space on the counter. Surely, he must have noticed the intermittent signal, yet made no effort to play back the recording. She wondered if Matthew would refrain from playing back his messages because he wouldn't want her to hear who the caller might be. She hadn't seen or heard from him for some time and wondered what he had been up to.

The phone on the counter rang. Quickly, he grabbed up the receiver leaving Rachael wondering even more.

"Look, I'm busy," he said sternly. "Well, I haven't been home. I'll call you tomorrow. Yeah, sure, I'll see you tomorrow."

He returned to breaking up leafage for the salad without looking her way. "My guys," he said. "They can't do anything without me." It sounded more like a lie.

Soon they were talking and enjoying their meal to the sound of waves lapping at the sides of the boat. It rolled to and fro on the choppy water and occasionally bumped the dock.

Matthew refused to allow Rachael to help him in the galley, particularly not to clean up after their lunch. This was his treat for her. She went to the windows to look out over the activities, standing on her knees on the sofa. Matthew finished cleaning up and came to her putting his hands around her waist. "Look at all those boats," she said in an attempt to divert his attention. Instead, he pulled her to him and she fell backwards against his chest. He wrapped his arms around her squeezing her snugly to him. His breathing was erratic.

"Matthew?" Rachael squirmed inside powerful arms that seemed to lock her in. "Matthew!" He released his hold and she twisted until she could face him. "Don't you ever give up?"

He smiled and grabbed her before she could move away, pulling her down on top of him as he fell backwards onto the sofa. She struggled to get up but he wouldn't allow it.

"Would you lay here with me. Just lay here." He wouldn't release her.

This was the first time Rachael found herself in a prone position with Matthew. She was reminded of lying across the car seat with Rodney. Her mind flashed on how she and Rodney, when they met in the evenings instead of attending dances, used to find a dark corner of the park. If they didn't stay in the car, he'd put his jacket on the ground to sit on. Soon they'd be lying down and she'd be putting him off. Rachael had been in this same position with Rodney too many times.

She squirmed again. Matthew wasn't going to let her go. "Would you relax? I want you to know what it's like to be at ease with me, without having to worry that I'm going to jump your bones every time we're together."

Laying rigid and quiet, with random memories of Rodney roaming through her thoughts, she remembered wanting him terribly. Now, in that same predicament, with memories too strong, emotions began to stir. She relaxed on top of Matthew as he rubbed her back. Soon, he shifted his position pinning her back against the sofa cushions.

"Rachael, take it slow, okay?" He held her chin and looked at her reassuringly. "Don't be afraid of me."

He pressed against her and kissed her with gentle light touches of his lips and tongue as if testing her reaction.

The memory of having been in that same position helped her unknowingly respond to Matthew. She began lightly returning his kisses. She hadn't noticed her own breath quickening. Her hands tightened around his shoulders.

Suddenly he whispered, "Do you ever want babies, Rachael?"

He had struck another chord from the distant past. A dizzying parade of memories and feelings floated through her mind.

The last time she had been in this position was when she had anticipated marriage and wanted Rodney's child. Now to hear Matthew ask how she felt about babies, and not realizing her own vulnerable state, Rachael's response was autogenetic.

"Yes," she said, whispering emphatically. "Yes, I want babies!" Her entire body moved against his. Her head began spinning. She began to shake. He brought his mouth down on hers and kissed her voraciously while pressing his body hard against her and pinning her to the sofa back. Rachael could only respond to the fire raging inside her.

Suddenly, the phone rang again.

Matthew froze. "No! Damn it." He shook his head sharply.

He pulled Rachael to him, sighing heavily as the phone began its fourth ring. The answering machine kicked on and soon she would be able to hear who the caller was. He rose quickly and snatched the phone from the cradle. "Oh, hi Linda," he said, breathing out a sigh and rolling his eyes.

So what if the caller was Linda. He had explained about her. Then why did he not check his answering machine earlier? It seemed he didn't want her to know who might be calling, or what the conversation might be about. Why had he now seemed relieved?

Rachael jolted back to reality. She stood, straightening her clothes, and paced.

He was in the galley leaning on the edge of the counter looking out. He made an open handed apologetic gesture to show he was sorry and that he didn't like the interruption one bit. He let Linda ramble. He didn't say much, a few grunts and sounds once in a while. Rachael balanced herself as the boat rolled and bumped. She was sorry that she had allowed herself to become sexually aroused. She almost lost control. Matthew motioned for her to come to him. She hesitated. He motioned again. When she went to him, he wrapped his arm around her, and didn't seem to care that she might hear the idle conversation coming through the phone.

"What else, Linda?" he asked impatiently. "Okay. I'm busy. I have to go." He hung up and wrapped both arms around Rachael.

On the rear deck of the ferry back to San Francisco, he leaned on the railing and stared pensively at the frothy water below. "She's changed her name to Star," he said unexpectedly.

"Who?"

"Linda. She's going by the name of Star. If I call her, I'm to use that name. That's what she called to say. Why would I call her?"

"Wouldn't you?"

"Why should I? She calls me. I find these lengthy messages on my answering machine. Sometimes she calls me in the middle of the night. I don't answer anymore. I know she's high on something. Her calls are starting to be more frequent now because it's getting close to the holidays."

"You won't see her?"

"I'm not seeing her, Rachael. She probably thinks I'm another sucker who'll buy her one more expensive gift she can hock." He shook his head. "Damned, I wish I could get my ring back. She's got a piece of me and I wish I could sever everything we ever had together." He paused again, then spoke softly. "And it's probably best if she did have an abortion."

Regardless how he tried to disguise his feelings, the inflection in his voice was a dead giveaway. His desire to know was eating at him.

When Matthew left Rachael at her door, he simply told her to take care of herself. Again, something in his voice set her nerves on edge and left a sinking feeling in the pit of her stomach.

In the weeks that followed, Matthew called twice, leaving messages and asking about her well being. She returned both calls but hung up each time when she got his answering machine. She didn't try to call him again and he stopped calling her.

Chapter 24

Rachael was inundated with paper work for her brother's business. In addition to working with the CPA's, Brandon found misplaced invoices and miscellaneous expenses. They looked legitimate enough. Rachael brought some work home, checking and double checking her figures to assure she had been accurate all along.

The pressures of closing were eating at Brandon. At one point, he released the brunt of his frustration on her, yelling and screaming and spreading spittle on her face, a careless habit of his. Like their dad. He hadn't before come that physically close to her in his rage, inches from her face. He flailed his arms in the air while screaming. She saw her father's face and thought he might at any moment strike her.

"If you won't do anything to help me, why don't you go away and don't come back."

"That's fine with me," she said quietly. "You've become like our father."

She talked back to Brandon for the first time in her life. The experience left her drained and weak. Five days later, he called.

"I haven't been able to find anyone to help me close my books. You'll have to come back."

Who the hell did he think he was? "I beg your pardon, dear brother. I may not wish to come back. What makes you think I want to endure more of the same treatment from you that Dad dished out?"

When Brandon spoke again, he sounded desperate, resigned. "You're the only one who can help. Please help me put an end to this mess."

"On one condition…"

"What?"

"You leave the house while I'm there. Or you bring your paperwork here and pick it up when I'm done."

"I hate San Francisco. I'll leave while you're here."

In tones that suggested he forgot his abusive outburst, Brandon asked her to fix the books so he could somehow come out ahead. He had made some big plans and needed money. He snickered into the phone. "You know how to handle those things, don't you?"

Greed and gluttony made him stupid. How dare he think she would stoop to doing something like that. If she was able to fix things, his books always balanced because she knew what she was doing. He couldn't admit that maybe she was pretty intelligent.

"First of all, Brandon, I wouldn't do that if I could. As things stand, you'd better be happy I know enough about what I'm doing to save your skin. I don't intend to jeopardize my own."

"Excuse me," he said, exaggerating. "Sorry I asked."

"When the equipment and property are sold, there isn't much you or I can do. You'll get what you get."

She rushed to finalize her dealings with Brandon completing everything less than two weeks before Thanksgiving.

Rachael had to contend with her contract at the bank. However, that was structured and orderly diversion from the problems that plagued her. Office gossip said they wanted her to remain on contract until the end of January. The bank was to come under new ownership and she was to stay until new officers and employees could be installed.

Again, to her chagrin, she saw the resumption of working on her novel pushed back even farther. At that point, she needed to make a decision to stay and continue to accumulate funds, or delay upgrading indefinitely by terminating her contract and resuming her writing.

Her rationale was that while she had no difficulty locating work when she needed it, the overall employment picture in the Bay Area was pretty gloomy. Too many people were unemployed and not finding jobs. More people were ending up in the streets. She was thankful for the temporary position, however, toyed with the idea she might be taking a job away from someone who desperately needed one. Then she remembered she'd be there two more months until the new people were hired and their training was completed.

She mentally reviewed the renovation on the guest unit and some minor details throughout the house. Important as it was, she waited a long time to see everything about to happen. Finally having her property updated carried as much importance as finishing her book. Completing every last bit of refurbishing was a pet project of hers about as many years as writing had been.

When she did make time to write, details would flow smoothly, ever since her meditation deepened. When different parts of the story would come to mind, problem areas seemed smoothed out. Her mind worked on the story though she wasn't able to consciously think about it. Somehow the words would be there when she fully resumed. Until then, she would continue with yoga and meditation, practices she wouldn't relinquish and that helped her make the best decisions.

Finally, swayed in a fit of loyalty to her friends at the bank, she decided to stay on as requested. Worldly demands were pulling her away from sanctuary. She called David Sullivan and made an appointment to discuss a draw against her investments.

"I can't remember when I've seen you smile as much," David said. "Everything's going well, I take it."

Her smile didn't have anything to do with things going well. She was remembering that Matthew coincidentally employed the same stockbroker. She ate her lunch and kept the conversation focused on her investments.

"I thought I might withdraw some money to finish remodeling. It's either that or keep working to save. I'd rather be writing."

"You've been able to write till now."

"Yes, but I get frustrated with having to put it aside."

"Say, I thought you gave up writing, not enough profit or something."

"I've got to try again. I have many great story ideas."

"I assume you need experience in many life situations," he said. "So you'll have something first hand to write about."

"That's the best, I'm told."

"Then don't shut yourself away from life."

"Shut myself away?"

"That's right. Don't let your investments be an excuse to shut yourself off from the world. If you begin to spend your savings, it's that much easier the next time. Go out and work. Your book will be there when you resume. You said you may look for a new publisher. Until then, you have no deadlines and no dire need to remodel. Your life's not on hold."

"You know, you're right."

"Get some diverse experiences, work, meet people. Hold onto the financial security you have and don't let any of it slip away."

Wise old fatherly figure that he was. He spoke in tones that were convincing, even loving and caring, something not too frequent in her life. Of course, he was right.

Since Matthew hadn't called for a long time, Rachael haggled over whether it would be appropriate to call him. She remembered the sinking feeling in the pit of her stomach the last time he left and told her to take care of herself. His words sounded final. It might also be too close to the holidays and he certainly must have made plans by now which didn't include her.

She wasn't sure about spending Thanksgiving with Brandon. She had an idea what that would be like. Since Matthew was close to his parents, Thanksgiving would be a personal holiday between them. After all, people go home for the holidays. She tried to see it from all angles.

Against her better judgment, she called Brandon. "Why don't you come to San Francisco for Thanksgiving this year?"

"Can't," he said. "I'm having friends over. You're welcome to come too. Stay through the weekend."

"I don't know."

"This might be the last time you get to see Dad's equipment."

See their father's equipment? In the past years, his invitations contained an ulterior motive. What could he be up to this time? The accounting was completed. She went to Brandon's for Thanksgiving sensing the upcoming liquidation might be easing his frustration over debt worries. Now they could spend this time in peace together.

When she arrived, he immediately presented her with the turkey and trimmings which he insisted she prepare for his friends. "Remember," he said. "You always did the cooking in our family."

Chapter 25

"This drives you crazy more than one week," Rosa said, whining. "Better you decide now."

"If I buy the books at Mona's store, and he sees me there," Rachael said, "it'll look as if I'm spying on him."

"*Pero*, why not?" Rosa asked, teasing and flicking her eyebrows.

Some of Rosa's advice sounded as though it came from the annals of the time worn tradition of pulling out all stops to get your man. Rachael couldn't imagine what Rosa must have been like in her younger years when she, as Rosa claimed, chased her boyfriend till she snagged him. She must have been a power to reckon with. Rosa's sense of humor, left unchecked, could enlighten a funeral. Yet, her way was not Rachael's way. "I don't believe in acting out of desperation," Rachael said.

"It would put your mind at ease, *chica*."

"No, he must be seeing someone else by now."

"You no know that."

Finally, in early December, Rachael drove to Sausalito. From the bridge to the store, she kept alert for a bright yellow Corvette or white construction truck without seeing any. Passing along the yacht basins on Bridgeway, she looked toward the parking lots for his car. There was no polished yellow anywhere around there either. She breathed a sigh of relief.

Again, Mona expressed strange surprise at seeing her. Rachael caught Mona looking at her suspiciously from time to time. Rachael browsed the racks, choosing stacks and stacks of books for the children in the Pediatrics Ward at Colliers Hospital. She chose some for all age groups covering myriad subject matter.

"Starting a children's library?" Mona asked through a forced smile.

Rachael's custom was to spend Christmas day with the children in the hospital. She'd spend hours sitting on the floor reading or playing games with them, adding her light to their isolated and, oftentimes, frightening confinement. Being with the children helped her get through the part of winter that made her feel lonely. She always took books which she and Rosa wrapped in bright papers, ribbons and bows.

One past year in particular when Rosa was feeling depressed and alone, Rachael invited her to go along to the hospital. From that time forward, Rosa's life changed. Each year, she'd beg Rachael to take her again. She didn't have to beg. Rachael was well aware of the good that happened for those confined kids. Plus, Rosa possessed an enviable knack for helping the children feel special. She played games with them to start them learning Spanish.

"They're for the kids in Colliers' Pediatrics," Rachael said as she tried not to pay attention to Mona's curious expression that seemed nothing to do with books.

Mona smiled with an expectant look. "Thanks for shopping here. I appreciate your support." She seemed a bit awkward ringing up such a large order. Rachael chatted about the way the racks were newly rearranged, trying to take Mona's mind off her embarrassment. She helped Mona pack the books into bags as each was rung up on the cash register.

"Wow, Rachael. That's nearly five hundred dollars worth of books," she said. "I'm going to give you our quantity discount."

Rachael grabbed her arm quickly. "That's okay, Mona. I have it to spend, I mean, this is for the children."

"I insist. This is such a large purchase." Mona looked searchingly into Rachael's eyes. "Take the discount and save your money. We both benefit."

"It's no problem. I do this every Christmas." She handed her charge card to Mona, who smiled warmly, shook her head, and rang up the discount anyway.

Rachael went to get her car and parked in the loading zone. Mona helped her carry the heavy bags out to the curb and load up.

Mona smiled when she saw the car. "Matt told us you drove a Porsche. This is a beauty." Rachael looked at her hoping she wouldn't say Matthew's name again. "Rachael, tell me. Do you know yet if you and Matthew are going to be dropping in for Christmas? Cam and I would love to have you share our Christmas celebration. We take off to Hawaii right after New Year's."

Rachael had to think twice about how to explain. She took a deep breath. "I don't think I'll be coming, I mean…" Rachael looked sadly into Mona's eyes. "I haven't seen Matthew since Fleet Week in October."

Mona's jaw dropped. "You weren't… you haven't… uh… you didn't…" Her face turned red. Mona busied herself with the bags of books unable to hide her surprise. "I guess he's busy. They're both busy. They've nearly finished that apartment complex in Daly City. They're working pretty hard." She looked away sadly. The questionable expression in Mona's eyes told that Matthew must surely be seeing someone and Mona was surprised to learn it hadn't been her.

Rachael wondered if he and Linda got back together. Matthew was probably not a man to go without a sex life. Holidays pulled people together. A deep sadness crept over her. Her father had been right. Men were that way. "Yes, they must be busy," she said quietly. She didn't want to linger. Mona, too, was experiencing a lot of discomfort. "Well, thanks a lot, Mona. I'd better be going. There's a lot of wrapping here and I have so little time."

Why did she say that last part? She hadn't meant to imply she was too busy, too preoccupied, too happy, despite not seeing Matthew. At times, she could stick her foot into her mouth deeper than most people could in theirs.

Mona reached for her. They hugged. "Take care of yourself," she said tenderly. "Have a great Christmas."

"Thanks for everything, Mona," Rachael said. "I'll always remember the boat trip up the river." She bit her lip and turned away. "Merry Christmas to you and Cameron." She walked around her car to get in, wondering what on earth possessed her to mention the cruise.

Rachael made a crescent turn across the double yellow lines. In a quick sideways glance, she caught a glimpse of Mona standing at the curb, her head cocked to one side as if trying to figure something out.

Chapter 26

Tina's deli was always decorated and festive around the year-end holidays. This Sunday, the deli was closed to the public with a party for employees and their significant others. Rachael decided to pay Tina a visit and present her the gift of 14K ruby earrings she knew Tina would love. The small corner deli was packed with happy people and well-wishers that spilled out onto the sidewalk. The crowd was boisterous. When Tina caught a break, she presented Rachael with her gift. They stepped into the kitchen in the back and opened their gifts. Tina immediately replaced the earrings she wore with the new ones and happily threw her head side-to-side, making the earrings dance and sparkle.

Tina's gift to Rachael was a gift card to Paulette's, a new designer boutique on Powell Street near Market. "No, no, no," Rachael said. She once mentioned admiring the clothes at Paulette's and knew the prices were out in the ozone. "Tina, why? You can't buy so much as a half-slip in there for under a hundred dollars. That store is too expensive."

"And dazzling 14K ruby earrings aren't?"

They hugged and returned to the storefront. Tina gasped when she saw two girls working the crowd out on the sidewalk.

"What is it, what's wrong?" Rachael asked.

"Uh… nothing." Tina kept staring at the girls.

Rachael tried to figure out who they were that would take Tina's attention. Then suddenly, the dark haired girl looked straight through the glass window at Rachael, and for a moment, froze. The next moment her expression was one of triumph.

"It's me," Rachael said to Tina. "That girl's looking straight at me. Am I supposed to know her?"

"It's nothing," Tina said. "They're not supposed to be here, but let's just enjoy ourselves."

That was hard to do with the dark-haired girl sneaking glances at her. She came into the deli to ogle. Finally, Rachael had enough. She found Tina again. "I have to know who that girl is. She's hanging on me and listening to my conversations. C'mon Tina, what aren't you telling me?"

Tina sighed heavily and nodded again toward the back room. Once away from the prying eyes of the black-haired girl, and her blond friend as well, Tina sighed heavily. "You're not going to like this."

"I'm a big girl."

"Okay, that girl, the one with the dyed black hair, she claims she's been going out with Matthew."

Rachael couldn't stifled a gasp. Her heart sank in her chest. She couldn't speak right away. Once gathering her composure, she said, "I haven't seen him since October. I thought he went back to Linda, his previous girlfriend. She's a tall blond model. Did he ever bring her here?"

"Well, this isn't Linda, whoever she is. Her name is Britt."

Then Rachael remembered the day she and Matthew walked from the park to the Deli. The black-haired girl and her blonde friend moved close to Matthew's chair and tried to get his attention.

Rachael was choked up, felt anger rising. "How did they meet? Matthew and her?"

"Matthew's been here a couple of times. He sat outside. I thought he might be waiting for you. He kept looking in the direction you might appear from Lake Street. One of those times, Britt showed up with a guy. After he and Matthew shook hands, Britt glommed Matthew's arm and clung to his side."

"Clung to Matthew? Even though she came with someone else?"

"Maybe it's me, Rach. It looked like Britt wanted the guy she came with to know she and Matthew were tight. She really rubbed up against Matthew."

"Maybe the other guy was only a friend."

"Maybe. Britt's been in a couple times without a guy. The other time Matthew came, she grabbed onto him again. I guess Britt made moves on him."

"And he fell for it."

"You're not seeing him anymore, are you?"

"How long…?" Rachael couldn't finish the question.

"You don't want to know." She dropped her gaze to the floor.

"Tina, you are and I friends."

"Better friends than most."

"That's right. So tell me what this girl's been saying and how long it's been going on. I feel like I'm being played."

Tina's expression softened when Rachael admitted her feelings. "Maybe a month and a half or so."

"Nothing before? How long has she been coming here?"

"Nothing before the day that you and Matthew were here together, that I know of. She's new in the neighborhood. She and her roommate live catty-corner over there." Tina motioned diagonally in the direction of the intersection. "Two or three doors down."

"So she's been bragging about dating Matthew?" Again Tina hesitated. "More," Rachael said, motioning with her hand to pull it out of Tina. "If I'm being played, I need to get him out of my head."

"Britt said she's dating him, talks about the places they go, things they do. She wants people to know she and he are an item.

Rach, I don't think they are. Britt's been here with a couple of construction guys. She flashed a bunch of pictures. I saw some. They looked to be at a construction office party, but Matthew wasn't in any of them."

"Has Matthew ever brought her here?"

"Not that I've seen."

Rachael was near tears. Her anger would not let them fall. She was reminded about how Matthew openly discussing Linda and the undercover cops. Back then she thought he might be too loose in his lifestyle, open to taking chances, a bit too carefree and trusting. "I don't get out much. I haven't seen his car around the neighborhood and I haven't been to the park." Rachael grimaced, trying to remember.

"Maybe he's with her. There's something else, Rach."

"Spill it now so I can be done with this."

"Britt and her girlfriend sometimes hold hands and act real lovey."

"So what?"

"I believe they are lovers."

"Okay, so what?"

"If Matthew is seeing one, is he involved with both?"

"Are you suggesting a *ménage a trois*?"

Could that be why Matthew hung onto Linda? Was he looking for a third person to round out his own triple delight? Not with me, Buster!

"Those two girls, they're always overly friendly with guys mostly, like trying to draw them in. I've been on this corner a long time. I see all kinds of stuff happening."

Rachael exhaled a long breath. "That's sick."

"Whatever primes your pump."

Matthew not showing up at the deli with Britt was a slight relief. It didn't hide the fact that Matthew might start a relationship with someone new while leaving her dangling. No wonder Mona was surprised when she admitted she hadn't seen

Matthew since Fleet Week. For sure, both Mona and Cameron knew that Matthew was dating someone, thought it was her and evidently had no way of knowing it wasn't. At least that meant they hadn't met Britt.

Chapter 27

"We need another month out of you," the bank officer said. "Till the end of February."

Rachael agreed to stay. No longer having to make the trips to Stockton, she spent time writing evenings and weekends. She had slipped into a blue funk. Surprisingly, it helped her climb into her mind and pour out awesome material for her novel. As she re-read while editing, she realized she lost the connection between Matthew and Hunter. The story character was upstanding, treated his love with respect, admiration and patience, unlike how Matthew turned out to be.

Brandon called to say he sold everything, the equipment, the trucks, and the property with its grand old Victorian. Surprisingly, before spending all is money, he followed Rachael's advice and purchased another home, located in South San Francisco. The town was not her recommendation, however. At least, he was able to pay cash for a small home and was totally out of debt.

"I bought two vans," he said with renewal in his voice.

"What on earth for?" Rachael asked.

"I rented a small office and started a new delivery service out of the edge of the SOMA District."

"Brandon, I'm proud of you." Her hopes for his new life soared.

"I figure I can service San Francisco and the Peninsula as well as the East Bay from the location near the Bay Bridge. I hired a driver to service this side of the Bay. He used to own his own smaller delivery service. He was forced to close when the economy started to suck. He maintained connections with most of his customers and managed to convince a lot of them to give my start-up company a try."

"Some breaks are coming your way."

"It's hectic," he said, now complaining.

"Different from hauling and drayage on the farms, I'm sure."

"I've been studying street maps of the Bay Area to learn truck routes," he said. "Gotta' keep an edge on competitors."

"Getting around within San Francisco is easier," Rachael said, "as opposed to the outlying areas of the East Bay."

"Yeah, I thought about changing routes with my driver," Brandon said, as if thinking out loud. "Or at least alternating with him. I hate it when I get a late rush delivery somewhere in the East Bay."

"You find routes over there that confusing?"

"I always seem to get stuck in rush hour traffic at a time when executives and business owners like myself should be sneaking home early for the day," he said boastfully. "I'm definitely considering alternating."

Though his head was in the clouds, Brandon found renewed incentive with his new life. Maybe ridding his life of anything that remind him of their father was the breakaway that Brandon needed to find his own strengths. The time had arrived when Rachael could stop her preoccupation with her brother's well being. Or so she thought.

One major concern lingered. Brandon began clearing his throat a lot, as if he were congested, for no apparent reason. Their father cleared his throat constantly. Rachael wondered about Brandon's lungs. A few days later, she asked him to see a doctor, reminding that their father died from complications following collapsed lungs due to obstructive atelectasis.

"A-tel-a-what? What do you know about it?" Brandon asked, sarcasm biting. "When in hell did you get a medical degree?"

Shortly after settling into his new home, which Rachael visited, she noticed he kept the louvered blinds and curtains closed in each room, keeping the house dark. The house didn't have the stale smell of his former home. This house just smelled tired. If only he'd allow it, she would hire a housekeeper for him. By the size of the fresh tree trunk stumps, he had cut down the two tall trees on the side of the front yard. He seemed attached to firewood, but not for the same reasons she loved her fireplace.

He bought hundreds of dollars worth of potted plants. Then he covered the patio and back yard with a screen and misting system that blocked out any vital sunlight the plants and grass needed to thrive.

"My plants are dying," he said.

"Could it be you're over-watering? There's no direct sunlight in here either."

He took two paces away and half-way turned to look back at her. "Why is it no matter what I do, you think you have a better way?"

The fireplace was kept burning every day when he was home, to save on electric bills, he claimed. Cords of wood were dumped haphazardly in the side yard. Dust from the fireplace and general lack of cleaning lay thick over everything throughout the house and Brandon's bronchi were becoming more and more congested.

With the contract at the bank completed, and not working for and receiving compensation from Brandon, Rachael decided to look for additional work. Having saved quite a sum toward remodeling fueled her desire to get the job finished.

The original estimate was outdated. She'd have to get another. The cost of everything was skyrocketing and the new bids would probably be substantially higher than the older ones. Or maybe some companies would be desperate enough to bid low to win the work, yet, she wouldn't allow anyone to skimp on materials. One thing for sure, she wouldn't allow Matthew to bid now.

Rachael telephoned several of her contacts to let them know she was again available for work.

"You're welcome to the job," her friend at ConverTech said. "The position's coming available the first of May. You'd have to stay six months."

"That's a biggie."

"It's yours, if you can stay that long. The job's complicated. Ideally, we want to train one person once."

"What's involved?"

"A worldwide systems conversion program. That's why we don't want to teach it twice."

"That's a long commute every day for six months," Rachael said. "About fifty eight miles, one way."

"Well, Rachael, we know your work. If you can stay the duration, I think I can get you two dollars an hour more than the rate you last billed. It's that important to us."

She quickly calculated. The total amount to be earned over six months, added to the money previously saved, put her way over the expected amount she needed and would probably cover unexpected cost overruns.

"I'll take it… with the extra two bucks," she said.

Matthew hadn't called since the end of October. Rachael thought about him from time to time as she thickened the steamy plot of her novel. Matthew's brief presence made her character come to life. That's probably all their chance meeting was meant to show her. That had been the way she wanted it in the beginning. At some point, her fictional characters developed lives of their own, surprisingly parallel to hers. Her characters and plot were becoming a depiction of everything she felt and feared and had yet to overcome.

After thinking at length about her writing progress, she decided to continue with the same story line, and not worry any longer about Hunter's similarities with Matthew or changing them. Development of the story was too far along to think about major changes. Matthew would probably never see the book. If he did, she'd have disguised the characters so well, he couldn't claim relationship, nor would he want to.

She had two months off between contracts. When she began to write again, words and ideas flowed easier. Writing sometimes as much as fifteen or sixteen hours a day, she was finally getting caught up.

Often, Rachael recognized parts of her writing where she experienced difficulty describing the motivations behind the father character's brutality. At those times, she would remember and scrutinize her father's teachings, his admonitions or outright accusations, and merciless lack of warmth and understanding. Thank goodness the couple she remembered arguing by the pond in the park weren't around every time she thought of her father. It was too cool this time of year to sit in the park to write. At home, she felt safe from intrusions.

She thought about how she responded to her father, and how she might have responded differently. Finally, she was seeing herself as being strong and determined, even aggressive. Strangely though, she was not able to express herself that way with the few men in her life and was forced to imagine doing so for the sake of her story.

In creating challenging transitions for her characters, she included these concepts as part of their growth processes. Further developing the characters of her dual protagonists, she wrote:

Melissa knew Hunter was not going to try to contact her and have his ego bruised again. He was a man, and there were more willing women out there. Not calling was Hunter's way of avoiding being hurt, just as Melissa needed to protect herself. He had been patient with her, yet not diligent enough in his efforts to be a gentleman after all. At least as far as she was concerned. Melissa believed her man should pursue her. Attention was one way she would be assured of his lasting interest. That's what her father had taught.

Hunter overlooked her needs. Maybe she had been too pensive, too withdrawn, and simply failed in making her wishes known. Perhaps she simply hadn't been responsive enough. She certainly wasn't about to fall all over herself. Smothering him with appreciation every time he did something nice would put her in a very vulnerable position.

Rachael realized she was creating Melissa in her own likeness. Melissa was also writing a novel. Writing about a person who was writing a book was easy for Rachael. All she need do was elaborate and define experiences that happened in her own life. When Rachael became distracted from writing by needing to work for money to update her home, she created a situation for her protagonist. Melissa was distracted from her writing because of a conflict demanding her attention.

Creating the character of Hunter was more difficult. She struggled to accurately portray the male perspective. At times, she turned to Gestalt therapeutic techniques she previously experienced in her own therapies. It was an effort to access Matthew's mind, to create a plausible Hunter.

Using a Gestalt technique, she placed two chairs facing each other and moved from one to the other, back and forth, playing out the parts of herself and Matthew as Melissa and Hunter.

When acting out the part of Matthew, Rachael would remind herself to remain focused on what any man might think, what he might feel, and how he might react in certain situations. She would speak aloud and gesticulate into the air around herself. Thank heaven Rosa never caught her.

Chapter 28

Late one evening, dressed to ward off the late March chill, Rachael entered the Yoga Center and was greeted by Taj, the owner. The Center was a soothing place. Taj looked at her strangely. Rachael wondered why people sometimes looked at her that way. It was a look of knowing, as if they knew something she didn't. His gaze followed her as she hung her coat and scarf. He watched from the doorway as she entered the meditation room and sat down quietly. Candles were lit on the small altar against the far wall in the separate meditation room. Several others sat in lotus positions. Rachael took several long quiet breaths and relaxed into meditation. When at last she opened her eyes and reoriented herself, she turned slowly looking around the room and found Matthew sitting to her right, a little behind her.

"Hello, Rachael," he said, whispering, sadness in his voice.

She couldn't speak and put a hand over her mouth, staring with wide-eyed surprise. They spent a moment looking at each other. He looked haggard and listless. Then he reached for her hand. His was trembling.

In the stillness of the room, he leaned close and whispered. "I've missed you."

She looked more intently at him. "I supposed I'd see you here eventually," she said dryly, though whispering. She looked at his hand holding hers and withdrew hers. "What do you want of me, Matthew?"

Their lives, or their timing, was always off. They certainly hadn't made an effort to work on any relationship issues. She could have called him more frequently to sustain contact, but he had come onto her too strong. That would have meant having to face sexual issues. In the back of her mind, she knew desires were normal, but she was taught to suppress her libido till she married. His motivations seemed geared toward sex. That type of relationship by itself wasn't the same intimacy she wanted.

"Is there any way I can see you again?"

She whispered. "I don't see why."

"I guess it's my turn to learn a few things the hard way." He nodded toward the doorway. "Can we talk in other room?"

Rachael went through bouts of missing Matthew and wanting to get to know him better, and then wishing she'd never met him, which caused much confusion. She didn't feel ready for a relationship. She recently wished to see him once more to decide whether to give it another chance or end it permanently. She talked herself out of needing a man in her life. She felt a great pulling inward, a place Matthew nor anyone could disturb. She should make this her last goodbye. She stretched out her stiffened legs and allowed Matthew to take her elbow and help her to stand.

Alone in the neighboring room, keeping his voice down, he said, "I want to try to rekindle what we started, if you're willing. I still care. What happened to us?"

"I don't know. I'm not ready to jump into your bed and I don't think you could have changed that much in so short a time."

"I once told you," he said, straining to whisper. "I won't beg, but here I am."

"Then don't beg," she said quietly. "Say what you feel."

"I want to see you again. I haven't stopped caring about you." He drew in a breath as she eyed him. "Look where we are,

Rachael. I wouldn't lie to you here, in this place. I wouldn't lie to you ever. Please give us another chance."

She was silent as flickering candlelight softly played across their faces. He seemed his usual self, going after what he wanted, despite his expression of anguish, like one teetering on the edge of depression. She looked into his eyes. "I have mixed emotions about us," she said. If only he knew how mixed they were.

"Rachael, I tried to show you I cared. I guess I acted in a lot of wrong ways." He fought becoming emotional, swallowed hard. His voice cracked as he spoke. "I guess I can't make you love me if you don't feel it."

The emotion was overwhelming. Her hand shook as she reached for his. "I'm probably not the person you want to build a relationship with." She thought of Britt carousing the neighborhood with her dyed black hair and heavy eye makeup. Was she someone he slept with till he got tired of her? Was he that desperate to be with someone, anyone? She remembered what he told her about his ex-girlfriend, Star. Maybe she, Rachael, was the most decent person he'd known and he was finally coming to his senses.

"We can make this work, Angel."

Again her emotions see-sawed till she thought she would faint. Here was the most decent guy she'd ever met laying his heart out to her. He couldn't have known that she knew about Britt. She wondered how forth-coming he might be. Then again, maybe he needed to meet a decent girl. Her sometimes denied desire of wanting to know an up-standing guy won out. "We can try," she said gently. "I guess we can try."

They drove back to La Fleur and searched frantically for two parking spaces. After finding one, she jumped into his car looking for a parking space for him. They missed the dinner crowd and talked for hours huddled on a tufted chaise in a corner. With caution, they finally made some headway in disclosing to each other what each wished from a relationship. Not surprisingly, they both wanted to same respect and understanding.

After the conversation changed directions, she told him about writing and about Brandon. She didn't mention the duality between their own lives and her story. Matthew wouldn't understand that writing her novel was helping her to understand him.

Matthew kept the conversation off himself personally and talked about work. "I was able to scare up the renovation of a beautiful old mansion on Terrace Drive in St. Francis Wood," he said. "That's where Dad and I are currently working."

"You're finding jobs, then?"

"Barely, and we still want a chance to bid on the work at your house."

After brief discussion, she surprised him. "You and your dad can do my house."

"Did I hear…?"

"Yes. That's if you're not going to charge me so much I spend the rest of my life paying your bill."

"What made you decide so quickly?"

"I took another consulting contract."

"To pay for the renovation, right. Where will you be working?"

"Santa Clara."

He sat up straight in his seat. "Where?"

"Down the peninsula, for six months."

"Not again." That meant they would again see little of each other and his disappointment was evident.

"I want to get my house done so I can write. I have other books," she said, pointing to her head. "In here." How many times would she have to remind him?

"Rachael, tell me you didn't have to."

"I accepted. I start the first of May."

He swallowed hard, said nothing more, and sat quietly, playing with the curls in her hair. That meant long tiring hours of driving for her and limited time they would have together. He could only accept things the way they developed in his absence. She had only herself to look after her life.

"It's just as well we don't spend a lot of time together," he said.

"Why do you say that?"

"I tried to rush things a bit before. I can't do that this time. I've got some things to take care of too."

"Then it's just as well."

"And I promise," he said, trying to tease. "I'm not going to pursue you with the intent of taking you to bed. At least, not right away."

"Don't expect me to respond to that." Her words contained a bite meant to tell him she wasn't about to let him backslide.

"I know you're real special, Rachael. If that's what it takes, that's how I'll be. Talk to me if I come on too strong, okay?"

Come on too strong? With his riptide of a libido? At that moment, a lie became the truth and truth became a lie.

Chapter 29

In the next five or six weeks they saw a lot of each other. Rachael seemed to deal well with missing an evening of writing once in a while. He was exhibiting great self-restraint to show her he meant everything he said. Not having to deal with the threat of becoming sexual put her more at ease. They were growing close in a very special way. They relaxed together and did and said things only accepting couples shared. Yet, one day, she would have to face the fact he'd want to take the relationship farther. The thought filled her with unease and age-old guilt. "Why can't I sort out my feelings?" she asked herself one day. "Was I meant to not understand any of this?"

To keep a balance in the relationship, Matthew took her to meet several of his friends who invited them over for dinner. They ate several dinners out with Mona and Cameron. Matthew and Rosa finally met.

"Rosa fell in love with you," Rachael said. "She fussed over you like a doting aunt and you ate it up."

"She likes my Mexican accent," he said, smiling broadly.

After two mediocre picks, they decided the movies were not one of their favorite pastimes. As often as their schedules would permit, and as many times as Rachael would allow, he went to her house from the jobsite for dinner. Sometimes he'd cook in her kitchen, or they'd go out to one of the local eateries.

They tried meditating together, which didn't work out that well. Both were too inhibited or too tired.

"Let's not be discouraged," she said. "We can try again when both our schedules are not demanding."

"When we're more comfortable with each other, too."

When possible, they went for walks and talked, beginning to understand one another. Once, he said, "I love it when you let the little girl in you come out to play."

"When you talk that way," she said. "You make me feel childish."

"Vulnerable? The way your father made you feel?"

"Not that you remind me of Dad."

"Tell me what vulnerable feels like."

She sighed heavily. "My stomach churns. I have a sense of losing control."

"I noticed," he said cautiously. "Anytime the conversation makes you feel like a child, you change the subject."

"You do know about such things, don't you?"

In their more active moments, keeping things light, they'd go ballroom dancing out on Taraval Street on Saturday nights. They even learned Lambada. Rachael's new black sequined dress made her a standout in the crowd. The experience was fun. They laughed a lot and loosened up, especially with the polkas. When they slow danced, one thing neither resisted was having their bodies locked together. They'd float effortlessly as if they were practiced partners.

"How am I doing?" he asked during a slow dance when they were pressed close.

"You dance divinely."

He laughed. "How am I doing with us?"

"We've both changed," she said, then teased. "But don't press your luck."

While dancing tightly locked in each others' arms, sometimes the sensuality between them became overwhelming. Rachael wondered if she was strong enough to resist and for how long.

One evening at Rachael's, Matthew said, "I've been talking to a therapist."

"You?" The admission took her by surprise.

"I'm not in therapy," he said. "A friend of mine at the Haight Rehab is a therapist. I chat with her one in a while."

"Didn't know you needed to work out anything serious."

"Not me. I try to understand my kids at the Rehab, the ones going through some heavy stuff. We who work with the kids share with the therapists and counselors."

Maybe he needed to work on himself. Or maybe by learning why things happen the way they do might help him better understand himself. "I'm happy you're into those kids. They must need a lot of help."

He seemed like he didn't know where to take the conversation. Perched on her sofa, he scooted forward, placing his elbows on his knees and facing her in the chair. "I'm understanding a lot about you too."

The hair prickled on the back of Rachael's neck. "I hope you weren't discussing us with the therapist."

"Not at all. In learning about those kids and how their teen years affect them, I've come to understand a lot about you."

Rachael paused. Their conversations hadn't delved into personal dilemmas and how far apart they caused her and Matthew to remain. Maybe now was the time to air some laundry and get past it. She smiled nervously. "You think you're getting to know me, huh?"

"You had no control over what happened to you in your younger years. Now you're left to try to understand how life comes at you and how you react to it."

Rachael began to feel uneasy. The conversation was about to discuss her problems and, true, she wasn't sure how to deal with them, nor Matthew digging into them. "Do we need to do this now?"

He was too deep in thought and probably didn't hear. "I'm finally beginning to comprehend your strong sense of self-preservation." When she tried to talk, he said, "Please, let me finish. Being reclusive is a common method of protecting one's self when a person has difficulty coming fully to grips with life."

"It's not like I'm hiding from life, Matthew."

He rose and went to her and waited for her hand. "Come sit with me on the sofa."

She paused a moment then offered her hand and went to sit beside him. They turned half-way to face each other.

"The reason you meditate is to be in touch with the part of you that knows how to make everything right."

"Maybe. It feels right for me."

"Angel, I'm resentful of you more easily entering into a meditative state than me."

"You're accomplished too, aren't you?"

"Not as adept.

"Let it go, Matthew. That comes with practice."

"I guess I do talk about myself with the therapist."

"You don't present as a person with deep-rooted problems. You're always up here somewhere." She motioned with a hand in the air over her head.

"I guess I get side tracked a little about Linda." He clenched his teeth. His jowls tightened. "The therapist said that all our nervous systems can do is treat a thought, like the aborted child, as if it really occurred. I finally realize some of my hopeless feelings were rooted in the thought of the abortion."

"Does that advice hit home with you?"

"Understanding myself helps me have more patience with us."

Once Rachael began working at ConverTech, little or no time was left for them to be together. The job turned out to be more complicated than anyone expected. She would sometimes work until eight in the evening, and sometimes both Saturdays and Sundays. Her erratic schedule put immense pressure on their relationship. She stopped writing once again, vowing not to take another job until her novel was finished.

Fortunately for Rachael, through therapy, Matthew learned to understand her unquantified loyalty to her commitments. Regardless of unexpected demands placed on her, if she made good her promise to endure such an employment contract because she gave her word, she would certainly be as devoted to any commitment she might make to him.

He started sending her a fresh bouquet of flowers each week. He bought a bunch of humorous greeting cards, and though he sometimes signed his name without writing a message, the cards spoke for him. He was truly making a gallant effort.

So was Rachael. One evening, he sat waiting in his car in her driveway. Arriving home weary, she insisted she could prepare a light meal. "I've got one of Rosa's great vegetarian casseroles in the fridge. I could pop it in the microwave, and steam some…"

"After your fourteen hour day? Not a chance."

In a little Asian neighborhood restaurant on Clement near Funston, hot rice crackled as it was introduced into the bowl of mixed vegetables and hot broth at their table. The doors closed at ten o'clock. They had enjoyed two precious hours together.

Saying goodbye was becoming more and more difficult. In the weeks that followed, Matthew showed up late one evening and handed her thirteen long stemmed red roses and a beautifully wrapped box with green foil and a large, puffy white bow. She unwrapped it in the living room as he sat by her side. "Oh my," she said. It was a copy of the picture Cameron had secretly taken of her and Matthew at the helm of the Mona Lee II and mounted it in a shiny white frame trimmed in 24 karat gold etching.

Chapter 30

Rachael returned from Santa Clara shortly after seven one Friday evening and headed straight downstairs to check her answering machine. She expected another off-the-wall message from Matthew. If not urgent, he began the habit of using the house phone instead of her cell phone to leave messages to cheer her when she came home depleted. He would call to let her know what time he'd pick her up for dinner. But the playback wasn't Matthew's voice.

"Rachael, this is Mona. I'm at Bay Side General. Please come as soon as you can. Don't hesitate, please! Just get here. Any hour. We need you!" Her voiced cracked and she was crying. "Come to the second floor and ask someone to show you where I am. Please be careful, but please… hurry!"

Stunned, she stood speechless. There were two more calls with no messages left. By the hospital noises in the background on the voiceless recordings, she knew the caller was Mona both times.

Rachael's hair stood on end. Her nerves shot rampant energy through her body. Why? Who? Something's happened to Cameron. Maybe he had a heart attack or was injured on the job. We need you, Mona said. Of course, Matthew would be at his father's side. They were both working at St. Francis Wood. Maybe there was an accident at the jobsite. That's why they'd be at Bay Side General. Emergency cases in San Francisco were taken there.

She took chances in the evening traffic, keeping watch for patrol cars as she sped as fast as she could.

Stepping off the hospital elevator, she was overtaken by a strange feeling of foreboding. She glanced around realizing she was on the surgical floor. She walked to the desk and asked for Ramona Knight.

"They're down that way," the nurse said, motioning. "In the waiting area outside of surgery."

Now surgery. Rachael's uneasy feeling intensified. What on earth could have happened. She rushed in the direction given.

Mona jumped up from the chair as soon as Rachael came into view. Cameron stood slowly. They were crying. Rachael saw them both and froze. Her eyes widened as she realized who was missing from the room. Her knees started to give out. Mona grabbed her, and held her up. Two others in the room first turned away then soon left.

"It's Matt, Rachael! Our Matthew!"

Rachael trembled violently. "What do you mean, 'It's Matthew'?"

Cameron came to them, putting his arm around them both. "Our boy's… been in an accident." He choked, barely able to speak.

Rachael suddenly stopped trembling and became still. She stared at them blankly. "Not my Matthew," she said quietly. "Not my Matthew. We're going out for dinner tonight."

Cameron guided Mona and Rachael back to the chairs. Mona blew her nose and Rachael sat quietly staring at the muted TV.

"Talk to her, Mona," Cameron said. "She has to know."

"Rachael, honey…" Mona sniffed. "Matt's hurt pretty bad. He's unconscious. They're doing surgery." She couldn't go on.

"They rushed him in by helicopter," Cameron said. "He's busted up bad. He's been unconscious since the accident. We don't know if…" He paused, his face contorted in pain. He wiped his eyes with a handkerchief, then blurted, "He may not make it!" Suddenly, he jumped up and walked hurriedly to the window and blew his nose, then stood clutching the window sill silently staring out into the darkness. He rocked back and forth with each heavy breath.

"Honey, he called out for you," Mona said. "He's unconscious. The E.R. doctor said he mumbled something like 'Rach… Rach' when they first started working on him."

Rachael still stared straight ahead without blinking. Her chest jolted and she swallowed hard, crying inside, without tears. "How… bad… is he?" Her whispered words and breath were spasmodic.

Cameron pulled himself together and returned to sit again. "His left leg's broken in two places. They have to put pins in. He's got broken ribs that punctured a lung." Cameron swallowed hard. "He has a dislocated shoulder and a fractured jaw. Worse, he's got a massive concussion. That's why he's unconscious."

"How did it happen?" Rachael asked, her whisper strained.

Mona and Cameron looked at each other. "It happened," Mona said. "You don't need to know the details."

"You have to tell me," she said. "What is it you're not saying?" Matthew was a careful driver because of his Vette. A car accident? Unless someone ran into him, it had to be something else. Then she remembered. He was trying to get his ring back from Linda, trying to put an end to her idiotic pestering. Had he been with her? Had she been high on who-knew-what and caused an accident? "Does this have something to do with Linda? Is that what you don't want me to know?"

Mona and Cameron exchanged another glance. Cameron looked at the floor, then started slowly. "Earlier this afternoon, Matt told us he was going to meet Linda to get his ring back. She was to give him the damned pawn ticket. He was going to pay to get the ring out of hock."

"Rachael, he was happy this whole thing with Linda was coming to an end," Mona said reassuringly while dabbing at her eyes. "He's been happy for the first time in his life, with you."

"He hasn't been happier, Rachael, than when you two got back together," Cameron said as he wiped his eyes again.

"Linda was on drugs again."

"Matthew knew that," Rachael said.

"Eye witnesses said they were parked at the curb in the Mercedes…"

"On 24th Street near Dolores."

"That the woman in the car kept taking swipes at the man."

"Hitting him, Rachael. Linda was striking him," Mona said, nearly screeching.

"Then she took off. She was driving. The car lurched across the lanes on 24th. It fishtailed into the intersection, hit the curb on the island in the middle of Dolores, and threw it into the on-coming lane."

Rachael was crying, weeping, but needed to know it all.

"Linda must have been wiped out, probably before she went to meet him," Mona said.

Rachael couldn't believe what she was hearing. She didn't care that Matthew went to meet Linda. She trusted him. He said that relationship was over and she'd never known him to lie. What she couldn't believe was that her Matthew, the perfect manifestation of what she idealized in a man, was now lying nearly lifeless while others worked to save him. Her energy left her. She wished to be as numb as he must certainly be.

Cameron swallowed hard. "Witnesses said when the car hit that abutment, it flipped over and over…" He couldn't stop his tears. "The car they were in, Rachael, rolled almost all the way down that long hill on Dolores Street. Rolled! Over and over and over!"

"No-o," Rachael said. She covered her face and shuddering at the terror Matthew must have known.

"Another car turned to go uphill and the driver saw it rolling down toward him. He managed to impact the Mercedes to stop it from tumbling."

"The driver of the other car wrecked his own car to stop the Mercedes from rolling," Cameron said.

"They worked for over an hour to extricate those two from that car." Mona shook her head again. "They used the Jaws of Life."

"They cut the car almost in half with a Hurst tool to lift it off those two."

"Were they pinned underneath?" Rachael asked fearfully.

"No. The car pancaked with them inside and finally stopped upside-down, squashing them inside."

"Why... God?" Rachael asked, praying.

"They found Linda crumpled upside down under the steering wheel. Her head was ripped open. Her gray matter was oozing out!"

"Oh, geez," Rachael said, covering her face with both hands.

Mona and Cameron kept talking, as if they needed to purge themselves of the gore. "They found Matt wedged on the console between the seats and said he kept fading in and out," Cameron said.

Mona touched her arm. "They had to decide which one got to ride in the chopper."

"Which one?" Rachael asked. "Weren't they both critical?"

"They got Linda out first. If they transported her about the time they got Matt out..." Cameron said. He shook his head. "They decided Linda with her head busted open like that didn't have a chance. They brought her in by ambulance and saved the chopper for Matt. Thank God."

"The StatEvac chopper couldn't land in the intersection because of electrical wires and tall trees. They were forced to go four long blocks down the hill and do a hot land in Dolores Park."

"And wait?"

"Till the ambulance could transport Matt to them. Then they flew him in."

"What about Linda?" Rachael asked after calming. "Is she in surgery too?"

"She isn't going to make it," Cameron stated flatly. His voice contained a twinge of pity. "She's alive. Her skull's been ripped away and her head's laying wide open. She's in another operating room." He thumbed the direction. "They're trying to do what they can for her. She's barely alive, and Doc said her blood's loaded with drugs. They can't give her anything for the pain. They're trying to clean debris out of what's left of her brain. They don't know if she can feel what they're doing to her." He stopped talking and swallowed hard again. "Damn her anyway!"

"The police found dope, blocks of cocaine, crack and ecstasy pills, even drug paraphernalia in the wreckage. The doctors are keeping us posted. They tested both Linda and Matt's blood," Mona said. "Linda was loaded with stuff. They thought Matt and Linda were transporting a shipment. Until we got here."

"They found our phone numbers in Matt's wallet." Cameron said. "We told them about Linda with her drug problem, and about Matt going to get his ring back. They found his car parked on 24th Street. They impounded it and dusted it for drugs."

"They won't find any," Rachael said, trying to reassure them. Then she wondered why she said that. She wondered if there was anyway Linda had drugs on her at any time she was in Matthew's Corvette. If so, how long ago.

Mona choked back crying. "Thank heavens, the police said they didn't find any." She blew her nose. "Shit!" She stomped a foot and clenched her fists. Her body shook. "Matthew just might have traded his life for a lousy thirty thousand dollar Marquis diamond ring."

Even though Rachael was in a daze, the amount he paid for the ring was staggering. No wonder Matthew tried diligently to get it back. Thirty thousand dollars? What kind of a person could

Linda have been to toy with him like she did? The shock of it was more than Rachael could bare. She slumped against Mona and began sobbing. Mona held her and cried too. Cameron placed his hand on Rachael's shoulder, staring straight ahead, glassy eyed, shaking his head from side to side.

"Matthew's not going to die," Rachael said finally. "He's not going to die."

"They don't know. They said they don't know. They told us to prepare for the worst. His concussion's bad. His brain was bleeding. He doesn't respond. He's been unconscious, even while they're working on him. They can't give him anything for the pain either, because of the concussion."

"Matthew's not going to die," Rachael quietly said again. She stood, walked out of the room, and swaggered away in a stupor. Mona came up quickly behind her. "Where's the chapel, Mona? Doesn't every hospital have a chapel?"

Chapter 31

The two women staggered toward the chapel, hanging onto each other. They entered the tiny room furnished with a small altar, a cross, and chairs. Cameron stayed in the waiting area.

"Nothing short of his own demise could convince him to leave that spot now," Mona said.

Inside the sanctuary, they held hands and prayed silently in their own ways. Rachael's eyes were closed. Tears poured silently from between her lashes and ran down her face and neck. After a while, Mona slipped out of the room.

Rachael returned to the waiting area and stood quietly at the windows. Mona and Cameron slugged down black coffee and consoled one another.

The eleven o'clock news began to air. The news flash was the accident that happened earlier in the day on Dolores Street in the Noe Valley District. Sound was muted on the TV. Rachael read the captions across the bottom of the screen. A witness on the street used his cell phone to capture the Mercedes 380SE as it tumbled. He had turned the video over to the police. Clips from the video showed the car throwing off windows, fenders and other parts, as it flattened more and more with each roll. Water and fuel sprayed out in all directions as it tumbled. It showed the good Samaritan who wrecked his own sedan to stop the Mercedes from its death roll. It, too, had its front end and windshield demolished as the Mercedes rolled up onto its hood, then slipped down to the pavement. Thankfully, neither the sedan nor the Mercedes had caught fire.

Rachael sat numbed to the core, glad she couldn't hear the description as the news showed flashes of first responders attempting to open the wreckage. Abruptly, Rachael turned away, and stared out the window into the night. She didn't want to see them lifting Matthew out of the wreckage. He was here, in this hospital, with doctors working on him. He was here. Them saving his life was what mattered now.

After what seemed like an eternity, a doctor wearing perspiration soaked scrubs appeared at the waiting room doorway. He looked fatigued. "Are you the Knights?" he asked.

"Yes," Cameron said, jumping to his feet. "Yes."

"I'm Dr. Fullerton." He shook their hands. "Your son's being moved into Post-op. We're going to hold him there till we're sure he's stable enough to be transferred to the Intensive Care Unit."

"How is he, doctor? How's my boy?"

"Would you come with me first," he said, leading them into a smaller room. When they entered, he switched off the room lights. Multiple x-rays hung on a screen and other assorted films were strewn across a table. "We did a CT Scan, then a pneumoencephalogram. These arteriograms show several small subdural hematomas.

"Please, doc, you gotta explain that to me."

Rachael watched from behind Cameron and Mona. She wouldn't be able to help Matthew recover if she didn't know the extent of his injuries.

"Subdural hematomas are blood clots from concussions in deeper areas of the brain." The doctor pointed on the films to the area of Matthew's head trauma. "Though intracranial bleeding seems to have stopped, your son is far from being out of danger," he said as he switched films.

Mona took one look at the jagged leg fractures on the films and ran from the room wailing.

The doctor continued, pointing to the various images. One film showed a jagged break of both the left tibia and fibula below the knee. Another film showed the leg bones after being reset. "His leg's in a cast now and the left arm and shoulder are being supported in a soft sling to set the dislocation."

Rachael stepped close, reaching up to touch the x-ray of the shoulder. "Did he feel any of this pain when it happened?"

"He may have been unconscious when the breaks occurred." He smiled warmly, then continued. "I don't know if you can see this. Let me explain." He pointed to the rib x-ray. "Because of his broken ribs and punctured lung, we did a VATS." He knew they wouldn't understand. "That's Video Assisted Thorascopic Surgery. We made small incisions in his chest and used a tiny camera and instruments to stitch up his lung. Matthew's going to be bound to the bed with restraints in order to avoid sudden trauma should his body spasm while he's unconscious. He won't be able to thrash about, if that should happen."

"When can we see him, doc? I gotta' be with my boy. Please, doc…"

"You can visit him now, if you like. I'll go with you so I can explain what's going on with him."

Matthew lay bare except for a sheet loosely draped across his pelvic area and between his legs with the busted one elevated in a cast. His right arm and leg were tied to the bed railings. The left top side of his head was shaved showing a long laceration on his scalp that was stitched closed but left uncovered. His chest and rib cage were shaved, still coated yellow with surgical disinfectant. His left arm lay in the soft sling bound over his chest. A tube protruded out of the left side of his ribs below the armpit with fluid sporadically bubbling through it. Numerous bags dangled from a multi-armed IV pole, their contents dripping through tubes connected to veins in various parts of his body.

The doctor pointed to the chest tube sticking out from between his ribs. "That's to allow air to escape that entered the chest cavity when the lung was punctured," he said. "And to draw out blood and other fluids from the lung. He's hooked up to a cardiac monitor, standard procedure. Just a precaution. We'll know what his body's doing while he's unable to tell us."

"He's so hurt," Rachael said.

The doctor looked at her curiously and nodded.

"Rachael's his girlfriend," Cameron said, placing a hand on her shoulder.

"That tube... stuck in his throat," Mona said.

"We did a tracheotomy to help him breathe." The doctor smiled knowingly and patted Mona's shoulder. "Matthew's mouth is wired into position to assure his jaw remains stationery until the fracture in the upper portion of the mandible heals. See here," the doctor said, separating Matthew's lips. "It's like he's wearing braces."

"That's why you did the... uh, that tube in his throat?" Cameron asked. Dr. Fullerton nodded. "And this is what plastic surgery?" Cameron asked again, looking over the stitched areas where skin had busted open, now stitched into swollen and nasty looking welts.

"He won't be able to eat," Rachael said. "He'll wither away."

"He'll get all the nutrients he needs through the IV fluids."

"Is there no end?" Mona asked.

"He's pretty banged up. You need to know these things, what he's facing," the doctor said. He waited till Mona calmed again. "That laceration on the top of his head took eighteen inner and outer stitches."

While the doctor spoke, Mona kept shaking her head from side to side as her body tried to keep up. She whimpered loudly as Rachael tried to comfort her. "This can't have happened to our son, please," she said. "Not Matthew."

After more than four hours of almost steady vital signs, Matthew was transferred to the Intensive Care Unit. Rachael, Mona and Cameron returned to the waiting area.

Cameron clicked the remote to turn on the TV. Though it was four o'clock in the morning, as if they had no new news to report, news of the accident was airing. Most likely filmed earlier, a reporter stood below the accident scene on the hill on Dolores Street. The camera panned up the hill a couple of yards to where two cars sat blocking the uphill lanes. The body of the Mercedes, earlier split in half, rested with its trunk and hood leveled flat on the pavement. Tow trucks had arrived. A glimpse of the horror, then the camera panned back to the reporter. The news told them nothing much they didn't already know. Rachael, Mona and Cameron sat gazing at the TV not aware the news anchor changed to another topic.

The doctor walked in as daylight began to appear. He looked haggard, and surely must have stayed in the hospital to keep watch on Matthew. His prognosis wasn't any more encouraging. Matthew remained in a coma and wasn't showing any signs of improvement. "I won't lie to you," he said. "We can't tell about this sort of thing. He could be the same for a couple of days or maybe weeks before regaining consciousness. Or he could slip away from us. We can't know the extent of damage to his brain until he regains consciousness and we can perform more tests."

"Damage? More tests?" Mona sounded fatigued.

"There could be further complications. Your son has evidently kept his body strong and healthy. That's going to help him through this. His brain's been severely traumatized. I'll be honest with you," he said, pausing as if deciding whether to say the rest. "He's not the worst I've seen, but it doesn't look good for him either. We've done what we can for the moment." He threw up his hands and shrugged. "Now we wait and watch. Go home, folks. Get some rest. We'll notify you when there's any change."

"Uh, doc," Cameron said. "The other guy, the one who used his car to stop the Mercedes from rolling. Is he okay?"

"No injuries, checked and released," Dr. Fullerton said.

"Can the hospital give me his name and number?" The doctor looked suspicious. "I wanna thank him for saving my boy," Cameron said.

"Check with the police."

Mona didn't seem strong enough to stand up by herself. Cameron went with her to have a last look at Matthew before leaving. By the time they returned, Mona was again shaking, barely able to walk.

"Rachael," she said. "You may not want to see him."

"On top of everything else," Cameron said. "Both his eyes got black."

"I have to see him. I have to. I need to touch him and tell him I'm here." Rachael burst into tears at the ICU doorway.

A nurse stopped her. "You're family?"

"She's family," Cameron said quickly. "Uh… she's our son's girlfriend."

"Not quite family," the nurse said, looking her up and down.

Panic welled up in Rachael's throat. Being denied access to see Matthew took her by surprise. Peering into the dimly lit room, she could see him in the bed closest to the nurses' station with its monitors. "Please," she said.

The charge nurse appeared. "You the one they said he kept calling for? Are you Rach?"

"Yes, I'm Rachael."

The charge nurse took her by the elbow and guided her to Matthew's bedside. The room was warm. As before, a sheet covered his hip area to allow the stitched areas access to the healing effects of circulating air. His face was discolored, swollen and distorted. He lay on a blue Chux sheet and a catheter tube passed from under his meager covering to a plastic bag clipped to the edge of the mattress.

"You come in any time. I'll tell the others. In a case like this, it's better for you to spend as much time with him as possible," the charge nurse. "Let him hear your voice, honey. Talk to him and touch him. Don't be afraid to touch him."

In a case like this? What the charge nurse said played over and over in Rachael's mind. The choice of words sounded like there may not be a lot of time left. Silently, tears ran again. She studied Matthew with total disbelief. He was mangled, unrecognizable. The circles around his eyes were not only black, they were red and blue and purple. Tubes remained in his nose and out his throat and the side through his ribs. IV lines remained stuck into the back of both hands and the top of a foot. Electrode pads were stuck everywhere, the trailing wires monitoring vital functions. The numerous lines running to different monitors and equipment looked ominous.

Suddenly she turned, running from the room. If there was any way he might, she didn't want him to hear her cry.

Unwillingly, they left.

"I feel like we're turning our backs and walking out on Matthew," Rachael said.

Cameron and Mona accepted the invitation to stay the night at Rachael's house to be on the San Francisco side of the Bay and nearer the hospital. They left their telephone numbers at the nurses' station. They made a quick trip home to get a change of clothes. Later, to occupy their time, Rachael showed them through her home, talking about the things that Matthew loved. She admitted she had not let him see the inside of her bedroom.

Cameron shot a glance of disbelief at Mona. Rachael realized she shouldn't have mentioned something like that.

Rachael called the department manager at her home and got a week's leave from work. After a few hours of fitful rest, they returned to the hospital. Several men from one of the construction crews stopped by. They were not allowed into the ICU. Cameron filled them in on Matthew's condition and they went away disheartened.

Later in the evening, Mona said, "We want to spend tonight at home, to help us feel closer to our son. We don't want to leave you alone though. Will you come to our place?"

Rachael accepted. For distraction, they repeated the routine of the previous night, showing her around their home in Sausalito and talking about Matthew.

Rachael shared some of the things she and Matthew spoke of. "We made a sort of commitment," she said quietly.

"What was that about?"

"That we try harder to understand one another."

Mona and Cameron sat, quietly attentive, wanting to hear more. Both had swollen eyes. Mona's were the worst, nearly swollen shut and no makeup would hide it. No one cared. They each shared the same heartache.

"We both feel the same about meditation. We understand it. Most people don't. It's hard to find someone with these interests. Yoga's what brought us closer. It doesn't work when only one is interested."

Hearing about their son seemed to help. Especially the part about the commitment she and Matthew made. After a while, they couldn't talk about him anymore. Later, Mona led Rachael to the guest room at the end of the upstairs hallway across from Matthew's room. "If he doesn't stay on the boat, that's his room." They were exhausted. After Mona and Cameron retired, Rachael went into meditation. The next morning, Mona found her in the room and in the bed where Matthew had slept.

The end of Rachael's week off came quickly. Matthew remained unconscious with no change in his condition. The doctor advised them to get back to their regular routines. They needed to stay occupied to remain strong.

Reluctantly, Rachael began the long drives to and from Santa Clara once again. The demanding nature of the work provided desperately needed distraction to help get through the days despite feeling numb. How could life be that cruel? She finally believed she could trust someone, trust Matthew. She was learning to let go of her fear of being hurt. She and Matthew had everything going for them. She gritted her teeth until her jowls ached. She would wait this out. Matthew would get better and then they could get on with their lives.

Every evening and on weekends, she spent in the hospital. Ever since the ICU charge nurse mentioned it, Rachael rubbed Mathew's free arm and persistently talked to him even though he remained in a coma. People can hear when under anesthesia, maybe some when unconscious too, the nurse said. Hopefully, there wasn't enough brain damage that would prevent him from comprehending.

Chapter 32

Days passed before the police were able to locate Linda's mother. Even then, she hadn't arrived immediately upon learning of her daughter's condition. Then she finally showed up in a drunken stupor. She was a tall thickly built middle-aged woman with a full head of lavender-tinted hair and heavy makeup. Each day, she would look in on Linda through the window of ICU for a few moments. Sitting beside her dying daughter's bedside was not her way of handling grief.

The following Friday, Linda expired, not having regained consciousness. She clung to life in a vegetative state for three long weeks, then simply slipped away.

On Saturday, while Rachael waited for Cameron and Mona who were inside the ICU, Mrs. Berringer arrived noisily at the unit desk in the hall. She unknowingly stood right beside Rachael.

"I wanna see d'asshole that killed my daughter," she said, slurring spittle at the nurse. "Where is that son-va-bitch that got my daughter strung out on drugs." Her breath reeked of stale cigarettes and alcohol that cheap cologne couldn't mask. She was boisterous. Someone called hospital security who commandeered two police officers passing through the hospital. "I'm Mrs. Berringer, Linda's mother," she said, lifting her chin arrogantly. "We're impor'ant people. That asshole ain't gonna' get 'way with this. I know people in high places." She fumbled nervously twirling the many rings on all her fingers. Especially the ill-fitting one on her pinky with a stone so large it could only be a *Cubit Zirconia*. People noticed her nervously rotating the rings. Rachael saw it too. Mrs. Berringer looked down at the rings and quickly turned a couple into her palm and closed her fist around them.

The stone on the ring looked similar to the Marquis diamond that Amanda used to wear. At that size, Mrs. Berringer's ring was probably an exaggerated CZ. She hid it to keep anyone from knowing it wasn't a true diamond and that she wasn't as wealthy as she would have people believe. Rachael stepped away.

"What're they gonna think back home? This is gonna make me look like a fool. Where you keepin' that son-va-bitch?"

The police tried to calm her. She continued to rant about her daughter being a big star until some guy got her into drugs. She was obnoxious and attracted the attention of other nurses and attendants. Cameron and Mona poked their heads out of ICU to learn what the raucous was about.

"Here I was, sendin' her money every month," Mrs. Berringer said, whining. "A career like hers takes a lotta' cash for clothes and public'ty and things. Some guy's been takin' my money and fillin' her full o' drugs."

"You don't know that for sure, Mrs. Berringer," an officer said.

"I been staying at my daughter's place," she said. "Been going through her things to help me remember. She had a fine life, lots of nice things, till that guy got her on drugs." She nervously twirled her rings. Rachael watched her every move. Her rings looked cheap.

A police officer stood close to her. "I think you should get ahold of yourself, ma'am, and do what's right by your daughter, which is arranging how you're gonna take her home."

"I wanna see t'asshole…" she said, continuing to slur her words.

"I'm sorry. That's not possible. Now, if you haven't already, I suggest you claim your daughter's body—"

"Oh, whadda you know?" she asked. Her mouth turned down grotesquely at the corners.

"I know," the officer said, leveling his eyes at her, "that if you don't take care of your business and leave this place, I can take you in for being drunk and disorderly."

"Humph," she said, snubbing the officer and staggering backward a few steps to cross the hall, accompanied by the security officer.

Rachael watched quietly. Mrs. Berringer poked at the down button several times, finally striking it. Two officers exchanged glances. Then, claiming to be dizzy, she groped her way to a nearby chair.

"Don't know what I'm gonna' do now," she said to the security guard. "As soon as her career got going, Linda was going to help me out."

"She was, ma'am?" The guard was being polite.

"I'm retired, you know. Getting up in years. Your kids are 'spose to help. Don't know how I'm gonna' manage. She's all I had. I was countin' on her."

"You'll do find, ma'am."

Rachael couldn't help glancing over. She didn't have to strain to hear the loud conversation. The elevator doors opened and closed.

"We're impor'ant people back home," she said again, pulling a piece of paper from her purse. She fumbled to unfold it while weaving forward and backward in the chair. "See here." She offered it to the guard. "I'm gonna' have to write something for our hometown paper. What d'ya think of that headline, *A Star Comes Home to Rest*. That was her movie name, you know… Star."

The guard looked around as if longing for help. He punched the elevator down button.

"I ain't gonna' tell 'em she had drugs in 'er." She sniffled. "I been going through things at her house and I found…"

The elevator arrived. The guard sighed as they stepped inside and the doors slowly closed.

Chapter 33

"I don't advise moving him," Dr. Fullerton said. "While he lingers in a coma, it's absolutely vital that his brain not be shaken in the least."

"Doc, it's been four weeks," Cameron said. "If not to Marin, how about to Colliers across town on Geary?"

"He'd be closer to us," Mona said.

"Sorry folks. Can't consider it."

When Rachael, Mona and Cameron arrived at the hospital one evening, Cameron said, "Yesterday at lunch time I walked in on a nurse clipping Matthew's mustache. It had grown down over his lips."

Matthew had lost much weight. His thick hair lost evidence of having been styled and had grown back in around the area of the laceration where his head was shaved. The restraints had since been removed, yet he lay unmoving. The tube sticking out of his rib cage was out and the incision healing. The pins in his jaw and clamps attached to his teeth to hold his mandible in position were to be removed at the end of the following week, along with the trachea tube. The dislocated arm and shoulder lay in a sling. Additional x-rays were taken of his leg to check on the healing process of the fractured bones. The tibia mended perfectly. The top of the fibula was healing slightly out of position from its natural location.

"How did something like that happen?" Cameron asked impatiently.

"It happens sometimes. There's nothing we can do right now," Dr. Fullerton said. "Once your son's well and strong again, he might consider surgically breaking the bone again and resetting it."

"What do you mean 'might consider'? What you mean is if he wants to look normal again, right?"

"We have no choice. We have to wait. When he's up and around again, time and a little exercise might do wonders for the leg."

"When he's up and around again? So far he hasn't so much as twitched."

"We can't control that," the doctor said, patting Cameron on the back. "I will tell you this. Because he's in a coma, it's likely your son's wounds are healing much faster than if he were active and burning up energy otherwise. His ribs appear to have healed well."

"Because they were allowed to set?" Rachael asked.

"That's right, and the punctured lung is clear. He will, however, require respiratory therapy when he's conscious again."

"Well, that's some progress," Mona said, nodding. "Thank heaven for that."

Physical therapists regularly massaged and flexed Matthew's limbs to assure adequate circulation to his muscles to stave off atrophy. The medical staff agreed Matthew's amazing state of physical fitness was sustaining him through his ordeal.

"The oral surgeon wants Matthew to have a check up every six months for his jaw, in addition to other exams," the doctor said, continuing to keep them apprised. Sometimes he and Cameron talked like old friends. It was good for Cameron to be treated that way. "When they set that jaw, the nature of the fracture was such they made a tiny hole high on Matthew's left cheek into which they would insert a scope to watch the procedure."

"That's that shiny little spot back on his cheekbone?" Mona asked.

"That's right. Follow up examinations of the jaw will entail running a scope down through that same area, to assure the jaw bone is not deteriorating instead of healing."

"Is there no other way? Through the mouth, maybe? What about x-rays?"

"An invasive procedure is the way to accurately view the area," Dr. Fullerton said. "The oral surgeon can fill you in when Matthew's conscious again."

"When he's conscious again," Mona said, whispering.

As Matthew lay nearly lifeless, Mona, Cameron and Rachael went through their days more like robots than humans. They had to endure and not lose hope Matthew would be back with them soon.

"I've located some obscure books on eastern philosophy that Matthew will welcome," Mona said. "I haven't put them on the shelves. They're for him. Unless I miss my guess, he'll spend recuperation time with his nose buried in a book."

"He does have an active mind," Rachael said, voice full of hope that he would still be that way, considering his brain injury.

From the day of the accident, Cameron doubled up and took over his son's management duties. "I let the men know I was counting on them to get the work done," he said. "I knew they'd come through." Not being allowed into ICU, they constantly asked for updates on Matthew's condition. Their attention and concern was a reflection of Matthew's rapport with his crews. "Who would've thought feeling proud of my son would make me feel so sad?" Cameron asked.

The Knight Homes' business attorney was to handle a law suit on Matthew's behalf and had wasted no time jumping into the process. Albert Taylor was both personal and business attorney for the Knights for nearly twenty five years. Now, he threw himself wholeheartedly into Matthew's case. Following through on Cameron's request, Taylor was able to contact the man who used his vehicle to stop the Mercedes from rolling. The man signed papers attesting that he would not hold Matthew liable for any and all future claims of any kind possibly arising from his decision to use his car as a barrier. The day of the accident, he was released from a check up in Emergency with a clean bill of health. Luckily, he sustained no nicks or cuts, not even a hint of a bruise. Cameron announced that he met the man and his wife, Jose and Virginia Martinez, and bought them a brand new Chevy sedan of their choice. Then the conversation turned again to how Taylor was proceeding.

"Linda was driving a car that was registered to Stage Center," Taylor told them as he enjoyed dinner at the Knights' home. "That production company was doing a multi-million dollar business. However, police narcotics investigators were in the middle of a long-term investigation and surveillance of the company, along with the dealings of its top executives."

"None of it ever leaked to the media?" Mona asked.

"Surprising, isn't it? Officials weren't able to accumulate sufficient evidence to indict anyone," Taylor said. "The owners of the production company were suspected of having established the modeling business as a front for drug running."

"How long has this been going on?" Rachael asked.

"Who knows? I'm sure the organizers were amazed when their bogus little company developed into a legitimate, thriving corporation promoting dozens of talented models and show people. They developed the perfect front, right there in the public eye." Al Taylor shook his head and then motioned that he'd like another slice of the pot roast. Taylor loved to have dinner with them. The way he put it, "That Mona can cook."

Cameron stood to cut off a thick slice of the pot roast. "What do they have on those guys now?"

"Well, the way I see it, they're pretty certain that at least the top executives of the company were involved in smuggling illegal substances across the border from Mexico. With the discovery of drugs found at the scene in the company car, the Grand Jury had enough for their indictments."

"They got 'em?" Cameron asked eagerly.

"Like that," Taylor said, snapping his fingers. "They've arrested the top four officials of the company, along with six employees."

"Thank God," Cameron said. "I want to see someone pays for what they did to my son."

"And to Linda. You didn't see this on the news?" Taylor asked.

"We musta' missed it. We been working long hours."

"You know? It doesn't matter whether or not Linda was involved in drug trafficking," Taylor said. "Members of the production company supplied her with drugs for personal use. She probably didn't know she was transporting large quantities when she was given use of the company cars. That's one fact, I'm afraid, may never be made clear."

"Then Linda might have been a pawn in someone else's game of greed and corruption," Rachael said. "As she drove from one location to another, it's possible she never suspected she was picking up or delivering."

"That's right. So it's the production company that's liable to Matthew." Al Taylor worked diligently building his case and preparing for a lawsuit against Stage Center and the individuals who were indicted. "I want Matt to get enough out of this to take care of his physical problems," Cameron said thoughtfully.

"And his future health problems," Mona said.

Al Taylor grinned. "I've started the wheels rollin' in that regard. We're going in for twenty mill."

Mona dropped her fork.

Then Taylor added, "Linda's mother's suing for one million, for her pain and suffering." He swallowed another bite of the food. "She's claiming Linda was to repay her for monies borrowed to sustain her career." His sideways glances said he didn't believe a word of Mrs. Berringer's claim.

At the sound of Linda's mother's name, goose bumps traipsed over Rachael body. "Oh, no, it can't be."

"Rachael, what is it?" Mona asked.

"The ring... the ring Matthew gave Linda." The thought left her breathless. "Mona, you said it was a Marquise diamond?"

"A monster diamond, too expensive for Matt's budget. That girl would take him for anything he could give, and he tried hard to make her happy." Mona totally broke down and Rachael leaned over and wrapped her arms around her and let her cry.

Cameron turned to Rachael. "Why do you bring that up now?"

"I think I know where the ring is."

"Spill it."

"In the hospital, Mrs. Berringer wore rings on every finger and she twirled them nervously. When she saw me watching, she turned a pinkie ring into her palm and hid it. It was a big monster Marquis cut stone." Rachael was breathless. "She said she was sorting through Linda's belongings. It must have been the Marquis that Matthew gave Linda."

Taylor raised an eyebrow. "How much are we talking about, dollar wise?"

"Doesn't matter now," Cameron said quickly. "We covered it in our advertising losses. If you can get a good sum on Matthew's behalf, let's leave it at that. We don't want to see the dammed thing again."

Rachael sat quietly through the rest of the meeting. If that was the ring that Matthew gave Linda, and Mona said it was a Marquis, Rachael's love of that cut of diamond had to end. If there was any way she and Matthew would end up together, she wouldn't want a Marquis now. Anything that looked like that stone would remind both of them of Linda. Yet, Rachael was getting ahead of herself. Matthew still lay in a coma with no sign of improvement.

Back when Rachael began returning to work each day, she offered her home and a set of keys to Mona and Cameron. They could stay in town when they needed to, or use her home as a stopping off point between their trips to and from the hospital.

Some days Rachael would come home to find them there and was comforted. Often Mona spent the night. Cameron wouldn't without Mona. They were getting to know her and Rachael knew she had gained their respect. As much as Rachael was getting to know Mona and Cameron, she recognized them not solely as Matthew's parents, but as his two best friends.

Rachael felt both envy and love for them. They lived the way she wanted her family to live, and which hadn't been the case. A fleeting thought reminded her not to give up on Brandon, her only family. And when she'd eventually have children, she could see herself bringing up her own family the same way one day, with the love and caring Mona and Cam showed their son. Like them with Matthew, when Rachael's children grew too old to mother, she would be an ally.

Desperately needing to occupy her mind, Rachael returned to writing her novel and plunged headlong into creating once again. As was her habit, she developed ideas speaking into her mini-recorder in the car during the long commutes. She could transcribe them into her computer when she found time. At least she wouldn't lose any of her ideas, regardless of distractions.

Another month had passed. Matthew remained in a coma and was moved to a private room adjacent to the ICU. He was connected to a monitor and intravenous lines. He was thin, his brawn having wasted away. Rachael was no longer spending entire weekends at the hospital, even though she did spend three or four hours each Saturday and Sunday. She stopped in on the way home from work the evenings she didn't work late.

"The plastic surgery has healed nicely," Rachael said to the nurse while trying to sound upbeat. She needed to keep her emotions buoyant.

"His face and upper torso should, in time, be almost completely clear of scarring," the nurse said. "In case like this, cosmetic surgery is a blessing."

"What about his throat?" He was still getting oxygen through a tube in his nose.

"Tracheotomy scars can recede."

Matthew seemed to be sleeping. There was no change in the condition of his coma.

Rachael was growing more and more despondent and weariness was getting to her. She began having minor anxiety attacks. People at work noticed. Working through lunch hours and break periods, she spent more and more time to herself. Staying occupied helped keep her mind off the rampant nervous energy that visited unexpectedly. She felt guilty going on with her life while Matthew lay withering away and showing early signs of atrophy. She needed to do something for him. He was becoming desperately thin. So was she.

Speaking into her mini-recorder, and sometimes aloud to herself at her computer, she wept and poured out her heartache and, finally, wrote about her sadness.

She developed an incident in her book about the gentle, lovable, assertive, positive giant named Hunter Lockwood who lay in a coma. Having been thrown and trampled by a horse, Hunter almost had the life kicked out of him. Hunter's patience and kindness was clearly evident while the story progressed, mirroring hers and Matthew's moods. So was his need to get on with his life, like Matthew, until the day of his accident.

Writing about Hunter enabled Rachael to more thoroughly express her feelings for Matthew. "I'm doing this for you," she would say over and over. She decided to dedicate her book, *Sea Cliff*, to him.

Working feverishly at times, she was able to capture on paper the things she wondered about and for which she found no answers. Somewhere along the way, she realized she didn't have to relate actual occurrences from her dreary past. What she needed to do was create new plausible scenes. The fact that the scenes may not have existed didn't matter. She would allow herself to feel and write the emotions, something of which she maintained a storehouse full.

Weaving a heart-wrenching counterplot for her characters provided the opportunity to vent troublesome feelings from real life. She was working toward resolution for her characters, yet, everything she wrote was pure fiction as far as she was concerned.

Chapter 34

Matthew's body was well on its way to healing and his vitals remained stable. The sling on his shoulder and the cast on his leg were gone. They finally put a hospital gown on him. He lay unmoving.

On Sunday, feeling more desperate than ever, Rachael spent the entire day in his hospital room. "More than two months have passed," she said to his face. "Come back to me."

She needed to have an active part, do her share in helping him survive. She remembered from her own therapies, when feeling helpless, to do something, anything. Chances are, she'd find the right thing to do. Take that first step. Though feeling quite timid about touching his body, weeks earlier, she learned how to massage Matthew's limbs and twice that day, again, performed his physical therapy. Assisting helped her overcome her feelings of helplessness. When speaking to him, she poured out her heart, as if doing so might be the last time she could. She'd concentrate on him and try to direct her words into his mind. She spoke like there was no one else in the world with whom to share. She touched him, lightly rubbing his face and arms and hands. Now leaning as close to his face as she could, she told him exactly how she felt.

"We have such a good thing going," she said softly. "You can't check out like *Ripp Van Winkle*." She didn't say she loved him, nothing like that. She reminded him of the great times they spent together and the ideas they shared in common.

"My meditation is deepening, Matthew. I want to share many things with you about what happens in the mind. I know you're coming back. You want to know these things, too. You want to experience them yourself. Have you been able to feel me meditating for you? I'm sending you healing. You'll be back with us any time now."

She stopped, momentarily gathering her thoughts, then leaned close again.

"Remember dancing? I miss dancing with you, Matthew. I miss having you hold me. There's a lot waiting for you. You have a very special family. The way you are with your mom and dad, that's the way I wished my family could have been." Her voice cracked. Then she begged, "Please, Matthew, please come back. I'm lost without you." She was feeling sorry for herself. She felt like a victim again.

She suddenly remembered the nurse had told her long ago that maybe the unconscious could hear and they she should talk to Matthew. She remembered Linda, lingering three long weeks in a coma. No one, not even her mother, had been there to talk to her. Rachael wished she had thought to go to Linda, to try to give her peace before she passed. Rachael cried for Linda.

The emotional roller coaster was taking its toll. More than once she wanted to scream, then reminded herself that Matthew was worse off. She rubbed his cheek tenderly and realized how sallow he looked. He had become his opposite, now emaciated skin and bone.

Suddenly, Mona touched her shoulder. She sat back in surprise.

Rachael looked into Mona's eyes, then to Cameron. Had they heard her talking to Matthew? Mona smiled lovingly. Rachael looked away, embarrassed, not wanting them to see how vulnerable and defeated she'd become. She stood, ready to leave.

"Stay with us, Rachael," Mona said. "Stay with us. We're so grateful."

"You give us strength," Cameron said. "Don't go."

Rachael wiped her eyes. That was the best thing Cameron ever said to her.

Mona glanced at her son and did a double-take. Her eyes opened wide. "He blinked!" she said, pointing to his face. "He blinked!"

They looked. Suddenly, Matthew's eyes opened wide. One knee flexed upward. His head and shoulders lifted off the pillows. His chest heaved and he vomited, shooting a projectile of foam and bile down the front of his gown and onto the sheet.

Rachael backed away and stood in front of the window. Relief flooded through her and made her dizzy. She grasped the sill for support, praying silently that he be okay. Mona went to the other side of the bed. Two nurses rushed into the room in response to signals on the monitor.

Matthew was disoriented. One nurse checked his airway to make sure he was breathing clearly, and took his vital signs. The other cleaned him up and changed his gown and sheet. They left when they were sure he was stable, saying a doctor would be coming in shortly.

Mona leaned over and embraced her son as Matthew grasp his father's hand. Soon Mona stepped aside and motioned for Rachael to come to the bedside. Weakly, Matthew reached for her, eyes filled with questions. Tears held back for months streamed down Rachael's cheeks. As she leaned over to kiss him, tears fell in wet sloppy drops into his beard.

He rubbed a hand in disbelief through the shaggy mass and seemed surprised at the length of his beard. "How l-long?" he asked with a raspy voice.

"Two months, Matthew. More than two months," Rachael said, whispering as she stroked his cheek lightly with trembling fingertips.

Slowly, he lifted his scrawny arms and hands and studied them. Then he looked again at each of them, tears filling his eyes. "Lin… da," he said. "Lin…da…?" He had remembered the accident.

At first no one spoke. It seemed Cameron was about to say something. His dislike of Linda may not allow him to say anything nice. "Matthew," Rachael said, taking his hand, but found she couldn't speak. She shook her head. Matthew turned away, pain clearly evident in his expression.

Matthew was kept in the hospital two weeks more. He remained quiet and moody after Dr. Fullerton explained about Linda. Though Rachael tried to get Matthew to talk, evidently his way of processing what he learned was in his mind and he didn't want to share any of it. He concentrated on getting his strength back through various recuperative therapies. The doctors continued to perform additional tests. His left leg was painful to begin walking on again and he was having physical therapy twice a day to strengthen the muscles around the break area.

At times, he had great difficulty speaking. He either couldn't remember the words or couldn't enunciate them properly. He stuttered. Some things he couldn't remember.

"An after-effect of the concussion," the speech pathologist said. "Difficulties should pass, or at least ease to a point as to be barely noticeable."

He began speech therapy and was to maintain regular appointments with the speech pathologist to assess any damage to his linguistic ability and to receive proper guidance to overcome any impediments.

A psychologist visited offering counseling and emotional support. He declined saying he knew a therapist, should the need arise.

"W-what bothers me m-most is the... plethora of aches and p-pains," he said. "From one move... ment to the next, my b-back twinges, or my neck stif... fens."

"The physical therapist said to expect this as you get re-acclimated," Rachael said.

Then his lumbar and sciatic area would act up. Tendonitis tightened both shoulders, arms and wrists. His joints seemed to cry out for attention, even his sternum ached. Facial tics plagued him. His bladder and bowel were affected.

"These symp... toms generally f-fade," he said, mimicking what he was told. "Each thera... pist says the... same thing."

"Then listen," Rachael said softly.

"I h-have no... no choice..."

"Patience. Have patience."

"For w-what? Someone took a... c-chunk out of... my life." He might have pounded a fist on the tray table. Instead, he let out a loud frustrated sigh instead. "C-can't wait. Have to d-do something..."

Anger and rage were boiling in him. Yet, despite himself, he was regaining strength quickly and would have checked out of the hospital against medical advice if not for the excessive dizzy spells that would force him into the nearest chair.

Finally, physicians gave their approval and he was released, with some sound advice.

"Bed rest, no work," Matthew said, again mimicking the specialist. "Yeah, sure."

"If you insist on being up and around, ride with your father," Rachael said. "You're not to drive until the dizziness is completely gone and you have medical approval to climb behind the wheel."

"Yeah, yeah," Matthew said again.

"They told you," Mona said, "to pay attention to how your body's recuperating, to allow time to heal and to live accordingly. Is that so hard?"

"Guess I c-can't…do m-much more than t-that."

More than once, the doctors suggested bed rest for at least the first couple of weeks at home. They were speaking to deaf ears. In the beginning, Matthew was to cease all activity when his head began spinning, and to report if the dizziness became more frequent. When they felt he was ready, he could cautiously resume an exercise program in addition to physical therapy. He was to eat lots and lots of the best body building foods. They didn't need to remind him. That much he knew.

Additionally, he was to report without fail for his periodic exams, like the one for his jaw bone, no matter how much he might resent the inconvenience. Those checkups would make the difference in saving his face. They would talk about the fibula, which hadn't healed properly, after he regained some weight and was fully walking on the leg again.

No surprise to anyone, Matthew refused to go back to bed and would lean his head against something, like the car window or the back of the recliner, when he was dizzy. He was given a set of crutches in the hospital before he left. He used one for a couple of days, opting instead, for a hand carved walking stick his grandfather had made. Cameron saved it as a remembrance. Matthew kept his full beard and mustache, and trimmed them nicely. The beard helped to distract from the fading tracheotomy scar.

Mona and Cameron organized a small party for Matthew a few weeks after he returned home. The construction foremen came with their spouses or significant others. In addition to being a rowdy bunch of construction workers, they were jubilant that Matthew was on the road to recovery. When they thought Rachael wasn't in earshot, they asked him if he'd felt up to getting laid yet.

For a while, Matthew acted as if he was glad to be alive. He bragged to his friends about the special parents he was fortunate to have, and the girlfriend. Rachael got her point across by teasing about how she thought he was accepting his temporary incapacitation miserably. He tired easily and left the party to go to bed without saying good night to anyone, not even Rachael, who felt stunned and embarrassed in front of his friends.

"Have patience, please," Mona said, begging.

After the party, Rachael drove home feeling abandoned. She tried to shrug off Matthew's rudeness, reasoning she was being too demanding of him in the aftermath of his crisis.

Strangely, a couple of weeks passed before he finally called late at night.

"I haven't called much because I'm commuting back and forth to Santa Clara," Rachael said.

"W-what about w-weekends?" Matthew asked.

"Actually, I'm working those days, too," she said. "I can get to the end of this job sooner."

"You volun… teered for over…t-time? What about w-writing?"

"I'm doing that, too, way into the night."

"Y-you're not avoiding me, a-are you?" he asked.

"No, I thought I'd allow you this time to recover and be with your parents," she said earnestly.

"Guess you're r-right," he said. "W-we can't expect to k-keep up the same pace as be…fore."

At various times, he called and left messages on Rachael's cell phone, usually kept turned off at work. His speech impediment frustrated him. He wondered how he must sound to the listener. He'd cut his messages short when he recognized how angry or frustrated he sounded. "W-well, it's okay not to see t-too much of e-each other right now," he said once. "I have s-something left over that I have t-to clear up. We'll talk soon."

Surely, he referred to the law suit and didn't want her to be a part of that mess. Rachael called back a few times and left a couple of conversational messages. She stopped calling when the phone wasn't answered. She began to feel there was no real reason for their exchanges. She began to feel like she should give him space, stay away, retreat to that place of serenity inside herself.

During the nights when sleep wouldn't come, Rachael's thoughts dwelled on Matthew and how she portrayed him in her book. She compared the two men, the fictional one she could have on a whim, and the real one who seemed to be passing from her life.

Possibly facing that she and Matthew were drawing apart, Rachael telephoned Mona.

"He's struggling with recurring headaches and speech," Mona said. "Matthew is in a mental rush to recuperate. His body is moving slower, regardless what his mind tries to dictate."

"I wish I could do something to help him."

"It's okay, Rachael. He's talking a lot to his dad. Cam will settle him down."

Chapter 35

"He wants to see my book!" Rachael waved the letter at Rosa.

"It's good, no?"

"Yes. Dennis DeBaer said the people who published my other books are interested in Sea Cliff. They want everything I've finished so far."

"*Que buena, chica*," Rosa said, twirling a cleaning rag in the air.

Rachael read further. "Oh, my," she said suddenly.

"*Que?*"

"I have to give them a tentative date when *Sea Cliff* will be finished. They want outlines of my next two books." She looked up, breathless. "Rosa, this is more than I expected."

"*Por que no*? You work too hard."

"Finally."

"We celebrate, no?"

"Oh, no, Rosa," Rachael said. "Not until the royalties roll in."

Rachael sat down at the kitchen table and leaned back in thought. "I've got a little more than two weeks left at ConverTech," she said. "After the end of October I'll be able to write without distraction."

"What about Senior Matt?" Rosa asked cautiously.

"You'll get to see him again, Rosa," Rachael said, teasing.

"*Si, si?*" she asked eagerly.

"He and his construction help will be underfoot. They'll be remodeling the guest unit."

"And you still write?"

"Don't worry about that. I can concentrate through anything."

A few days later at work, the Tracking Department completed world-wide computer conversion. They were celebrating the early wrap-up. Some staff from peripheral departments joined in. About seventy five people attended. They gathered at an outdoor picnic in Santa Clara behind a bar-restaurant under a tented awning. The weather was curiously warm.

Music blared. Most had finished a meal of barbecued ribs, chicken, baked beans, salads and trimmings. Some were seated or standing and talking in groups. Others played volleyball, video games, or table tennis.

Suddenly, everything began severely vibrating. The ground under them started moving up and down in places, and rolling like a choppy earthen sea.

"Earthquake!" several shouted.

Sharp cracking sounds and loud popping could be heard from the distance in several directions. The noise sounded like thunder.

Karen, sitting beside Rachael said, "I'm getting out of here. C'mon." They ran past the barbeque pit and ducked under a tree in the open field behind.

Most of the others ran toward the gate near the corner of the restaurant wall and into the adjacent parking lot. Many panicked as they pushed and shoved and screamed and almost trampled one another to get through the gate.

The ground jerked sharply up and down. The rolling wasn't like other earthquakes Rachael had experienced. The earth now jerked and ground against itself. The noise was horrific, sinister. Odd rumblings came from everywhere and filled the air.

"Fire! Fire! Get away from the building!" a cook shouted as he swaggered out the rear door of the restaurant, barely able to keep his balance. Smoke belched out behind him. "The gas lines in the kitchen are broken!"

When the ground stopped moving, everyone seemed breathless, caught in slow motion. The quake seemed to last minutes, the mind in shock fooled.

"Fifteen seconds," someone yelled, having timed the duration, typical of those who work with logic and figures.

"Rachael, that was a big one. That was *the* big one. That was *It*!" Karen said, babbling, excited.

Someone yelled the fire in the kitchen was extinguished. One wise soul flipped off the gas switch as soon as she recognized they were having an earthquake. The remaining gas in the stove burned and some cooking oil burned itself out.

Slowly people crept back under the awning. Some sat, some stood, seemingly ready to run again. All talked at once, shocked at the severity of the quake. People were completely disoriented. Several didn't react greatly and must have internalized their feelings with their food. They kept right on eating. Some went to listen to their car radios. Electrical power was out.

Suddenly, a severe aftershock rumbled through with a force almost as severe as the original jolt. People ran again, out into the open field. Moments later, a milder aftershock hit.

Many stood punching numbers into their cell phones. Rachael called Matthew and connected with his message center. The same when calling his dad. Would Matthew have been out somewhere with his dad? Mona would be across the Bay at her store. Rachael wondered how widespread the quake might have been. She thought of Brandon driving in the East Bay and tapped his name on her phone. The call rolled to his message center. She thought about her house sitting on the steep cliffside. This had to be the most severe earthquake the Bay Area experienced in many years. There was yet no way to know how it registered on the Richter scale.

People were pulling themselves together and deciding what to do. The managers would return to ConverTech to inspect the offices and the warehouse for structural and content damage. The rest were released to head home.

She climbed into her Porsche and turned on her radio. The scanner found the only station now broadcasting as she pulled out of the parking lot into the biggest traffic jam ever.

"This is going to be a long fifty eight miles," she said, talking to herself. She glanced at the gas meter and sighed with relief. For the first time in a long time, a positive memory of her father came to mind. *"Don't get caught with an empty tank."*

It was strange that her father would pop into her mind. She thought about him less and less and when she felt free of him, a memory would come to her. At least this one was positive. As mean as he was, some things he taught gave her strength. Maybe, just maybe, his meanness gave her incentive to face almost anything.

The sporadic radio news announced roads, overpasses and bridge closures, and for people to stay off their cell phones. A large sink hole opened on a road in Oakland and a delivery van was sucked down with it. There was no word on the driver.

"Where did these people come from?" she asked out loud again as she eased onto Hwy 280. All five northbound lanes were filled with traffic. On any normal commute day, there were sparse pockets of traffic during the heaviest commute hours. Staggered work shifts helped keep traffic thin. Now, everyone was commuting at the same time.

Listening to intermittent reports about bridges possibly being weakened, bridges she would have to cross to get home, was making her paranoid. She turned the radio just low enough to catch anything new.

After many bumper-to-bumper miles, she realized she was near where Brandon had moved. She quickly jostled into the right lane and left the freeway at the next exit.

Brandon unexpectedly walked outside as she arrived. "Yeah, I'm here," he said. "Wouldn't you know it? Two weeks ago, I worked out a way for my driver and I to alternate shifts. He's got the East Bay routes Tuesday, Thursday, and Saturdays this month." Brandon's grin was smug. He managed to save himself from harm, at the cost of someone else's peril, and he gloated.

"That sinkhole in Oakland, could be your driver and van trapped in that pit right now," Rachael said. "How can you stand there and smirk?"

"What the hell can I do about it?" Brandon asked, his expression suddenly souring. "What can anybody do?"

Chapter 36

What could anybody do? While no one could change what happened, she was irritated at his lack of concern. "Show some compassion, for heaven's sake."

"I think he's okay," Brandon said, trying to sound sympathetic. "Every time he delivers in the East Bay, he gets back real late. I think he's got drinking buddies on that side."

Rachael felt great relief knowing Brandon was safe and herself having completed the freeway portion of the journey home.

Streets and yards were littered with glass and debris and fallen trees or branches. Cracks in the roads were slowly filling with shadows as the sun fell lower. Calls were put on the air for volunteer workers to report to their facilities and how to get there via detours. Types of help most urgently needed were named.

After innumerable delays and a couple of detours, she arrived at the San Francisco city limits. Her usual one way commute took two hours. Now it had taken five long, nerve-wracking hours. Many cars overheated or ran out of gas. The sun had gone down. With electrical power out everywhere, cars and the waning moon provided the only available light. At each successive intersection, local people had parked their cars and directed traffic using flash lights. Seeing men in white shirts and slacks, women in high heels and business suits, and teenagers guiding traffic, drove the point home about the seriousness of the whole ordeal.

The radio aired cautions about cars driving over the Golden Gate Bridge. She was thankful that Sea Cliff was located before the entrance to the bridge. At last, she turned onto Sea Cliff Avenue.

Surprisingly, Cameron's truck was parked on the street at the top of the driveway. She hoped Matthew would be there, too, to know he was safe.

As she eased down the driveway, both came out of her front door waving for her to stop.

"Don't drive into your garage," Cameron said as he bent down to peer into the Porsche. "Don't park in the garage until we inspect your whole property in daylight."

She shut off the engine and climbed out of the car shaking, collapsing into Matthew's arms, totally exhausted.

"R-rough drive?"

"We made a preliminary inspection of the house. You have some structural damage on the rec room wall below the garage," Cameron said. "The window in there has a big stress crack. There's a hairline crack over there, too." He pointed to the front wall near the garage that none of them could see at that moment in the dark.

"We t-taped… the glass."

"Your neighbors, the Shylers…?"

"Skylars, Keith and Willa," Rachael said, stretching her back.

"They saw us and came over to ask about you."

"About me?"

"They said they didn't know much about you, but were concerned. You ought to get to know your neighbors, Rachael," Cameron said. "It's not good to be isolated, even here."

Rachael didn't comment. She didn't like to be scolded. The people in the bigger wealthier houses did a lot of socializing, parties and such. Rachael lived in a remade house in the back, albeit down on the cliff side with a fantastic view. She felt uncomfortable around the neighbors and shared no desire to mingle with society.

"The Beckwith's over there," Cameron said, pointing to the other side of the driveway. "They got some broken windows high up. We carried the ladders over and taped them. They seem like good folks too."

Again, Rachael said nothing. She didn't know how she could visit her neighbors one day. What did she have to talk about? Sitting around the kitchen table discussing the latest party or function that she knew nothing about wasn't her style. What an intrusion she would be. "I guess I don't know them," she said. "I'm sure they're grateful for your help."

Finally inside her home, Rachael stretched to remove the kinks from sitting so long in the car.

Cameron returned from the kitchen carrying a tray of juice and glasses. "The stuff from your fridge is in a cooler from our truck. It'll keep a couple of days."

"You guys have thought of everything."

They drank quickly and then Cameron said, "Okay, right now, I need to get across that bridge."

"Does Mona know you're okay?"

"Yeah, we got through on the cell. She stayed in the store to pick up some books that fell."

"I'm glad you were able to reach her." Mona could manage on her own in probably any situation and Rachael knew it. She felt a great kinship with Mona.

Cameron turned to Matthew. "You going to stay here with her, son? I've gotta' check out things at the office too."

"I'll be okay now," Rachael said before Matthew could answer.

"You don't sound that sure," Cameron said. "Matt should stay."

"I'll be okay."

Cameron knew that she and Matthew had never spent the night alone together. If Matthew stayed, he may not care to sleep alone and she wasn't in the mood to have to put him off the rest of the night.

"I-I'll go home," Matthew said. His faltering speech made him seem vulnerable, even cute. His actions were strong and definite. Him and his mom and dad seemed strong in that way.

"Then grab some things, Rachael," Cameron said quickly. "You're coming with us."

"I'll be okay, now that I'm home."

"It's not a night to be spending alone. C'mon, hurry up now."

Finally, Rachael went downstairs to pack a few things. On the way back, she paused at the bottom of the stairs to change into more comfortable shoes. She listened, wondering why they were talking in hushed tones upstairs.

"Dad, s-she's okay b-by herself. She's pretty tough. I-I don't want her to s-see me like…"

"Since when did you ever want to leave her alone?" Cameron asked. "Despite your condition, I guess she'd probably be running away from you all night. Anyway, we're not leaving her behind."

"W-well… in my condition, h-how fast, do y-you think I could c-chase her?" It sounded like a joke. Then, as quickly, he was serious. "I d-don't want her to know about my b-bad dreams."

"Son!"

"I'm stiff and I-I ache. I can't talk r-right. I'm not myself yet."

Rachael strained to hear more.

"Son, did you ever stop to think she might be the best medicine you could get?" Cameron seemed not in the mood to put up with Matthew's flimsy excuses.

"Oh-oh. I t-thought you were *Mr. Cautious*." Matthew said, teasing again. "Y-you were worried s-she might be too s-stuck in her p-past. You were uncertain about her future."

"Listen, I have a whole new view of that little girl, from the way she treated you when you were laid up in that hospital. She was there nearly day for you." He enunciated the words. "If anyone could overcome a mountain of troubles, it's that one. You ride in her car."

"With her?"

"Yeah. She's been to the house only once, right after your accident. If she ends up down on Bridgeway, she may not find her way to the top of the hill again in the dark. Besides, she shouldn't park in her garage yet. If she leaves her car outside here, looters could strip it. There'll be a lot of troublemakers out tonight and it's anybody's guess where they'll strike. You ride with her. I gotta' get over to your mom now."

When Cameron was getting to know her, he couldn't hide his curiosity about her hesitation in everything, even commented about her strong self-preservation. He probably saw her as a person retreating from reality, or at least having found a safe haven for herself, not making an effort to improve her lot. He didn't understand why she was quiet. She once heard him tell Matthew that he thought the intensity in her eyes hid some deep dark secret lurking below the surface, waiting for an opportunity to rear its ugly head. Her passivity gave him an unsettled feeling and made him aware of the things he had heard affecting people abused in childhood.

Certainly having watched and overheard a few conversations Rachael directed at Matthew while he was suspended in some unknown purgatory, Cameron drastically changed his opinion of her. According to Matthew, his father admitted that he saw her sensitivity unblemished. Her unending devotion to Matthew, to say or do whatever she might, to help bring him back to consciousness without hint of reward for herself, seemed incomprehensible to him. Maybe Cameron was finally seeing her personal problems as a thing of the past.

"I guess I'm ready," she said, directing her voice toward the two upstairs. Their conversation ended as she started up the oak staircase.

Chapter 37

Sausalito and most of Marin County hadn't lost electrical power. After Mona and Cameron went to bed, Rachael changed into light sweats. She and Matthew relaxed on the sofa watching fog slip in over The Bay below, illumined by moonlight. Volume on the radio was kept just loud enough to hear quake updates.

Each aftershock was announced. Sausalito barely felt the milder ones. The announcers were in San Francisco where aftershocks were being felt the strongest. The man who drove into a sink hole in the East Bay was rescued after he climbed onto the top of his vehicle. Within a few minutes, the sinkhole swallowed the entire van. Rescue crews were looking for several people missing in the collapse of several apartment buildings in San Francisco's Marina District. Finally, Matthew switched off the radio.

"This earthquake m-makes me feel m-more helpless. It's frustrating."

"You needn't be self-conscious around me," she said confidently. "I can imagine how you must feel. I have deep empathy for you." Occasionally, he would lift his arm and rub the shoulder that had been dislocated. "Why don't you lie on the floor," she said. "I'll give you a back rub."

Much surprised at her offer, he threw sofa pillows and an afghan to the carpet. She tried massaging while sitting beside him. The position was awkward. She straddled him, sitting on his buttocks, the boldest thing she'd ever done. Realizing where she was, she suddenly climbed off, in total disbelief that she had spread her legs over him.

Sensing what happened, his smile stretched across his face. He rolled over and pulled her down to lay beside him. "I'll bet you can g-get pretty frisky, w-when you let yourself l-loose."

"No," she said, moving away quickly.

"Rachael, c-come here," he said, pulling her back. "I'm n-not going to do any…thing. And besides, I'm not s-strong enough." He smiled that devilish grin she both loved and abhorred.

"Not strong enough?" she asked, almost laughing.

"If I were s-stronger, w-we might wrestle."

She relaxed. He was evidently open to talking, however much he struggled. He sat up and pulled his weak leg into a cross-legged sitting position. She did the same facing him.

"Angel, w-we have to be…more open, i-if we expect to get closer."

"Speak for yourself. Sometimes we're like two people who've just met."

Staring out the window, he began to talk, hesitatingly at first, as if fearing she may not like what he had to say.

"My b-body's been traumatized. I'm h-having difficulty…" He looked away from her expectant gaze.

"With what?" she asked.

"It's effected me." He seemed embarrassed and gestured toward his pelvic area.

"You don't need to tell me that," she said with surprise. "Our relationship hasn't gone that far."

"T-thought you should know…"

"Why?"

"Y-you might notice. It has n-nothing to do… with you. My body's not b-back to normal."

She sensed something more behind his words. What could he be hiding. "Of course. The shock has been too much."

His reasoning sounded plausible, yet he couldn't look at her while he spoke. To admit such a thing was embarrassing, for sure. Something felt missing. What was he not he saying?

"Don't want you to f-feel I'm l-losing interest."

"Matthew, would I be here if that were the case?"

"I d-don't want to lose you again. You're the m-most important person in m-my life."

"I'm surprised to hear you say that."

"You d-don't know what I've been t-through, Angel. S-so much has happened to me... three roller coaster years with L-Linda, the accident, other things... even you. It's affected me." He struggled to get the words out. "I've put myself... through a lot of t-trauma. It's d-drained me. I'm not the m-man I used to be but I will b-be again."

The effort to vocalize his shortcomings took a lot of courage. Whatever the depth of his problem, coming face to face with it, he was on his way to healing.

They were high-strung, both from the earthquake and from being together again. Neither thought of sleep. They lay on their stomachs on the floor, propped up on cushions, looking out over the sparse lights of Sausalito below.

"Dad and I will inspect y-your house... w-work up a quote for... quake d-damage... renovations."

"We should start repairs immediately. You guys are going to get busy again after the holidays," she said, finishing his thought.

"I have a g-great idea." She waited. "I-I've always wanted..." He was too excited. "A party."

"You?"

"Y-yes. Can't do it... on the boat. Your house... before repairs?"

The idea made her cringe. "I don't know. I couldn't bear the thought of people traipsing through my private space."

"N-not inside your house… the rec room, the yard, p-pool."

She realized if she wanted Matthew in her life, she would have to allow other friends in too. This man was not going to shut himself off from the world. If she wanted to keep his interest, she'd have to open up a little. The thought played on her like anticipating a surprise knowing it may not be what she would like. "Well, that might be doable."

"Say yes. It would be p-perfect."

"You must be feeling a lot better."

"Say yes. Before r-renovations."

"We could have a New Year's party," she said, surprised at her own enthusiasm.

"W-wait that long…to finish your house?"

"Yes, it's okay. I could use the time between now and then for writing. You'd be much stronger, too. Besides, I don't think I want my house up-side-down with construction debris during the holidays." Afterward, she would need peace and quiet again to write. She knew better than to remind him at that moment.

"Well, we won't be busy… d-during that time."

Then their conversation drifted back to the work to be done on Rachael's home. Matthew described some of the changes necessary and suggested a few antiquated items in her home be updated.

"The outer door," he said, "to your b-bedroom. Salt air's t-taken its toll. Anyone could… kick it in. You need a solid core. And the l-locks stick."

She sat up suddenly. To know about the locks, he must have been on the inside. "You went in my bedroom?"

"Well, y-yes. We walked y-your house… Dad and me."

"How could you?"

"You d-don't think we could… leave you there. That w-wall of glass could c-come down on you. I mean, at first, we assumed y-you'd stay there."

"It won't come down."

"We're having a-aftershocks, Rachael."

"Is that the only time you went in there?"

"W-what are you implying?"

"Oh, forget it. I guess it's okay." Rachael put her head down and was quiet. From the beginning, she made it clear that was her private area. Now she had to accept the fact that he went in for the sole reason of assuring her safety. The idea of him being in her bedroom made her feel exposed, naked.

He clutched her arm. "Rachael, give me a b-break. It was... for your own g-good."

She heaved a sigh. "It's all right, Matthew. It's okay." She wasn't sure if it was. "I'm grateful for your concern."

She tried to relax. He kept touching and rubbing her back as they talked. Her mind preoccupied, she was vaguely aware of his hand under the back of her shirt. The gentle massage felt good. She wasn't wearing underclothes beneath the sweats. He slipped his hand down over her buttocks and she quickly pushed him away. If he teased one more time, she'd leave the room.

She encouraged Matthew to talk about his accident. Vocalizing was a valuable therapeutic technique for healing.

"Poor lost L-linda," he said. "I thought... I l-loved her once."

Rachael was envious but realized Matthew felt confident enough in their relationship to talk openly about Linda.

Later, he said, "Rachael, we haven't made love, n-never got that far. I c-can't believe... you waited for me. Someday soon, I'm g-going to lay you down and... l-love you completely."

Rachael's emotions came apart. She shouldn't be led by his words as her body responded against his.

"It's been a l-long time... for us," he said.

"Almost a year and a half."

"That long? Angel, s-somewhere in there... I m-missed your birthday, didn't I? When was it?"

"I don't put much emphasis on birthdays, Matthew." Her dad, the one adult she counted on, hadn't paid attention to hers or Brandon's birthdays. Recently, she was disappointed when Matthew hadn't told her about his birthday the day they sailed up through the Delta.

"P-placing less emphasis on y-your birthday... is that part of y-your selfless philosophy?" he asked. "Or another aspect of your self-denial syndrome?"

"What?" she asked, jumping up to a sitting position again, totally surprised by his remark.

"When is it?"

She stared away from him.

"When?" He took her arm and shook it gently.

"Tomorrow," she said quietly.

As quick as he could, he raised on an elbow. "Are you k-kidding me?" She shook her head. "Where have I been? Oh, baby, I'm s-sorry. I'll make it up to you. I p-promise."

"That's okay, Matthew. You coming out of coma is all that mattered." She meant it too.

"I can't believe y-you waited," he said again. "Do you know w-what that does to me? I want, even more, to get close to y-you."

She pulled away again, mumbling she'd better get some sleep. He grabbed her wrist.

"I said n-nothing's going to h-happen. I meant it." He pulled her down hard against him again. "Hold me, Angel," he said, begging and sounding frightened. "Life's too short."

They fell asleep together on the floor. During the night, he woke in a cold sweat, trembling and gasping for air. She covered him with the afghan and whispered his name again and again. She cuddled up to him and tried to reassure him everything was all right and she was there for him.

Half coherent, he mumbled about occasional bad dreams, about rolling in the car, and about lifting out of his body and flying away. He wished he had flown away and not returned.

She wiped tears from her eyes and quietly whispered, "You had to come back. We haven't finished what we started. Together, we'll make your body a good place to be again." She leaned over to kiss him and found he had slipped back into fitful sleep.

The next morning, they went first to the construction office, then to Mona's store to make a thorough inspection for damage. San Francisco took the brunt of the earthquake, though the epicenter was found to be some eighteen miles below San Jose. Sausalito sustained almost no damage. Cameron's office was secure. The bookstore, however, developed a long irregular crack across the ceiling in the back corner and up the back and outside wall.

Rachael found Matthew in the Eastern Philosophy section holding several books and thumbing through one. A picture on one cover caught her eye. Against brilliant blue, and under the title and other print, a silhouette of a person with a stream of bluish white light traveling up the spinal column into the brain and beyond. Accompanying the light, a scattering of sparkling energy along the periphery.

"Oh!" She seemed dumbfounded. He waited for an explanation. "Matthew, look at that. That's what happens to me in meditation. That's what happens to me!" She grabbed the book from him and stared at the cover.

"You? You're that far?"

"I saw the lights real strong several times. The streak went up my spine and into my brain, like a silky river of blue-white light!" She was breathless. The other books he held were by the same author. She grabbed them from his hand. "I've got to have these. I need to read them."

"I'll g-get these for y-your birthday."

"Okay," she said, mumbling while perusing the pages.

"You're worth far m-more. I could never d-do enough for you."

"You don't know what validation this picture gives me," she said, excited. "Now I'll be able to understand what's happening to me."

Chapter 38

Somehow Matthew needed to get back the feeling of euphoria that was a constant with him. Rachael was seeing him through a lot of changes. Going to the yoga center and the gym on a regular basis were the best places to begin. She went with him for meditation when she could.

"Exercising has helped strengthen my leg," he said.

"You've gained back a lot of weight too."

With the long brown locks and facial hair, he looked rugged, even had a savage quality about him. He no longer had his hair styled every week and was finally able to fill in his trendy clothes. Although he occasionally expressed anger and frustration, his self control was improving.

Rachael couldn't wait any longer to break the news to him. She had to proceed cautiously. "I'll be going to Brandon's for Thanksgiving.

"What?" He was hobbling around a lot better lately and turned quickly to face her. "You're not going to spend it with me? With Mom and Dad?"

"Brandon is the only family I have," she said quietly, not buying in to his outburst. "If you feel that strongly, come with me."

"I don't care to meet your b-brother. At least, not now. Got to heal… t-talk better."

Rachael stayed quiet, unexpressive.

He softened. "I'm s-sorry, Angel." He paused, thinking. "I guess I'm a-apologizing a lot lately. I'll meet Brandon later, on a more casual b-basis. I don't think... I could relax enough r-right now... to be good company."

She listened and waited, feeling a little let down.

"Angel, maybe at the New Year's p-party, okay?"

She reluctantly agreed, wondering if Matthew cared about meeting her brother ever.

That night, she expressed her disappointment through Melissa and Hunter.

Melissa wondered why Hunter seemed reluctant to meet her brother. Was there something about Hunter that made him feel above other people? It was true that her brother mingled with some low-life characters, but he had a mind and could hold his own. All he needed to do was clean up his act. If it were true, that Hunter felt superior to her brother, she wasn't sure how to manage the situation should they ever meet. She wasn't about to write off her brother, not for one moment, not for anyone, not ever.

The weeks passed. Matthew was able to get around a lot better although the doctors hadn't released him to driving. A construction buddy or his dad chauffeured him. Rachael took him for a drive up the coast.

Stinson Beach was closed due to earth slides and road cracks. They detoured and found themselves in the heart of a wilderness preserve area that smelled of pine trees and fresh, clean damp air. They crossed a dammed water shed area in a valley then climbed back up into high country. Suddenly a utility truck appeared right in front of them from behind a blind turn. "No!" Rachael said, screaming as she swerved sharply across the speed bumps bordering the shoulder, while the truck driver honked and darted back into his own lane.

With the rocking motion of the car Matthew panicked. He yelled and grabbed the steering wheel, looking around wildly.

"Matthew, don't!" Rachael said. "I've got it! I've got it!" Wild eyed, he maintained his grip. "Let go! It's me, Rachael! We're okay!"

Yanking his seat belt loose, he threw open the door and dragged his shoe on the pavement trying to get out. She pressed hard on the brake. The car slid onto the shoulder. Before the car came to a complete stop, he lunged out, most likely needing to feel sure this time he could get free. Reaching him as he collapsed against the rear fender, Rachael wrapped her arms tightly around him as he stood shaking.

"What a trauma you've been through," she said. "What a horrible memory,"

"Damned it," he said. "W-why do things have to haunt a p-person."

They held each other for a long, quiet time.

He was still plagued with severe dizzy spells and continued to rest a lot. The spells worried Rachael. His speech remained slow and affected and his reflexes were nowhere as sharp as they used to be. Other than occasionally mentioning shooting pains throughout his body, he stopped complaining, though he would flinch from time to time. The facial tics persisted. His muscles seemed to have memories and, thankfully, were rapidly filling out again with his workouts. As his face began to fill in, he shaved his beard and mustache, then wished he hadn't. He had his hair styled to a new, fresher look, shaved at the sides with the top slicked back in a kind of wet look that covered his scar. Despite handicaps, he was becoming more and more positive about his recuperation.

Chapter 39

One day in mid-December, Matthew was at Rachael's house working up plans and costs for the work to be done. He had taken apart one of the light switches in the spare bedroom to check the wiring. In the course of conversation, Rachael mentioned going to Brandon's again for the up-coming holiday.

"What? You s-spent Thanksgiving there." He blurted it angrily, completely losing his composure. "Christmas is f-for us. I was counting on y-you being with us."

She hesitated, completely shocked by his assumption. "Brandon's my family. I love him regardless of his faults."

"What about M-mom and Dad? Aren't they like f-family to you?"

Rachael hadn't thought of them that way. That would be like chasing idle fantasies.

"I'm not spending time with the kids at Colliers this year, Matthew, so I can spend more time with Brandon."

"Why's that i-important?"

"His business is flourishing. His problems are minimal. I thought this would be an opportunity for him and me to get close again."

"How close can…you g-get with somebody like him? He's not g-going to change."

"I can't turn away. I'm going to spend some time with him."

"When?"

"Christmas Eve, I'm going there Christmas Eve."

"You s-spending the night?"

"I don't know."

"I don't w-want to hear anymore. I was h-hoping you'd spend Christmas…with m-me."

"Well, maybe I'll come over Christmas Day, if you'll be in a better mood."

He sighed heavily. "I guess I can live with that."

Like it or not, he'd have to change his attitude. He remained sullen the rest of the day. During his tantrum, he neglected to put the light switch back together. Seeing the loose parts laying on the night stand irritated Rachael. She should probably leave the dusty old hardware for him to find later when finishing repairs. Yet, the thought of that mess lying there for an unspecified time would intensify her frustration. Rather than instructing him to replace the parts, she waited till he was gone and reinstalled the pieces herself.

"I don't like sloppiness," she said, mumbling to herself, tightening a screw into the plastic plate. "I won't pick up after a man and you'd better know it, Mr. Builder."

During the last days before Christmas, Rachael didn't see Matthew, nor did he call. Why was he making things difficult for her? Finally, on the Friday before Christmas, she picked up the phone and called him without giving herself time to change her mind. He sounded totally dejected. She couldn't tell if his sadness was real or fabricated. In any event, she had purchased a wonderful gift for him and knew everything would be okay once they were together again.

In the late afternoon on Christmas Eve, she drove toward her brother's house in South San Francisco. In her heart, she longed to be headed in the opposite direction, across the Golden Gate Bridge toward Matthew. She didn't know if she was doing the right thing. Why did everything have to be complicated?

If he wanted her to accept his family, he could as well accept hers. Along the way, the increased number of *For Sale* signs in windows of homes confirmed that peoples' lives were changing, brought about by the downturn in the economy and the earthquake. She sighed. Her chest was tight, anxiety becoming unbearable.

When she arrived at Brandon's, she found the front lawn had been used as a parking lot. What grass remained was either dead or dying, the yard turned into a rutted dirt parking lot. She hoped his neighbors would complain because she wasn't about to.

Brandon seemed relaxed and happy to see her. His patronizing demeanor was a warning she knew too well. He either wanted something or was hiding something. She placed his gift under the tree.

He hadn't yet cleaned his house for the holidays. As usual, thick dust from the fireplace covered everything. He cleared his throat frequently. Rachael knew better than to comment on his condition or prompt him to see a doctor. They sat and talked while several of his friends drifted in and out for beers from the refrigerator. She was shocked by his choice of new acquaintances. While she and Brandon hadn't grown up in the most perfect of situations, they were taught to be clean in body and mind, as well as in the home. Brandon's new friends were dirty and one smelled horrific, desperately needing to be introduced to the wonderful concoctions known as soap and deodorant.

"Hey, my new girlfriend's coming over," Brandon soon announced.

"You met someone?"

"Yeah, Denita," he said. "When she gets here, the three of us better do the cleaning before the real crowd shows up."

Rachael gasped, unable to speak. "You're expecting people tonight?" she asked, trying to keep her composure.

"Yeah, we gotta hurry, and tomorrow, you can cook the turkey this time, okay?"

Being taken for granted was more than Rachael could bear. In his own way, her brother was now being abusive. If he wanted to have someone cook for him, why couldn't he come to her house when he was invited. Or why didn't he hire a cook? Or why didn't he go to the super market and buy a prepared turkey to reheat in the microwave? She wanted desperately to walk out.

Brandon mentioned earlier that he wanted her to meet Denita, saying she was the best thing that happened to him. Rachael would stay to meet his lady friend. After that she needed to think of a way to leave.

"What's Denita like?" she asked. "Is she nice to you?"

"Uh-h-h," Brandon said, rolling his eyes and cupping his hands in front at his waist. "She's got big chaboongas."

Time passed. Brandon picked up a gift from under the tree and handed Rachael the package. He lifted his eyebrows several times as if to signal something special.

"You've shopped a lot this year. Looks like you've got a gift for everyone on the block."

"Those are for Deni," he said proudly. "I want her to like me."

"Brandon," Rachael said, almost blurting. "You're buying her affection. There are things more impor—"

"Hey, keep your beliefs to yourself," he said. "I run my life. I'm free from Dad now and no one is ever going to tell me what to do again. Not even you."

Brandon launched into a tirade about always being bound by other people's rules, then finally threw his hands into the air and left the room before his rage got the best of him.

Wishing she hadn't voiced her opinion again, Rachael meekly followed. "I'm sorry, Brandon. I want the best for you." She wondered why she was always the one having to apologize. She certainly meant no harm. She was always there for him. He was the one who, unknowingly, withdrew from her. She stood at the sliding doors looking out into the darkened back yard while Brandon busied himself elsewhere.

Soon, her mind drifted back to Matthew and the peace they shared, despite some hardships. During one of their deeper conversations, words he quoted Eleanor Roosevelt as having spoken came drifting back into her mind. *"There are no victims, only volunteers."* Finally, Rachael understood what that great woman's words meant.

Denita arrived knowing she was late. She was tall and thin with a plain face and Brandon had been right. She had big chaboongas, down to her waist, poor thing. She had the type of body that would expand unrestrained in middle age. She treated Brandon well. Otherwise, she seemed distant. The two of them, together, acted as if they shared a great secret. Finally, Rachael realized she didn't belong with her brother's crowd.

"Brandon, I'm going to leave. You two can manage. I want to be with my friends. I don't want to be the one single person in the crowd again."

"Oh, don't leave," Brandon said, for once begging. "We need you."

"Yeah. There'll be 'nough guys floatin' 'round," Denita said, her gaze rolling down and back up Rachael's body. "You could have yer pick."

"I'm sorry. It wouldn't be the same."

"Guess you're stuck with the bird," Brandon said, turning his sheepish grin to Denita.

"Yuk," she said, raising the corner of her lip.

Rachael absent-mindedly walked out without her brother's gift and would certainly have left the package behind had he not run after her. They embraced warmly exchanging holiday wishes. Despite the hug, Rachael was left with an empty feeling about Brandon. The small boy she loved with all her heart and wanted to protect was buried somewhere deep inside a now indurate ego. She no longer knew the man who walked away compulsively clearing his throat.

Rachael arrived home after nine o'clock. She trifled with the idea of the hour being too late to call Matthew to explain what happened. She longed to be with him, but couldn't bring herself to admit he might have been right. She shouldn't have gone to Brandon's after all.

In the stillness of her office, she opened Brandon's gift. It was a silver heart with a tiny diamond and dangled on a dainty silver chain. She hoped he would like his *Versace* watch.

Still angry at her constant indecisiveness about Matthew, she busied herself in her office, then found she couldn't concentrate enough to write. Instead she began rummaging through files, sorting materials and accumulated notes saved for additional novels. Scraps of paper contained bits of information, from the strange to the absurd to the startlingly true, written to last into perpetuity, lest the mind forget.

Suddenly, there it was, staring up at her from the folder which included the papers from her creative writing class in college.

Chapter 40

Old notes quickly jotted, with ink bled into the tiny piece of scratch paper, were saved to remind her what the psychic reader predicted years earlier.

Unhappy past
Several years, then meet special man,
Architect… something like that
Children, a boy first, girls
Boy like father, past life connection
Must believe things will change
Working through much karma
Must be true to spiritual beliefs
Great unexpected changes

Her hands shook. She stared at the faded piece of paper wondering if any of the predictions would come true.

"Children? I want to be married first," she said aloud. "At the rate I'm going, not sure if I want to be."

Remembering it was Christmas Eve, her thoughts went again to Matthew. She couldn't help wondering if he might be the man to whom the psychic alluded. *An architect… something like that.*

Finally at eleven o'clock, she convinced herself to call him to say goodnight.

"Hello?" His husky voice was quiet on the phone.

"It's me," she said plainly. "I'm home."

"You're n-not staying at your brother's?"

"No, I don't belong there."

"Of course, you don't. We should be...spending Christmas Eve together. Mom and Dad have turned in. When we spend Christmas at home, the big event is... Christmas morning." He paused. "Angel, I'm sitting by the fire, remembering the time you and I... fell asleep on the floor." He sounded sentimental, then his tone changed. "Get your body over here. Let's finish what we started."

Rachael concentrated on his diction. "You're speech. it's wonderful. You didn't stutter or pause too long mid-sentence."

"I'm telling you, Angel. I keep getting... better and better." He sounded confident again. However, sadly though, he sounded like he was trying to convince himself as well.

Christmas Eve was quickly passing. People were where they wanted to be to celebrate. The highways were empty, not a cop in sight. For a moment, she felt incredibly alone, then reminded herself where she was headed.

Matthew had readied fixings for hot tea. They talked on the sofa. Soon Matthew suggested they get some sleep because Mona would be up before sunrise.

"In the morning," he said. "We're like robots, following Mom... directly to the tree to get our delights."

"Sounds like you both approve and disapprove."

"Someone else's tradition," he said, shrugging. "A throw-back from childhood, and theirs too."

"Strange, Matthew," she said. "I've felt a need to shed some of this tradition for a long time."

Alone in the guest room, she closed the door and quickly changed into her nightgown and snuggled deep beneath a layer of soft covers. Feeling comfortable and secure, sleep came easily. Then, the sound of a door handle penetrated through sleep. She mumbled and rolled over. The bed shook a little, not enough to cause alarm. She was tired. Something warm touched her face.

"I love you, Angel," he said, whispering softly. He kissed her lightly again on her forehead.

In a hypnogogic state, with the sound of his recitation floating into her mind, she sighed and turned her face toward him.

His hand pushed the hair from her face as she stirred.

"Matthew?" she asked dreamily, not fully awake.

He pressed his lips briefly against hers and she responded without hesitation as his words fully penetrated her mind. She opened her mouth to speak. Before she could utter a sound, his tongue lashed into it. He clutched at her pulling her hard against him.

Rachael was aroused before becoming fully awake. She responded instinctively and naturally. Now fully awake, she realized the danger in what was happening. She struggled to free herself from his grip and his relentless demanding kiss. He was too strong for her, his kiss too tempting. She found herself submitting to his strength and relaxed in his arms. She held him, and actually encouraged with her tongue and wanted more of his!

As their passion raged and threatened to consume them both, he slipped one hand down her body which had become uncovered. Her gown was up around her thighs and his hand went quickly under and brushed against her pelvis.

She froze momentarily, then struggled to get free. She drew her legs up to hide herself and pushed, almost tumbling backwards off the bed. She sat up with one arm folded across her chest, the other tugging at the sheets to cover herself. One strap of her gown hung loosely off her shoulder nearly exposing a breast.

"I thought you said nothing would happen in this house." Her breath was rapid.

"I did," he said, smirking in the dim light. "That was… a couple months ago. I told you. I keep getting better and better."

"Get out of here," she said. "I don't like your games. I'm not ready for this."

"When will you be?" He stared piercingly through the semi-darkness into her eyes, demanding an answer.

She shook her head. "Not here, not now." But she didn't know when.

He grabbed her wrist a little too firmly. She gasped and pulled back. He wouldn't let go. Whispering loudly, he strained to make his point. "One of these days you're… going to want me, and I'm going to be… gone."

A hint of resignation shaded his voice. Her heart skipped a beat at the frightful thought of losing him.

"Come here," he said, suddenly yanking her to lie back on the bed. Her hair spread out over the pillow. "No other guy would… take this from you. Why don't you try to… figure out why I do?"

He stared at her intently for another brief moment. Then he lightly kissed her lips. She tensed. "Someday, Rachael, some-day…" He forced a smile, then quickly climbed off the bed and disappeared beyond the closing door.

Rachael lay on her back and listened while her heart pounded out a wild rhythm. He had acted strangely. Regardless of his condition, he wouldn't expect anything to happen here in this house. The way he left. Too easily. Was he getting better and better, or was he sexually dysfunctional and trying to prove something to himself?

Then suddenly, she realized she was the one who had become aroused. He was always in control. He was merely testing her, playing a game, to learn if she could respond to him. She remembered his words. She might lose him. Her heart thumped again. She didn't want to lose him. The idea of making love with him persisted, yet, she didn't want to submit to keep him. She thought about how cold she must seem to him, when sex was free and easy to find everywhere. No, she couldn't get close, not for the reason he presented.

The signals from her body were strong as she lay imagining what making love to him might be like. *Put it out of your mind, girl!* She had to get some sleep. Rolling over onto her stomach, she buried her face in the pillow and locked her hands beneath it.

Chapter 41

Christmas morning found Rachael unsure how to approach Matthew following his strange behavior the night before. She felt timid, convinced she must have done something wrong. Now he would probably avoid her and she'd end up feeling out of place at his parents' home. She'd have to leave. She dreaded facing him. She woke the same time as Mona and surprised her by being there. After showers, they talked over tea and sat in front of the windows watching the city lights shut off below as daylight crept in. Mona had a way of making her feel close.

A little later, Rachael was standing at the kitchen counter with her back to the open dining room talking to Mona when, suddenly, Matthew came up behind her and slipped his arms snugly around her waist. He bent around, kissed the side of her neck and whispered good morning in a tone that sounded totally sensuous. Mona watched as Rachael felt her face flush.

"I think I'd better look in on Cam," Mona said. She smiled approvingly, diverting her eyes away from them and walking past, firmly patting Matthew on his upper arm. "Good morning, son," she said playfully.

With his morning cup of coffee in one hand, Cameron directed the family to gather in the living room to receive their gifts.

Matthew gave Rachael a 14K gold dinner ring which was set with a glowing pink pearl and two large sparkling corn flower sapphires. A few small diamonds nestled in the crevices of the mounting.

"O-oh, my. It's too much." Her mouth dropped open.

"Don't say no. Let me do this." He took the ring from its case and reached for her left hand. She offered her right. He expressed disappointment at that by glancing up at her.

"See, see. I told you it would fit." He held Rachael's hand up for his parents to see. He was excited and proud as a small boy with a straight A report card.

When Matthew finally settled down, Cameron presented Rachael with even more gifts.

"Here's another from Matt, and this one's from us," Cameron said, gesturing as Matthew dragged a large heavy box from the tree toward her. She could remember a time when he would have lifted something like that. There was a small flat package sitting on top of that one.

The smaller package, from Mona and Cameron, contained a sizable gift certificate from the bookstore.

"Thank you," she said to both of them. "At times, I guess I can have a voracious reading appetite."

The other box from Matthew, contained a stack of books on Eastern philosophy he'd not found in her library while he walked her house noting repair work to be done. On the top of the stack lay a thick volume of the *Bhagavad Gita* and another on the *Yoga Sutras of Patanjali*. She held them to her breast and shook her head, thoroughly pleased.

The tenets of Eastern philosophy teaches one does not give or receive gifts other than as charitable acts and deeds. That belief was the reason she felt confusion around Christmas time. She sat hugging the books, deep in thought. Certainly Matthew must believe the same, but why had he given her the ring and why had she chosen what she bought for him?

Mona tapped her shoulder. "Here's your gift for Matt."

Snapping back into reality, Rachael offered her gift to him with an enticing look. He reached. She withdrew, teasing. She offered and withdrew the small package again when he reached once more.

"Will you stop?" He snatched the gift from her hand.

The look on his face was one of utter surprise and sheer delight. He lifted the tidal chronometer gingerly out of its case and studied it with his mouth agape.

"I've been meaning to…get one of these." He slipped the watch on his wrist and held up his arm. "How did you know?" He glanced at both parents who shook their heads as if denying they had anything to do with the purchase.

Mona and Cameron bought Matthew a larger iPad to replace his older one.

The gifts kept coming. Rachael gave Mona and Cameron four large floor cushions for the foot of their tall bedroom window. They were decorated with corner tassels and covered in peach colored shantung.

"Isn't this fabric similar to the small cushions in your family room?" Mona asked.

"Yes," Rachael said, smiling and nodding.

"They're beautiful," Cameron said as he examined one.

"You made these, didn't you?" Mona asked, thoroughly pleased.

Matthew surprised his father with a new, larger cross bed tool chest for his work truck. They made a trip to the basement for the unveiling.

Upstairs again, in appreciation of her husband always lavishing her with expensive vacations, Mona presented Cameron with an all-expense paid vacation for two. Of course, Hawaii was the destination, Maui this time. They would depart after the New Year's party.

Then Matthew withdrew a large flat gift wrapped in silver from behind the tree. He carried it like a serving tray on which sat a monstrous gleaming red bow.

"This is from Dad and me," he said, offering the package to his mother.

She seemed to hold a very special place in the hearts of her husband and son. Mona accepted what might be a wall picture of some kind. "I'm not even going to guess," she said. "You two have always outdone yourselves."

She worked gingerly loosening the brilliant mound of ribbon. Suddenly, giving in, she began ripping the wrapping paper. To her surprise, a framed wall picture. She studied the strange art as Cameron and Matthew waited, exchanging expectant glances and trying not to smile. Mona's expressions went through many changes as she tried to make out the message of the drawing. Rachael scooted over beside her for a look.

Tables with colorful umbrellas and chairs sat on elevated decking. Sketches of people sitting here and there with coffee mugs and reading books added color to the artist's rendering of the terrace drenched in sunlight pouring through tall trees. A professional rendering it was, but not something they might hang in their home.

Mona knitted her brow and looked again. "What am I missing?"

The artist had positioned herself on a hill behind the building when she drew the sketch. Suddenly, Mona said, "Hey, that's Sausalito Harbor in the background, and—and the San Francisco skyline with the Transamerica pyramid building across The Bay." She couldn't decipher the message.

Cameron and Matthew played dumb. "Better look again," Cameron said.

"Am I dense? Why am I not getting this?"

No one said anything. She looked again, holding the picture at angles, studying the direction of the view of the harbor. Suddenly, she knew. "Oh, no," she said, pausing momentarily to study the drawing again. "This is a rendering of the area behind my store, from high up on the hill in the back." The sketch was of the back of the building that housed her bookstore. In the drawing, a terrace filled the area presently occupied by overgrown weeds, insects and a stray cat or two.

"What do you make of that?" Cameron asked, feigning innocence.

"You're going to do this for me? You're going to build a terrace? We don't have a lease on the back, and no permit to serve coffee or edibles."

"Don't need a lease," Cameron said proudly.

"We can get a permit," Matthew said.

"What are you saying?"

"Don't need a lease," Cameron said again. "It's yours. The building. The whole property, it's yours."

"Mine? Cam, how?" Her hands began to shake. "What are you saying?"

"You know, 'ole Reub's getting too old. The neighboring property owners were after him to improve that corner. It sticks out like a sore thumb, right there on that busy street. Especially since it cracked in the quake. He decided to sell it. Matt and me, we bought it for you."

"You didn't."

"The building, the yard, the whole lot, it's yours."

She was close to laughing and crying at the same time. Matthew took the picture from her lap as she stood to embrace her husband. "Oh," she said, moaning into his shoulder, then opened her teary eyes and reached for her son.

Rachael watched, smiling, feeling the love they shared as family. Although she wasn't involved in the purchase of that building for Mona, experiencing this moment with them made her feel very much a part of their happiness. She always wished for a Christmas like this, where giving and sharing were acts of loving kindness, despite this day being over-shadowed by com-mercialism.

Then Matthew leaned the picture against the sofa and reached for Rachael. She stood and hugged with the three of them. Mona wrapped an arm around her. Rachael belonged.

Chapter 42

New Year's Day was quickly approaching. Rosa was to sleep over on the weekend to do last minute cleaning and preparation for cooking food to be served at the party. Several of her widowed friends would arrive Sunday after church to handle last minute food preparation and stay to help serve that evening.

Although Matthew was plagued by headaches, facial tics, transient soreness, and a plethora of other symptoms, his euphoria had continued. Between therapies and some repair work to the Woodland Sports Center gymnasium, he and his father stopped by frequently, collecting and verifying last minute details for the renovations. Like many others, Knight Homes dipped into a slump, so they were happy to have the work on Rachael's house. Business will get better, Cameron continued to say. Sooner or later, all structures have to be repaired.

A makeshift office was set up in the kitchen of the guest unit. Matthew and Cameron came and went without Rachael sometimes knowing. Matthew continued getting prices on materials and calculating as if Rachael's house was were the most important job of his career.

Workmen came at various times to take final measurements before ordering needed materials. Sometimes Rachael had to leave. Matthew had his set of keys to the house. Mona and Cameron still had theirs. Rachael didn't care. She knew the

Knights were people she could trust with her life, if any situation came to that.

Occasionally, Rachael discreetly watched Matthew. She felt proud to know him, and to be as intimate in as much as they shared. At times, she found it difficult to believe someone like him could be interested in her. His endurance was finally returning. Strangely, his strength reminded her of his gentleness. How big he was, and how brutally mean he could be with his power if he wanted to be. Yet, he chose to express his life through kindness and understanding.

Sometimes her thoughts of him made her feel small and childlike, even protected, something she'd not known when younger. Matthew always encouraged her to abandon her inhibitions. *Letting go of one's fears is healthy*, he had said. He hadn't mentioned how to go about doing it. Perhaps that was what he meant when he pointed out her expressing girlish delight in some of their happier moments. The child inside her was learning there was nothing more to fear. She was firmly aware she needed to be the adult. When adult feelings prompted, the childish euphoria would disappear.

Work being finished for the day, Matthew was in the lap pool strengthening himself. Both the spa and lap pool was heated. Rachael and Rosa were in the recreation room decorating the walls and tables with colorful satin bows, streamers, and balloons, and setting out vases for lots of fresh flowers. Rosa was on a ladder. She had to constantly call Rachael's attention back into the room, or ended up practically hanging in mid air until Rachael handed up another thumb tack.

"Sweetheart," she said as she descended. "You need this man." Rachael looked at her. "You watch him always. Do you know you love him so much?"

Rachael wasn't sure what Rosa actually meant.

Rosa smiled, trying to project her thought, being motherly. "I say something to you, no?"

Rachael exaggerated a smile that said why not.

"Why you no get close to Senior Matt? He's one fine *hombre*."

"Close? What do you mean close? We are close. I'm not seeing anyone else. I'm close to his mom and dad. I don't think he's seeing anyone either," she said. "But, I guess I don't know." Rachael hadn't worried about that lately.

"No, *mi'ja*. Let me tell you this…"

Rachael was about to hear another of Rosa's opinions.

"I think Senior Matt is, uh, very healthy." She paused. "Uh, *como se dice en Ingles…* you know. *El hombre es muy caliente…* very sexy." She lowered her voice. "Needs someone to sleep with."

The words startled Rachael. She remained quiet for a time as Rosa worked, then slipped into her office to make note of another bit of information for her characters:

Melissa thought many, many times about making love with Hunter, so many times she lost count of the sleepless nights she endured because of indecision. She certainly wasn't going to go to bed with him just to save him from the surge of a hormonal riptide. First thing she knew, she'd be expected to abandon her dreams to keep him pacified. She had plans for her life. If writing was her way of spending sleepless nights, that was her prerogative.

Puzzling over how to balance her time, Rachael remembered the day after Christmas, having received another communiqué from her editor through her literary agent, Dennis DeBaer. They were asking that the balance of her manuscript to be forwarded as soon as possible. They read the first two-thirds of the book. They loved it. They wanted to publish immediately. *Readers are ready for this*, they had written. She wondered why the rush. Her two previous books weren't published till about a year after completion. Perhaps with the downturn in the economy, the book markets were also in a slump. Maybe her book was thought good enough to bolster sales. Whatever the reasons, they didn't matter. At this point, she couldn't afford to flatter herself. Surely now, she must be writing much better than before.

In the exhilaration of the moment, she responded saying she would send the final chapters in three months. Now she realized once the renovations were completed, finishing her book would mean hibernating. The publisher also wanted one or both of the next two stories she told them about. Matthew wasn't going to like that. What's more, she had additional stories in outline form or rough notes begging to be told. Having long ago accepted the fact that she wanted a writing career, her creativity exploded with additional plots for novels, short stories, essays, just about anything she cared to make of them, and they kept pouring out of her mind.

Somehow she and Matthew were going to have to work things out between them. With the interest shown in her current novel, there was no way she could see herself doing anything else. Early in January, they would have to have that long de-layed talk. Both were going to have to make compromises. For the time being, she wasn't going to trouble herself. One step at a time. The party was next. She sneaked back into the recreation room where she left Rosa.

"*Chica…*"

Rosa's insistence interrupted her thoughts. Rachael hoped she had heard the end of Rosa's well-intentioned counsel. Right now, she didn't need the pressure of Rosa's nudging on top of everything else. "Tack the streamer a little higher in that cor-ner," Rachael said.

"Rachael," Rosa's voice softened. She wasn't through with her advice. "Senorita, you love him, no? More than you admit, *si*?" She paused and took a breath, checking to make sure she wasn't speaking out of turn. Rachael waited expectantly. "Why you no get close to him? He loves you. He's a strong man, should have woman."

Strong may not have been the most appropriate word for Rosa to use though Rachael knew exactly what she meant. Though Rosa considered herself to be a good Catholic, she liberalized much of her thinking in the years since moving to the United States. Most often, Rachael would laugh at the classic examples of Rosa's metamorphosis. She was always amazed by something else the woman might say or do. Now Rosa had taken her boldest stance yet.

She looked at Rosa suspiciously, playing naive. "You mean, go to bed with him?"

"*Si, si. Aye, Dios mio.*" She swooned, hugging herself. "Tell him you love him. Make him satisfied." She paused with a wild look in her eyes, then waved a hand toward Rachael as if to shoo her toward him. "Go for it, chica. Be in love. You live in A-me-rica."

Chapter 43

After the catering van from Tina's Italian pulled away, Matthew blocked off the driveway at street level. Directive arrows were affixed along the driveway retaining wall pointing to the doorway to the guest unit and to the outside steps which descended the grounds on the east end of the property. People made their way to the recreation room and pool area after finding a place to park somewhere on the street. Typical of San Francisco, where they parked was anybody's guess.

The house was locked up tight except for the recreation room and guest unit, where people could mingle inside and out. The lap pool was warm and the hot tub hot. The weather was crisp, drought usual, no rain expected. Water was a scarce commodity and getting scarcer by the day. At least, they wouldn't be forced indoors. At the last minute, Rosa's crew hung streamers throughout the garden area and across the back bordering the cliffside. Although there was a low ridge of decorative rock intermingled among the plants, an inebriated person might trip and fall down the craggy hill. The arbor lights were on, creating an enticing, romantic retreat for those who might vie for a brief moment of seclusion.

Dress was casual. People came in droves. Matthew's crews arrived with their spouses, significant other's and friends. Some of the staff from the Haight Rehab were expected. So were the police officers with whom Matthew was closely associated. Rachael's small selection of friend's from her day jobs came and must have brought all of theirs. Some people with whom Rachael worked at ConverTech came all the way from cities in the South Bay. Others who worked at the bank in the Financial District were expected. Jose and Virginia Martinez arrived. When Virginia met Rosa, she insisted on helping the Latina ladies doing the serving. Lastly, Mona and Cameron wouldn't think of missing this party. Their personal contribution was the music. They also brought their neighbors, the Claytons.

"I sent Brandon an invitation," Rachael said.

"You sent it?" Matthew asked. "What happened to a simple phone call?"

"Actually, I wanted him to see the words, *By Invitation Only*."

"He probably won't come now."

"Why do you say that?"

"Because that phrase would sound to him as being too… how did he once put it, *uppity*?"

Rachael signed. "Maybe you're right. I was trying to keep him from bringing his hangers-on friends."

"Well, if he needs them around, he'd feel out of place here."

"I don't understand how Brandon and I have grown estranged," she said with a sigh.

Food smells and flower scents circulated in the small rec room. People floated in and out. Surprisingly, there were no complaints from any neighbors who might have wanted to spend a quiet year end at home. A couple of police officers passing by wandered into the party, having recognized Juan Carlos's low rider parked at the top of the driveway to block it. They patrolled the area well during holidays, when people were attending various festivities and the wealthy neighborhood homes might be deserted.

The officers, along with the others, feasted on plates heaped with deli meats and imported cheeses, hot or cold pastas, tacos, enchiladas and pasteles, with chips and tubs of salsa and guacamole. Rosa must had leaned a little heavy on the chilies. Quite a few people took turns dancing around fanning their mouths.

There was a selection of different breads, sliced fruits and vegetables, and tubs of dips and various other finger foods and vegetable sticks from which to choose. Matthew set up the outdoor barbecue and oven and with Juan Carlos, kept a supply of barbecued game hens from Tina's Italian rotating on a spit. A skillet was kept ready for braising tofu to be mixed with stir-fried vegetables. Then finally, there was an assortment of rich cheesecake wedges, Mexican pastries, and other small deserts for those with a sweet tooth.

There was beer on ice in the sink in the laundry room. Wines were on the tables and more wine, along with mineral waters and sodas cooled in Coleman chests out on the sidewalk. If anyone wanted hard liquor they were told to bring their own.

Thanks to Rosa and her friends, and Tina's Italian, the quantity and variety of delectable edibles was unimaginable. More people than expected arrived. Word of the party had spread. Rachael was overwhelmed at the response as Rosa's crew kept replenishing seemingly an inexhaustible supply of food and drink. Rachael wouldn't venture into her kitchen. Rosa was in charge of the mess in there.

"Whose idea was it for the costumes?" Matthew asked.

"Rosa thought it would liven up the party if her friends wore Mexican style skirts and blouses," Rachael said, smiling at the idea.

With much delicious food, no one could get drunk. When a couple of guys got close, they were treated to a dunk in the pool that quickly subdued their attitudes.

The officers who drifted in and out on their rounds were told if there were any other souls in blue out there unfortunate enough to have to work, they should stop by for a meal.

Dooley and his cop friends kept an eye out for any drug use. Most of both Matthew's and Rachael's friends knew of their attitudes toward drug use and evidently respected their wishes, or kept their habits well hidden.

Soon, the Skylars found Matthew who steered them to Rachael. They were in their mid-sixties. Like most of the others attending, they dressed in denims and warm sweat tops and carried cell phones.

"I hope the noise isn't too bad," Rachael said, apologizing.

"The noise is what brought us," Willa said. "Other than some of our own stuffy cocktail parties and dinners, this area hasn't come to life like this in many a year."

"Then we're glad you decided to come. I wasn't sure if I should invite anyone from—"

"Think nothing of it," Willa said. "Most people in this neighborhood are distant from one another. Too busy, you know." She smiled and looked around.

"You don't mind if we photograph your event?" Keith asked.

"Be our guest," Matthew said.

"This place is much different from the time we sold our half." Willa stood looking around.

"Actually, this is a one-time party," Rachael said. "I'm going to be renovating the guest unit afterwards. C'mon, I'll show you what I've done to the place."

Music was mixed. They danced to everything from progressive jazz to rock to salsa to polka and to 50's and 60's oldies. Matthew still limped. He danced a slow one with Rachael every now and then. He'd whisper sweet wonderful nonsensical words in her ear to fit the mood or music. They laughed together as if nothing mattered. Others noticed.

Rosa put on a CD from Mona's favorite 50's era collection. Oldies blared across the grounds. Matthew wrapped Rachael in his arms and they swayed in one spot with him singing an entire song to her.

A little later, when someone played a polka, Dooley sought her out. Matthew bowed deeply from the waist, sweeping his arm out widely in an exaggerated gesture toward Rachael in approval. Leaning back against the toe barre, he watched them spin around the room.

"You're such a smooth dancer, Rachael," Dooley said. He was all teeth, even when he spoke. He had a permanent smile.

"Ah, c'mon," she said. "I'll bet you say that to all the girls."

Several times during the evening, Rachael, watching from inside the rec room, noticed Matthew shake his head. Once out by the barbecue, holding the spatula, he placed the back of his hand on his forehead. He must have been having dizzy spells. She didn't know they were that intense. As she was about to go to him, Britt walked up and tended to him. Who invited her? Matthew was having some difficulty and Britt was hanging over him and he wasn't sending her away. She leaned over for no apparent reason and her boobs almost fell out the front of her nearly nonexistent dress, and he hugged her!

Chapter 44

Unbearable jealousy reared its ugly head. Why was Britt cuddling up to him? Why was she hanging around and happened to be nearby when he had a dizzy spell? Rachael swallowed the lump in her throat and looked away feeling paralyzed.

Rosa watched the clock, and then banged a spoon against a metal pan. "Two minutes to midnight!" she said, making sure she was heard.

Rachael looked for Matthew. He was nowhere in sight. Waves of panic washed over her.

"Everybody ready?" Rosa asked at the top of her lungs.

Where was he? The knot in Rachael's throat threatened to close off her windpipe.

"*Un minuto!*" Rosa said in her excitement. "Aye, Dios. One minute!" She changed the music to *Auld Lang Syne*.

Suddenly Matthew came up behind Rachael, spinning her around and lifted her into the air as high as he could. He was beaming. Her fear melted to nonexistence. They were both exuberantly happy. Midnight arrived. They kissed, first tenderly, as he lowered her to a standing position. Then he wrapped her up in his mighty arms and kissed her fully as they stood locked together. Everyone blew horns and waved noise makers. Rachael and Matthew were in another time. Someone tooted a horn right beside their ears and brought them back. When they broke their embrace, they found a group gathered round them yelling and blowing noise makers and clapping while they stood locked tight together. Fernando stood grinning, getting an eyeful of San Francisco heat.

Someone put on a waltz and Rachael and Matthew danced along with a few others. As they moved past the doorway, Britt peered in at them looking somewhat dejected. The dance ended. Matthew whispered sweet personal words into Rachael's ear, then went to tend the barbecue once again. People were getting out of their clothes and into their bathing suits to swim or sit in the hot tub. And maybe to sober up. They'd been told the party would last as long as people cared to hang around. No one seemed to want to leave.

Again Dooley came to dance with Rachael. Then Juan Carlos cut in. Soon, Dooley cut in again. The attention must have been their way of showing they accepted her. "So when's the wedding?" he asked.

"What-a-at?" It was then that she realized that his eyes were green too.

"You know. Isn't that next? You two have been an item a long enough."

"Now, Dooley, don't you try to win me over for him."

"Would I do that?" he asked, flashing that devilish grin.

"I think you're trying."

"Nope. I don't think anyone has to push either of you. Fate's taking care of everything."

The next time Rachael caught sight of Matthew, Britt was standing beside him and several other guys near the edge of the pool. She had changed into the skimpiest of revealing bikinis that sliced right up what looked to be her silicone derriere. Evidently, the need to exhibit her false attributes was greater than her need to keep warm in the brisk night air. She danced, using suggestive hand gestures and begging come-hither glances, while thrusting her pelvis at Matthew in time to the music.

Her breasts floated behind her string bikini and revealed the edges of implants. Rachael wondered before. Now she knew. Britt had been teasing a lot of guys and some had left without her. Now she was after Matthew. Rachael's blood began to boil. Fear clutched at her emotions. Britt reminded her of Myna in high school making the rounds of their guy friends till she landed Rodney. Surely girls chased Matthew everywhere he went. They couldn't help themselves. He was everything a girl could ask for, especially when they learned he was a bachelor, successful enough, and unimaginably well built. If that wasn't enough, he was a decent human being. Definitely worth throwing themselves at his feet. Especially since Britt hadn't scored with anyone else all evening.

This was the first time Rachael saw anything like this happen to Matthew. Britt had watched her and Matthew together. Still, she persisted. Rachael wasn't about to go to them and show her jealousy and make a fool of herself. If Matthew was truly hers, he would not allow himself to indulge in the cheap thrills that Britt offered. Rachael would allow Matthew to decide for himself what was right for him. Tightness welled up in her throat. She busied herself with the table arrangements waiting for the waves of fear to pass.

"Hey, Rach. Guess I can't call you Greta anymore, huh?"

"What? Oh, Tina, you startled me. W-what do you mean?"

"You can bet Garbo never had a party like this under her roof."

"Guess not." Rachael smiled and looked around. "Tina, who invited Britt?"

"She came with two of Matt's construction guys. Guess she and her boobs are making the rounds, huh?"

"Why is she floozing up to Matthew?"

"Don't know why all the single ladies aren't after your guy," Tina said. "Can't say I blame anyone, Rach."

Rachael sighed unhappily. "You think he's seeing her?"

"You've got nothing to worry about. You're much better look-ing," Tina said. "How long has it been for you two? Nearly two years, right?"

"Something like that." Rachael couldn't concentrate.

"You must have him trained well to keep him that long. I mean, he could have anybody. You must be pretty hot in the sack, babe, to keep a guy like that."

Tina sometimes had an off-the-wall compliment. She didn't know Rachael and Matthew hadn't been *in the sack* to-gether. Somehow, Rachael knew admitting the truth, to anyone, wouldn't be a wise decision.

Maybe she should be spending more time with Matthew. Then Britt could go shake her body parts at someone else. Rachael went to look for Matthew but couldn't find him. She looked around trying to locate Britt, thinking he'd be near her. She was gone, nowhere to be found. Rachael's mind flashed back to Rodney in high school when, more than once, he disappeared from her. Panic gripped her. Rachael finally asked someone if he had seen Matthew.

One of the construction guys said, "Matt was feeling dizzy, said he'd lay down for while." Rachael thought she would find him in the guest bedroom or on the sofa in the living room. If he was feeling poorly, she would stay with him for a while. The party could take care of itself. Thank goodness Rosa was there.

She walked through the house. Matthew wasn't in the guest bedroom nor living room, nor her bedroom, for that matter. She headed back outside.

Most had gathered around the lap pool and some were timing one another to see who could swim two laps the fastest. Rachael walked toward the guest quarters.

"Tina," she said, motioning for her to come close. "Where's Britt?"

Tina motioned toward the east end of the property. "She might have gone up the side steps by the guest house to leave." She shrugged. "I saw her headed in that direction."

Rachael turned to go back to the party then noticed, curiously, the drapes in the guest quarters were pulled closed. She walked over to try the door knob which, surprisingly, was locked. She stepped back and studied the window. Interior lighting cast moving shadows onto the curtains. Suddenly, she couldn't believe her eyes. Silhouetted onto the drapes was the shadow of two nude bodies atop the bed undulating frantically in the heat of passion!

"Matthew!" Rachael choked in a loud whisper. Tears poured from her eyes. "Matthew!" He had gone to lie down and Britt followed him. Or maybe he took her.

Once again, Rachael's father's words came back to haunt her. *"Don't you do anything with these guys. You don't know what they do behind your back."*

The words echoed through her brain until she could hear nothing else. Stumbling over a couple of deck chairs, she hurried away. Others stared, not understanding. The outer door to her bedroom looked far away. She'd never make it past the hot tub before losing her composure. She fumbled with her keys and entered the house through the second bedroom, slamming and locking the sliding door behind her. Making a dash for the sanctity of her own bedroom, she collapsed onto the bed where she wept and stayed for nearly an hour.

When she finally emerged and peeked out through the curtains, Matthew was climbing out of the lap pool. He quickly ran a towel over his body and dried his hair, then threw on a hoodie to ward off the chill.

Damned you, Matthew. After what you did, now you take a bath in my pool?

That was how he took care of himself, right here, in her house, on her property.

Matthew! Her brain screamed. *I've been faithful. I haven't been with anyone. How could you?*

She could no longer cry. She was seething. Her heart was irreparably broken. She found Rosa in the lower foyer. "Maybe I should have put my writing aside in order to get enough sleep to stay up tonight," she said, lying. "I'm exhausted."

Rosa looked at her curiously. "Sure it's tired you feel?"

"Yes, yes," she said, a little too angrily.

"Aye, Dios."

"I'm tired, Rosa. Please pack the food after the party. Take it home and share it with you wonderful ladies who helped this evening."

"All this food?"

"*Si, si, todos*," Rachael said, forcing a smile. Then she retreated to her bedroom without saying good night or goodbye to anyone.

Chapter 45

The phone rang. Rachael knew it would be Matthew again. Each time he left messages, his voice was cheerful, positive and reassuring. He wanted to meet with her to go over work to be done on her house. He was eager to get started. Ignoring the phone, she walked into another room wishing not to see his face or hear his voice again.

She wasn't about to return his calls. How dare he pretend nothing had changed between them. Was he so unconscionable as to have no guilt about what he did, and right in her own home? She agonized over how to bring in another contractor.

Where there once was love, there was now abhorrence. Rachael seethed with desire for revenge. She was reminded of the despair she felt with her first love and how she wouldn't, or couldn't, retaliate to help herself through her ordeal. Now history was repeating itself. Her wounds lay open and raw. She would delay talking to Matthew as long as possible. She needed to find another contractor.

"Rachael? Call me," his insistent voice pleaded on the answering machine. "You weren't...supposed to go back to your writing...until after the house was finished...so, let's get started."

He came over once, walking completely around the house, trying to see if anyone was home. For a while, he stood at the front door. Again hiding behind the cafe curtains, she watched him struggle with uncertainty. Then slowly, he reached for the door knob. Panic gripped her when she thought the door might be unlocked. But she was getting to know him. As much as he might want to barge in and make his presence known, he wouldn't. He left a note on a business card under the doormat.

Rachael knew if she didn't respond, the next time he would come over when Rosa would be available. Rachael dreaded the confrontation. She couldn't bring in yet another contractor for a new quote. That meant additional delays in finishing the house and painful delays in getting back to writing. Somehow, she would have to see this thing through. She had to face Matthew. Of course, he would play innocent while she, in her discomfiture, would be forced to play along. She wished no part of the game. Somehow she needed to come up with a way to heal her fragmented hopes and restore some semblance of order to her shattered dreams.

Remembering what life was like after Rodney married Myna, Rachael found the numbness she now felt not unlike what she succumbed to back then. After she lost Rodney, she turned into a zombie. She neither ate nor drank much. Instead of sleeping, she cried a lot, lost weight, and became dull and listless. Then Amanda stepped in, coaxing her gently back to life. Rachael learned to accept her loss as her lot in life, like the rest of the animation she lived out. Back then, there was nothing she could do.

A lot of time passed since she loved Rodney and learned to live without him. Though Tina had told her she lived in a world of semi-naiveté, Rachael knew she must have matured some. Tina once said her innocence was more a hindrance than it was becoming. Rachael found her senses obtund. She lost her appetite again. At best, she experienced great difficulty trying to write with such a distraction draining her creativity.

Long before, in therapy, she learned to write her thoughts as a means of understanding her plight. Practicing that technique now, she included a disparaging episode in her book and, once again, vented her pain and anger through Melissa and Hunter.

Stunned and fairly certain Hunter was seeing other women, Melissa shuddered at the thought of what might have become of her had she allowed their relationship to be consummated. She would most certainly go insane. She shook her head to release herself from the thought. Finishing her book was too important to be delayed due to a bout of depression. She sat down to write but her jumbled thoughts played on. After a while, she showered with stinging hot water. By the time she stepped out of the shower, she knew exactly what she would do.

Rachael felt much relieved after creating a new episode for her dual protagonists. Absorbed in writing the ending to yet another chapter, she became aware of a small vindictive voice within beckoning her toward forbidden indemnification. She knew what she must write for Melissa and Hunter, and in doing so, realized resolution for her heartache was now at hand.

Yet, how could she hurt the man she deeply loved? How could she hurt anyone? That kind of behavior went against her spiritual beliefs. Yet, how could she stand by and allow herself to be blatantly taken for granted for yet a second time. Try as she might, she couldn't bring herself to hurt him outwardly. Screaming and scratching his eyes out, or kicking him in the groin, would be temporary, superficial. There had to be something else she could do.

Experiencing that kind of pain twice in her life was too much. This time, there was no Amanda with whom to take solace. There was no one. Not even Rosa. Rachael had to muster her strength. She would be alone in her revenge. Then a cruel possibility came to her. If she had to know that kind of pain twice in her life, maybe he too, should know the same in his. Suddenly, she knew what she must do.

Sensing the time of retribution need be close, lest he forget, Rachael conjured her plan, resolving to stay calm and collected to carry it off, whether or not her love for him burned deep again. Whether or not affection turned to passive disregard. That afternoon, with vengeful determination, she telephoned him and said she would pick him up and take him to dinner. They could discuss renovations at that time.

Matthew was jubilant. "I'll call down the hill and have my friend reserve us a private table at Trudeau's on the pier."

Chapter 46

They were shown to a corner booth at a window.

"See here," Matthew said, lifting a pant leg to his knee.

She flinched and looked away, embarrassed that others may notice.

"Look, Rachael. Any noticeable difference in the shape of my leg is here, where the fibula fractured."

She looked timidly. The small round bone at the top of the fibula protruded under the skin only a bit more than normal.

"Working out's been helping this," he said, dropping the pant leg.

Working out regularly was building and strengthening his entire body. His outward appearance was helping him regain his emotional stature. Rachael sensed his positive familiar presence. His speech hadn't hesitated, which meant damage in his brain had healed or was close to it. Neither had he stuttered, but she wasn't about to offer a compliment.

Even before they ordered, Matthew opened a folder containing numerous drawings and plans. As he did, he commented on the success of their New Year's party. Without comment from her, he began explaining the details of the renovation. His excitement at being able to work again was evident. Or was he glossing over his New Year's *faux pas.*

The plans for the work she requested weren't intricate. The job could be done in no time.

"You sustained no structural damage," Matthew said. "The thermal window in the rec room will be replaced. The quake cracked the stucco where the guest house and the garage join together."

Refraining from showing enthusiasm, she followed as he pointed to different areas on the drawings.

"I suggest," he said, leaning across the table toward her, "that we build in a joint at both the front and back of the house in that same area." He pointed with a pencil. "When there are more shakers, and there will be, the joint will absorb the shock and the stucco won't crack."

The plans were simple. Yet, there remained a large quantity of papers Matthew hadn't shown her.

"And those?" she asked with businesslike curiosity. Actually, she was seething. How could he sit there. Fooling around must be a normal thing for him. Lay one woman. Go to dinner with another. Maybe he'd been doing that all along. The candle on the table made the gold specks in his eyes dance. She purposely kept her gaze on the papers in front of them.

He pulled out more pages and separated them into a second and third batch. "Okay this," he said, pointing to the second stack, "represents the upgrading you want done." He pointed to the third stack. "And these represent additional changes you might want to make."

"Additional changes?"

"I know you're proud of that house and I want to do what I can to help you." He smiled warmly.

Rachael cringed. She was out to deceive him and there he sat, offering to do more for the betterment of her home. Maybe he was trying to make up for what he did. She quietly studied the artist's drawings, following as Matthew explained.

"Some changes I think you'll find indispensable, like touch light switches instead of those old fashioned flip things. Then I think we should rip out the old carpet in the guest unit. I found some that nearly matches the green carpet you have upstairs." He paused only a moment. "For that matter, you should rip up all that green carpet upstairs in the main house too. Bamboo hardwood floors would better match your tropical decor."

"I've thought about replacing that," she said flatly. Even she didn't like the sound of her voice.

"You said you wouldn't rent to anyone again who was short of perfect and that you might save the unit for friends who stayed over. In that case, you should put a little money into the flooring."

The thought of finally renovating the entire guest apartment was exciting. "You remember what I told you, Matthew? That I've always felt my home represented a part of me that needed some work? Do you think that by fixing things, something in me will improve?" At that moment, she forgot her pretentiousness and bubbled like a school girl.

"Whether it's the apartment or something personal, you're talking to the right person to get the job done."

A hint of flirtatiousness snapped Rachael back into the moment. She felt sickened. Regaining her composure, she leaned forward to examine the rest of the materials. The waiter appeared with the salads. As they ate, they continued to discuss the plans with the papers lying on the corner of the table. Unexpectedly, it began to shower. Rachael stared at the window with its streaks of rain and wished she were home alone, in front of the roaring fireplace that soothed her mind and helped her forget all else.

By the time their stuffed colossal mushrooms, stir-fry vegetables, and herb rice pilaf arrived, Matthew had explained the renovations which might make Rachael's house more appealing. Included was a new garden area outside the master bathroom.

The tub presently sat under a full length window that looked out onto the side pathway coming down from the upper level. The view was of occasional rocks and wildflowers and weeds. For privacy, they would add a fence and gate at the top of the west end pathway off the kitchen on the upper floor. New landscaping would be put in on the incline facing the bathroom window. The view would be pleasant and private should she wish to bathe in the garden setting without pulling the blinds.

There were other changes. A new kitchen and bathroom for the guest unit, and a sturdier staircase. She could choose another spiral one or his men would build an L-shaped one. The plumbing fixtures in the bathrooms in both the house and guest unit should be updated, as well, some electrical wiring too. She might consider replacing the old glass doorknobs with lever handles of shiny polished brass. There were many other renovations suggested in the plans, some small, some not that minor, all adding to dollars.

"How can you sit there devouring your dinner?" he asked. "And look like Miss Manners." He was sensing something different about her and it seemed to unnerve him.

She watched him squirm. Her rigid attitude about the plans confused him and forced him to treat her like a business client. Rachael had no plans to relax. She acted like a businesswoman and treated him as if nothing more existed between them than a contract for a job. But Matthew might soon be onto her. She warmed to him to divert his attention.

"I do want to update a lot of things in my house. For now, I'll get by with the way it is. I have an aversion to delving into my savings. To accomplish everything you've mentioned here, I'd have to rob a bank or go back to work again."

He cringed and started to say something. She wasn't finished.

"I'm not going back to work again until my book is done. Maybe not then either. I have many more stories I want to write."

"Rachael, Rachael," he said, finally interrupting. "I have no intention of throwing you into debt or making you do things you don't want to do. Don't you think I know you by now?" He smiled, shook his head and rolled his eyes. "I have a plan."

The waiter cleared the table.

"I'd like to see the desert menu," Rachael said.

"That's something you haven't done." He studied her curiously.

She held to her nonchalance. "I eat sweets once in a while." She looked at him through cold green eyes. "Didn't I ever give you a piece of Rosa's carrot cake? Anyway," she said, "I'm a little too skinny, don't you think?" She assumed a very affected sitting pose.

You just think you know me.

Rachael scraped the frosting off the chunk of carrot cake and pushed it to the edge of the plate. Matthew sipped hot tea, studying her strange behavior, evidenced by the way he glanced at her every movement.

"Rachael, our business has been lacking over this holiday season due to the sluggish economy. Dad and I have decided to make more TV commercials."

"Oh, really?"

He spoke as if he knew he must proceed cautiously. The commercials with Linda years before hadn't worked out, not for any reason other than the fact that Linda wouldn't complete them. His hesitation said he wanted to approach her with a similar offer but didn't want her to feel like she was playing second fiddle to Linda. She was way ahead of him.

"We'd like to use your house."

"My house?" Rachael swallowed hard and almost choked.

Matthew quickly reviewed the first set of changes Rachael asked for, telling the cost involved. Then he reviewed the additional major changes he suggested and told her the cost of those.

"That's a huge difference."

"Like I said, Rachael, it's not my intention to throw you into debt or anything. If we could use your house in the commercials, it would save us a lot of money that we'd have to pay someone else."

"What do you mean 'pay someone else'?" She frowned.

"Actually, Dad and I want you to be in the commercials."

"Me? In your commercials?" Rachael was well aware of what happened to the commercials with Linda. None of that was ever an issue, but Rachael couldn't honestly see herself in front of a camera. She forgot about her duplicity and thought for a moment.

"I have the details worked out," he said.

"I'm sure you do."

"You're by far the best one to do this. We know your qualities. We think they'll come through in the filming. You're a special person, Angel. No one knows that better than I."

Rachael's heart started pounding. She swallowed hard and looked away. *You don't know me, Matthew, and you never will.*

Chapter 47

"I'm going to be directing the whole thing, if you'll agree." Momentarily he seemed to need to bolster his self-confidence. "I've worked with the filming crew before. They let me direct our own commercials." He sounded proud of his versatility.

"I remember seeing some of your commercials," Rachael said suddenly. She remembered seeing the older commercials with a different girl when she first arrived in San Francisco, only now realizing they were advertising Knight Homes. "Saw them a few years ago where you show the inside of a house—which you probably built—then the outside at night. After the announcer finishes the talking part, a woman's low, sultry voice says, 'Knight Homes!'" When Rachael pronounced the name, her voice was even more sultry than the woman's in the original commercial.

"That's it, that's it. I know you can do it. Don't you see? If you'll do our commercials, we won't have to pay an actress. You'll get this work done for the cost of the lesser quote. It's a trade off." He was excited. "Those older commercials brought us more business than we could handle. I know that's what we need now."

"You're sure?"

"Despite the economy, a few people are out there building new homes or making renovations after the quake. We need to get a piece of that action."

Rachael sipped her tea. She reminded herself why she was there. She'd have to deviate from her deceitful plan. She could make this work for her. Her mind went back to Matthew. How could he be sitting there innocently expressing himself, and knowing what he did?

Like a polished salesman, Matthew seemed to have yet another strategy to apply. He pulled out a sheet of paper on which were printed three phrases.

"This is what you'd say. There's one line for each commercial."
She read:

Knight Homes—for Knight people
A Knight place to come home to
Knight life

He described what each filmed sequence might consist of and the part she'd have in each one. She would be the last person the viewer would see, with a room from her home in the background. She didn't live in a Knight Home, but her decor resembled one. That's what mattered since the Knights produced custom homes which wouldn't be duplicated.

Suddenly excited, she grabbed the pen. Below the three quotations, she jotted two more.

Are you a Knight person?
We can make you a Knight person.

"Your creativity amazes me," he said. "Angel, you're the right person. You're photogenic. You're goodness shows in your face and you're beautiful. Please do this for me." He put his hand on hers. She pulled hers away. He noticed, hesitated, and frowned.

Again, he said she was beautiful. He was trying hard. This particular time his flattery held no significance. She determined to somehow make the deception work the way she intended. Above all else, she would have retribution.

"I'll do it." she said after a long moment of silence. "On one condition."

He expelled a long sigh of relief and leaned back. "Anything, Rachael. Name it."

She looked at him knowing he was about to regret his words. "You give me your promise to give me time to finish my book."

He didn't frown. He didn't get upset. He smiled warmly, gorgeously. "Is that it? Is that what you want me to promise?"

Somehow, he hadn't reacted the way she expected he might. "You don't understand, Matthew. I started this book over two years ago. True, a lot of things have happened..." Her voice cracked with emotion. She pressed long fingers against her lips. He watched intently. She couldn't crack now.

They both knew they'd been through a lot, and they were together, despite their now fraudulent alliance. She wondered if she was doing the right thing. Maybe she should have talked to someone first. Maybe Tina. Maybe not. Maybe she should swallow her pride and drop the whole pretense. And suffer like before? Not on her life. She regained her composure.

"I've managed to complete about two thirds of the story. I need more time. I'm not working now. I plan to write day and night if I have to. My publisher is demanding I send the rest. I have deadlines."

"I can handle the house."

"Fine. You handle the house. Let me write. The work on the house, how long?"

"Two weeks. Three on the outside. What about the commercials? Can you leave your writing long enough?"

"I'll do the commercials. How many and how long will the filming take?"

"Depends on you. One for each of these." He pointed to the five slogans. "We might be able to get them done in one day. One very long busy day."

"I'll do the commercials. Then you'll let me write?" She wanted to hear him verbalize his agreement.

"Are you saying after the house and the commercials, you want me to walk out of your life till you finish your damned book?"

She said nothing. just sat there glaring at him.

"Look, we're at a point in our lives when we can finally spend time together. I'm almost healed. You're not working anymore. There are twenty four long hours in a day, for Heaven's sake." He was becoming aggravated. Suddenly, his eyes opened grotesquely wide. Then he strained to close the lids and opened them again. Rachael watched. He breathed out heavily. Something was wrong.

"Matthew, what is it?" Her concern was genuine.

"Dizzy," he said, letting out another long breath. He grabbed hold of the table edge. "Dizzy."

"Is that still happening?"

"Less and less, but once in a while, it grabs me." He squeezed his eyes shut and shook his head again. "Do you know what the doctor told me?" he asked, looking like even he couldn't believe what happened. "He said months pass before the body totally washes away bruises in the brain. If a blood clot breaks loose and migrates I could have a stroke or a heart attack."

Rachael lost her composure. She reached across the table and found his hand. "Oh, Matthew," was all she could say. "Oh, Matthew."

"If that happens... you'll have all the time you need to write your book." His voice carried a twinge of self-pity, and of indignation directed at her.

"Don't hang that on me." She yanked her hand away. "You gave your promise."

"My life has always been quite full. I'll have no trouble occupying my time," he said.

"I'm sure of that."

"I'll be busy after this," he said, gesturing to the papers on the table top. "I have those ridiculous therapies to contend with. I'm due for that surgical procedure to check my jaw next week."

"Oh, that," she said. Now he was sounding like a bleeding heart.

"Damn it, Rachael." He leaned over the table and whispered loudly. "We're not much closer than when we first met. I want us to be close. You hear me? I want to be able to touch you without having to worry that I've offended you. I want to hold your body next to mine without you worrying I'm gonna' jump your bones every chance I get."

She almost laughed. She glanced around hoping other patrons hadn't heard, then managed to maintain her innocent stare.

"There's this wall here," he said, motioned in the air between them. "We're not relaxed around each other, never been completely spontaneous." He sighed. "Okay, no two lives run parallel, but can't we set aside some of our time for each other?"

"Maybe."

"Look, Mom and Dad said you came to the hospital every day. Can't you give me some time now when I can respond to you?"

She remained stoic.

"Rachael?"

"I need to finish my book."

"I gave you my word."

"Then we'll have to work things out, I suppose."

"I'm not going to let you fade from my life again," he said.

She was suspicious. Was his dizziness real or faked. She had no way of knowing. He was super intelligent and might have suspected she was up to something. Had he staged that whole scene to evoke her sympathy? Would he stoop to something like that?

Rachael's mind was cloaked in bitterness. Driving home alone in the darkness, she spoke out load. "You haven't seen anything yet, Matthew. You really don't know me."

Chapter 48

Canvas coverings were laid over the carpeting and tile and people traipsed in and out and around her. Rachael wrote right through the commotion. She ignored them all. Despite her contemptuous feeling for him, she had complete faith in Matthew's ability to improve her home. The work on the house was about completed. Through it all, Matthew was playing right into her little scheme.

"I don't know how you can work on that computer through this commotion," one of the workmen said.

"She's got the most fantastic level of concentration," Matthew said, bragging, evidently having found new respect for her diligence. Truth of the matter was sinking in for the first time. Writing was the career she was serious about and intended to pursue. She needed to get this book completed to seal the commitment she made, not to him, not necessarily to her publisher, but to herself. Certainly he had to interpret her commitment as a classic example of any devotion she might have for him.

Rachael held to her wicked scheme. She knew of no other way to heal her wounds. Pretending to ignore him, she allowed Matthew to pour every bit of his creative effort into her house, leaving him to think she'd be appreciative when the upgrading was completed.

Continuing to develop her novel, she encountered more difficulties than she had experienced thus far. She had included many of the occurrences that happened between Matthew and her, concealing the facts in the imaginative schemes and maneuvers of her characters. Originally, she intended to close the book with a surprising and happy epilogue. Now she could not conjure up the simplest of words to move her characters toward exultation.

The weeks ahead were set. Melissa intended to meet her editor's deadline regardless how many obligations she must set aside. She'd make Hunter wait, then finally tell him she wasn't going to see him anymore. He could go back to the girl reflected on the curtains and make more shadows. He should film that for a risqué commercial. She could care less. Everything was beginning to fall into place.

She went to the library and perused various novels. Most ended happily. A few didn't, and those left her feeling disheartened. Disappointment and depression wasn't the message she wanted to convey to her readers. Reality was. Then she found a copy of Margaret Mitchell's *Gone With The Wind*. Remembering the story well, especially the ending, she didn't have to open the book. That ending seemed to lend credence to the direction of her contorted plot. Standing between the racks, she hugged the thick volume to her heart, knowing what she must do.

Late one afternoon, while talking with the building inspector, Matthew experienced another severe dizzy spell. Rachael, again, wondered if the whole scene was contrived. She allowed him to rest in the guest room. He succumbed immediately, sleeping fitfully into the night.

He must have awakened in the early hours after midnight. Sometime during the night he had opened his bedroom door which was directly across the downstairs foyer from her office. She didn't dare close it for fear the slightest noise or movement might wake him. By the time he woke again, she had been at her computer for hours.

Even with her back to him across the lower foyer, she sensed him watching her.

You'd better try to understand my determination, Matthew.

Her fingers flew over the keyboard as the words flowed through her fingertips in a never-ending stream from her fertile brain.

How many more words, how many more books she might produce, seemed incomprehensible to him. She wondered how she could allow time for him or anyone else. Writing was what she wanted to do. She imagined him lying in the bed, silent and wanting.

So sleep in a tent, Mr. Builder!

She heard him begin to stir and pretended not to notice.

He called across the foyer. "Angel?"

She turned slowly finding him motioning her to come to him.

"What do you want, Matthew?" she asked, with a look of amusement.

"Come give me a morning hug."

"Go back to sleep." Surely he slept in his underwear since he had gone to sleep right after work. Did he honestly think she would go to him when he could be naked?

"No, Rachael. Come hold me a few minutes. Just a hug."

The front door opened and closed upstairs. Rosa had arrived for the day. *Synchronicity!* Rachael walked toward the guest room, smiling smugly at Rosa's timeliness. She closed the bedroom door, much to Matthew's chagrin.

Chapter 49

Work on Rachael's home was finally done, except for the lush green carpeting being replaced. The house was clean and beautiful once again. The filming crew and entourage arrived and began setting up equipment outside the front entry. People accumulated on the street to watch and ask questions. Technicians scurried about, testing equipment, erecting, then moving, then again erecting reflective screens, spotlights and backdrops. The hurrying and scurrying didn't seem to accomplish much. What on earth could they be trying to prove, since filming the front of the house wouldn't begin till dusk?

Additional camera crews were in and out the house, asking Rosa and her aides to open and close doors, windows and drapes, and turn lights off and on. They had to get a feel for the place. The entire day, with its transpirations, would not be successful without the ever present and dedicated assistance Rosa offered.

Cameron and Matthew were excited about being able to make five commercials instead of three. Rachael had practiced a little, saying each one of her lines in the most provocative voice she might articulate. More importantly, she practiced the way she wanted to appear on camera, which would be a vital part of her deceit.

Mona came to watch the filming and to be a part of one clip. Her being present made Rachael nervous. Surely Mona and

Cameron had no idea about the difficulties between her and their son. Matthew, himself, wasn't fully aware of any new issues between them, issues like the real reason Rachael was becoming more and more reticent. What could his parents suspect, unless Matthew discussed their standoff with his dad? He shared everything else with him. Yet, what importance could a few idiosyncratic mannerisms hold? She dismissed the thought. Nothing happened that could give anyone reason to suspect her vicious scheme.

Extras arrived, to be used when additional people were required in certain scenes. Finally, a security company was asked to send over two guards to keep gawkers from walking down the pathways to the lower level at either end of the property. Once people discovered the access paths to the rear yard, they ended up wandering about trying to get filmed.

Stills around the pool area were completed though rain wasn't expected. They were doing the yard scenes first in case fog rolled in. Powerful bright lighting was in place creating an atmosphere of summer on the terrace. Space heaters were strategically placed out of camera range around the pool and hot tub to negate the January chill.

A hairdresser styled and fluffed Rachael's thick curly hair and stood by for additional primping. For the first scene, her hair was piled loosely on top of her head. A few loose wisps trailed down here and there at the sides and back and over her forehead. Rachael wore one of her own bathing suits, not necessarily a seductive one. This one would cover her scars. The color was a vibrant teal that contrasted strikingly with her shiny hair and skin tones. A daring low cut neckline did justice to her muscular cleavage. A white terry cover up hid what Rachael's bathing suit did not. To the men, she probably looked seductive, but she remained aloof most of the time.

"Hi," the voice said. "I'm Benji Simon." She turned to greet him. "I'm head of the film crew, and we're about ready for you to drop the jacket."

Rachael was suddenly tense. "It's time, huh?"

"Don't worry," he said. "Both guys and girls feel nervous the first time they're in front the camera. Remember, this is a great thing you're doing for my good buddy. You know, he really cares. He's always talking about you. Don't pay attention to anyone else. Relax and be the best you can be."

She stared at the ground, wondering how many times he might have offered similar advice to others. He sounded rehearsed and that could make the day awfully boring. Had he said something like that to Linda? Or was Linda a professional who needed little coaching? Had he used another line on her considering she was a model?

Slipping out of the jacket and dropping it into a deck chair, she was aware of all eyes upon her. The only thing she cared about was whether or not Matthew noticed guys looking at her. She hoped he hungered for her. She hoped he'd suffer. To those present, this was another filming like so many others. They filmed women's bodies all the time and could probably tell a lot of stories. She was sure no one suspected she and Matthew had never slept together, though Matthew might have led his closest buddies to believe they had. No one would have any idea how much he might be lusting for her. She carried herself like a lady, retaining perfect composure, yet intending to drive him to desperation. She looked around slowly and smiled warmly, disguising her real thoughts. Now he was about to get a taste of how his unconscionable act made her feel.

Benji continually pointed the camera toward her even though no particular scene was being filmed. Finally, after seeing Matthew and Benji huddled together too many times, and the way they stopped talking and smiled when they saw her looking, she guessed Benji was taking some extra shots of her for

Matthew's benefit. This was her chance to give him something to remember her by.

You can't take your eyes off me, Matthew. Stand there and pretend and burn inside!

"This is Armand," someone said. "He's going to do the hot tub with you."

Benji's team had chosen the perfect compliment for her. Armand was tall and tanned and great looking with a shock of jet black hair that fell over his forehead. He got into the tub without hesitation. He reached for her hand as she slowly eased into the tub of hot churning water. Soon they were sitting side-by-side among the froth and bubbles.

"I love hot tub scenes," he said, jokingly. "Gives me a chance to get close to the ladies." He snuggled up to Rachael. The video crew was not yet taping their voices.

The hot water soothed and Rachael relaxed and slid closer and smiled at him warmly.

Benji cued her. She turned to face the camera, offering her vixen smile. "A Knight place to come home to," she said, suggesting fun and frolic, then slowly turned that teasing look toward Armand again.

"Cut!" Matthew said, nearly screaming it.

"Perfect, perfect," Benji said, throwing a fist in to the air.

The makeup girl ran over with Rachael's terry jacket and towels as they climbed out of the hot tub. Armand grabbed the towel and began rubbing down Rachael's back side. Of course, Matthew watched, as her wet bathing suit stuck to her skin and displayed every contour of her tight buttocks. She allowed Armand to help her into the terry cover-up, thanking him graciously. How perfect! His flirtatious nature added to the deceit. She knew Matthew watched, and allowed Armand to continue. Her need for vengeance had seeped too deep inside. She would take advantage of every chance possible to make Matthew jealous without compromising her respectability. She hoped no one caught on. Benji's expertise with the camera would make more of it than she could possibly exhibit. Matthew would notice. That's what mattered.

"Take it easy, man," Benji said to Armand. Then he turned to Rachael and said, "This work is a lot of play, sometimes a lot of fooling around. The guy's harmless."

"Okay, the remaining scenes are indoors," Matthew said, calling out for all to hear. "Off with the shoes."

Several people groaned about having to work in their socks again. If they didn't, those who remembered, knew Rachael might stop the filming faster than Linda had.

For the scene in front of the fireplace, Rachael chose to wear the black sequined cocktail dress Matthew was crazy about. *Black. The color of our future.* She stepped into the dress.

That sequence finished with her sitting on the raised hearth by a roaring fire. She was to sit with a pleasant expression, then speak her line and resume the look once more. She knew how to play this. Instead, she turned sideways leaning toward the camera and against her arm which pushed her breasts together and exaggerated her cleavage. Lighting fell perfectly across her bosom, casting interesting shadows. Her face was framed by firelight dancing in the aura of her sparkling brassy curls.

"Knight Homes… for Knight people," she said, lulling with eyes inviting company.

From the crowd came a lot of oohs and ahs. Even Mona nodded and smiled.

The next shoot was of a dinner party and two additional stand-in couples were dressed for the occasion. Cameron changed his shirt and jacket and added a tie. His work denims wouldn't show as he sat tucked in at the head of the table. "Maybe I'll start a new fad," he said. "This formal shirt does a lot for these old jeans."

Mona, wearing a blue designer dress and evening diamonds, was placed opposite Cameron at the long table. Matthew dressed for this scene and Rachael had changed into a pink lacey dinner dress. She and Matthew sat next to each other. Barely able to contain her delight about being included, Tina was paired with an actor opposite Rachael and Matthew. The stand-in couples sat opposite each other.

The table was set with rented china, crystal and silver. Even the linen table napkins and Rosa's apron and arm towel were props.

At the last minute, Matthew asked Rosa to play herself and pretend to begin to serve a meal. Why should they hire an actor or actress when they had someone who knew the part, and who had personality and a sense of humor to boot?

Rosa was thrilled. She told her friends she was going to be in the movies. Matthew and Rosa had hit it off from the day they were introduced. Now he had endeared himself to her forever.

Too many people made having each doing appropriate things at the right moment difficult. Not everyone was smiling or acting happy, or even acting like they were at a dinner party, which was a little unnerving. Finally, all were again positioned. On cue, Rachael leaned toward Matthew in a feigned brief *tete-a-tete*, then turned her face slowly toward the camera. In a voice sounding much pampered, she said, "Knight life!" That time, the scene was perfect. She didn't make mistakes.

Chapter 50

Lunch break was called. Again, Tina's Italian was pleased to cater the day. Food tables were set up in the guest quarters after all the necessary videos and stills needed in that area were shot. Rosa didn't go near the tables, except to choose her plate of food.

"No working now," she said. "Today, I'm actress."

Benji found Rachael. "You're great! You're super!" He always seemed hyper. "Did you know sometimes to shoot one scene could take more than a day? Now I know why he's crazy about you. That Matthew, he's one lucky guy."

"Thanks," she said.

Too bad he doesn't know that.

"Have you done this before?"

"I practiced my lines," she said in the innocent childish way Matthew taught her to recognize in herself. She felt embarrassed, having caught the mood of the day, and felt good about being in some commercials regardless of motivation.

Mona left after lunch and Cameron spent a lot of time talking shop with the crews. Rachael was greatly relieved. The last two clips were to be filmed in private. She needed to be as uninhibited as possible to pull off a climactic ending to her charade.

Finally, her bedroom was set up. Her hair was left hanging loosely down her back and falling where it may over her shoulders. Wispy curls softened her face. The lightest strands of hair would be kept buoyant as she passed through forced air gently circulated by a small fan out of camera range.

She wore a floor length night gown and matching sheer peignoir. She had wanted to buy one to assure proper fit, then decided against spending money on her deception. Because of that, she wouldn't want to wear the thing again. The prop crew supplied her with what she needed in lavender lace, another color to enhance her features. The gown was too big. A few pins at the waist in the back took up the slack and accentuated her waistline magnificently.

She was to walk away from the camera through the sliding doorway into her bedroom. The camera would pick up the room beyond. Inside the doorway, she was to turn slightly and speak her line.

Matthew attentively watched Rachael perform, his curiosity plainly evident. No longer demure or hesitant, Rachael offered a facet of her personality he'd never seen. In fact, she knew she was vibrant, an aspect of herself she'd never known either. The fact that she hadn't said too much to Matthew seemed to be irritating him. Luckily, most of the day, she remained preoccupied with someone else. She was enjoying the attention of other men and ignoring him.

Rachael was directed to her starting point. The light shining from within the bedroom would highlight her hair. She floated through the doorway and turned to speak her line. Instead of doing so provocatively, she tossed her chin out, slanted her eyes, and dropped the sheer peignoir, dragging it along the floor and asked, "Are you a Knight person?" Her voice taunted, eyes again focused directly into the camera. Then she turned and walked into the bedroom, dragging the peignoir on the floor behind her and finally casually tossing it to the edge of the bed. Again unexpectedly, she looked over her shoulder at the camera with a sultry smile, beckoning with her eyes.

There was immediate pandemonium. Those of the crew allowed to view the bedroom scenes expressed their enjoyment with everything from smiles and clapping to sensual groans. The crew was excited, but agreed she was too sexy for public commercials. They made her film the scene again. Matthew watched in disbelief. She was better than he'd expected. That was one scene, among others, the loyal Benji might save for Matthew.

Watch it and suffer!

A break was called. Some of the guys crowded around Matthew who stood nearby and boisterously told him how lucky he was to have a girlfriend like Rachael. Some intentionally wanted her to hear as they slipped glances her way. They bragged that she was terrific, something special, and mostly, sexier than anyone they'd seen in a long time. They wanted to know about her, and could he get her to do more commercials. Rachael made herself look preoccupied with the makeup girl. Matthew made excuses and walked away seeming to be angry. Of course he'd be. He was probably questioning how she could disregard what she was told to do. Why was she being sexier than the commercials required? He'd never want others to see her that way. The plans they made for filming were enough without her flaunting herself in front of that crazy bunch.

One day, you'll figure it out, Mr. Builder.

Beginning again, the camera panned her bedroom, pausing at focal points for effect, getting a shot of the sweeping view of the Bay through the wall of glass. Then to the meditation mat poised under a tall, profuse floral arrangement of red bamboo with leaves and several other sprigs and vines. A glimpse of the large elevated bathtub, and the garden beyond, was framed through the open bathroom door and large window beyond.

Next, Rachael's reflection was caught in the wall-to-wall mirror at the back as she floated into the room through the pocket doorway. Then they paused again to prepare Rachael for the final sequence.

The scene was a simple one. Originally, an actor was to be in bed with Rachael. They were to look cozy, propped up, reading or watching television. Matthew cut the actor. Benji with the camera, the girl positioning the overhead microphone, one guy with the white reflective screens, and Matthew, were to be the only people in the room with Rachael in bed. Matthew must have had a lot to do with those arrangements. Still, they would be filming toward the mirrors at the back. If they caught anyone's reflection, they'd have to shoot the scene again.

Rachael chose to wear the same white gown she found lying on her bed rumpled up in a knot after Matthew and Cameron had inspected her home the night of the earthquake. Memories of seeing the gown lying that way flooded her mind. She never left her clothes rumpled like that, wadded into a ball. Surely, Matthew had picked up and examined it, maybe even sniffed it.

Why are you looking surprised, Matthew. Haven't you seen this nightie before? This time, see how it fits, because you'll never see it again.

The look on Matthew's face was one of utter pain. He paced, finally leaving the room, returning sometime later having regained control of himself.

Rachael was positioned in a not very seductive position leaning back on pillows stacked against the headrest. A sheet was pulled up over her chest. The sheets were tamped down around her to suggest her pose beneath.

"What I want now," Benji said, "is for you to be reading that book. Then look up with a smile and say your line."

The lights were dimmed, casting soft, suggestive shadows across her and the bed. Light from a small reading lamp illuminated the book. She waited for the microphone to be positioned above her knowing what she had to do. When the filming started, instead of looking up and speaking, she sat up quickly, drawing her knees up under her and leaning toward the camera. She tipped her head back, with eyes and mouth suggestively half opened. Her breasts almost rolled out of the top of her gown!

"I... can make you a Knight person!" she said, gushing and allowing her mouth to remain provocatively expectant.

"Wow," Benji said.

"Rachael," Matthew said. "What on earth?"

She sat, innocently smiling, covering her chest with the book. "You don't like dry commercials, do you?" She turned slightly, smiling at Benji out of the corner of her eye like a naughty child.

Matthew's jaw dropped. "Rachael, you're supposed to say, '*We* can make you a Knight person.'" Fumbling with his notes, he pretended not to be effected.

Rachael saw signs of him coming apart. "*We*, Matthew? Who's '*we*'?" she asked, playing on his nerves.

"Rachael, it's been a long day. Can you just follow the part?" He was fidgeting and pacing again.

Rachael gloated. The retake went perfectly.

"That's a wrap, folks," Benji said, motioning for the crews to pack up.

When Matthew was able to corner Rachael, he asked, "Why have you been displaying such extremist behavior? Some of the stuff you pulled was totally uncalled for."

And I'll bet you watch each clip over and over too.

"That was a sample of my creativity," she said, innocently teasing. She tried hard not clenching her teeth when she spoke. If ever there was an opportunity to show him she was not a person to be taken for granted, this day had been perfect. Clean and direct.

"Sure," he said.

"I wanted to give you something to remember me by, while I'm sequestered finishing my book." She looked directly into his eyes, teasing with hers and added, "Enjoy your videos."

Chapter 51

Making an honest effort to honor their agreement was difficult at best. Matthew called several times leaving messages on her answering machine. She hadn't responded. Surely, he was used to that by now.

In the meantime, Rachael needed to know more about child abuse in order to further round out her book characters. Back at the main San Francisco Public Library, she found a wealth of new books and read voraciously. She was finally understanding more about healing from abuse than she might have learned in the next ten years of therapy. In bits and pieces, the scenario of her story plot came together. She carried an armload of books, found a table, opened her laptop, and began to write a scene in her story.

The child in Melissa had been battered and abused. When Hunter showed her any affection, one of the two, the love starved child or the adult responded. The child had always been admonished about not allowing anyone near her or to touch her. The child was who always pushed Hunter away.

Rachael paused to think and allow the information to sink in. She was onto something significant. Her fingers pounded the keyboard in a blur.

As a child, Melissa was taught that affection was naughty, dirty. The child she was could not comprehend her father's harsh directives. Even though Melissa was now a feeling, sensual adult woman, she cowered from life, the child not having been allowed the curiosity and expression that encourages any adolescent to mature.

When Hunter exhibited affection for her as any healthy, red-blooded male might, her adult self with mature needs responded to that attention. The obedient child in her was the one who pushed him away when sexuality became a threat.

Melissa the adult, had no choice but to try to appease and protect Melissa, the child, who had not been. When the child would be allowed to experience, express and mature, would be when the child and adult merged and became a whole person. Then the whole person would respond in more mature ways.

That explained some of the curious childlike qualities she often expressed in some of their happier moments. Even so, the child-like expressions of the little girl sometimes annoyed Hunter, yet, he made no effort to rebuke this strange behavior. Now, slowly recognizing there would be no further reprimands or punishments for her curiosity, the little girl was finally coming out to play. Melissa's inner child needed approval and praise and acceptance for simply being. Then the fragments would begin to mesh.

How much Hunter might learn would help. Melissa needed to experience her own transformational shift from within. With his knowledge, he might nurture and support her. She was now an adult, and as such, had to find the connection within herself. Only then would she be freed of the devastating effects of having been brutalized.

Rachael continued studying until something inside clicked, combined with the personality and understanding she created for Melissa. Rachael had undertaken therapy on her own which meant she was willing to accept help. Additionally, she was determined not to be like her parents, carrying forward senseless brutality, generation to generation.

The books presented her with the worst scenarios about how the abused grow up to abuse their own children, spouses and others. They presented the best scenarios, the hopes for the future of abused and battered children as adults. She read about some cases where the abuse was not carried on and how the perpetuating effects were overcome by the few.

In a short time, she learned much. She felt empathy and understanding that she could now fully flesh out the character of Melissa. She wrote that Melissa finally understood her need to be alone and it was okay to be any way she needed to be.

Returning home, just as Rachael entered the front door, her cell phone rang. Dennis DeBaer was full of surprises that would play into and make her deception a huge success.

The searing image of two bodies casting shadows on the drapes in the wee hours of New Year's morning was indelibly scarred into Rachael's memory. Since then, her scheme had gone better than expected. A trip to New York was totally unscheduled, but ratified the choice she made to end the relationship. She left immediately. Once settled there, she worked feverishly to accomplish the goal she set for herself long before meeting Matthew and becoming distracted.

"*Si, si*, I tell Senior Matt you are in *Nueva York* with your book," Rosa said over the phone.

New York was cold and foreign, a place that would be nice to explore in warmer weather. "What was his reaction?"

"I watch his face. He have shock. He say you no tell him you leaving." Rosa paused a minute. " 'She's where? *Nueva York*?' he say. 'When?' " Rosa sounded frustrated, having to deal with Matthews persistence. "Three weeks ago, Senior Matt, I say. After commercials."

As far as Rachael knew, Rosa hadn't figured out what was happening with her and Matthew. "You know I had to leave fast," she said, hoping Rosa would not read between the lines. "I appreciate your daughter finding me this loft to rent, Rosa, right next to her place."

"*Si, si.* I tell Senior Matt my daughter in *Nueva York* help you. I thought you tell to Senior Matt already."

"No chance, had to leave too fast." It was a flimsy excuse. Rosa would see through it. "My publisher wanted me to come here to finish the book. They want to publish it right away." Rachael felt pure adrenalin. Her publisher loved her story. "They're working with me on promotion too."

"I tell Senior Matt you work with spirit writer."

"A what"

"*Como se dice...* spirit writer?"

"Oh, you mean ghost writer?" Rachael laughed into the phone.

"Ah, si. Then I tell Senior Matt they asked for another book. *Dios mio, es imposible.* How you can finish another book because first one not finished? They say come to *Nueva York* and work with ghost writer. Rush. Rush." Rosa sounded out of breath relating what happened.

"I appreciate you letting him know, Rosa."

"You have fight with him?" she asked cautiously.

Rachael knew that Matthew was caught in a very embarrassing predicament. Nervous energy ran rampant throughout her body. She hoped he was paying the price for what he did. "A little disagreement, Rosa."

"I give your messages, Senorita. He say you no call yet. *Porque no?* Senior Matt is—"

"Rosa, I'll explain when I come home, okay?" Rachael knew she would have to keep Rosa appeased while she was in New York.

Rosa acquiesced knowing she didn't have the right to pry. They ended the call with Rachael's assurance that she would explain once she returned to San Francisco.

After three weeks since filming the commercials, and three weeks she previously told Matthew it would take to finish her book, he must be frustrated not having heard from her by now. Then he learns she's gone to New York without a word.

"Get a life, Matthew," she said out loud. "One without me."

Chapter 52

The loft was sparsely furnished and not too modern, but clean and warm and comfortable enough for the short time she would live there. It was a spacious sunlit attic of a large Brownstone bordering Central Park, which had been converted to private guest rooms and studio apartments. There was privacy enough. At the front end were large paned windows, with each of the many tiny corners harboring a share of drifted snow. Across the street, Central Park lay under a blanket of white.

An unmatched sofa bed and chair in the middle of the room faced the fireplace on the side wall opposite the stairwell. Rachael immediately moved the chair to face one of the gable windows. That would be her meditation area.

An old refurbished kitchen was tucked in at the rear. A small balcony off the back door held frozen potted plants and offered a view over the tiny cramped snowed-covered back yards of the neighbors. The long wooden table in the kitchen area was set up as work space with two laptops and peripheral equipment on loan from Rachael's publishing house. By sitting at one end of the table, she could see out the dining area gable while working, when she occasionally looked up. She was working against time.

The next thing she did was change the dedication of her book from Matthew to Brandon.

Richard Barron arrived punctually each morning at seven. "Call me Richie," he said almost immediately.

Of the two stories she'd presented him in outline form, he made a quick choice and set to work. Rachael would supply him with pertinent details she wanted included in the plot. Richie gave them life with words. She would proofread, correct and change the story to suit her desires as they went along. With the outline to follow, Richie's talent at ghostwriting was pure genius.

"Why don't you write you own stories? You're gifted in the use of the English language."

"You said it. The English language. I can't come up with the plots. I've tried it. Mine sound juvenile. It's frustrating at best."

"Have you taken any classes?"

"Yeah." He chuckled. "I've a degree in Marine Biology."

"You're kidding."

"I became a political activist, fighting to save the oceans." Richie raised his eyebrows and shrugged sadly. "I had big dreams. Once I got to New York, via Washington, I discovered a flair for theatre and the arts. When I can find parts, I do some acting. Ghost writing's what's keeping us from starving."

"I think you should consider taking classes or getting some kind of help to free your creativity," she said. "You sound like a person with much experience. You could turn that into books."

She felt good being able to offer that kind of encouragement, considering the life's events she kept tucked away inside her mind.

"I guess," he said with an air of dismay. "I haven't made enough to go back to college or study. I get a salary from this publisher. Well, it's a little bit better than a salary because I work the same long hours as you. Still, I'm writing other people's stories, and right now, my wife is pregnant with our second."

While Richie worked on one of the laptops, Rachael worked on the other. She was nearly finished with *Sea Cliff*. However, even the calm, benign presence of Richie sharing space inhibited her to the point of frustration. She began to work more with him to finish the second book, resuming work on *Sea Cliff* in the middle of the afternoon after he left for the day. She'd work feverishly as late as she dared, then get some rest in order to wake at four in the morning for meditation.

Excitement about finishing *Sea Cliff* was mounting. This was a major milestone, a turning point in her life. She determined to finish the other stories rattling around her mind. Then one sleepless night, the thought came to her that she might want to disassociate herself from her first two books, which had limited successes. Beginning with this new book, she would use a pen name.

Some days, Rachael was called to proof galleys. There was a photography session which produced a few shots of her to be used in promotion and advertisements. She was allowed to work with the artist drawing renderings for the cover. "You don't need my help," Rachael said. "You're excellent at what you do." Rachael felt right allowing her the full range of her creativity. When she was shown her photo and the final sketches for the dust jacket, was when Rachael realized *Sea Cliff* was to be published in hard cover.

Her head reeled. They were doing this for her, because of a story she chose to write. She couldn't believe what was happening.

Late one night, Rachael visualized the end of her story coming clearly into focus. Her dual protagonists, Melissa and Hunter, had gone their separate ways with pain and bitterness. Rachael had created Melissa in her own image. She first lost her mother, then her first love, and then her father. Eventually, her brother had forsaken her. In the only way she knew, Melissa had loved and needed Hunter, more than she realized. Yet, his indiscretion in front of her very eyes would never allow her to commit to him now.

Melissa renewed her strength with regular visits to the ashram. Hunter stopped going for a while and finally found another place to attend classes in Marin. More than likely their paths would never cross again and Melissa would not yet experience intimacy with a man.

Nearing the end of the final chapter, Rachael wrote that Melissa's book was published and she was well into writing yet another.

Melissa received a lot of healing through writing and determined to set in words every possible human emotion she might explore and come to understand. She would write about people with the heart and fortitude to rise above life's difficulties and be wiser for having braved the struggle.

The loft was quiet, almost eerie. Rachael sat at the end of the kitchen table staring out into the black sky of the New York night. Except for someone angrily honking, traffic on the street below was relegated to nothing more than background din as the main events of the plot of *Sea Cliff* passed through her mind in orderly procession.

"It's almost over," she said aloud and clasped her hands tightly together. "Now, to wrap this up." She wasn't sure how to finish it. Then she had a brilliant idea. After having Melissa and Hunter parting ways, she would have time pass. Then one day they happened to accidentally meet.

Melissa sat at an outdoor cafe, perusing a copy of Around the Neighborhood. Quietly, someone sat in the chair opposite her at the table. That would be okay. All tables were usually taken and here she was sitting alone at a table for four. She glanced quickly, intending to offer a smile to let the person know it was okay to share the space. She did a double-take. Hunter sat across from her.

Her heart began to pound. She looked into his hazel eyes. They hadn't changed. The gold specks sparkled.

"How have you been, Melissa?" he asked. Then he seemed embarrassed. "I mean, other than with your bestsellers?"

She almost swallowed her tongue. "Personally, I'm doing well, secluded, writing. You remember, people call me Greta."

It was his turn to swallow hard. He paused, then spoke. "I think Greta should get out once in a while and have some fun."

Her heart pounded even harder. She thought she was over him, felt overwhelmed that he cared to contact her again. Then she remembered the image of two bodies reflected on the curtains. "I'll need time to think about it," she said. She really couldn't decide till the hurt went away. One thing she learned from that experience, she had gained an even deeper respect for herself.

"I've done it. I'm finished." Her voice quivered and her hands began to shake as a rush of adrenalin filled her. First she laughed, then she cried. She paced back and forth, her slippered feet shuffling on the hardwood floors. She paced in the kitchen, then made a cup of hot Darjeeling tea, then went to stand at the steamy front windows. She wiped the moisture away and watched the darting blurred lights of traffic on the street below until she realized her tea had cooled. Where a couple of hours before, she was consumed with finishing the book, now her mind was filled with apprehension about how well the readers might accept her style of storytelling.

She couldn't understand how anyone would want to publish a story containing parodies of her life. Yet, someone important liked her story. Pure and simple. Even if the resolution for her protagonists separated them in the end, she was able to create their separation happening in such a way that both Melissa and Hunter were able to go on with their individual lives with positive outlooks for the future. She intended that she would go on with her life too.

Chapter 53

When she left San Francisco, she turned her back on Matthew with no intention of seeing him again. Now that her thoughts weren't being consumed by writing, the feeling, the hope, and the hurt she felt connected with him came rushing in. Closure for her hadn't happened, but now she would go her own way and meant to keep going.

She looked at the cup in her hand. It was empty and she hadn't remembered drinking the cold tea. Nearing total exhaustion, she sat again at the end of the dining table, staring out the gable until black began turning to powder blue.

After electronically sending the completed manuscript to her publisher, two days passed before a message came from DeBaer saying they accepted the story as written. She could go home.

An hour later, her cell phone rang.

"Rachael? Are you still here?"

"Richie? Yes, I'm here, barely. I'm packed. What's up?"

"I'm at the office. They asked that I catch you before leave. They want you to come in for one final meeting."

"Is something wrong?"

"No, nothing. They thought since you're here, they could go over a few last minute details with you. Wrap it up, sort of."

"Are you sure there's nothing wrong?"

"Sure, I'm sure. It's normal procedure when the writer's in town. This meeting is important. Can you come in first thing tomorrow?"

"Important? Richie, what do I wear? How should I look?"

"Wear that dark blue business suit you wore the day you first came to the office. They know you're living out of a suitcase. This is the last time most of these people will see you and you'll want to leave a good memory behind."

"Are you sure there's nothin…"

"Rachael, trust me. Get here, okay?"

When she arrived the next morning, people were casting looks that said they knew something she didn't. Richie Barron was there and said they should go right into the conference room. They would meet with a few of the others who were instrumental in the publication of her novel. Something was happening.

Richie opened the door and they walked into a conference room full of happy smiling people wearing both business suits and some in casual clothing. All rose from their chairs around the huge oval table and began to applaud. An enlarged replica of the poster to be used for advertising hung high on the back wall. Beaming down at her was a large reprint of her photo. In beautiful script along the bottom corner, the words:

SEA CLIFF
A Love Story of Transcendence
by Rachael Daye

Caught totally unaware, her eyes widened. A hand went up over her gaping mouth. Dennis DeBaer waved from near the head of the table and she was shown to the empty seat beside him. He made quick introductions all around. Rachael made sure she shook hands with Ms. Geri Daniels, the CEO of *Romantique.*

The meeting began immediately with discussion about an addendum to her contract. The verbiage included a clause stipulating that she reserve rights of her next two books, beyond the present four, for their consideration before submitting elsewhere. In plain English, they were to have first right of refusal, within a certain length of time, before she could submit to other publishing houses.

The idea they wanted more from her sent Rachael's emotions soaring. She read again. DeBaer smiled and nodded his approval that she sign the addendum. With shaking hand, she accepted a pen and signed at the bottom.

Immediately, Geri Daniels rose from her seat and went to stand below the large wall poster. DeBaer rose and nudged Rachael to do the same. A photographer positioned himself as Rachael and DeBaer took positions of either side of Ms. Daniels.

"In view of the fact that you've consented to give us a total of two additional stories—that makes six all together," Geri Daniels said, "we look forward to an even longer and mutually profitable relationship." People clapped. "We are rushing to publish this hot new novel, your *Sea Cliff.*"

Another round of applause and cheering sounded throughout the room.

Ms. Daniels continued. "Therefore, the board has voted to present you with a sizable advance, which will run against your royalties." She handed Rachael an envelope. Both held onto an edge for photos to be taken.

"Thank you," Rachael managed to say, smiling proudly, unable to hide her emotions. Tears filled her eyes. She glanced at Richie for assurance.

"Speech. Speech," someone called out.

"Go ahead." DeBaer prompted quietly. "They're good people."

Rachael discreetly wiped at tears. "Thank you," she said, looking at others around the room. "I-I'm not sure what to say. I'm having difficulty believing this is me standing here." They laughed while she paused. "I hope I can feel for all my books, what I feel for *Sea Cliff*."

"Here, here," someone called out.

"Thank you, all of you. You don't know what this means to me. I appreciate that Romantique has faith in me. I appreciate everything you have done on my behalf. Thank you."

The conference room doors were thrown open and the rest of the office staff joined in. A bar was opened at the side of the room and the celebration began.

Rachael hugged Richie. "You knew."

"Of course. Do you know what this means?"

"I'm trying to absorb it."

"They're going to republish your first two books."

People wanted to hug her or shake hands and extend their congratulations. The party lasted another half hour. Then some began drifting back to their work places.

"Well, it's over," Richie said. "You should say your goodbye to Geri before heading home."

What would she have done without Richie Barron. He was a savior and a blessing when their schedules were the tightest. He had been her coach in a city with a people and a lifestyle as foreign as a country anywhere else on the globe. How would she ever show her appreciation?

Chapter 54

"*Que te pase, mi'ja?*" Rosa asked one morning. "More than two months pass since *Nueva York.*"

"Nothing's going on, Rosa." Rachael said, unable to produce a smile.

"Something different with you, supposed to be happy, have three books published. Another one soon and many more. *Que maravilloso.*"

Instead, Rachael became retracted and morose. Having immediately started writing a new story, she occupied herself at the computer as many hours as ever, except to make the choice of eating or fainting from hunger. She no longer became rejuvenated by exercising and did little. Meditation became an escape. A few simple necessary errands were delegated to Rosa or delayed as long possible. She saw no one.

Rosa tried to cheer her by calling her attention to the television every time she saw one of the Knight Homes commercials. Rachael realized she should join Rosa and watch at least the commercial in which Rosa appeared. Rosa was a changed person for having been in front of a camera. She felt special and had a higher opinion of herself. Although she wished she could have had time beforehand, Rosa went on a diet and lost over fifteen pounds from her stomach and hips. She was a new woman.

Why should Rachael now destroy the good created by passing the commercials off as something too trivial to bother with?

One day she found Rosa standing in front of the family room television, dust rag and furniture polish in hand, hoping to see herself on the screen again. Rachael went in to join her. "Now you can say you're an actress, Rosa."

"Ah, senorita. Soon the commercial comes. Stay, please. Maybe it's mine."

They watched Rosa gracefully serving dinner, her chin held forward and dignified. The camera panned to the rest of the seated guests. Rachael was reminded this was the clip where Matthew participated. She watched him sitting beside her as she spoke her line. At the time of filming, his arm rested across the back of her chair and he smiled warmly at her. Because of her pretense at that moment, they represented a divine couple.

Rachael moaned and ran downstairs. Rosa followed and peeked in to find her sitting on the bed sobbing.

"*Aye, que te pase, otra vez?*"

Rachael turned away.

"Senorita, something happened you no feel so good about. I know you no see Senior Matt, Now you cry. Why you no go to him? Patch up."

Rachael needed to talk to someone. The pain was too much to bear. "You don't know what he did, Rosa."

"*Que?*" she asked, tucking her chin in disbelief.

"The night of the New Year's party? He took someone into the guest quarters and… and… had sex with her."

Rosa gasped and nearly choked. "*Dios mio.* Not Senior Matt." She sat down on the bed beside Rachael putting her arm around Rachael's shoulder.

"Yes, it's true."

"He was cooking outside. Maybe you wrong."

"It was after midnight. He told someone his head hurt and he was going to lay down." Rachael whimpered. "When I went to see how he was, the guest house door was locked. I saw his shadow on the curtains. He was on top of someone on the bed, with her legs in the air… and they were… moving. They were… doing it."

"At what time this?"

"I don't know," Rachael said, whimpering, "Twelve-thirty, or a little later."

"No, Senorita!" Rosa said. She stood suddenly. "This time, you make big mistake."

"Rosa, I know what I saw."

"*Si, si.* You saw what you see. Two people." She shook her head. "You no see Senior Matt."

"I did… I did!"

"Rachael, let me tell you this." Her finger pointing in the air asked for silence while she spoke. "Senior Matt is with me in the kitchen after the Old Lang Sign—"

"*Auld Lang Syne.*"

"*Si*, whatever." She waved a hand in the air impatiently. "After singing and the kissing, he was with me till one o'clock *pasado.*"

"Don't protect him, Rosa."

"No protect."

"I know you like him and you want to see us toget—"

"No protect. You no see him on the curtain. That not his way." Rosa was bold, adamant. "Senior Matt can have woman anytime. He don't do this here. Senior Matt not the hurting kind. He no do this to people, not to you."

Rachael was consumed by anger. She stood quickly and pranced to the windows, turning abruptly, staring Rosa straight in the eyes. "He dated a girl named Britt even after we were going together. I think that's who was in the room with him. I saw her—"

"Believe me, you no see—"

"Don't you tell me what I may or may not have seen. I'm not blind. His foreman told me he went to lay down, and it was right after Britt headed in that direction too."

"Aye, Dios. Senior Matt is with me in the kitchen. He say head hurts. I offer cup of tea. He put his feet in the chair and say to me to rub his head. He tells me how to do pressure therapy on his shoulder and neck. He has much pain. All he talks is you, always you."

"Rosa, please…" Rosa had stuck her nose in where it didn't belong.

Rosa knew she had gotten too angry, and her expression said she anticipated repercussions. Her look said she didn't care. "I'm sorry, Senorita. I go now. This not my business." She hurried out of the room. "I sorry for you."

For weeks, each time she came to do her cleaning, Rosa avoided Rachael. When she needed to work in the master bedroom, she entered through the outside doorway to keep from crossing through the office where Rachael sat at her computer. Rachael would be sitting idly at her desk staring blankly out the window, and noticing out the corner of her eye that Rosa sneaked glances at her from inside the bedroom doorway.

Once Rosa offered sweetly, "Senorita, why you no telephone him, please say you make mistake. He is good man, would understand."

Rachael was good at protecting herself. From childhood, cowering became one of the very best things she learned to do.

Weeks passed. Rachael's new book was progressing well enough. She tacked a large note in bold print on her bulletin board reminding herself to thoroughly edit her current work when she was in better spirits. During the writing of *Sea Cliff*, when she was happy, she wrote enlightening passages. When she was despondent, even that was woven into appropriate story scenes. Whatever her moods may have projected, she was able to utilize. As she wrote her way deeply into the story line of her next book, she couldn't help wonder if her present state of depression might be all she was committing to print. Finally, one day, she couldn't write anymore. Yet, this book was promised, and the next one. She was obligated to finish. Her publisher waited, but her ambition and drive left her. She was simply unable to begin again.

One day the phone rang. With cell phone in hand, Rosa found her in a deck chair where she retreated to get away from even the phone.

"It's *Nueva York*," Rosa said, handing her the phone.

She accepted it. "Richie? How are you? It's good to hear your voice," Rachael said flatly.

"I'm okay. We're fine, but you sound like you've lost your best friend. What's up?"

"I'm not doing too well with my current story. I don't seem to have it."

"You? I can't believe you have nothing to say. Have you got a delayed case of post-Big Apple blues?"

"I guess I'm feeling kind of down after the excitement of being there."

"That was quite a while ago. Are you sure that's it?"

"Well, no. I've always been able to write, no matter what. Recently, I learned about something that happened a while back and I've been depressed ever since."

"That's too bad. Maybe I can tell you something to cheer you. Are you ready for this?"

"What is it?"

"I'm not sure if I'm supposed to tell you this. You're going to be hearing from your agent real soon."

"I am?"

"Yes. I heard a rumor that *Sea Cliff*'s coming out in September".

Rachael's heart began pounding. "Are you sure?"

"Well, that's the word, and from reliable sources."

"That is good news. I can't wait to see something I've written in print again."

"There's another reason I called. We're coming to California for a vacation. I got a big bonus for the work I did for you. My wife would like a vacation before the baby arrives. It's good timing. I'm on leave from writing because I've landed a part in a new play."

"That's wonderful. Things are going great for you."

"Yeah, we thought we'd go to Los Angeles. I'm hoping some of the creative vibes down there will rub off," he said. "I got some positive feedback on a script that popped out of my head after I finished working with you. Anyway, I want to poke around and see if I can look up some people in the industry. We're staying a week. We might stop by one night in San Francisco to visit you on our way home."

"That long a trip for one a week?"

"Yeah. It wasn't a super big bonus."

"Richie…" She paused, gathering her thoughts. "I've had a brainstorm."

"I don't doubt that."

"If you have the time, stay a second week, here in San Francisco."

"Oh, no. Even L.A. is a stretch for us."

"No problem. Stay here, in my house."

"Wha-at? That would be a total imposition."

"No, it's not. My brainstorm is that you could jump start me back into this story I'm working on. Stay for a week. I won't take all your time. Then you'll be able to see some of the Bay Area too."

"It's out of the question. We're bringing our son, you know."

"You don't understand, Richie. I have a spare bedroom and a convertible family room. And I have a super guest unit that's just been refurbished. You'd be the first to use it. I don't rent it. It's for special occasions like this. The guest unit has one bedroom. It's private and separate from this main house. Please, Richie, please."

"I'll have to ask Carrie."

"Are you home? Ask her."

"I'm home. She's not. Call you back?"

"Yes, but don't say no."

When Richie called back, their vacation was settled. His wife was thrilled for a longer time away from New York. She hadn't been outside of the state for over four years.

Rachael emailed him the first draft of the current novel which he would mark up before arrival in San Francisco.

The following Monday, Dennis DeBaer sent a fax confirming that *Sea Cliff* was to be released around the middle of September. Someone from his public relations department would be contacting her in the next few days to discuss autographing sessions at some of the Bay Area bookstores. He would be sending several cases of advance copies and suggested she make the circuit of as many book stores as possible promoting her latest effort. Actual autographing sessions were to be referred directly back to the public relations representative at his office. Arrangements were being finalized for a live interview on the morning talk show, *Heart of The Bay*, which would air to coincide with release of the book in the Bay Area.

"This is big," she said aloud. "This is big!"

In the past, they accepted her little stories and published without much contact after signing the contract online. There was no reading of galley proofs, nor dust jacket, nor cover art, no close contact every step of the way. She should have known when these things were requested of her in New York, this time would be different. She had dreamed about autographing sessions and talking to others about her books. Now, a live talk show too?

Inspired beyond her wildest imagination, even before Richie and his family arrived, she was diligently back at her computer doing the right thing.

Chapter 55

Summer was passing. Richie, Carrie, and Richie, Jr. spent a productive yet relaxing week and left. They were a congruent family and Rachael struggled to hide her envy. They were yet another example of togetherness, the way Rachael knew family could be, the family she could only see in others or conjure in her fiction.

Nearly finished with her current book, she was scheduled for four autographing sessions and the live talk show taping in the month of September. Her professional life had taken a turn for the better, much better. But her emotions were in a state of disaster. Beneath the required façade of happiness, all else was gloomy.

When she allowed herself to think about the grave error she made concerning Matthew, what presented was that any effort of salvaging the relationship was already too late. Too much time had passed. Calling him after so long would be futile. The very eligible Matthew Cameron Knight probably found someone else. He longed for an intimate relationship, and for a son. She hadn't been ready to provide either. At least not until she was sure he understood everything from her perspective.

When he came to mind, she would force the memories away. Suppressing was much easier. Somehow, she'd get over him, maybe find someone else. She began thinking again about her father, and blaming him for her misery. She wondered if other parents and children ever talked about such things, or if they blindly bumbled their way along and alone through life's experiences. Was humanity degenerating into a state of neuroses from their so-called lives?

Her father told her never to let a man do things to her. He had warned about not getting intimate before marriage. Who was the right man? How would she know? According to her father, if a guy like Matthew had been serious, he'd have proposed marriage. Would she ever be lucky enough to enjoy a relationship that went that far? What was the missing link?

After each bout of struggling with questions that provided no answers, she would suppress her thoughts and immerse herself with plans for upcoming events, though the questions kept returning. Each time they puzzled her, she became more passive, more saddened.

In an effort to stay connected, she began calling friends she hadn't seen in months, to say hello, or to arrange to meet them for lunch. She tried talking with Brandon on the phone. His new answering machine was more foreboding than Matthew's had been. One day, she and Tina went on a shopping spree. While Rachael dressed well, she seldom maintained closets full of clothes. Now she shopped for the upcoming public appearances as if she were trying to change her image. She bought trendy clothes, shoes and bags, a full wardrobe of unmentionables, and even a few new nightgowns and pajamas. She hadn't been able to again wear that white nightgown Matthew had touched and donated it to the Salvation Army Thrift store.

When the two returned from shopping, Rachael went through her closets and pulled everything off hangers she no longer wanted. Especially the ones she wore with Matthew.

"What's gotten into you, Rach? Is it off with the old, on with the new?"

"I'm going back to natural fibers. Getting real, I guess."

"All at once?"

Rachael's clothes were expensive. She had no qualms about offering some to her friend.

Tina selected a few pieces from the pile on the bed and the rest would go to Rosa who would donate them to a charity in the Mission District where she lived.

Regardless of activity, nothing could keep the thoughts from rolling in at a time when Rachael needed to be quiet and contemplative. Nothing was solved, merely glossed over. She was living her days and falling asleep each night with a tight stuck feeling in her throat. For the first time in a very long time, loneliness was about to get the best of her.

Two days later, taping her interview for Heart of The Bay was about to begin. A select group holding tickets for the live filming were supplied with copies of *Sea Cliff* to read beforehand. They were told they would be required to provide audience participation after its author was interviewed. Actors were planted in the audience to ask questions, Rachael being forewarned, in case no one spoke up.

Rachael managed her life alone. However, this was one event she was not strong enough to tackle by herself. Rosa accompanied her and didn't have to be asked twice. Not wanting to be embarrassed if the book didn't sell well, Rachael avoided spending time at Tina's Italian among neighborhood acquaintances.

"Why you think the publisher spend much money on advertising?" Rosa asked.

"They have to," Rachael said. "They do their share. Besides, I paid to arrange a lot of my own signings. It's a shared responsibility."

"No, senorita, they pay because you write good story."

Rachael smiled. Rosa had not read her story, in fact, none of them. Yet, she had undeniable faith that Rachael's efforts would prevail. While waiting off set, Rachael began to pace.

"*Chica*, calm you down."

"I'm nervous. I don't know why we have to do this. Why couldn't we advertise in the book clubs and magazines and things like that?"

"Senorita, you no mess up now. You have career success. You come long way with this. It's your dream." She paused to take a breath. "The first books maybe come good again because of this one. This one big. Keep together. Don't blow the last minute."

Again, Rachael smiled. Rosa, her cleaning lady, had always been more than that. She was a trusted confidant. For a moment, Rachael despised having to think about Rosa as her maid. Rosa's composure was enviable. Then someone signaled time to begin and Rosa wasn't the one being interviewed.

"Keep your chin up, proud, like when filming commercials," Rosa said as Rachael walked away.

As expected, response to the book by this select group was mixed. With the wide range of responses, most agreed the book was going to cause a stir.

After the taping, Rachael and Rosa were shown to an alcove with a table and chairs near the building exit. Everyone, including those who voiced strong objections about the book, passed through for an autograph.

The show would air October 3rd, after *Sea Cliff* had been on the racks a couple of weeks.

Chapter 56

Each time Rachael happened to be anywhere books were being sold, she would poke her head in to see if hers was available. Several of the larger chain stores where she was scheduled for autograph sessions displayed a colorful banner atop the racks where *Sea Cliff* was being exhibited. The racks were usually in a prominent location inside the front doors, in windows, or on the check-out counters. The banners were copies of the one at the party in New York. On additional signs, emblazoned with large artistic letters, the words beckoned:

SEA CLIFF
The very best of
RACHAEL DAYE

After one autographing session, the day seemed unbelievably long. Her hand was cramped and ached. She collapsed onto the bed lying spread eagle on her back. Her mind drifted back over the day's events, remembering those buying her book and others eagerly waiting in line for her signature. One woman admitted she didn't know anything about the book, but since Rachael was signing, she had to have one too. Her insinuation didn't matter. What mattered was that Rachael wanted this novel to be a success, a huge success. She wanted sales to last, if not sky-rocket, instead of falling off quickly like her other books a few years earlier.

Now she wished there could have been someone close with whom to share the moment, this time of turning away from the clamor and coming home to sanctuary; an empty room. The entire house seemed eerie and sadness came slowly creeping. In a few moments, she intended to move to her meditation corner and give thanks to the powers that be. Instead, she fell asleep, fully clothed, where she lay.

After some time, she woke, feeling groggy and depleted. The day was gone. A glorious full moon hung in the sky. She turned out the room light and sat on the window cushions on the floor staring out from darkness. Moonlight illuminated patches of fog slipping over the shimmering water below, hiding, then exposing the towers of the Golden Gate Bridge as the drifts passed on.

The world outside was quiet and tranquil. What was she supposed to do now that she longed to talk to someone. She didn't know the hour, didn't know how long she slept. It was probably too late to call anyone. She was alone, and for the first time in her life, truly wished she wasn't.

Under any other circumstances, what came next would be to go to her computer and industriously resume writing. Yet, now, the idea repulsed her. She should be celebrating. She should be laughing and sharing her good fortune. An incredible array of people came to the autographing sessions. More were sure to come in the future. Yet, she'd come home alone.

Looking across The Bay to the lights of the Marin Headlands, she wondered if Mona was aware her book was published. Mona probably wouldn't call her even if she knew. Though she held mild apprehension about her son, she wasn't one to stick her nose unnecessarily into his life. Her calling would seem to be simply satisfying her own curiosity about Matthew's relationships. She and Mona would see each other again someday under different circumstances.

Tears began streaming down Rachael's face. She wondered why everything couldn't have worked out so Matthew could be with her to share this moment. How could she have made such a disastrous mistake? In trying to keep herself from being hurt by a man, she instead, brought hurt upon herself in the process. More than that, she hurt the man who genuinely cared for her.

"It's your fault, Dad," she said, crying. "You taught me to be this way. How could you do this to me? You taught me the wrong ways." She covered her face with her hands and wept, then was silent again.

"Why couldn't you tell me how to make a relationship work? Always warning, 'Don't do this! Don't do that!' Why didn't you tell me the right way to allow a man into my life?" She doubling over onto the cushions. She wept bitterly again, for loneliness and failure, and for loss of Matthew, the one man who cared about her. The only man she loved, even more than two-timing Rodney in high school. There was no comparison.

After a while, she straightened and sat motionless looking out the window. She believed in and followed the guidelines her father demanded of her. She had been filled with fear of him, and went on trying to live up to his expectations in order not to be punished or hurt again.

"Even from the grave, you have a hold on me. Why can't you let go?" she asked, screaming.

Then swiftly as a searing tide, a revelation swept through her mind. The unceasing flow of thoughts drastically reversed like a movie projector suddenly thrown in reverse.

"You're dead!" she said. "You can't hurt me anymore. You're six feet under!" Her breath came out in a gust. "You can't yell at me. You can't strike me again. You can't make me do anything." She exhaled a deep healing breath. "You'll never be able to pun-ish me again. You're six feet under." Both fists lifted. She cried hysterically. This time, the tears were for freedom. "You can't control me anymore. You're dead!"

Not caring to stop the onslaught of tears, she wept bitterly. When she finally calmed, she spoke into the night with quiet determination.

"You listen to me, Dad. I know you can hear me in Spirit, so listen. I'm not following your way anymore. From now on, I'm on my own. If I make mistakes, they're mine, not yours. In the future, how deeply I might suffer from my mistakes, that's my punishment. Not the kind you doled out." She paused, pressed her hands flat together and brought her fingertips to her lips. "At last, I'm free to be me." Choking on tears, she screamed it again. "I'm free to be me!"

For the longest time, there was silence as she slipped into a reverie, carrying the point home within.

The flood of tears purged her demons. Later, she soaked in the tub, refilling when the water cooled. She lathered then scrubbed her entire body with a loofah, concentrating on the old being washed away. After that, she took a hot steamy shower and shampooed her hair. Emerging, she felt renewed. A strange new calm pervaded. "I'm free to be me," she kept saying.

After blow drying her hair, she slipped into one of her new nightgowns with thin straps and a diagonal ruffle accentuated the bodice. Opaque pearly swirls fell to the floor on light billowy folds, carrying the slightest hint of lavenders and pinks.

Surprisingly, she caught herself wondering how much time might pass before she met someone new. She would hide away no longer, but enjoy the man's presence. Who knew where their friendship would lead? Maybe Greta had been banished along with her father. Next time, she intended to manage things a whole lot differently. That is, the next time she met a decent guy. A guy like Matthew.

She frowned, needing to stop comparing. How could she even think about meeting anyone new? Getting over Matthew would take time. She had lost him. That didn't mean she would try to smother the hurt with a next guy who paid her some attention. She'd be patient. Someday love would find her again. In the mean time, as long as Matthew came to mind, she needed to heal his memory.

Chapter 57

Absolute silence filled the house and she drifted into deep sleep. A sudden noise roused her with senses on high alert. A rustling noise, as if something was dropped to the floor in the office, just outside the bedroom door. The sound was similar to Rosa's nylon garment bag. Once in a while, when she anticipated a lot of extra chores, she would arrive the night before to get an early start the next morning. Why was she arriving so late? Why would she leave her bag in the office? Had someone else gotten into the house? A lot of people could have gotten hold of keys.

Rachael started to rise as a light tapping on the closed pocket door sounded. Her nerves went on high alert. As she passed the corner of the bed she grabbed a flashlight from a shelf in the closet. She needed a weapon, just in case.

The tapping sounded again.

She opened the door slowly expecting to see Rosa, though feeling great uncertainty.

"Matthew!"

She jumped backwards, dropping the flashlight. Her mouth hung open. Their eyes locked.

He merely stood there in the light of the full moon filtering in through the windows. His eyes caught the light and threw off golden sparks, but he looked tired and haggard. One elbow leaned against the door jam, the opposite hand turned backwards behind his hip. He'd even remembered to remove his shoes. A flicker in his stare said he was seeing the rest of her exposed as she stood there in her flimsy nightgown.

She felt paralyzed. Her knees began to weaken. She crossed her arms over her chest. He stood there drinking her in with his eyes.

Why had he come? She had ended her book with Melissa and Hunter not seeing each other for a very long time. Now seeing Matthew at her door was unimaginable. At her bedroom door, no less. How dare he be so bold as to keep a set of keys and sneak in?

Slowly, he began to smile, seeming totally pleased with himself.

As she continued to tremble, she gestured, trying to ask him to wait till she could get a robe. All she could do was feebly lift a hand as if to tell him to stay where he was.

His stare was intense, dead serious, absorbing her total reaction. Certainly, he couldn't be perceiving what she was feeling. The confusion and fear, the embarrassment, and even the flicker of relief. But he always read her. His hesitating smile said he knew he had been right to come.

Her feelings for him were there and must have rushed to her face. He aptly read them in the past and in the intensity of this moment, stood there calm, waiting, while she couldn't suppress her relief if she tried.

Then his smile disappeared. He knitted his brow, almost frowning. "It doesn't have to end like this, Rachael." His voice cracked. He raised the hand from behind his hip and waved a copy of *Sea Cliff* in the air. "It wasn't me in the guest bedroom. Have you learned that yet? It wasn't me."

She nodded stiffly.

"I know your secrets now. I know why you always pushed me away." He paused only a second.

Rachael was lost for words. "You… you don't under—"

"Why couldn't you tell me you were saving yourself for the right man?"

His words hung heavy in the air. How could she have told him she needed to protect herself until she was sure of his intentions? How could she say she needed to be sure he wouldn't be mean like her father had been? How could she tell him she wasn't sure what a good relationship was, and that the need to protect herself created a barrier she never understood till a few hours ago?

"Rachael, the writer of words, has been unable to express herself to me." He tapped his chest with the corner of the book. "To me."

Now she needed to tell him nothing mattered anymore. She wanted to throw herself into his arms and surrender with wild abandon, yet, some shred of moral fiber deep inside tugged at her conscience and wouldn't let her to move. Her feelings surely showed on her face. He picked up his bag and stepped into the room, sliding the pocket door behind him, closing out the world.

"All this time you've been evading me. You've either kept me dangling or pushed me away, and it's happened long enough. This story says it all." He waved the book in the air again. "This is about us. You've manipulated the story line so well, no one except you and me would know it's about us."

All she could do was stand there and face the truth.

"It doesn't have to end the way you wrote it." He shook the book in the air yet again. "I thought you pushed me away to finish this damned book, or because you were paranoid about being hurt again." He shook his head gently from side to side. "Angel," he said, voice filled with emotion. "I couldn't hurt you. You must have known that. It had to be something else."

Quickly, he reached for her and pulled her close. She listened to his heart racing inside a massive chest. She breathed in his masculine smell, something she remembered and longed for and denied.

"Rachael," he said. "You've never been with a guy because your father taught you it was wrong to be in love."

Tears spilled down her face as she looked up at him.

"Did you mean everything you wrote in this book? That you wanted to tell me, but didn't know how to talk about sex?"

"I wanted it all," she said, whispering. "I didn't want you to walk away after we…"

"Do you love me, Rachael?"

Every facade created for her own protection was being stripped away. She felt a pang of guilt at having been found out. Blinking back tears, she looked searchingly into his eyes. If he wanted to, he could take her now and make up for all the teasing, the wanting and suffering. Then he might simply leave. She doubted she was strong enough to prevent anything from happening. She closed her eyes and prayed for a sign. "Matthew…," was all she could say.

He pulled away and looked deep into her eyes. "I've been a man obsessed. I went to Hawaii to forget you. My feelings for you are incomparable. This whole thing's been driving me insane. You haunted me even in Hawaii. I went to a concession stand to get something to read on the beach and found your picture and this book staring back at me from the rack. Rachael Daye!"

"You read it?" she asked, whispering and swallowing hard.

"Every word. Then drove myself crazy trying to decide whether or not to come back."

She hadn't expected him to read the book. She resigned herself to picking up the pieces of her life and going on without him. He had read her story and returned. His unexpected appearance meant one thing. Her heart quickened.

Suddenly, he leaned down and kissed her. First gently, with his hand moving smoothly across her back, pulling her tightly to him. His tongue found hers and his kiss became demanding and forceful. Finally, he hesitated.

"I'm back now, and I'm not going to let you push me away again." The inflection in his voice hinted at more. "I love you, Rachael."

She felt his warm breath on her ear and neck and flowing through her hair.

"You're mine." His voice rang with tones of the proud victor claiming his reward. Her breath quivered uncontrollably. Chills ran unchecked up and down her body. His fingertips responded to them.

"You're mine," he said again. "And tonight, I'm going to love you completely."

The implication of his statement took her by surprise.

"Matthew, please," she said, cautioning, but powerless to resist. She wanted him, more than anything, and had to face the fact she was about to have her wish. Her shiver was a clue he didn't have to verify. Her excitement was mounting. She remained apprehensive knowing he was intuiting her every response. "Can't we talk? I thought you had problems…"

"Not anymore, and I'm not going to let your bad memories keep us from being happy together. Your father…" He shook his head slowly.

"My father's dead now," she said quietly.

He held her at arm's length, absorbing her words. His eyes said he knew what she meant. Suddenly, he threw the book to the floor sending it skittering across the carpet. It came to rest at the cushions by the window, the volume laying open with some of its pages gently flapping back and forth.

Quickly, he scooped her up in his arms, and carried her toward the bed.

"No, Matthew. Not like this," she said. "It's too fast!" Still, she couldn't resist. There would be no getting away, no more excuses. Having no time to think was not the way she would have liked this moment to happen. He wasn't going to allow her indecision to influence him any longer, nor allow her to talk herself out of the moment. Not since she wanted him probably as much and he knew it.

Pausing at the side of the bed, he kissed her full and hard on her mouth until she struggled. She pushed frantically against his chest. He relaxed somewhat. She wouldn't resist any longer than it took to show him she needed to breathe. She began returning his kiss, slowly at first, curiously.

"You're mine, Rachael," he said, whispering against her lips. "No one will ever hurt you again."

Waves of relief washed over her. She needed to hear him say those words to help erase her fears. She wanted Matthew. She loved him and even if he climbed out of bed later and walked away as punishment, at least she allowed herself to show him her love.

He lifted a knee onto the bed, bending over to lay her gently down, then moved back a bit to view her fully. He fumbled with the buttons on his shirt and finally peeled it off over his head and flung it aside.

Rachael had admired his bare chest inside his tank tees and by her pool. His broad shoulders and muscular torso looming naked over her now made her feel small and frail. Not as a child, but as a mature woman longing to be possessed by her powerful man.

He was wearing shorts over longer stretch cotton bike shorts. Kicking off his shoes, he dropped the outer shorts to the floor, exposing anatomy that bulged from inside the bike pants. He laid down beside her and kissed her again.

"I love you with all my heart, Rachael," he said, whispering into her ear.

Rachael's heart kept pounding, as if about to jump out of her mouth. His constant admission of his love was the answer to her hopes. "Yes, Matthew, yes. Love me always."

"You don't know how I've suffered wanting to make love to you."

Laying side by side, he watched his hand slide over her covered breasts, down over her flat belly, over her thighs and between. He moaned in satisfaction.

A groan shook loose from her throat as her libido sent messages. His hand retraced its way back up her body, bringing the gown up with it. Her nipples were now painfully rigid. Her nerves shot hot streaks of lightning to every part of her body. He kissed her neck lightly, seeking the frantic pulse beneath her soft skin. He nibbled her ear and squeezed the lobe between his lips and followed the outer edge with the tip of his tongue, all the while massaging her muscular breasts. She gurgled with breath becoming deeper and more labored. Her fingertips dug into his skin.

Quickly, he lifted her and eased the gown over her head and she sat there stark naked with a man for the first time in her life. She trembled in anticipation while expelling quivering breaths. Her breasts stood straight out from her rib cage, with dark, hard nipples protruding toward him. Her brassy hair fell over her shoulders and down toward her breasts. She sat with legs tucked under her, but the top of the curly camarillo colored mat between her legs couldn't be hidden.

She felt awkward and pulled the edge of the sheet up to cover her front. As quickly, he snapped the sheet from her hand sending it to the foot of the bed. His quick look of warning told her she dare not deprive him further.

He turned and sat on the edge of the bed and slipped out of the bike shorts, then pulled the sheet up as they lay back. She's never been in bed with a man, never made love, and he knew he'd have to take his time with her and she was thankful.

She trembled frantically. He undulated against her, his erection pressing, demanding, hot against her thigh. His lips again searched for her mouth and pushed it open. His tongue shot inside seeking every crevice. She hesitated, then gently pushed her tongue up to meet his.

327

In the excitement, she gasped for breath. Her conscience, cautioned though her body demanded something else.

"Matthew," she said, whispering. "You know much more than me."

"Trust me," he said, whispering softly.

His strong hands ran smoothly over her body, fingertips tantalizing sensitive areas. Her skin tingled.

"I can't." She stiffened and tried to draw away from him. He was being too rough! "I don't understand."

"You don't have to," he said, whispering and searching her eyes. "Give yourself, Angel."

Her desire had not stopped. Her libido raged. She pressed her body against his. "Be gentle," she said, her body not aware of any caution.

"Yes," he managed to say.

Giving in to desire, she found his mouth and probed with her tongue and welcomed his against hers. When she could get a breath, she panted. Her head reeled. She was losing control. She turned away.

"Don't stop, Angel. Let go. Let it happen." His mouth sought hers again.

She knew what was about to happen and was powerless to stop. Resistance vanished. Her passion exploded. She concentrated on the strange new feelings, being both frightened and eager. He rolled her onto her back and parted her knees and lowered himself in between. She was vaguely aware of clawing at him. He groaned savagely. Her submitting was turning him into a man possessed.

She dug her fingertips into his shoulders. "Push, Matthew. Push!" she said, begging with a new lusty whisper.

"Not all at once," he said in a voice that sounded more like he'd like to have her that way.

Her fire was raging out of control "Push me… have me." She braced her feet to the bed and pushed with her arms, arching her entire body toward him.

Without hesitation, he shifted his weight to his knees. His muscles tightened and quivered under her fingertips. With a labored groan, he pushed, tearing forcefully through her last shred of resistance.

She yelped as a sharp pain cut through her nervous system. Tears sprang from her eyes and ran down her temples into her hair.

"Easy, Angel. It won't hurt like that again." He remained still, kissing her face, her eyes, and licking tears from her temples. "Love me, Rachael," he said, barely managing a whisper.

She had abandoned all control. She was beginning to understand. She was incredibly full of him. Concentrating on his movements and listening to his breath and the sounds he emitted, taught her what passion was. She visualized him inside of her. As her thoughts shifted back to her own body, her sensations intensified. She had yearned to submit to him. She heard the animal sounds of her own passion, as his thrusts rocked her body in time with his.

He lifted above her and watched her face, surely seeing her pain and pleasure. Beads of perspiration flew from the ends of his matted hair, his entire body thrusting, again and again.

Her fire spread, threatening to consume her. He continued without let up, heightening her pleasure, and his. She was wild in her excitement, gasping for breath and gouging at his hips. She heard her own guttural sounds as the intensity of her orgasm overtook her and she quaked with heat. Then his body jolted with spasms that filled her to overflowing with his hot liquid love.

Chapter 58

"Rachael Connor. Rachael Daye. Rachael Angeline Knight."

She began to awaken and heard his teasing voice as if through a dream. "Hmmm...?"

"Angel, wake up." He shook her gently. "Wake up."

"What...?"

"Wake up."

Rousing, first the smell of the sheets caught her attention. Was that the smell of sex? She opened her eyes and found him dressed and groomed. Panic gripped her. She reached for him. Was that all he came for, and now they were finished? "You're leaving?"

"Are you kidding? Angel, we're not going to be apart ever again. You need to take a shower so we can get out of here."

She breathed a sigh of relief. "Out of here. Where are we going? It's not even daylight."

"To Reno," he said with a smile.

"Reno... why?"

He leaned over her. "We're going to be married, Angel. Now."

She stared up at him wide eyed. He waited patiently. She always dreamed of having a special wedding ceremony, not the traditional kind, but one that she and her betrothed might have planned together. She wanted to be married. She wanted

Matthew and no one else. Now she could have exactly that, but Reno? "I thought when I got married, it would be—"

"We will have a formal ceremony later, whenever you want. I'd like that, too."

"Then why don't we wait?"

"Not a chance."

"On what? Separating again? It wouldn't be me—"

"Not that." He lifted her to a sitting position, sat beside her, and kissed her softly, then held her close. "You've broken through the garbage that's been heaped on you. You've renounced your father's hold on you. In case there are any of his old tapes playing in your sweet head, I don't want you to build up any guilt over what we've just done."

"I have no guilt. We couldn't have been close if I thought—"

"You don't know that, Angel. Childhood programming is a powerful thing. You've evidently been taught sex without marriage is a horrible sin." She nodded, agreeing. "I'm not taking a chance something like this can fester in your subconscious and cause you to resent me later if we put off getting married."

"I wouldn't."

"Maybe not. You do love me, don't you? You've never said so."

"Yes, Matthew, I love you." They kissed passionately. "I love you," she said, whispering against his lips.

She fell backwards onto the bed and he fell on top of her as their passion exploded. Then suddenly, he pulled away.

"Stop, Angel. If you don't let me up, we won't get out of here. Three times the first night—"

"Four," she said, teasing.

"Will you go take a shower?" he said, laughing. "Rosa will be here pretty soon."

"That's right, and she may faint at finding you in my bed."

"Oh, yeah?" he said, laughing. "Wait till she gets a look at those sheets."

Later, they arrived at Union Square which was nowhere near freeway access to the Bay Bridge. Downtown traffic was hectic, starting and stopping, with many dodging cable cars and pedestrians.

"Whatever are we doing here?"

"I'm test driving your car," he said, being silly. "In the time we've known each other, this is the first time you let me drive this little green machine."

"C'mon, why are we here?"

"Another one of my surprises for you, Angel," he said, smiling mysteriously.

They parked underground at Union Square and sauntered up to Post Street with their arms around each other's waist, peering into shop windows. Then he stopped.

"A friend of mine owns this shop. Actually, I met him several years back at the gym. Dad and I remodeled this store for him before he opened for business."

They stopped in front of one of those small expensive jewelry boutiques bordering Union Square through which doors the most well heeled set foot.

"Are we doing what I think we're doing?"

"You got it. Can't get married without a ring."

"They're not open," she said, looking into the empty window. "It's barely daylight."

He motioned her toward the front doorway. "The very best for you, Mrs. Knight." Then he crooned, smug and well pleased, changing the words in the Cole Porter song. "Knight and Da-a-aye… you are the one. Only you beneath the moon or under the sun…" He smiled constantly. "I called John while you were in the shower. He owes me a favor. He's been coming in early to do pre-season inventory anyway." Matthew used a car key to tap on the glass door.

Rachael met John Jessup who locked the door after them and reset the alarm. Bypassing empty store front display cases, they entered a rear showroom and were shown to seats in front of a massive custom built desk. A large tray of expensive looking jewelry lay open where he had been doing inventory.

John disappeared into the walk-in vault which stood wide-open, leaving the entire tray of easily a few hundred thousand dollars worth of valuables sitting in front of them. John's walking away without a care told Rachael an awful lot about Matthew and what, at least, this friend thought of him. She felt a momentary lapse of disbelief that someone like Matthew happened into her life. Shaking her head and staring at the jewels under the light, the sparkle seemed confirmation everything was true.

Soon, John returned with a large tray full of tiny pastel colored velvet boxes. He began opening them, exposing some of the most exquisite jewels Rachael had ever seen. Diamonds, rubies, sapphires and emeralds of all shapes and sizes, twinkled up at her under the desk lamp.

"Many of these custom pieces aren't displayed out front," John said.

Various stones were set in platinum, white, or yellow gold. Rachael looked doubtful. A large Marquis sat in a white gold setting with the wedding band and guard ring each containing two large round diamonds clustered on each side the Marquis. Rachael studied the ring set, knew she would never want a Marquis, at least not a Marquis wedding ring. Somehow the ring set brought out an uneasy feeling. For sure, Matthew wouldn't want another Marquis either. She looked at other rings. "I prefer yellow gold," she said.

"Anything your heart desires," Matthew said. Opening some of the delicate velvet boxes, he smiled suddenly, then sat back waiting for her to choose.

Rachael studied the stones in 14K and 18K yellow gold. "I'm going to have trouble deciding." She didn't want to choose something and not know if Matthew wanted to pay as much. She remembered his loss of thirty thousand dollars on Linda's Marquis. Maybe he wouldn't want to take a chance of losing another ring worth many thousands. She frowned suddenly. Why was she even comparing herself to Linda in the first place? That should have no bearing on what she chose. She vowed never to compare herself to anyone again. Matthew was marrying her, not Linda.

She studied some sets with the least ostentatious stones and design. All the rings with smaller settings and stones looked similar. She wanted something different. She reached for a ring with a multi-carat solitaire in a Tiffany setting. It was quite a piece of ice. She studied the tall mounting, then decided it looked too garish, pretentious for her. She examined a few of the more expensive pieces, rings with one major stone surrounded by a bevy of tiny diamonds that continued down the sides of the bands. Several were enticing, but she couldn't decide.

"Check this out," Matthew said, offering a box hidden in his palm. "I would sort of like you to have this one."

She held her breath and opened the lid. Three huge round emeralds mounted in Tiffany settings atop a band in antiqued 14K gold twinkled. The matching wide wedding band and guard ring each contained large brilliant channel set emeralds over the tops. They waited as she examined the set. She realized her mouth hung open. Finally, she said, "Matthew, this must cost a fortune. Even a simple gold band would be okay."

"That's not good enough for you. Do you like these?" He didn't wait. He slipped the rings onto her finger. They were about a half size too large.

Disbelieving, she held her breath as her hand shook. Yes, she wanted them. They were stunning. Mathew chose them because he knew she loved the color green. Probably, too, because wearing them would make a definite statement about his wife. Casting a quick sideways glance, John seemed amused at her reaction.

"We'll take these," Matthew said, reaching for his checkbook. This will come out of my line of credit. You should have no problem."

"Do you have time for sizing?" John asked.

"You mean you'd do that now?"

John measured her ring size. "There isn't that much difference. Sizing won't take long."

"Wait," she said. "What about yours, Matthew? Will you wear a wedding band?"

"I'd be proud to."

Without hesitation, John returned from the vault one more time, with a small black velvet tray containing a half dozen rows of wedding bands. Matthew stared at them. He tried a few and put them back. She waited to see if he found any to his liking. "Not sure," he said.

"I'll choose yours," she said playfully. "I think this one would look smashing against your tan."

Six channel set diamonds nestled in two white gold trenches cut diagonally across the wide 14K yellow gold band. He let her slip the ring on his finger. The fit was slightly loose.

"Cut this one, too?"

"No, I don't think so. Once I start power lifting again, my hands and fingers will get thicker. I'll take it as is."

Rachael offered a credit card.

"I'll get this one, too," Matthew said, pushing her hand away.

"Not on your life."

They ate breakfast standing at a window counter in a tiny sandwich shop on the corner while waiting for her rings to be sized. The two sitting tables were either taken or got taken as soon as they were vacated. People scurried quickly, buying coffee and sweets to take to work, some gulping on the run. One well groomed young woman, wearing an expensive business suit and sitting at a window counter, quickly read page after page of a rather thick book.

"Hey," Matthew said quietly, poking at Rachael's arm with an elbow. He signaled with his eyes and Rachael looked. The woman was reading a copy of *Sea Cliff*.

Rachael's heart fluttered. "Mathe-e-ew," she said under her breath, crinkling up her nose and grinning from ear to ear.

"If she sees you, maybe she'll want you to autograph it for her."

Someone moved away from the window counter and they slid their cups closer to the woman reading. Rachael wasn't sure exactly how to strike up a conversation. She stared at the book in the woman's hand. The woman took another bite of pastry without taking her eyes away from the printed page. Out of the corner of her eye she noticed Rachael watching and looked up.

"Early morning rush," she said, showing embarrassment over her table manners. "A friend gave me this book yesterday evening and I haven't been able to get my nose out of it. I hope my food's not missing my mouth." She dabbed with a napkin.

"I've heard of that book," Rachael said. "I understand an interview with the author is going to air on Heart of The Bay next Wednesday."

"Next Wednesday? Oh, I'm gonna' be sick from work. I've got to see that show."

"Is the book that good?"

"Good? It's great. What a story. If I could write like this, I'd give up banking. I didn't know they were doing an interview. I'd have gotten tickets. I'd give anything to meet the author. I tried to write several times. It never came out like this."

"You're in banking?" Rachael asked, smiling.

"Yes. I'm a lending officer. There." She pointed to a bank building across the street. "I'm supposed to be a professional and here I sit going gah-gah over a romance novel."

"I have a friend who's looking for a business loan," Rachael said. "Do you have a card?"

"Oh, yes. My name's Phyllis Baker," she said, reaching into her jacket pocket and handing each a card.

"Well, enjoy," Rachael said, smiling as they made their excuses and left the woman to however much time she had left before heading to work.

"Why did you entice her like that?" Matthew asked when they were out of ear shot.

Rachael couldn't keep from smiling. "She hasn't put my face together with the makeover image on the back cover. When she watches the interview, she'll remember us being here. After it's over, I'm going to call her and ask if she'd like to join me at my next autographing session. She is going to be shocked."

"You little schemer."

Chapter 59

"Oh, no," he said with great disdain.

They waded across plush pink carpet inspecting the garish style decor.

"At least the art work's not bad," she said.

"To think I asked for their least ostentatious accommodations."

"Can we convince ourselves we're somewhere else?" she asked with a wry smile. "Turn up the heat and pretend to be at the beach, maybe?"

Standing in the kitchen area and looking around, he said, "There's a lot of space here. We wouldn't have to climb over the bed to get to the bathroom." He snickered. "Driving around looking for suitable place is not how I had intended for us to spend our time." He smiled deviously.

"So much pink," she said. "What about colors representing the man?"

"That's what the mirrored walls are for," he said, teasing and grinning broadly.

He came into the bedroom with some liquid refreshment from the fully stocked refrigerator. They unpacked and then freshened up. He refused to allow them to sit down to rest. If they got too cozy, they wouldn't leave the room.

The ceremony in a little chapel was short and simple, though not lacking in feeling and commitment for one another. The minister's wife was their witness. After the kiss was finished, Matthew clutched his wife tightly to himself saying, "Finally, finally."

They stayed in, ordering their meals from room service the entire week, leaving once about mid-week to have dinner elsewhere, regretfully. The end of the week arrived too soon. They had talked a lot about beginning their new life together.

On their way back to San Francisco and crossing through the East Bay, he asked, "What do you think about this? Instead of going to your place, let's head over to Mom and Dad's and surprise them."

They drove directly to Sausalito and, at long last, parked in front of the garage. They climbed out of the car and stretched and groaned from the long sitting spell. They stepped inside the doorway.

"Mom? Dad? You home?"

"Matthew? You're back from The Islands?" Mona asked from the living room. "We're in here."

"I have a surprise for you," he said, raising his voice to be heard.

They walked into the room together. Mona and Cameron looked as if they had seen a ghost. Mona rose out of her chair as if she'd sat on a needle.

Matthew wasted no time. He stepped behind Rachael, lifting her left hand in a manner on top of his so both their wedding rings faced outward. "We got married," he said proudly.

Mona and Cameron were speechless. Then Mona rushed to hug Rachael. "I'm so happy. Welcome to our family," she said joyously. "You always were a part of us."

As Rachael hugged her and looked over to Cameron, she noticed a copy of *Sea Cliff* lying on the coffee table.

Matthew walked to where his father sat. Cameron seemed hesitant, then stood slowly, shaking his son's hand, then finally embraced him. "I didn't think you two would go this far," he said.

Matthew was a little hurt by his father's words and stepped back as Cameron turned and stiffly embraced Rachael. Then they took turns looking at the rings and crying, then hugging again.

"We read your book, Rachael," Mona said finally.

"She's promoting you big time," Cameron said. "Right up front and throughout the store."

"Oh, thank you," Rachael said. "Thank you."

"This abuse thing," Cameron said suddenly. "I don't know enough about it. It scares the bejeebers out of me."

"Would you leave it alone, Cam?" Mona asked. "The kids are going to be fine." She turned again to Rachael. "You've come an awfully long way."

"And I'm a better person for it," Rachael said.

"So am I," Matthew said.

Cameron raised a dubious eyebrow.

Rachael's cell phone pulsated again. Later, when she had a moment to check messages, a brief one among many, was left in Voice Mail.

"*It's a boy. We've had our second son. October eleventh, straight up at four in the morning. We've named him Phillip Roger Barron, after his great grandfather. Carrie and Richard, Jr. send their love. Please call when you can.*"

"My ghostwriter," she said. "They've had their baby."

She was beaming. Matthew said nothing. He managed a weak smile, then turned and walked away, leaving her alone to listen to the rest of the messages.

Matthew's transition into Rachael's house at Sea Cliff was uneventful, as if he belonged there from the beginning. He walked around the rooms until he found suitable places for his few personal possessions. Most of them either went into the bookshelves or into the closet and dressing room. The actual moving in process took no more than an hour.

Remodeling of the building purchased for Mona had long been completed. Afterward, Cameron moved the construction office from Caledonia Street into half of the second floor above the book store, and none too soon. With the economy slowing, he did well to get out from under the expense of leasing a separate office.

Now they were advertising for another tenant to fill the rest of the space. The building was in a choice location in Sausalito, a town that thrived on tourism. They didn't expect the space to stay vacant long.

Rachael telephoned Phyllis, the banker. They had a good laugh. Rachael invited her to join in at an autograph party at Mona's store.

In sporadic conversation between signings, Rachael commented, "Now, if Mona could rent the space upstairs…"

"What space?" Phyllis asked. "How much?"

"About a thousand feet. Mona and Cameron are looking for a long term tenant."

"Well, surprise," Phyllis said, "I happen to know of a start-up business looking for a home."

"No kidding," Rachael said. "What type of business?"

"The business office for importers of herbal teas and assorted natural products. They're distributors. They have a warehouse. If they can find an office location soon, our bank will finance their start up costs."

After Mona and Cameron decided to speak with the potential new tenant, Mona said, "We should thank our lucky stars for the day we met Rachael. She's been a good omen for of us."

Cameron said, "We'll wait and see."

The next day Rachael received a call from Celine, her high school friend in Rio Vista. She previously sent Celine an autographed copy of *Sea Cliff*. Celine excitedly reported the whole town was reading the book and would Rachael come for a hometown autographing party?

Rachael postponed calling back immediately. She needed time to think. "Going to my hometown as something of a celebrity would seem too much like gloating," she said, confiding to Matthew. "Especially since no one cared who I was while I was growing up."

"All the more reason," Matthew said. "Strut your stuff, woman!"

"Not a good enough reason."

"Where's your self-confidence, Angel?"

"Well, being married to you," she said, smiling, "has given me a huge jolt of it. Maybe when I can do it for the sake of the invitation."

"They did invite you. That speaks for itself. Better not wait too long."

"I wouldn't want anyone to think I was snubbing them."

"Do it for a day, or one afternoon."

"Do you think we can squeeze it in?" she asked. "I mean, I've got that cross country tour coming up in less than two weeks."

"You do want to make the best seller list, don't you?"

One week later she did exactly that with Celine by her side. The whole town must have shown up. Former casual acquaintances acted like dear friends. People she barely knew in school were warm, friendly and lavished congratulations. Even newcomers to the area who knew nothing about Rachael's youthful years attended.

"See what I told you," Matthew said.

"About?"

"Those people aren't the people you thought they were."

"How do you figure?"

"The way you were raised, you perceived them to be one way or another. You didn't have a chance to learn who they were."

"Or they me."

After returning home from a hectic two week book signing tour across the country, things began to calm a bit. Matthew continued to do what came as second nature, and that was to scrutinize every square inch of the Sea Cliff house. Anything found that needed updating or repair got fixed. Other things he'd like to improve were planned and carried out. Not that much needed changing, considering he and Cameron had recently finished major refurbishing. He lived and breathed to build, remodel, or repair. Rachael wondered how he might keep himself busy once the house was free of flaws. Heaven forbid, the recession should worsen to the point where he'd have no work at all. Maybe now was the time to install the new bamboo flooring he'd mentioned more than once. It really would enhance the island decor, give the house a facelift, and a fresh start with him there.

His health was robust again and nearly back to normal. Yet, the economy was slipping deeper into recession. Many houses damaged by the earthquake languished silently as profound reminders.

A court date was set for a hearing in Matthew's case against Stage Center. He became quiet, poised, gathering tenacity. Waiting was going to affect him.

"I'm not sure my conscience is in agreement of this complicated lawsuit Taylor has launched," he said one day. "After all, I survived."

Al Taylor and his father squelched any notion of Matthew backing out.

When adjusting to their new life was too hectic, too scattered, Rosa couldn't do enough for either of them. Now she had two children to care for. She never complained. Instead, she loved them. If she knew they were staying in on Friday evenings, after her day's work, she'd leave having set the table adding candles and fresh flowers. She received a whopping raise for caring for two, and for her effort and good intention. No one was more deserving.

Rosa had her very first conversation with Brandon on the telephone. "A real piece of work," was how she described him. "I going straighten him out."

The next morning, in a tone that suggested Romantique was more than pleased, Richie reported from New York that sales of *Sea Cliff* had skyrocketed. Envy sounded on his every word. Envy that said things were not right with him.

For a while, Rachael confined her writing to hours when Matthew was not at home. Not that she was conceding anything. Her hunger for intimacy and love was being appeased in the closeness they shared, and anything else was relegated to no better than second place. Except for their meditational practices, which was the one of the strongest factors that had kept their lives entwined regardless or not they knew it.

Not until the first royalty check arrived did Rachael realize how fortunate she was. She held the check and thought about the events, the struggles, and people involved that led up to that moment. Despite the way her life began, she was coming out on top. She had so much and others had much less. She needed to give something back.

She remembered Richie Barron and his undeniable genius. He alone was responsible for her being able to meet the deadline on the second novel, which was to be published in six months. Something in his voice during that last conversation haunted her. The next day, having remembered the name of the hospital where Carrie delivered, she called and asked if there might be a balance on the account. She knew they had no insurance. Half the bill was paid and the balance was supposed to be taken care of by the time mother and baby went home. She asked for the balance owing, then paid the amount with her credit card.

"When you send the paid-in-full statement to Richard and Carrie," she said to the accounting clerk. "Please include a note saying, 'Wishing you a wonderful life - from Rachael Daye.'"

Chapter 60

Matthew stood at the sliding doors in the living room looking out. "I have an idea," he said cautiously.

"Give it up."

"We could have a small wedding sooner if we don't have to bother with a lot of plans." He looked at her hopefully. "That is, we need to come together on this."

"Right, no huge wedding, just something nice for our one and only day."

"How many people would you invite?"

Rachael mumbled names to herself while counting on her fingers. At least twenty." She looked dubious.

"Wow," he said as she watched his mind work, tallying up those he would invite. "Besides family and close friends, I'd be remiss if I didn't invite at least my construction supervisors and Dad's crews too."

Wedding plans and writing personal vows occupied the few empty hours between Matthew's work and her writing. The wedding would take place in February after Mona and Cameron return from The Islands. They first thought about having the ceremony in the yard on the cliff in front of the arbor, drought conditions prevailing. The reception would then take place in the guest unit. That idea did not bode well with either of them. Recalling the weather during the previous winter when they had their party, the moist sea air would be too cool to put their guests through outdoor festivities. Too, the bay fog was sometimes so thick, a person could feel it on their skin back there in the yard.

A week later, preliminary plans were established and those few who needed to be contacted immediately were happy to assist. The service was confirmed to be held at a neighborhood church out on 19th Avenue at Junipero Serra Boulevard. Tina secured a small banquet room at the nearby *Stonestown Shopping Mall* for the reception and would cater it.

In a quiet moment one evening, Matthew announced he had made reservations for their honeymoon in Carmel by the Sea, a quaint one square mile village nestled down the California coast.

Rachael called Brandon. "I still would like you to walk me down the aisle and give me away."

There was a pause on the phone. Why would he not consent? Then he said, "I don't know, Rachael. It's not like this is something new. I mean, you're already married."

With most of the plans going smoothly, and pending convincing Brandon to be a part of the ceremony, Rachael launched into designing her wedding dress. Rosa's widowed friend, Consuela, would be seamstress. She made many of Rosa's nicer clothes. That was confirmation enough.

Rachael remembered the deadline for her next book. Time wasn't running out, however, she liked the idea of being ahead of schedule. The book wasn't due on her editor's desk until the first of April. Still, she wasn't about to fall behind and have that worry on her mind during the wedding. Till then, she couldn't allow herself to be away from writing for any length of time.

Christmas was spent quietly at Sea Cliff. Mona and Cameron arrived Christmas Eve and spent the night. The Clayton's, with whom the Knights usually celebrated, arrived early in the morning. The Skylars accepted an invitation and walked over a little later.

Brandon and Denita, of course, didn't accept.

"From our last conversation," Rachael said in a quiet moment with Matthew. "Brandon's relationship with Denita is in trouble."

"What about the wedding?"

"He won't commit," she said. "He doesn't have to bring Denita. I have faith he won't let me down."

"Not with something this important," Matthew said.

"Each guest brought food for the Christmas meal. Rachael and Mona prepared a turkey for the meat eaters. As soon as all arrived and settled in, exchanging of a few simple gifts took place around the fireplace. It was kept burning to stave off the bitter cold snap that plunged the entire West Coast into a deep freeze. The blazing fire and the scent of burning wood was also synonymous, for Rachael, with peace and security.

The mood was low key, mellow, unpretentious. Matthew talked with Willa Skylar about possibly remodeling the back portion of her daughter's house to accommodate the arrival of their second grandchild. She wanted to get the job done as soon as possible. She and her husband could begin traveling soon after his retirement in June.

Matthew announced he'd be delighted to create a children's room. His mood further enlightened. Maybe he was seeing it as practice for building something for his own children. After all, he was dying for a son and he and Rachael had not used protection when making love.

"I'm busier than ever with the store," Mona said. "I've hired another clerk along with the new food and drink counter persons."

"Mona was able to keep the new deck open because we installed a canvas awning and space heaters," Cameron said. "A few people sit back there, even though it's cold out."

"Albeit, dry," Mona said. "As soon as the cold snap's over, the terrace will become the local hangout again."

When Matthew was out of the room, Rachael brought out the drawings of her wedding dress which was being sewn at Consuela's apartment to keep Matthew from peeking. After that, most of the conversation centered on the topic of the wedding.

"What is it, Rachael?" Mona asked. "You looked sad just now."

"It's my brother. He hasn't consented to walk me down the aisle. I'll have to find someone else for back-up, just in case."

Mona glanced at Cameron and raised her eyebrows.

Two days after Christmas, Juan Carlos, disappeared. An insider rumor had it that he had been pressed into an undercover sting operation. No one knew for sure in a situation like that, not even their close-knit circle of friends. Some shifting needed be done among the groom's Honor Attendant and the Groomsman.

Rachael called Brandon again. "Please don't tell me you're not coming."

"I said it before. It's no big thing. You're already married."

"I want you to be in my wedding. You're the only family I've got. I wanted you to be a part of it and to give me away. This is a real special time for me, Brandon. You can count on me if you get married."

"Well, I'm not going. Deni and I broke up. She hung around long enough to get her Christmas presents. To think I spent a hell of a lot on her. I don't want to have anything to do with relationships or marriages or anything like that for a long time to come."

"You could have called," she said, trying not to nag. "I've never let you down."

"Oh, no?" he said, sounding hurt. "Well, think back, way back. Think real hard."

Chapter 61

Knight Homes was managing to capture its share of the repair market, landing a contract for an apartment complex on Chestnut Street in the Marina. Even though the big earthquake happened nearly two years prior, many houses and buildings stood vacant, attesting to the effect of worsening recessionary times. Surprisingly, Cameron was able to secure a couple of contracts for new homes in Marin County as well.

Time passed swiftly. Rachael's third book was nearly done. Now she was seeing the chapters of her next novel already forming in her mind. "Two a year is my goal," she said.

"Your schedule is chaotic," Matthew said.

"With each new book, I've got to do the autographing sessions and publicity interviews."

"I have to hand it to Dennis DeBaer and Geri Daniels," he said. "They've kept you in the forefront.

"Excuse me?" she asked, teasing. "I'm the author. I'm doing my part."

"I hope they don't want you to start traveling more than you do."

"How selfish."

"Well, I kind of like having you underfoot."

She snickered. "Who's under whose foot?"

"I guess people want to meet their favorite author," he said. "You realize how the activity takes you away from meditation and yoga, don't you."

"It's a tedious balance, but I make the time."

Al Taylor did his homework, and then some. Over dinner at the Sea Cliff house, he said, "In addition to you needing physical strength for your line of work, I've based your case on the fact that you, Matthew, were the *golden boy* at the gym."

"The wha-at?"

"That physique you were blessed with," he said, gesturing toward Matthew's body. "You've graced everything from posters and advertisements to multiple ads in telephone books."

"You were their spokesperson," Rachael said, "in a most visual way."

"The way I see it," Taylor said, "is that with a slightly crooked left leg, those perpetual scars on your cheek and throat, and some remaining over your body and legs, you can no longer participate in the promising career for which you'd been groomed and well paid. And for which you would've had many more years to contribute."

"I wasn't paid that much, and besides, the scars are fading."

"Ha," Taylor said. "I did some checking. "Did you know out of all the guys pumping iron and posing for gyms, you were the third highest paid model in northern California?"

"You're kidding."

"You didn't know that?" Rachael asked.

"Didn't care."

"Then there's the collapsed lung, lingering dizziness, occasional stuttering." Taylor rolled his hand with each phrase. "Along with everything else, that contributes to a diminished physical capacity vital especially in your construction business."

"I didn't know you were going to be this thorough."

Al Taylor looked at Matthew and smiled. "I got your orthopedic surgeon to give a convincing deposition saying that future problems might be avoided by re-breaking and straightening that bone in your leg."

"And what about your neck?" Rachael asked. "You're neck's always stiff and you keep having to go to the chiropractor."

Matthew exhaled a quick breath. "That'll clear up."

"You should have told me that, Matt," Taylor said, surprised and scolding.

The claims were true. Though Matthew was nearly fully recovered, certain persistent after-effects remained. He had regained some weight, but had not been able to restore his body to the massive pre-accident physique he was proud of. It would take more gym time.

"Then there's a little matter of that pain and suffering," Taylor said, as if he hadn't said enough. "The doctor said some of the physical trauma has the potential for future complications. We're going in for all of it." He ran his thumb over the edges of the thick stack of papers and fanned them. "So refresh your memory about the accident."

"What little I remember."

"Well, you've got to get yourself positioned for the grueling ardors of cross-examination."

"I wish this shady game was behind us."

"What's shady about it?" Taylor asked quickly. "You almost lost your life—two months of it for sure."

Rachael finished her current manuscript in the latter half of January. Due to her busy writing schedule, she spoke with Brandon only twice more, to no avail. Secretly wishing he would make an effort to read, Rachael sent him an autographed copy of *Sea Cliff*, to share the joy of her accomplishment. He might see it as more of her rich high life. Hoping Brandon would look inside, was too much to expect. Brandon did not write well, nor was he able to read well. He hadn't made an effort to transcend his dyslexia. She knew him well. If he kept the book, the sole purpose might be to brag to his friends. She wanted to share some part of her life with him and hoped some of his childhood curiosity would resurface strong enough to make him try to read. The characters' lives she wrote about might be a way to help him since he wouldn't see Rachael as part of the story. Besides, she wanted him to find the book dedication to him without being told about it.

Close to the end of the January, Al Taylor again showed up at Sea Cliff late one evening carrying his thick briefcase. He was breathless as he excused himself for not having called first. He came directly from a meeting with the legal counsel for Stage Center.

"We've got an offer." he said, following them into the living room.

"They want to settle?" Matthew asked. "Out of court?"

"Personally, if this thing goes to court, this case is complicated, with the drugs and illegal border activities. It could take at least another two years."

"Since we've come this far, would it be worth it? To settle now, I mean?"

"Well, they didn't counter with anything near what we asked. You know, I started with the twenty mill to make it high so they'd be happy if we settled for less. They got guilt written all over 'em." He chuckled, then paused, gathering his thoughts. "You two know, even if this goes to court, you'd be lucky to see anything near a million, maybe a whole lot less. Fact is, they'll say," he said, directing his comments to Matthew, "you didn't buy the farm. You weren't even maimed."

"So what's their offer?"

"Seven…"

"Mil-l-lion?" Rachael covered her mouth hanging agape.

"Then we should settle," Matthew said.

"Not so fast. I countered that offer."

"You upped it?"

"I got you ten," Taylor said, smiling.

"You got… they settled…ten…?"

"All big ones."

Chapter 62

The wedding day had arrived. The anteroom of the popular neighborhood church was crowded. Rosa's friends marveled over the magnificent wedding dress. Rosa fussed over the hemline to assure it fell correctly. Perfectionist Consuela tended to the train. One of the ladies arranged Rachael's shiny red hair, sweeping it to the top of her head with a bun near the back that would hold her jeweled tiara and veil in place.

The dress was strapless with a plunging center front and a tiny satin flower just below her cleavage. The open back dropped nearly to her waistline. Support for her bust was a sewn-in bustier. White Satin Piping ran around the top edges front to back. Dainty white Chantilly lace covered a full body dress of white satin all the way to the floor. It was form fitting, snug at the waist and hips, flaring out from above the knee. A slit started above the knees at center front with rounded corners at the hem. At the top of the slit was a white satin flower, its petals clustered around a group of tiny glowing seed pearls. Rachael designed the slit to tease with a light blue garter slightly peeking out from beneath. The hemline was longer in the back, trailing on the floor a couple of feet.

The same sheer Chantilly made up the veil, attached to the tiara. The veil hung to the top of the gown in front and dipped around her shoulders to her waist in back. It, too was bordered with white stain piping. Consuela fitted the tiara entwined with her piled up hair. A few wispy curls softened the hairline around her face and down the sides.

Her bouquet was white Stephanotis. Fresh green leaves trailed to knee length with more stephanotis. Two white Lady Butterfly orchids nestled in the center of the bouquet.

To complete her look:

Something old were the sparkly diamond earrings that Amanda bequeathed to Rachael.
Something new was the wedding dress.
Something borrowed was Mona's stunning necklace with its incredible pear-shaped diamond pendant that hung down to the top of Rachael's cleavage.
Something blue was the sexy lacy blue garter.

The ceremony was scheduled to begin in less than half an hour. Rosa left to take her place; Rosa as Matron of Honor and Tina as the bridesmaid, both wearing sea green dresses. Rachael didn't know what to do about replacing Brandon. This was a non-traditional wedding ceremony and requirements didn't need to follow ceremonial protocols. She could walk down the aisle alone, if need be. She thought of asking the church secretary to provide someone. She stuck her head out the anteroom doorway and looked around seeing no one.

Off to the side of the doorway, a friend stood smiling and preening like this was one of the most important days of his life. She reached out and took the hand and gently shook the long thin arm. He would do just fine.

"Dooley," she said quietly. "I don't think my brother is here to give me away. Would you consider doing it? I'd be honored."

He smiled. "Can't. I'm Matt's Best Man." He stuck out his chest and stood tall. "And Fernando's the Groomsman." His smile changed to that of one who had a secret. "I need to get inside there right about now." He walked away quickly.

She sighed heavily. "I guess I can walk alone. I wish my brother could have been here."

"You won't be walking alone," Dooley said over his shoulder. "Matt's been working hard on that problem. He took care of things. He's got someone for you."

"What do you mean? What did Matthew do?"

Dooley smiled his big toothy grin and moved quickly toward the side alcove that would take him to the front of the church. He looked back. "Just walk through when the doors open." He disappeared before she could ask what he meant.

Suddenly, from inside the church, a chamber group began to play the sweet melodic strains of *Ke Kali Nei Au*, the *Hawaiian Wedding Song*. Mona and Cameron had managed to slip one of their favorite tunes and their love of Hawaii into the ceremony. Rachael fought back joyful tears. The music was her cue. Up to that time, she had not felt the least bit uneasy. As she took her place at the closed outer doors, Consuela arranged the hemline behind her and assured the bouquet stems hung appropriately in front. Rachael suddenly felt tense. She let out a forceful sigh. She could do this. She would walk alone, if need be. It was toward Matthew and nothing would stop her now.

Two ushers began to slowly open the double doors. To her surprise, two young barefoot Latina flower girls standing inside, began to walk slowly up the aisle, spreading pink rose petals.

Rachael peered inside as the doors slowly opened. Everyone had turned to watch her walk through. She recognized a lot of Matthew's police friends and those who had attended the New Year's party. Both construction crews and their families and friends filled the seats on the groom's side. Mona, Cameron, and the Claytons sat up front.

Sitting on the bride's side were Rachael's neighbors, some of which she'd rarely seen while passing in and out of the driveway. Keith and Willa Shylar sat with the Beckwiths and quietly waved. Tina's crew from the deli were all smiles. She spotted her close business friends and Phyllis, the banker, was among them. Rosa's friends and their families filled the rest of the seats. Rachael had thought the bride's side of the seating would be empty. It was overflowing on both sides with people standing in the alcoves. She didn't know whether to laugh or cry. She wished her brother could have seen his way to be a part of his sister's life. If only…

Rachael took a deep breath and stepped to the doorway. As she stepped through, a rusty red head leaned toward her from inside and offered an arm. It was Brandon!

"Here I am, Rach," he said quietly and smiling genuinely. He wore a dark blue tuxedo and his hair was cut and shiny.

Rachael stifled back crying out loud, but her tears flowed like water. It meant everything to be on Brandon's arm at this special time in her life, and because she could not see through teary eyes where she was stepping as she walking toward Matthew, the love of her life. Matthew, who loved her with all his heart, must have used his in-your-face attitude to get through to Brandon. Brandon being here meant he was making big changes in his life as well. From this day forth, life would be perfect, no matter what.

About the Author

Mary Deal is an Amazon best-selling, multi-genre author whose books have won many awards. She has written suspense/thrillers, a short story collection, writers' references, and self-help. She is a *Pushcart Prize* nominee, and former newspaper columnist and magazine editor.

Mary's first feature screenplay, *Sea Storm*, and *Chin Face*, a short story, were nominated into the Semi-Finals in a *Moondance International Film Festival* competition.

One of Mary's many short stories, *The Last Thing I Do*, appeared in the anthology, *Freckles to Wrinkles*, by Silver Boomer Books, and was nominated for the coveted Pushcart Prize.

Mary is also an Artist and Photographer. In addition to originals and art prints, her paintings and photographs are available in her online galleries to create gorgeous personal and household products.

She has traveled a great deal and has a lifetime of diverse experiences, all of which remain as fodder for her fiction. A native of California's Sacramento River Delta, where some of her stories are set, she has also lived in England, the Caribbean, the Hawaiian Islands, and now resides in Scottsdale, Arizona.

Find Her Online
Her Web site: http://www.marydeal.com/
Linked In: http://www.linkedin.com/in/marydeal
FaceBook: http://www.facebook.com/mdeal
Twitter: http://twitter.com/Mary_Deal
Google+: https://tinyurl.com/y8j723lr
Goodreads: https://tinyurl.com/hvvomeo
Cold Coffee Press: http://www.coldcoffeepress.com/mary-deal

Her Art Galleries
Mary Deal Fine Art
http://www.marydealfineart.com/
Island Image Gallery
http://www.islandimagegallery.com/
M Deal Art
https://www.facebook.com/MDealArt
Pinterest
https://www.pinterest.com/1deal/